OUT

OF THE

DEPTHS

BARRY IVKER

ISBN 978-1-950818-67-9 (paperback)

Rushmore Press LLC
1 888 733 9607
www.rushmorepress.com

Barry Ivker
2559 Foothills Drive
Hoover, AL 35226
e-mail: drfbi1@gmail.com

Printed in the United States of America

Introduction

I was born in 1941 some months before the bombing of Pearl Harbor and our entrance into the war. News about the Holocaust began to permeate my consciousness at a very early age. Even from the apparent safety of a lower middle-class Jewish-Italian-Black neighborhood in South Philadelphia, there were intimations of danger. If you tolerated prejudice against Blacks, my father told me, then the Holocaust will have taught you nothing. If you allow discrimination against Blacks or any other groups, we are next in line. What happened in Germany under the right conditions could happen here. Human nature is what it is. Ordinary people have the capacity of perpetrating atrocities. There were horrors in the past. There will be horrors in the future. We build our lives and our homes on a thin crust of earth we suppose can support us. But periodically, that crust cracks and a great hairy claw rises up out of the depths, bringing death and destruction. When the crack closes, the survivors try to rebuild as best they can. Human passion is tempestuous, chaotic. It takes strong will to keep it in check, even in the best of us.

As a child, I found it natural to root for the underdog. We had a local movie theater I went to regularly. Back in those days, for a quarter, you could see newsreels, cartoons, serials, and one or two features. In cowboy and Indian films, I rooted for the Indians. In a film about fighting Zulus in South Africa, I rooted for the Zulus. And I rooted for local baseball teams, the Phillies and the As, who almost always wound up in the cellar of their respective leagues. There were wisps of family history. My grandparents left Eastern Europe to escape persecution. There was talk of hiding in pickle barrels on Easter Sunday to survive pogroms. One of my aunts watched as both of her parents were bludgeoned to death in one of those pogroms. I developed a paranoia about Christianity that made even pronouncing the name Jesus was difficult for me. And that was problematic, because we had to learn Christmas carols in public schools; and in junior high school, they read excerpts from the Hebrew and Christian Bibles at daily assemblies. This paranoia had to be worked out with my Christian friends, who were having their own problems dealing with long-standing issues between Catholics and Protestants. It was at that time that I noted a transformation from anxiety to excitement in myself, in dealing with others. In my early twenties, I went to workshops and retreats whose major focus was promoting dialogue with people of other faiths.

In the midsixties, I was involved in ecumenicism. I was one of the major spokesmen for the Jewish student body at Indiana University at interfaith conferences. This was the era when Americans of all backgrounds began identifying themselves with hyphens: Afro-Americans, Jewish-Americans, Italian-Americans, Polish-Americans, Serbian-Americans. People were searching for roots within the boundaries of the American dream. I celebrated this "beyond the melting pot" consciousness in ethnic dance. For three minutes at a time, I could be Serbian, Croatian, Russian, Hungarian—or Israeli—Chassidic, or Arabic. There was an implied message here. If we honored each other's culture, sang each other's songs, and danced each other's dances, maybe respect would overcome fear and animosity—a naive hope, perhaps. But during the civil war in Yugoslavia in the 1990s, during the ethnic cleansing, I led my folkdance group to dance Croatian, Serbian, Muslim, Macedonian, and Albanian in turn. And every week, I danced a dance from Sarajevo, a city where all the ethnic groups had intermingled peacefully. For that reason alone, it was being shelled into rubble. I had walked the streets of Sarajevo in 1963, eighteen years after Serbians and Croatians had fought each other and over 1 million people were killed. Eighteen years after I walked those peaceful streets, the ethnic hatred had been reignited. I watched men in closed giant metal crates being suspended over open pit mines dying from the heat as other men watched, singing songs that I had danced to.

The problem of human evil persists. The evil of the Holocaust, which was supposed to generate such horror that people resolved that it would never happen again, has not stopped other genocides from being perpetrated. There were mass killings of ethnic Chinese in Malaysia, of the Masai in Kenya, of Ibo in Nigeria, of Tutsis in Rwanda, of Cambodians by Cambodians, Arabs by Arabs in Black September, and in villages by the elder Assad in Syria, mass murders in Darfur, extinction of native populations in the Amazon. The list goes on and on. Terrorists target civilian populations waiting in bread lines, attending funerals and weddings, at nursery schools, and nursing homes. It seems that the Marquis de Sade's prophesies are being realized over and over again. When intellect serves the will to power, it seems, the greater the intricacies of evil.

In the face of this horror, there are, however, glimmers of hope and promise. In one village in Kosovo, one seventy-year-old woman, at the risk of her life, protected six Albanians from being killed by her fellow Serbians. Some Rwandans protected others from being massacred. Some Poles protected Jews from being rounded up and killed. One village in northern France, the king and head prelate in Bulgaria, the people of Denmark and Albania.

Yad Ve-Shem in Jerusalem sought to honor these people. It brought some of them to Israel, to interview them, to find out what made these people act in the name of goodness when everyone around them either stepped aside or participated in the horror. In the end, they gave up their efforts at explanation. There is seemingly a mystery to human goodness that rivals the mystery of human evil.

There is also a resilience in some people that defies explanation. Some people in the ghettos and in the camps were overwhelmed by the horror. There were suicides. Some were reduced to such dehumanization that they became like zombies—like the walking dead. Some never recovered from the trauma, even if they physically survived. But there were also those, who even as the Nazi bombardments were reducing the Warsaw ghetto to rubble, were studying the agricultural techniques that might prove useful for the few who survived and somehow made it to the Jewish state. There were those who taught watercolor and collage to children in

Theresienstadt so that the one in two hundred who survived might bear witness to what had transpired. There were those who composed and performed music—symphonies, oratorios, and operas—even as their fellow artists were being shipped off to the extermination camps. And among the survivors that had lost their entire families, the greater number dared to love again, to bring children into the world, to raise them to be decent people.

I remember seeing a movie at the height of the Vietnam War. *David and Lisa* was not a great film, but it dramatized something profound to me. A whole team of therapists spent countless hours trying to get two deeply disturbed children out of their shells—to take a first step at living a normal life with all its risks and uncertainties. At the time, the casualty figures kept coming in from Vietnam. As many as one thousand American soldiers killed in one week, countless others wounded and psychologically traumatized. No reports were made of the casualties on the Vietnam side. The contrast between the effort to save two disturbed children and the massive force of the destructive war was almost overwhelming. Years later, some of the survivors of the massive tsunami in the Indian Ocean sent a check to help the survivors of Hurricane Katrina in New Orleans. What else was there left for them to do?

The Holocaust was my touchstone for this confrontation of good and evil. That there were aspects of the Holocaust that were unique in human history may be true. But the genocides that followed were no less for the people involved. When I write of the Jewish experience, I hope that I speak for those people as well as for myself.

When I went to Theresienstadt fourteen years ago, we traveled with my son, my daughter-in-law, and my two-year-old grandson. I realized that I would have been two years old at the time the camp was operational, and that most probably I would not have survived, that the Czech women who delighted in my grandson's tottering steps would probably have tossed my ashes in the river that flows through town. For better or worse, I used the Holocaust to try to understand the drama of human history as it unfolds—writ large and in the human soul. This struggle is at the heart of everything that I write.

I envision bringing this work to the mass graves at Auschwitz and asking the victims if what I have written is worthy of their memory. I ask the survivors if it honors their experience. It is the nature of drama to present all characters as humans and not stereotypes—the ideologues, the perpetrators, the victims, the humanitarians, and the survivors. It is my hope that these plays will join the countless other works written about the Holocaust—scholarly, fictional, poetic, cinematic, musical, and artistic—and in some way will help us to confront the forces of good and evil in the world and in ourselves.

Hermann Broch said it best in a rather-somber trilogy he wrote just before the Holocaust began (*The Sleepwalkers*).

Do not despair. For we are all here.

Gute Nacht, Mrs. Calabash, Wherever You Are

(Two men, dressed in ghetto garb, on a bridge spanning a street in Lodz, Poland, early in 1941.)

1	What does it say?
2	Nothing special.
1	Tell me.
2	Read it for yourself.
1	You know I don't read Polish.
2	It's translated into German.
1	I don't read German either.
2	That's amazing.
1	What's so amazing?
2	It's a wonder you've survived so long.
1	I know people who read Polish and German who haven't survived.
2	Just my point.
1	Jurawicz.
2	Who?
1	Jurawicz. He died just this morning.
2	Oh.
1	He read in Polish and German. In Hungarian too.
2	Impressive.
1	He died of typhus.
2	That's too bad.
1	Typhus.
2	I heard you.
1	Polish, German, and Hungarian.

2   You said that before.

1   The intelligent ones die. While I, who don't read Polish or German . . . or Hungarian, I am still alive.

2   Obviously.

1   Tell me what the message says.

2   To change roles on command.

1   Now?

2   That's what the notice says.

1   That means . . .

2   Yes.

1   That you no longer can read Polish or German.

2   Not anymore.

1   So you are now the ignorant one.

2   Yes.

1   So I get to read the second page of the notice.

2   I suppose so.

1   So . . . what does it say?

2   You read it.

1   OK. Just don't hurry me.

2   What does it say?

1   It is strictly forbidden for anyone to interfere with a Jew who is trying to commit suicide by jumping off this bridge.

2   That's what it says?

1   Yes.

2   That's all?

1   No. There's more.

2   Nu?

1   Jews who wish to commit suicide by jumping off this bridge are requested to put their identification papers in their pockets before they jump.

2   Yes . . .

1   That's all?

2   That's . . . strange.

1   What's strange?

2	There are no penalties listed for people who don't follow the directives.
1	You're right.
2	Have you ever read a directive before that didn't include penalties for disobedience?
1	No. Never. But then again . . .
2	What?
1	I can't read the directives. They're always written in Polish and German.
2	That's . . . amazing.
1	What?
2	That someone as ignorant as you has managed to survive . . . while Jurawicz.
1	Yes. Poor Jurawicz. I knew him well.
2	He read in Polish, German, and Hungarian.
1	You said as much before.
2	No. You said as much before.
1	I suppose.
2	I heard that he read in Russian as well.
1	Impressive.
2	Although directives are never printed in Russian.
1	True.
2	And moreover . . .
1	Yes.
2	Jurawicz died this morning.
1	Of typhoid.
2	Typhoid or typhus?
1	Typhus. My friend said typhus. Definitely typhus. And I've never known him to be wrong before.
2	Really?
1	Or to lie.
2	You don't find many people like that around these days.
1	True.
2	People lie left and right . . . for no purpose, it seems, but to keep in practice.

1	In practice for what?
2	A good lie can save your life.
1	I suppose.
2	I ought to know.
1	You have lied before?
2	Only in extenuating circumstances.
1	Like when?
2	Well, of late, almost every day. And you?
1	Well, to tell the truth . . .
2	Yes.
1	I am not very good at lying.
2	I have gotten very good at lying.
1	Really?
2	I am, in fact, lying to you right now, and you didn't realize it.
1	That's quite true. (Sound of a shout Achtung signals a change of roles.)
2	I would never have known.
1	Suppose it would happen that a fat Pole and a skinny gestapo officer fell off this bridge at the exact same moment . . . Who would hit the ground first?
2	Let me see . . . I remember something like this from my science class in high school.
1	Nu?
2	OK, I forget . . . so . . . Who would hit first?
1	I don't know either, but who cares?
2	Say, that's very funny.
1	True, but you have to be careful who you tell it to.
2	I certainly wouldn't tell it to a skinny gestapo officer.
1	Or a fat Pole.
2	Or a skinny Pole, for that matter.
1	Not sure they would understand it.
2	Enough to do a number on you.
1	I already have a number on me.
2	Me too . . . What's yours?
1	13430.

2	That spells out Yigdal.
1	What?
2	Yigdal . . . you don't know any Gematria?
1	I don't even know what Gematria is.
2	Let's see how to explain it. (Achtung!)
1	Damn. At least they could have given me time to explain.
2	Yes. I want to know.
1	Me too.
2	No . . . you do understand. You were about to explain it to me.
1	I was?
2	You said you were. I'm really interested.
1	OK . . . Every Hebrew letter has a numerical equivalent.
2	Why?
1	It goes way back, before we had a number system. They used the letters of the alphabet. So every word has a numerical value. I worked back from the numbers on your arm.
2	You mean, on your arm.
1	Anything you get from that?
2	Yigdal.
1	Which means?
2	He will be magnified. It's the beginning of Maimonides thirteen principles of faith.
1	Wow, you really know your stuff.
2	I know a little. I could teach you.
1	While I stand on one leg?
2	Not everything, but enough.
1	Enough for what?
2	To alleviate one or two levels of tedium . . . anxiety . . . stress.
1	There's one really easy way to eliminate stress.
2	What?
1	Go to the fence.

2	I'm not sure I'm quite ready for that yet.
1	Or leap off this bridge.
2	I left my papers at home.
1	Pity. It's always good to be prepared.
2	Prepared for what?
1	For anything.
2	How can you be prepared for anything when they keep changing the rules?
1	That's true.
2	Like yesterday. They were gathering people together for a work detail.
1	There's nothing new in that.
2	This wasn't for a day. It was . . . far off, they said.
1	Oh, one of those work details. The usual promises.
2	Better than usual.
1	Good food. Good lodging.
2	Postcards to send home to the folks.
1	Postcards. That's a nice touch.
2	Isn't it?
1	To ensure that we think everything is fine and dandy.
2	Yes.
1	It's not clear why they're doing this. They usually ship off the weak . . . the elderly . . . babies . . . and keep the young, healthy ones around.
2	So . . . what do you make of it?
1	Don't ask me. You're supposed to be the clever one.
2	I thought it was you this time.
1	I've lost track.
2	Me too.
1	So how are we supposed to know who is who?
2	Does it really matter?
1	Who is the clever one and who is the ignoramus?
2	Precisely.
1	Someone has to be able to read the notices.
2	Read the words or read between the lines?
1	You read the words, and I'll read between the lines.

2	That's fair enough.
1	So?
2	So what?
1	So . . . I have another notice to read.
2	Good. Read.
1	Everyone is to turn in their fur coats . . . mink, sable, fox, beaver, raccoon . . . I don't recognize this word. You can keep rabbit, as long as the collar isn't one of the aforementioned animals.
2	I don't own a fur coat.
1	That's too bad. Winter will be very long this year.
2	Not even a rabbit coat.
1	They're not so warm anyway. A couple of sweaters is better than a rabbit coat.
2	Rabbits seem warm enough in the wintertime.
1	True.
2	So I wonder why coats made of rabbit . . .
1	Life is mysterious.
2	You can say that again. (Achtung!)
1	What?
2	Life is mysterious.
1	I think that's my line.
2	Whatever. (He bends down to pick something up.)
1	What's that?
2	It seems to be a script.
1	Of what?
2	Of a play.
1	What play?
2	A children's play . . . actually an opera . . . called *Brundibar*.
1	What's it about?
2	Children battling the forces of evil in the form of an old organ grinder named Brundibar. It's written in Czech.
1	You read Czech?
2	No.

1   Then how do you know?

2   I'm not sure.

1   You read it, perhaps, in translation?

2   Maybe. Let's see. It's written in September 1941.

1   This is February 1941.

2   OK then. It will be written in September . . . in Terezin. And there will be translations in a number of languages. I'm not sure which of them I will have read.

1   Where?

2   I'm not sure of that either.

1   But not here.

2   Probably not.

1   So you will survive this place. (Achtung!)

2   Or perhaps you will.

1   You or I.

2   That's nice to know. At the rate we're going, I didn't think there would be anyone left.

1   Hey, do you know old lady Hechstein?

2   You mean, the witch?

1   Yeah. That one. She looked into her crystal ball last night and told me, Hitler will die on a Jewish holiday. "Which one?" I asked her. "It doesn't matter," she said. Any day that Hitler dies on will be a Jewish holiday.

2   Oh, go on, she didn't tell you that. She's a real card though.

1   She'll tell your fortune according to the cards.

2   It doesn't take a fortune teller and a deck of cards to tell our fortune these days.

1   True enough. But I go there periodically to make her feel needed.

2   You have a good heart.

1   Let's hope my liver and kidneys hold up as well.

2   Hold up what?

1   Hold up my end.

2   Why, is it sagging?
1   In the end . . .
2   Look . . . down there . . . a milk wagon.
1   Amazing. Do you know how long it's been since I've
        seen a milk wagon?
2   We have to come to the bridge more often.
1   (From *Brundibar*, intoned, or one can use the actual
        tune from an English recording.)
        Milk, milk, fresh milk, butter, cheese
        Come and buy some, if you please
        For the children and their mothers
        For the pets and all the others
        Milk, milk, fresh milk, butter, cheese
        Come and buy some, if you please.

2   Hey, that's not bad. I didn't know you were a poet.
1   It's from *Brundibar*.
2   That play?
1   Yes.
2   In Czech?
1   Of course.
2   Let me see the play.
1   OK . . . here.
2   It's written in a language I can't understand.
1   Then it might be in Polish, German, or Hungarian.
2   True. Probably not German though.
1   Why do you say that?
2   No exclamation points.
1   True enough.
2   Oh . . . the milk wagon is passing.
1   Do you suppose he might be persuaded to toss a liter
        or two up this way?
        Milk and cream the jolly milkman
        Gladly pours into your milk can
        But if you don't have a quarter
        Your kitten must lap water.

2   I have some Rumkies left.

1   For Rumpkies your kitten must lap water.

2   Fresh water?

1   Water with fresh supplies of typhus bacteria every day.

2   We wouldn't want to catch typhus from stale germs now, would we?

1   What I wouldn't give for a liter of milk.

2   Really?

1   I would sell my soul for a liter of milk.

2   Sell your soul?

1   Yes.

2   To the devil?

1   I suppose.

2   These days I fear the devil has a German accent.

1   Oh.

2   I don't think we would be welcomed there.

1   Darn.

2   If we'd accept an alternative to hell, perhaps he'll agree.

1   What did you have in mind?

2   How about . . . Auschwitz?

1   Never mind. I'm not that thirsty. (Achtung!)

2   One day, Cohen was in a restaurant and he accidentally steps on Schwartzpfeffer's foot.

1   Accidentally?

2   That's the way I heard it.

1   You know what Freud says about accidents.

2   Which Freud?

1   Sigmund.

2   Ach . . . a German.

1   No . . . actually a Jew.

2   A Jew with a name like Sigmund?

1   Go sue me. I didn't know his parents.

2   Me neither. Will wonders never cease . . . a Jew named Sigmund.

1	Ziggy.
2	Ziggy is something else again.
1	Maybe they called him Ziggy around the house and Sigmund in school.
2	That already would make sense.
1	I'm glad you're happy.
2	Happy as a Pole with a pint of vodka?
1	Yes.
2	Happy as a Cossack with a whip?
1	Da shto ve govorit.
2	Happy as a German with a luger and a big dog on a short leash?
1	Jawohl!
2	I'm so happy I forgot what we were talking about.
1	Something about a Jew named Cohen. (Achtung!)
2	Yes. You were telling a story.
1	You finish it.
2	You sure?
1	Go ahead . . . it's a good story.
2	So. Cohen steps on Schwartzpfeffer's toe.
1	Are you sure it was Schwartzpfeffer?
2	Schwartzpfeffer . . . Weisspfeffer . . . something like that. Are you going to finish the story?
1	It's your pfennig.
2	OK. So he steps on the German's toe, and Weisspfeffer is highly insulted. "Hey, Jew," he says, "you just stepped on my toe."
1	"I'm sorry," says Cohen. "I didn't mean it."
2	"Sure you meant it," says Rotpfeffer. "Freud says there are no accidents. Deep down inside, you really meant to step on my toe. All you Jews are passive-aggressive types. You wanted to hurt me."
1	He quoted Freud?
2	Probably, didn't know he was Jewish.
1	Really?
2	With a name like Sigmund?

1   It's possible.

2   So he says, "I'm really insulted by what you did, especially in front of the lady."

1   He was with a lady?

2   Yes.

1   Not his wife?

2   I'm not sure.

1   He did call her a lady?

2   Yes.

1   Not his wife?

2   True.

1   So. He was insulted.

2   Very. He challenged Cohen to a duel. With pistols. At seven the very next morning.

1   He challenged him to a duel?

2   Yes.

1   Each one would get a pistol?

2   Yes.

1   Cohen would get a chance to shoot at Weisspfeffer?

2   Yes . . . but Cohen, you should know, was not such a good shot.

1   I can imagine.

2   In fact, he had never handled a pistol before in his life.

1   It figures.

2   While Weisspfeffer was a top marksman who had already shot six men to death.

1   Not to mention . . .

2   Please . . . don't mention it.

1   OK.

2   Especially not here.

1   I can be discrete.

2   The walls have ears. (Achtung!)

1   See, I told you.

2   What?

1   The walls have ears.

2   If you say so.

1   You can never be too careful.

2   That's just what Cohen was thinking.

1   You're right.

2   So what happened?

1   Morning came. And there was Schwartzpfeffer.

2   Schwartzpfeffer?

1   Weisspfeffer . . . with two pistols and his second, waiting for Cohen to show up. And then in the fog, he sees a man approaching in the fog . . . and he begins to feel really good.

2   I can imagine.

1   There's nothing like a duel to really make your day.

2   Especially if you win.

1   That goes without saying.

2   That's why I didn't say it.

1   Nothing like killing a man.

2   A Jew, no less.

1   That also goes without saying. (Achtung!)

2   That's why I wish you hadn't said it.

1   I think you said it.

2   Whatever.

1   So?

2   So?

1   So this man comes out of the mist, and it's not Cohen. And Weisspfeffer says, "You're not Cohen." And the man says, "No, I'm Freud."

2   Freud?

1   Yes.

2   Sigmund Freud?

1   Otto Freud. "I have a note from Cohen," he says.

2   "From Cohen," says Weisspfeffer. And he nods to the lady.

1   The lady was there?

2   Of course she was there.

1   You didn't mention her before.

2   Well, she was there. Of course. Weisspfeffer wanted to impress her. Women like to see their men in action.

1   She wouldn't have liked it to see him shot.

2   That would be OK too . . . to watch her man die for her honor.

1   I thought it was his honor.

2   Maybe he stepped on her toe.

1   That would make sense.

2   Or maybe Cohen just looked at her wrong.

1   Wrong?

2   Well . . . right for someone else, but wrong for him.

1   Oh.

2   So the man hands the note to Weisspfeffer and he reads it. It says, "Being a man of honor . . ."

1   Who . . . Cohen or Weisspfeffer . . . or Freud?

2   Weisspfeffer.

1   How do you know? Grammatically . . .

2   You know grammar?

1   You surprised?

2   Yes. You never cease to amaze me.

1   I know all kinds of things.

2   But not how to read Polish or German.

1   No.

2   Or Hungarian?

1   No.

2   Czech?

1   No. Definitely not Czech.

2   But you do know grammar?

1   Of course.

2   It was Weisspfeffer.

1   You're sure of that?

2   How do you know?

1   Context.

2   Context?

1   Let me finish.

2   Be my guest. (Achtung!)

1	I suppose now you'll have to finish.
2	My pleasure. "Being a man of honor," the note said, "you . . ." Notice *you*. That could only refer to Weisspfeffer.
1	That's clear enough.
2	So. "Being a man of honor, you, having challenged me, would offer to let me take the first shot."
1	Really?
2	That's part of the code of honor. Cohen knew that.
1	Very perceptive of him. How did he know that?
2	If you want to survive, you learn all kinds of things. Being ignorant is an invitation to disaster.
1	But then there's Jurawicz.
2	True enough. But Cohen did know.
1	Clever.
2	So the note said, "Since you would allow me the honor of the first shot and since it happens that I am not feeling very well this morning . . ."
1	He was not feeling well?
2	Up all night with a fever.
1	Figures.
2	"Would you," the note continues, "be so kind as to shoot yourself for me . . . and we can finish the duel at your earliest convenience."
1	That's what the note said?
2	Yes.
1	And what did Weisspfeffer do?
2	The story ends at that point.
1	Oh.
2	To tell you the truth, it's more of a joke than a story.
1	Rather far-fetched in any case.
2	I got it from Vanya.
1	Vanya?
2	The tailor.
1	From Lwow?
2	The very one.

1   If it's one of his stories, it's bound to be far-fetched.

2   Pretty feeble, if you ask me.

1   I did the best I could, considering all I had for breakfast this morning was a piece of moldy bread.

2   I had . . . a potato.

1   A real potato!

2   Not such a nice potato. Not very big at that. And by the time I cut around the rot from the frost, there wasn't very much at all.

1   Well.

2   But there was a distinct taste of potato. And an aftertaste. I have it now.

1   The aftertaste of potato. What I wouldn't give for the aftertaste of potato.

2   What wouldn't you give?

1   I might give my soul for the taste of a potato.

2   The taste or the aftertaste?

1   Either one.

2   Hard getting an aftertaste without having the actual taste first.

1   Actually, if I imagine very hard, I can conjure up the taste itself.

2   You are an excellent conjurer.

1   I can fill up my thoughts with the taste.

2   Really?

1   Unfortunately, my stomach tells me that it's still empty.

2   Of course.

1   My very soul.

2   We've been through this routine before.

1   I know.

2   There's no one that wants your soul . . . even for a single potato.

1   Not even . . . God Himself.

2   That's another question entirely.

1   What else do we have to do?

2   Not much.
1   We could work the garbage detail.
2   Getting rid of it or sorting it?
1   Either one.
2   It's amazing what you can find sorting through the garbage.
1   Tell me about it.
2   Potatoes, for example.
1   You work the garbage detail?
2   Not officially. I work the excremental detail now.
1   Oh.
2   Going on three months now.
1   And you're still around to tell the tale?
2   Look at me . . . am I still around to tell the tale?
1   Appearances can be deceiving.
2   You think maybe I am some kind of apparition . . . or an angel maybe.
1   Too strange looking to be an angel.
2   Angels come in all sizes and shapes.
1   In rags?
2   Have to get past the guards . . . not create suspicion. What would happen, do you think, if I wandered by in a white robe . . . with wings and a halo?
1   They'd think you were crazy and they'd put you away.
2   Away?
1   You know . . . away.
2   Kill me?
1   Don't need to feed crazies when the sane ones are going hungry.
2   Sane ones.
1   Relatively sane . . . still capable of working.
2   Oh yes . . . sane people.
1   Whatever.
2   You can't kill an angel.
1   I don't think so.

2	So . . . an angel. You could, maybe, take a message to God?
1	That's what I'm here for.
2	Really? Not to bring messages from God?
1	That too.
2	So . . . which one goes first?
1	I suppose the message from God, since I got that first. Besides, God being God, He should go first.
2	Kol Ha-Kavod. So. What does God want to tell me? (Achtung!)
1	That's not fair. I've never gotten a message from God before.
2	And I've never given one.
1	No?
2	I'm no angel.
1	I figured as much. I can imagine what God might say.
2	Really?
1	Well . . . not really. But I certainly have some things I could say to God.
2	Like what?
1	A petition.
2	Yes . . .
1	From the people of Lodz.
2	All the people?
1	No.
2	How many?
1	Well . . . thirteen actually.
2	That's not too many.
1	Quality will have to make up for quantity. When Abraham argued to save Sodom and Gomorrah, there was only one of him.
2	Did he save Sodom and Gomorrah?
1	No, but he could have, if he had been able to find ten righteous people in town.

2   God would have saved the cities if He could have found ten righteous people?

1   That's what the Torah says.

2   There must be at least ten righteous people in Lodz.

1   More than ten righteous people in the petition alone.

2   Thirteen.

1   I got three extra to make sure. Some people look pretty good on the outside, but deep down inside they're pretty bad.

2   I've known people like that . . . Our fearless leader, for example.

1   He's not on the petition.

2   I'm not surprised. He says wonderful things about protecting us, but that doesn't stop people from dying.

1   No.

2   Or from being shipped out.

1   That too.

2   Children . . . the sick . . . does he think we're blind or just stupid?

1   He's not on the petition.

2   Good. So who is on the petition?

1   The Rebbe, for one.

2   The Rebbe himself!

1   He was the one who gave me the idea. If Abraham could try to save cities like Sodom and Gomorrah . . .

2   Yes . . .

1   If Nineveh could repent and not be destroyed . . . surely this city . . .

2   You're right.

1   So . . . the petition. (Achtung!)

2   Petitions are dangerous.

1   Indeed.

2   But it's not like we're petitioning the authorities.

1   Certainly not.

2   Not the prince of the ghetto . . . or the gestapo.

1	No.
2	Just . . . God.
1	That's right. Just God.
2	And that's how it reads . . . to God, the Almighty, Creator of the Heavens and the Earth.
1	That's a good beginning.
2	Be it hereby known that the Jews of Lodz, Poland, hereby forbid the King of Heaven from punishing His people any longer.
1	Forbid?
2	Yes. Forbid.
1	That's pretty strong language.
2	The times demand pretty strong language.
1	And how is this petition to be delivered?
2	You told me you were an angel.
1	Oh.
2	I'll let you take the petition with you when you return.
1	I'm not sure that's the kind of message I feel comfortable bringing to the King of Heaven.
2	I'm afraid I'll have to insist on it.
1	How about softening the language a bit . . . how about *request* instead of *insist*?
2	I insist that the language remain as it is.
1	You . . . insist.
2	I'm afraid I have no other choice.
1	And if I don't comply with your insistence?
2	Then I will have to keep you here till you agree.
1	I have other pressing tasks to complete before morning.
2	All the more reason for you to comply with our . . . request.
1	And if I just take a running start and fly off the bridge and soar up to heaven?
2	I will hold you down and not let you get that running start.

1	I'm pretty quick.
2	I played soccer as a boy.
1	Oh.
2	And I was the champion wrestler on my block.
1	I have some rather unorthodox moves. You might find yourself a bit worse for wear tomorrow.
2	It's worth it to me.
1	You might wind up limping.
2	I seem to have heard this story before.
1	All the good stories seem to repeat themselves from time to time.
2	You're no angel?
1	No.
2	You were just pulling my leg?
1	You could put it that way.
2	Indeed.
1	So. What do you think of . . . Madagascar?
2	Madagascar?
1	Yes. There's talk of sending some of us to Madagascar.
2	I suppose it couldn't be any worse than here . . . Where is it anyway? (Achtung!)
1	I don't know.
2	Neither do I. (Achtung!)
1	It's in Africa.
2	Where?
1	An island off the east coast of Africa.
2	An island?
1	A big island.
2	In Africa?
1	Yes.
2	An island . . .
1	If they isolate us way down there . . . .
2	Yes.
1	It would make it easier for them to do away with us.
2	Then again.
1	What?

2   Here we are in Europe.

1   Yes.

2   And it doesn't seem to be much of a problem for them to do away with us here.

1   That's true . . . but down there, there would be savage natives, tropical diseases . . .

2   So . . . we have our own savage natives and horrible diseases.

1   True.

2   Still don't want to go to Madagascar?

1   Wouldn't mind going to the United States.

2   The golden Medina.

1   Yes.

2   Unfortunately, they have a quota on people from Eastern Europe.

1   They wouldn't relax the quota considering the circumstances?

2   They do purport to be a Christian nation . . . Oops.

1   You said it . . . Oops.

2   Well . . . how about England? The weather is not so nice, but it's still better than here.

1   England also has a quota.

2   France?

1   The Germans hold half of it . . . the other half is governed by collaborationists.

2   Oh . . . Spain?

1   Ruled by Fascists.

2   Italy?

1   Fascists.

2   South Africa?

1   Quota.

2   Israel?

1   The British won't let any more people in.

2   Even now?

1   What can I tell you?

2   You're making things awfully difficult for me.

1	I'm making things difficult?
2	In a manner of speaking.
1	In a manner of speaking, I think we're stuck here.
2	Russia?
1	You must be really desperate.
2	I am rather desperate.
1	You'd prefer a Soviet prison camp in Siberia to this?
2	Maybe not.
1	Or Babi Yar?
2	The subtle charms of this place kind of grow on you after a while.
1	Like a wart?
2	A beauty mark.
1	A cancer.
2	I'll settle for a wart.
1	There was some talk of Uganda.
2	Where's that?
1	Africa . . . East coast.
2	Africa again.
1	Not an island this time.
2	Thank God for small favors.
1	Or maybe . . . Argentina.
2	That's in South America.
1	Yes.
2	We're getting warmer.
1	They want to put us up north . . . in cattle country . . . with the gauchos.
2	Gauchos?
1	Cowboys.
2	Jewish cowboys.
1	Better Jewish cowboys than Jewish typhus.
2	You have a point there. You know, I once dreamed of being a cowboy.
1	Really?
2	The dream lasted till I had to get on a horse . . . then it became a nightmare.

1   If you put your mind to it.

2   It wasn't my mind that had the problems.

1   Oh.

2   I guess it all comes out in the end.

1   In the end. Yes. The end. (Achtung! A message comes flying onstage in the form of a paper airplane.)

2   What is it?

1   A flyer.

2   Obviously.

1   Rather well made.

2   Yes.

1   Look at the wings. Aerodynamically quite accomplished.

2   No one ever faulted these people with a lack of technology. What does it say?

1   Are you supposed to read it, or am I?

2   I've lost count.

1   You take it.

2   Are you sure?

1   Try it. If you can't read it, it must be my turn.

2   It's in German. Look at all the exclamation points.

1   I guess it must be my turn.

2   Nu?

1   It's announcement of a contest.

2   A contest?

1   To translate a sentence into German.

2   A contest?

1   The winners will be given jam for their bread for . . . two weeks.

2   Real jam?

1   Sort of real jam. A choice of two flavors. Sort of strawberry and sort of orange marmalade.

2   Sort of strawberry is my favorite flavor. What do you have to translate?

1   "This sentence is in English."

2   That's all?

1   That's all.

2   It seems too easy.

1   Try it out.

2   You're the one who knows German. (Achtung!)

1   Try it out.

2   OK. Dieser Satz ist in englisch geschrieben.

1   That's it?

2   Seems so. But wait a minute. The original sentence was in Yiddish.

1   It was?

2   Of course. That's the only language I speak.

1   What was it in the flyer?

2   I think it is in English. Your guess is as good as mine.

1   Let's assume that it is in English.

2   OK.

1   Then the English sentence is informing us that it is in the language it is in fact written in.

2   That would be true.

1   So if you translate it into German, what does it mean?

2   That the sentence is in English.

1   But then it wouldn't be in English. It would be in German.

2   So the sentence should read, *Dieser Satz ist in deutsch geschrieben.*

1   That's true now.

2   Yes.

1   But it's not really a translation of the original sentence.

2   No.

1   So what can we do?

2   I'm not sure there's anything to do.

1   That's too bad.

2   Yes.

1   I was sort of counting on having some jam for my bread.

2   You didn't have any bread this morning. You had some potato.

1	Jam on potato wouldn't be so bad. It would cover the taste of the mold.
2	True.
1	Especially the sort of orange marmalade. It has a sharper flavor.
2	All that is . . . water under the bridge.
1	There's no water under this bridge.
2	There is when it rains.
1	Not much at best.
2	I'm sure they do the best they can.
1	True.
2	While we, on the other hand, have to make do with mud.
1	Not much mud down there. They have cobblestones.
2	While we . . .
1	We specialize in mud.
2	Top quality.
1	We should package it . . . ship it to places that don't have any. We could make a fortune.
2	We can't even get a postcard out. How do you expect to get packages out?
1	It would be interesting to have them open up some packages and try to figure out what we were trying to do. The Germans are so logical. We could keep them guessing for days.
2	Address one of the packages to Hitler.
1	To Hitler?
2	Call it medicinal mud.
1	To help prevent arthritis.
2	Does it work?
1	Sure. See many people with arthritis around here anymore?
2	True.
1	QED.
2	If you say so.

1 I'd go further. Invite Hitler to come to live here with us.

2 You want him here with us?

1 Sure. Tell him if he moves here, he'll live forever.

2 Why should he believe you?

1 It's obvious. No one rich and powerful ever dies in the ghetto of Lodz.

2 QED?

1 QED.

2 Eh . . . what does that mean?

1 I'm not sure. Something I remember from school.

2 I don't think I remember anything from school . . . except how to make Molotov cocktails.

1 You learned that in school?

2 Yes.

1 You had a very progressive school.

2 We learned practical things. Molotov cocktails . . . how to till the soil . . .

1 We have no soil to till here.

2 In Israel.

1 How could I forget? Very practical. What else did you learn?

2 We studied Maimonides.

1 Maimonides?

2 Ethical questions.

1 Oh.

2 Like . . . is it permissible to sacrifice one life for another?

1 An interesting question.

2 If, for example, one person is weak and sickly and will probably die before long, is it permissible to sacrifice that life for someone with a better chance to survive?

1 And what is the answer?

2 I can't give it to you standing on one foot.

1 You told me you could.

2 I think that was you.

1	Whatever.
2	If two men are traveling in a desert and have only enough water for one person to make it to the next watering hole . . .
1	We are not exactly in a desert.
2	You establish a principle, then apply it to other circumstances.
1	How about . . . our circumstances?
2	I am not an expert on specifics. I never got very far in school.
1	Not motivated?
2	They closed the school.
1	Oh.
2	I used to go six days a week, from early morning till suppertime. In the winter, I would get home well after dark.
1	That would have been hard for me.
2	Why?
1	I'm afraid of the dark.
2	Really?
1	Traces back to childhood. In my school, when you were bad or didn't prepare your lessons well enough, they used to lock you in a dark closet.
2	That must have been terrible.
1	It was. I used to scrunch up on the floor and imagine that spiders were dropping down on me and crawling over me. I'm afraid of spiders too.
2	That's understandable.
1	And snakes.
2	Where do snakes come into this? There are not many snakes that live in dark closets.
1	Might be something I read in a book once. But I am definitely afraid of snakes . . . and marshmallows.
2	Marshmallows?
1	Yes.
2	How did that come about?

1	I choked on one when I was little. My father had a difficult time getting it out. I thought I was going to die. I have definite fears of being asphyxiated.
2	Don't we all?
1	I suppose so.
2	Actually it's probably a fast way to go.
1	That's not exactly what I had in mind.
2	Typhus is better?
1	That's not what I had in mind either.
2	Around here, it doesn't really matter what you have in mind. It matters a lot more what certain other people have in mind.
1	The best made plans of mice and men.
2	And rats. (Achtung!)
1	And rats.
2	You can say that again.
1	What?
2	Rats.
1	Where?
2	Nowhere that I can see now.
1	None down there?
2	There might be some, but I don't see any.
1	There are a lot by my house.
2	That is incorrect.
1	How would you know? You live somewhere else.
2	I was not talking about the rats.
1	You said you were.
2	I was talking of your grammar.
1	Grammar again. You're going to kill me with your grammar.
2	You're not going to die if I talk about your dangling participles.
1	That's all you have to talk about?
2	Can I help it if I like people to speak correctly?
1	The Germans speak correctly.
2	You mean grammatically.

1	Isn't that what you're talking about?
2	I was then, but suddenly I realized an ambiguity in the words we were using.
1	An ambiguity?
2	In levels of language.
1	I like to think I have both feet on the ground.
2	If the Germans catch us on this bridge, they will dangle more than our participles.
1	Will they speak correctly as we dangle?
2	Grammatically?
1	No use beating a dead horse.
2	If I had a dead horse.
1	Yes.
2	I'd be more likely eating it than beating it.
1	You couldn't do that.
2	Why not?
1	A horse doesn't have a cloven hoof.
2	But a German, on the other hand . . .
1	Does not chew its cud.
2	Too bad.
1	Why?
2	I just came across a cookbook.
1	What kind of cookbook?
2	A German cookbook.
1	Really?
2	I suppose all it would take is one German and some vegetables to make a very tasty stew.
1	Yes.
2	But I had no vegetables.
1	Oh.
2	And besides, I couldn't read the German.
1	I could help you with the German.
2	Good, because I don't think the German would cooperate willingly.
1	But the vegetables . . . still . . .
2	Rats.

1	That's what I was saying. If you want to substitute rats for the German, there are a lot by my house.
2	You're wrong again.
1	Come by my house this evening and you'll see for yourself.
2	You said . . . "there are a lot." You should have said, "there is a lot."
1	The rats are in the lot, right? Where the synagogue used to be.
2	The synagogue was there?
1	That's what I just said.
2	And now the lot is there. It doesn't really matter. Rats don't have hooves, and they don't chew their cud.
1	No rat I ever knew.
2	And we have no vegetables.
1	True.
2	And rats sleep at night.
1	They do?
2	Rats. And butterflies.
1	Maybe during the day as well.
2	What?
1	The butterflies. It's been about a year since I've seen a butterfly.
2	Plenty of the other variety.
1	Flies?
2	Yes.
1	But no butterflies.
2	No. No butterflies.
1	No flowers. No butterflies.
2	There were some purple flowers growing on the other side of the bridge.
1	Yes.
2	Well?
1	Nightshade. Poison nightshade.
2	Oh.
1	Right where the sign was.

2	What sign?
1	You don't remember?
2	Maybe. Sort of. I can't remember what is said though. I get a picture of the letters.
1	It was written in German and Polish.
2	That might explain why I can't remember. (Achtung!)
1	Exactly what they said.
2	The sign said, "It is illegal to remove this sign. Anyone caught removing the sign will be severely punished. Anyone turning in the name of someone who has removed this sign will be rewarded."
1	That's what it said.
2	As near as I recall, yes.
1	How reliable is your memory these days?
2	There was a time when I had a photographic memory.
1	And now?
2	Maybe only . . . 87 percent.
1	So you might have forgotten something?
2	Possibly. But the sign was . . . distinctive.
1	In what way?
2	The letters were painted with unusual flourishes.
1	You remember the flourishes?
2	They're as clear as day to me now.
1	And the words?
2	More or less. I have the gist.
1	It's a pity we can't check your memory out against the real thing.
2	True.
1	Someone has, in fact, removed the sign.
2	Yes.
1	So now we can't check.
2	No.
1	It wasn't you, was it?
2	Me? What would I do with the sign?
1	You liked the flourishes.
2	I did like the flourishes.

1   Well?

2   But not enough to take the sign. Why should I risk punishment if I could see the sign here every day?

1   But what would happen if you wanted to see the flourishes . . . at night . . . after curfew? There you would be, stuck in your house, far from your beloved sign.

2   I don't live that far from the bridge.

1   But it's dark at night. And dangerous. You could be shot. And the rats . . .

2   Rats sleep at night.

1   Who told you that?

2   You did.

1   And you believed me?

2   Have I ever known you to lie?

1   Well . . . I'm sure . . . I would never lie to you . . . willingly.

2   But you might . . . unconsciously?

1   Then I wouldn't realize I was doing it, and it wouldn't count as a lie.

2   You wouldn't realize it consciously. But unconsciously . . .

1   What can I tell you?

2   Did you take the sign?

1   No. I swear.

2   By all that's holy?

1   By all that's holy.

2   By your sainted mother's grave?

1   My sainted mother?

2   Yes.

1   My mother was no saint.

2   You know what I mean.

1   Actually, I don't. My mother was a mean-spirited woman who made my childhood a living hell. I told you that. Don't you remember?

2   You're the one with the photographic memory.

1	Eighty-seven percent. Only 87 percent. Tell me . . .
2	What?
1	If it turned out that I had taken the sign, would you turn me in?
2	You are my best friend.
1	Someone else could turn me in. Then they would get the reward.
2	Well . . .
1	If anyone gets the reward, why not one of us?
2	Betray a friend?
1	It has been known to happen. The temptations are there. If the perpetrator isn't caught, the whole community will be punished. You would be saving the community at the cost of only one person.
2	Namely yourself.
1	True.
2	My best friend.
1	Sometimes you have to sacrifice individuals for the sake of the community. For a higher good.
2	Such a dilemma. I wish I had paid more attention in class.
1	Class?
2	When we studied Maimonides.
1	Oh.
2	Then I could work this problem out.
1	Yes.
2	And not begrudge you your just rewards.
1	Virtue is supposed to be its own reward.
2	But a little extra jam now and then sweetens the pot.
1	Sell a friend for a bit of jam. You wouldn't do that if you were me.
2	If I were you, who would be questioning you now. (Achtung!)
1	If I were you.
2	Well, I didn't take the sign. I can assure you of that.
1	I'm glad.

2	So you don't have to face the predicament.
1	You mean, you don't have to face the predicament.
2	I'm certainly glad of that.
1	And me as well.
2	You know, there's a legend about this bridge.
1	So soon . . . they only built it last year.
2	Do you doubt my word?
1	Should I?
2	You have no reason to under the circumstances.
1	Under what circumstances?
2	The legend.
1	Yes . . .
2	Is . . . that if anyone tells a lie on this bridge, it will collapse in an instant.
1	Really?
2	That's how I heard it.
1	From reliable sources?
2	You checked them out.
1	I have never known them to lie to me before.
2	OK . . . for the moment, I'll assume that they are reliable.
1	OK.
2	Tell me again.
1	If anyone tells a lie on this bridge, it will collapse in an instant.
2	Anyone?
1	I think so.
2	German or Jewish?
1	I'm not sure.
2	Not too many Germans walk on this bridge.
1	I've noticed that.
2	And those that do . . .
1	Yes . . .
2	I've never noticed them saying anything.
1	Nothing at all?
2	Nothing at all.

1   They must be acting very carefully.

2   What would the problem be? They don't lie to each other.

1   You think the officers tell the rank and file everything that happens or is going to happen?

2   Isn't it clear to everyone what is going to happen?

1   To everyone who wants it to be clear.

2   Why would the Germans not want it to be clear?

1   You think ordinary soldiers would be a party to it if they knew?

2   You think there are compassionate ones among them that would come to our rescue?

1   It could happen.

2   Not likely. Think of loyalty to the Fatherland.

1   Jawohl.

2   Centuries of indoctrination—the church, the schools, the newspapers, speeches, posters, songs . . .

1   Yes.

2   After all that, you think you could find anyone who wouldn't want to see us all shipped from here to eternity?

1   They say there have been protestors that have been interred.

2   Germans?

1   Yes.

2   So I suppose.

1   It could happen.

2   One or two at most.

1   So they do have to be careful.

2   Or the bridge would collapse.

1   And then how could we get from here to there . . . and back again?

2   Without putting our feet on their street.

1   Contaminating it.

2   Unthinkable.

1   You want to test it?

2	What?
1	The bridge.
2	To see if it would collapse?
1	You're not tempted?
2	We are standing on the bridge now. We would collapse with it.
1	We could wait until we were at the very end of the bridge . . . and jump off as it collapses.
2	There is something about being in the middle . . . on one certain spot.
1	You wouldn't happen to know where the spot is?
2	I'm not sure I want to know.
1	You might accidentally find yourself standing on it and might at that very moment be telling a lie.
2	I don't make a habit of lying.
1	If there could be one German soldier . . .
2	I get your drift . . . except . . .
1	What?
2	I . . . lied about the bridge.
1	You lied.
2	Yes. There was no legend.
1	Then why?
2	I thought the story might be entertaining . . . might lighten things up a bit. (Their bodies indicate a tremor.)
1	Uh-oh.
2	What was that?
1	The bridge. (Larger tremor.)
2	I'm getting out of here.
1	You can't possibly make it in time.
2	We will fall to the street below. (Third tremor.)
1	We'll . . . be shot.
2	Wait.
1	What?
2	I think . . . it's over.
1	How do you know?

2	I have a feeling.
1	Should I trust your feelings?
2	I've learned my lesson. No more lying.
1	Even to save your life?
2	I think lying is permitted to save a life.
1	Maimonides again?
2	Something like that.
1	Education is important.
2	Especially . . . practical education.
1	Like how to till a field.
2	Yes.
1	In Israel?
2	Yes.
1	When you get there?
2	If I get there, yes.
1	What are the odds of your getting there?
2	I don't think I can count that high. Then again . . .
1	What?
2	They're not too high if I stay here.
1	There's talk of the Russians coming to liberate us.
2	To liberate us?
1	Well, maybe not to liberate us, to defeat the Germans.
2	That would liberate us . . . sort of.
1	Put us at the mercy of bears instead of wolves.
2	You're rather cynical these days.
1	Let's just say I'm a student of history. The way things are. The way things have been. The way things probably will be.
2	Probably?
1	Most probably.
2	What are the odds things might change?
1	For the better?
2	Yes.
1	I don't think I can count that high.
2	So we're damned if we leave and damned if we stay.
1	Probably.

2   So given the fact that it really doesn't matter what we do, what should we do?

1   I'd like some jam right about now.

2   What kind?

1   Kind of strawberry would do nicely.

2   For your sort of potatoes. (A woman in her early thirties walks past them, barely noticing them, leans over the railing without saying anything. At times, her body is shaken with sobs).

1   We have company.

2   Do you know her?

1   Never saw her before.

2   I know most of the people here.

1   People come and go. She might be one of the new ones, shipped here from another city . . . maybe from a village.

2   She doesn't look like a country girl.

1   She doesn't look terribly happy.

2   So who is happy these days?

1   Not much to be happy about, that is true.

2   She's no different than anyone else.

1   No different from you or me.

2   What makes you so special?

1   Nothing much. I'm starving. My mother and father both died of typhus this year. My wife went visiting her family in a town near Cracow two months ago, and I haven't heard from her since. Nothing special. And you?

2   I don't want to go into it.

1   Come on, I told you.

2   That was your choice. My choice is not to go into it.

1   We're supposed to be friends. Friends can tell each other everything.

2   Friends don't force friends to talk when they're not ready to talk.

1   Do you suppose . . . that she would want to talk?

2   Would you want to listen?

1   Perhaps.

2   There are thousands like her. Are you ready to listen to thousands of tales of woe?

1   Maybe not thousands.

2   Hundreds?

1   Maybe . . . one.

2   Hers?

1   Perhaps.

2   Why?

1   I don't know. It might be a nice thing to do.

2   Just like that?

1   Just like that.

2   She's . . . moving off.

1   You want to go after her?

2   She . . . probably wouldn't stop . . . for me.

1   You know she was probably thinking of jumping.

2   Yes.

1   She wouldn't do it because we were here.

2   Probably not.

1   She'll be back tomorrow.

2   Probably.

1   And if we're here tomorrow . . .

2   She probably won't jump, again.

1   And if we're not?

2   She probably will.

1   Are we going to come tomorrow?

2   For her?

1   Maybe.

2   To stop her from jumping?

1   Yes.

2   Is that our job now . . . to keep her from jumping?

1   I don't know.

2   How do you know she won't try something else? People take pills. They jump out of fourth-story windows. How far are you willing to go to save her?

1	Right now?
2	Yes.
1	Right now I will stay on the bridge. You?
2	That's OK with me.
1	It's getting late.
2	You have somewhere else to be?
1	Not particularly.
2	So here is as good as anyplace else.
1	It's getting chilly.
2	Is your place heated?
1	No.
2	Does it get chilly?
1	Yes.
2	So . . . here or there . . . it doesn't really matter. It might as well be here.
1	With you?
2	Yes.
1	Why?
2	I . . . don't want to be alone.
1	You're not thinking of doing anything drastic?
2	I don't want to be left alone.
1	I can stay here a while longer.
2	How much longer?
1	I am getting a little hungry.
2	You have food at your place?
1	Not really. You?
2	Nothing to speak of.
1	So?
2	Here is as good as any place else.
1	It does have a good view.
2	Of the trolley line.
1	Marvel of modern engineering.
2	You ever ride the trolley?
1	Before they put up the barrier . . . yes. Every day. I got a real kick out of it. It's funny. That's almost the thing I miss the most.

2   The trolley?

1   Yes. What do you miss the most?

2   I . . . don't want to talk about it.

1   I heard a story. (Achtung!)

2   Well?

1   Tell me about it.

2   It seemed that Hitler was running short of airplane fuel for his air force. His spies told him that Britain was also short of fuel. So he sent a letter to the King of England.

1   Don't you mean, the prime minister?

2   The way I heard it, it was the King.

1   The King has no power in England. It would have had to have been the prime minister.

2   King . . . prime minister, it really doesn't matter.

1   Then make it the prime minister.

2   Fine. So Hitler sends a letter to the prime minister of England.

1   In German or in English?

2   That's not important.

1   Of course it's important. The prime minister of England probably doesn't read German.

2   You don't think he has translators?

1   I suppose he does. But then again, I suppose Hitler also has translators.

2   I suppose so.

1   So it could have been either in English or German.

2   Right.

1   So which one was it?

2   Anything you want.

1   It's your story.

2   OK. He wrote the letter in German and had it translated. Does that make you happy?

1   Ecstatic. So what did the letter say?

2   It said, "Dear Mr. Prime Minister. I heard you are running out of airplane fuel."

1 He would say that in a letter? That's like admitting he had spies in England.

2 This is a story.

1 A true story?

2 A joke.

1 Oh . . . a joke.

2 So you don't have to question every little detail.

1 Of course not . . . now that I know it's a joke.

2 Good.

1 Some people think I have no sense of humor. But I have a very good sense of humor. Believe me.

2 I believe you. Now can I finish my story?

1 Please. (Achtung!)

2 This always happens to me.

1 If you remember, it started out as my story.

2 That's true.

1 So it's only fair that I get to finish it.

2 That's good, because I didn't know the end of the story.

1 So I better finish it quickly before we have to change again.

2 By all means.

1 So he says to the prime minister, my agents tell me you are also running low on fuel.

2 He would tell the prime minister he had spies in England.

1 We've been through this before. The prime minister knows there are spies. He just doesn't know who they are.

2 Oh.

1 So he says . . . I have a suggestion that could save us both millions of zlotys.

2 He said zlotys?

1 No. He probably said Deutsche marks.

2 Not pounds sterling?

1	Well . . . maybe he said pounds sterling. As long as he was writing in English.
2	Hitler knows English?
1	His translators.
2	Must be good translators.
1	The best.
2	They probably could have figured out the problem you posed me.
1	Which one?
2	About the sentence in English that needed to be translated.
1	For a two-week supply of jam.
2	Yes. That one.
1	I don't think Hitler's translators would make the effort to translate anything for a bit of ersatz jam.
2	Probably not. But being translators, they might do it for the pure challenge.
1	They might.
2	So?
1	So what?
2	So finish the story.
1	Yes.
2	Before the next Achtung!
1	Gesundheit.
2	Bitte. So. Hitler said, "Instead of you spending all that money sending planes out to bomb us and instead of us sending all our planes over to bomb you, why don't you tell us which targets you want to hit, and we'll tell you which targets we want to hit, and you could bomb your cities and we could bomb ours."
1	I heard that story before.
2	You couldn't have. I made it up just this minute.
1	Really? You're quite talented. You show a great deal of imagination.
2	You really think so?

1   You're better than most of the comics I used to hear in the cabarets.

2   Thank you for the compliment. I once thought I could make a go of it as an entertainer.

1   It's a hard life . . . working every night . . . working late . . . in smoked-filled rooms. Audiences can be very critical, you know. There's nothing worse than telling a joke to a crowded room and getting no response.

2   I can think of worse things than that.

1   Eating leftovers in the kitchen.

2   I would do anything for a plate of leftovers.

1   Anything?

2   What did you have in mind?

1   Join the Prince's police force.

2   I'm not that hungry . . . yet.

1   I heard they have no trouble getting enough to eat.

2   I suppose. It's hard work putting babies and children on trains . . . beating off their parents.

1   To save the rest of us.

2   Cooperating with the wolves.

1   What choice do we have?

2   We could fight.

1   Molotov cocktails against tanks?

2   Die like men, not penned animals.

1   The Prince . . . is buying time.

2   Time for what?

1   The Russians should be here soon.

2   They have more important things to do than to save Poles . . . or Jews.

1   They'd get to kill some Germans in the process.

2   I think what they're trying to do is figure out how to kill Germans without having to save Poles and Jews.

1   A tricky business.

2   Especially for a Russian.

1	Hey . . . how many Russians does it take to change a lightbulb?
2	I don't know.
1	One hundred.
2	A hundred?
1	Sure. One to hold the lightbulb and the other ninety-nine to turn the house.
2	Hey, you're pretty good yourself. You ever think of becoming an entertainer?
1	A gravedigger, did you say?
2	What's the difference?
1	One tries to slay you with laughter.
2	I've seen some pretty dead audiences in my time.
1	Ready for burial?
2	All of us.
1	I tell you jokes and you think about graveyards.
2	Graveyard humor.
1	Alas, poor Jurawicz, I knew him well.
2	This isn't working.
1	We talk. We joke. It doesn't do any good.
2	Better than the usual entertainment.
1	We used to have concerts.
2	They shipped off all our instruments.
1	There was a public hanging last week.
2	Yes. A woman and two children.
1	That was . . . different . . . a break in the routine.
2	Such differences I could do without.
1	The children were so light . . .
2	You don't have to remind me.
1	We had to stand there until it was all over.
2	What are you trying to do to me?
1	I can't get the picture out of my head.
2	They are paying us back for the Crucifixion.
1	For one death two thousand years ago.
2	The death of God.
1	That would explain everything.

2	What?
1	The death of God.
2	You shouldn't say such things.
1	The Rebbe Himself . . .
2	Petitioned God . . . Sometimes God hides His face.
1	Why?
2	It is not given to man to know.
1	So what are we supposed to do in the meanwhile?
2	Suffer and die, until He decides to save a remnant.
1	Why?
2	For the glory of His name.
1	Such glory He can keep for Himself.
2	I suppose He will.
1	I don't wish to talk of this any longer. In truth, I no longer wish to speak at all.
2	So what am I supposed to do if you don't speak? Talk to myself?
1	Do the best you can.
2	Are you going to leave?
1	Eventually.
2	You could stay here for a while and at least pretend to listen to me.
1	I'm not an actor.
2	That's too bad.
1	I . . . did play a role in a school play when I was six or seven.
2	What play?
1	*The Nutcracker.*
2	That's a Christmas play.
1	What can I tell you? I went to a Polish school.
2	Really? For how long?
1	Three or four years. I wanted to become a doctor.
2	What happened?
1	You know what happened. I was advised that my presence was no longer welcome.
2	And the play?

1   I was a wooden soldier.

2   A wooden soldier . . .

1   I didn't have any speaking lines.

2   Oh.

1   All I had to do was march around a bit and then fall over at the end.

2   How . . . glorious.

1   A foreshadowing. Maybe they were trying to tell me something.

2   Who were the other soldiers?

1   I forget.

2   No other plays?

1   One other . . . at Easter time. A Passion play.

2   Don't tell me.

1   So I won't tell you.

2   So tell me.

1   I got to deny the Christ. They got to curse me.

2   Strange how thing work out.

1   Who would have thought it?

2   They could have given you the role of Jesus. He was Jewish too.

1   I can't quite figure that one out. Why they adulate one Jew and condemn the rest of us.

2   I think I've figured it out.

1   So tell me.

2   They're not really angry at us for killing Jesus.

1   No?

2   They're angry at us for saddling them with a philosophy so foreign to their nature.

1   In what way?

2   Jesus said, "Love your enemies. Turn the other cheek."

1   So?

2   Do you see any of them loving their enemies?

1   Not particularly.

2   So . . . we saddled them with something they didn't want to hear and somehow they got stuck with it and

so they feel guilty, and they've been paying us back with interest ever since.

1   That's a novel theory.

2   I'm filled with novel theories.

1   Like what?

2   Like why Hitler has it in for us.

1   OK. Why does Hitler have it in for us?

2   He's part Jewish himself.

1   That doesn't make sense.

2   You never heard of self-hatred before? Jews changing their names . . . their hairstyle . . . their clothes. I heard that some men are trying to get uncircumcised again.

1   For survival purposes.

2   Some would do it anyway . . . They'd snip off the tip of their noses if they could.

1   Take it off from one place and put it on the other . . . They say I have a Roman nose.

2   You . . . a Roman nose?

1   A sort of Roman nose.

2   To sniff your sort of coffee with?

1   I . . . could use a cup of sort of coffee about now.

2   When is the last time you had one?

1   Tuesday.

2   Well, you had your cup for the week. I'm saving mine for Shabbos.

1   I'm not very good at delayed gratification. You don't drink your cup of sort of coffee by Tuesday, you could be sort of dead by Saturday.

2   Then you wouldn't miss it.

1   Why bother doing anything at all then? We'll all be dead some day.

2   Some sooner than others.

1   I try to get as much pleasure out of every day as possible.

2   Pleasure?

1	Simple things . . . The blue of the sky.
2	Today?
1	OK . . . today was overcast. But clouds are nice too . . . fluffy and layered.
2	And the cold drizzle?
1	Drizzle is better than rain . . . I found a flower in the lot by my place. Not much of a flower. But it was a flower.
2	What color?
1	It was sort of covered by dust. But what the hell. It was a flower.
2	I saw a rotting dog.
1	That's the difference between you and me. I look for flowers. You see only rotting dogs.
2	You misunderstand me. The dog was dead, but the flesh was alive with all kinds of different creatures.
1	Maggots and things?
2	Maggots . . . beetles. It was fascinating. One life giving rise to countless other lives.
1	You're impatient maybe to donate your body to Mother Nature for her proliferation of worms?
2	We have such a narrow view of things. We are so preoccupied with ourselves, we don't look at the whole picture.
1	Which is?
2	The world of nature doesn't really need us at all. If we all disappeared, the insects and the birds would never notice we were gone. They wouldn't miss us at all.
1	Jews?
2	Not just Jews. People.
1	Oh . . . I thought for a moment you were spouting Hitler's line. I wonder what he'll do if we all do disappear. Who would he have to blame then?
2	Slavs.
1	Not quite the same thing. The Protocols of the Elders of Moscow. Doesn't quite have the same ring to it.

2	He'd think of something. He has clever advisors. Theoreticians.
1	They'd have to recreate a history of animosity. Centuries of hatred.
2	It could be done in much less time than you think.
1	More time than I have.
2	More time than Hitler has.
1	You think he will lose the war?
2	He can't fight Europe, the United States, and Russia at the same time.
1	He's done fairly well up to this point.
2	Wait till the Russian winter gets to him . . . just like it did to Napoleon.
1	God's gift to Mother Russia.
2	In a way.
1	What's the difference between Hitler and the sun?
2	I don't know.
1	The sun sets in the west.
2	That's very clever.
1	It's not mine, I have to confess.
2	Whose is it?
1	Jurawicz.
2	Oh.
1	I tell his jokes . . . in memoriam.
2	I'm sure he'd be honored by your gesture.
1	I am perhaps the only one who remembers him. They took him off on the cart.
2	Oh.
1	He'll be buried in an unmarked mass grave.
2	Most everyone is these days.
1	Marked or unmarked . . . it all comes to the same thing.
2	You wouldn't want to have a marker on your grave?
1	They're using old markers to line roads.
2	You're letting things get to you again.
1	Why do elephants have such flat feet?

2 What?

1 Why do elephants have such flat feet?

2 I don't know.

1 From jumping out of tall trees. Where does a 250-kilo gorilla sleep?

2 I don't know.

1 Anywhere he wants to. What's worse than finding a dead baby in a garbage can?

2 I don't know.

1 Finding a dead baby in ten garbage cans. What's the longest word in the English language?

2 I don't know any English.

1 Neither do I. What's the difference between a duck?

2 I don't know.

1 One leg is both the same. What's purple and stomps out forest fires?

2 I don't know.

1 Smokey the Grape.

2 Knock, knock.

1 Who's there?

2 Cantaloupe.

1 Cantaloupe who?

2 Cantaloupe tonight. My ladder's broke. What do you get when you cross a Polish cow with a German giraffe?

1 I don't know.

2 An animal that feeds in Warsaw and gets milked in Berlin. (Achtung!)

1 What do you get when you cross a Nazi with a jackass? (Achtung!)

2 I'm getting tired.

1 You've been going at it for quite a while.

2 Twenty-seven years.

1 I didn't mean it that way.

2 But I did.

1 We can't give Hitler an easy victory.

2	It is over . . . for us. He has the victory already.
1	For the night?
2	For the night. For the week. For the year.
1	You're feeling that way now. Sleep on it. You'll feel better in the morning.
2	After I eat my potato.
1	Yes. After you eat your potato.
2	Without jam.
1	Unless you can figure out the translation.
2	I don't think well on an empty stomach. (Another paper airplane flies on stage.)
1	Another message?
2	You read it.
1	It's . . . another chance to win some jam.
2	What do I have to do?
1	You get your choice. Turn my name in to the Jewish police as an agitator . . .
2	What's the second choice?
1	Solve this puzzle.
2	What puzzle?
1	That puzzle. (It comes rolling out . . . across the stage.)
2	What do you have to do?
1	Work the cube until each side has only one color on it.
2	Hopeless. I've never been able to solve things like that.
1	Solve three puzzles and you get to leave the ghetto.
2	For where?
1	Your choice . . . Madagascar, Uganda, or a labor camp in Germany.
2	You do it.
1	I'll try. I'm pretty good at puzzles.
2	Good enough to figure out how to get out of here?
1	Oh, I've already done that.
2	You have?

1   No problem at all . . . there are places in the fence . . .
2   Then why are you still here?
1   I haven't figured out what I'd do once I got out.
2   I see your point. You wouldn't want to take the chance . . .
1   Can't count that high.
2   What's the difference between a Jew and a pile of ashes.
1   I don't know.
2   About five minutes.
1   Oh.
2   There . . . is nothing left to say.
1   There must be something.
2   Don't blame yourself. You tried your best.
1   You . . . don't have your identification papers with you.
2   Call it an act of defiance. I won't make it any easier for them than I have to.
1   Then this is it?
2   For me, yes.
1   And for me?
2   You'll do what you have to do.
1   I have to go on. I have to see things through to the very end.
2   For me this is the end. You remember the directive. You are not to try to stop me.
1   Was that a directive for Poles or for Jews?
2   In this case, the law is the same for Poles and Jews.
1   Ironic.
2   Fitting. And now I'll just climb over this railing. (Achtung!) No! It's not fair. It's not fair. (The other one climbs over the railing and jumps off without a word. There is the sound of a thud and a cry of pain.) Just his luck. The bridge wasn't high enough. (Black out. Quickly lights come on. The jumper is

lying on the street, gravely injured and in great pain. Two Poles approach, dressed in winter coats.)

Pole 1   The weather has turned cold again.

Pole 2   I've never seen the likes of that before.

P1   It doesn't bode well.

P2   Food will be scarce.

P1   Fortunately, my wife can turn almost anything into a hearty meal. You know the story of stone soup.

P2   I was the one who told it to you in the first place.

P1   A few onions . . . a few potatoes . . . some kasha . . . some gravy from the Sunday stew . . . and a piece of black bread. I am an easy man to satisfy.

P2   In the dining room . . . and in the bedroom.

P1   The simple pleasures of life are the best ones. Simple food. A good woman. Children around a fire in the hearth.

P2   But the Germans . . .

P1   Conquerors come and go.

P2   They talk about a reign of one thousand years.

P1   Conquerors come and go.

P2   There is one good thing about this invasion.

P1   Really?

P2   They'll take care of the Jewish problem once and for all.

P1   You've got something there. (They move off. Two children enter.)

Girl   You're it.

Boy   I was it last time.

G   I'm older.

B   I'm a boy.

G   I have blond hair.

B   But you have gypsy eyes.

G   I do not have gypsy eyes.

B   Sure you do. They're big and brown and close to each other . . . and your eyebrows meet in the middle.

G   My father's eyes are like that.

B	Your father's a gypsy! Your father's a gypsy!
G	Don't say that, or they'll come and take him away. And then we won't have anybody to work and we won't have any food and we'll starve to death.
B	Then you're it.
G	OK . . . I'll be it this time. But you're it next time.
B	I'll think about it. Go hide your eyes and count to fifty.
G	Twenty-five. Last time you cheated when I counted to fifty.
B	I did not cheat.
G	You didn't hide on this street.
B	You didn't say we had to.
G	You have to hide on this street . . . on this block.
B	There's no place to hide.
G	I'm counting . . . to twenty-five.
B	OK . . . I'm going to hide.
G	And this is base. (She crouches behind the body of the man who is still groaning periodically. Before the girl can hide her eyes and the boy can hide, they see two Nazi soldiers approach. They run off, visibly scared.)
Nazi 1	Would you look at that.
Nazi 2	Another suicide.
N1	Not quite a suicide. He's still alive.
N2	I can take care of that.
N1	No . . . let him suffer for a while longer.
N2	I don't know why they do it from the bridge. Can't they tell it's not high enough?
N1	Who can tell anything about these people?
N2	People?
N1	You know what I mean.
N2	Check to see if he has his identification papers on him.
N1	Nope.

N2   It figures. More work for us. That's why we issued the directive. You read it?

N1   Yes.

N2   It was clear enough . . . yes?

N1   For anyone with half a brain.

N2   I think you've hit on the central problem here. They don't have half a brain. They think ignorance is bliss. Well, ignorance is no excuse.

N1   So now we have to search through all the records and ask people to identify him. Time that could have been better spent.

N2   Playing cards.

N1   Drinking vodka.

N2   I don't know why they bother finding out the information. Who cares about a dead Jew?

N1   The directives are clear. Everybody must be identified. The records must be complete.

N2   Who cares what his name was or where he lived, for Christ's sake?

N1   They have their reasons. We must follow orders.

N2   I have wondered at times what would happen if we made up the name and address.

N1   You know what would happen if they caught you.

N2   I can imagine.

N1   Besides . . . the shame of it all.

N2   It was just a passing thought.

N1   Let it pass then. You take care of this one here. I will teach these Jews a lesson. You see there on the bridge. A man leaning over looking at us?

N2   Yes.

N1   And a young woman just coming onto the bridge with her daughter?

N2   Yes.

N1   Watch me pick off the woman and her daughter. Later we will print another directive. For every Jew who jumps without papers, two Jews will die. That should teach them how to behave properly. (N2 drags off the moaning man. N1 draws his pistol and fires twice at the bridge. A moment of silence. A shot from offstage. Blackout. Lights on quickly to reveal 2 alone on the bridge.)

2 Almost night. I am afraid of the dark . . . and spiders . . . and snakes . . . and marshmallows. And silence . . . A German and a Russian and a Jew died and went to heaven. They reached the pearly gate, and an archangel greeted them. And he said to them, "To pass this gate, you must answer one question." "Fine," they all said. So he asked the Russian to say the name of God. "Bog," said the Russian. The archangel nodded, and the Russian passed through the gate. He asked the same question of the German. "Gott," said the German. The archangel nodded, and he too passed through the gate. Then he asked the question of the Jew. "I don't know," said the Jew. "His name has been hidden since the destruction of the Temple nearly 1,900 years ago." The archangel shook his head, and the gate remained closed.

You ask me what that means? I don't know what that means. I just made it up right now. Don't get impatient with me. Don't leave me alone. I can play three musical instruments: classical, cabaret, even American jazz. True, I have no instruments at my disposal to play on, but I could sing for you. No. You don't want that. I can tap-dance. Well, I could before my ankle started to swell up. I could teach you a few chess openings. The openings. That's all. My middle game is weak. My end game is nowhere at all.

A joke . . . I'm always good for a joke.

The war is almost over. The Russians are waiting to advance until the Germans finish with the Jews, and there are only two people left in Lodz: the Prince and one of the members of his council. Another train

arrives to transport Jews to Auschwitz. The Prince turns to his council member, and he says, "You go. Otherwise, it will be hard on the rest of us."
A bit heavy for this late in the evening.
Well, you there, in the front row. I can tell you where you got your shoes. You tell the person next to you . . . Yes. And now I'll tell you where you got your shoes. You got them . . . on your feet. Sorry about that one. One more. Just one. I promise you.
Some Jews float up to heaven, compliments of the crematoria. They reach heaven, and they get to walk on the streets of gold, and they pass a wall. And on the wall, scribbled in crude letters are slogans repeated over and over again, "Beat the Jews," "Christ killers," "Zhid." The Jews look around nervously except for one who starts smiling and laughing. He can hardly contain himself, he is so happy. He dances around in a circle and starts to hum some old Chassidic Nigun. Why are you so happy? They ask him. And he points to the writing on the walls. There are no Germans here, he says with a whoop and a holler. Only Poles. (He bows slowly to the audience and walks off with a step that could almost be a slow, stately dance, a melancholy Freilach, if that is possible, as the lights dim to final blackout.)

Finis
1995

Aaron, The Shoemaker

[Aaron, a poor man, in the clothes of his trade—at least sixty years old—he is working in his shop—with minimal tools and supplies. Enter a working man in his forties.]

I.

Man	Aaron, my shoes!
Aaron	Let me see.
Man	My only pair of working shoes. Look.
Aaron	Already, I see the problem.
Man	The sole.
Aaron	Yes.
Man	It came off.
Aaron	Yes. You found it, maybe.
Man	I lost it in the mud.
Aaron	So you will need a new one.
Man	Yes.
Aaron	I'll see what I can do. It's so hard to get materials these days.
Man	You can help me?
Aaron	I have an old pair of work shoes from Reb Zissel.
Man	Ach. Reb Zissel. Who would have thought it?
Aaron	These are difficult times.
Man	Always difficult times for us.
Aaron	We have to be patient.
Man	I am beginning to lose patience.
Aaron	What good will that do?
Man	No more or less than having patience. It doesn't matter what we do or don't do. The results are always the same.

Aaron	So for the same money, why not be patient?
Man	My anger grows with each incident. It is like a ball of molten iron—a bubble that swells and is about to burst inside me.
Aaron	And if it bursts, what will you do then?
Man	I . . . don't know.
Aaron	So meanwhile, let me get Reb Zissel's shoe. That is something I can do something about. Reb Zissel doesn't need that sole anymore, and you do. A man has to work in this world.
Man	From sunup to sundown. And where does it get me?
Aaron	You have to put food on your table.
Man	I barely manage. But what if one day one of my children gets sick?
Aaron	Are they sick now?
Man	No.
Aaron	So enjoy them now. Tomorrow will be another day.
Man	That's what I'm afraid of.
Aaron	You'd rather be dead now?
Man	No.
Aaron	So you sit there while I put this new sole on your shoe so that you can work, so that you can feed your children and maybe put aside something for the next Simha.
Man	I should live so long.
Aaron	The next Simha could spring up before your eyes like a flower along your path.
Man	Who has time to look at flowers these days?
Aaron	If you don't look at the flowers, they might get discouraged and decide not to grow anymore.
Man	Aaron, you are a strange man.
Aaron	I am just a cobbler, a simple shoemaker.
Man	I watch you at your work. You are so intent.
Aaron	To mend anything in this world, you must do it right. A sole that is not attached right might come

	off and get lost in the mud. Then you wouldn't be able to work and prepare for the next Simha.
Man	You fix it right, Aaron. It will have to last me a long time. To buy a new pair of shoes these days is no small matter.
Aaron	Your shoes will be so happy, they will sing to you all day as you work.
Man	You are a strange man, Aaron.
Aaron	I am just a cobbler, a simple shoemaker.

II.

Asher	Aaron.
Aaron	I'm here.
Asher	These shoes—
Aaron	They are lovely shoes. Your wife's?
Asher	Of course my wife's. Who else's would they be?
Aaron	She is in good health, I trust?
Asher	She is—somewhat delicate—her health, her disposition.
Aaron	You have been a devoted husband, Asher.
Asher	Sometimes, it's very difficult, Aaron.
Aaron	A very devoted husband.
Asher	These shoes. They are her favorites.
Aaron	They are very well made. Anybody could see that.
Asher	I bought them for her many years ago. I had money then to buy her nice things, to make up for—
Aaron	You don't have to talk about it if you don't want to.
Asher	I have talked about it so many times, Aaron. What is one more time?
Aaron	Does it make it any easier, Asher?
Asher	No, Aaron.
Aaron	So maybe this time you don't have to talk about it. The shoes, Asher—
Asher	I was helping her to lace them for the other day. I pulled the laces tight. You have to pull the laces tight or the shoes wobble. She's not too steady on her

      feet. I wanted to make sure she wouldn't wobble and maybe fall.

Aaron   If a shoe wobbles, even the most balanced person can fall.

Asher   I pulled too tight, Aaron. I snapped the lace. She was disappointed, because she had to wear another pair of shoes. She wouldn't put on anything else. She took off her things and went to bed. I'm desperate, Aaron. For the sake of those laces, her whole day was ruined.

Aaron   Laces are important, Asher. They hold together what must be bound. They make movements possible by restricting movement. An interesting paradox, is it not? That freedom comes from restriction. Let me see. Laces. Very long laces. Let me check in the back. [Exits and returns.] These should be long enough. The color isn't perfect. I'll have to dye them. That shouldn't take too long.

Asher   I would like to give her back the shoes at dinner today. To cheer her up a bit.

Aaron   I'll have to mix some colors to get the shade right. Not too light or the laces will stand out. Laces are not supposed to stand out. Yet they are the most essential part. Without them, even the most beautiful shoes can't be worn. Not too dark and not too light. They will be all but invisible. There. That should do it. Take them home now, Asher. Let them dry. Surprise your wife. Nothing like a pleasant surprise to put a nice finish on a long day. A pleasant surprise. A prelude to a pleasant dreams, Asher. A prelude to a pleasant dreams.

III.

Aaron   You look sad, Levi.

Levi   My . . . daughter.

Aaron   I heard. How is she today, Levi?

Levi   She . . . wakes up in the middle of the night, crying. Sometimes screaming. It tears through my heart.

Aaron	What do you have there, Levi?
Levi	Her shoes. The ones she was wearing when—
Aaron	Let me see, Levi. They are tan.
Levi	Like her flesh, Aaron.
Aaron	I can sew them, Levi, from the inside. I can sew them so nobody will ever know that they were torn. Sit down, Levi. This will take some time. I will use small stitches, stitches so small it would take a magnifying lens to see them. When she is up and about, you will give her back these shoes, Levi. You will tell her that as the shoes have been made whole again, she will be made whole again.
Levi	Would that, you could sew her back again from the inside, Aaron. That you could repair the tears.
Aaron	When she wakes up, Levi, you will show her the shoes. You will tell her what I said. Let her dream about the shoes, about walking in the shoes. About skipping in the shoes, running in the shoes. Dancing in the shoes. Tell her that, Levi. It will help her sleep.
Levi	Thank you, Aaron. I will tell her what you said.
Aaron	All things can heal, Levi, if you take the time, just so. All things, Levi, if you stitch them . . . so.

IV.

Velvel	I . . . am going to be married, Aaron.
Aaron	So I heard, Velvel.
Velvel	Next week, on Sunday.
Aaron	*Mazel Tov*, Velvel.
Velvel	They say I am crazy to get married at such a time, that the axe is suspended over our heads.
Aaron	The axe is always suspended about our heads, Velvel. That has never stopped us from getting married before. It is written, so must a man leave his parents' house to be with his bride.
Velvel	My parents are dead, Aaron.
Aaron	The angels in the heavens above celebrate each wedding.

Velvel	They will have a hard time finding this place. They seem to have forgotten that we exist.
Aaron	We will remind them, Velvel. At your wedding, the musicians will play and everyone will dance. You and your bride will be like Adam and Eve in the Garden.
Velvel	Adam and Eve didn't have to wear shoes, Aaron.
Aaron	So Adam and Eve, with shoes.
Velvel	These shoes, Aaron.
Aaron	They have seen better days, Velvel.
Velvel	All of us have seen better days, Aaron.
Aaron	For you, Velvel, I will make these shoes fit for a king.
Velvel	I don't expect miracles, Aaron. They should look . . . presentable . . . for a wedding.
Aaron	I will make these shoes fit for a king. King Solomon himself, if he saw them, would ask you to take them off so he could dance with the Queen of Sheba.
Velvel	For next Sunday, Aaron. Next Sunday.
Aaron	The shoes will be ready, Velvel. But be careful. If King Solomon happens to be in the neighborhood, don't show him the shoes or you will find yourself walking barefoot to the Huppah.

V.

Guerilla Fighter	You must help us, Aaron. Shoes are critical. They must fit.
Aaron	It is important for shoes to fit.
Guerilla Fighter	We go on maneuvers. We travel many miles in all kinds of weather. If our shoes do not fit, we get blisters. People cannot travel with blisters on their feet. A whole operation could fail if our boots are too tight or too big.
Aaron	You will have to tell me each person's foot.
Guerilla Fighter	I have the outline of each one's foot.
Aaron	And the shoes—
Guerilla Fighter	They could be here by midnight.
Aaron	How many pairs?

Guerilla Fighter	As many as we could find. They must be finished before dawn. It would not do to have them discovered in your shop.
Aaron	I understand. I will need materials. Give me a few days.
Guerilla Fighter	We are pressed for time. Every day lost can have incalculable consequences.
Aaron	I think I have, in that closet—maybe it will be enough.
Guerilla Fighter	It will have to be enough. We cannot pay you for your work.
Aaron	I understand.
Guerilla Fighter	Every kopek must go for—
Aaron	Don't say it. You do what you must do.
Guerilla Fighter	Yes.
Aaron	And I will do what I can.
Guerilla Fighter	One day, perhaps, we will be able to—
Aaron	Each one does what he must do. Tomorrow will take care of itself.
Guerilla Fighter	Perhaps. I will return at midnight.
Aaron	Yes.
Guerilla Fighter	At the back door.
Aaron	Yes.
Guerilla Fighter	I will meow like a cat. Three times. I will scratch at the door.
Aaron	I will be waiting for you.
Guerilla Fighter	And I will return . . . before dawn.

VI.

Lupka	[A child.] It is so cold, Aaron.
Aaron	I know, Lupka.
Lupka	Our shoes have holes in them.
Aaron	Yes.
Lupka	Can you fix them for us?
Aaron	I have no more leather to fix them.
Lupka	What can we do then?

Aaron	What we used to do many years ago. I will take paper and fit it in the bottom of your shoe. Newspaper. It will be like a pad. Your shoes will feel like elegant slippers. They will keep your feet warm as toast.
Lupka	We do not get toast anymore, Aaron.
Aaron	You will remember what toast is like, and you will be warmed.
Lupka	What will we do if the paper gets wet, Aaron?
Aaron	Nothing is perfect, Lupka.
Lupka	I am afraid, Aaron.
Aaron	If your feet get wet, it's not such a frightening thing, Lupka.
Lupka	Masha's feet got wet, and she got very sick, and she started coughing up blood, and then she died.
Aaron	There is always more paper to put in when the old paper gets wet, or you can warm your shoes over a fire, and the paper will get hard like leather.
Lupka	I am afraid, Aaron.
Aaron	Do not be afraid, my child. Your shoes will feel like golden slippers. You will dance your way to the stars, and the angels will watch you and smile. Give me your shoes, Lupka. And get ready to dance.

VII.

SS Officer	Aaron, it is.
Aaron	Yes, sir.
SS Officer	Shoemaker—
Aaron	Yes, sir.
SS Officer	You are one of the lucky ones. There are no other shoemakers in the camp. Our boots are in need of repair. You will attend to that starting today. You will make sure that when you are done, they look like new. In perfect condition. With a shine that you could see your miserable face in.
Aaron	Yes, sir.
SS Officer	Officers must command respect. Everything must be spotless. Immaculate. In this godforsaken Drecknest,

this mudhole, this place of rags and squalor, we alone walk as if nothing can touch us. You understand this, Aaron? If there is one nick, one scratch showing, it will go bad for you. Very bad. Sooner or later, we could find another shoemaker to take your place. Is that understood?

Aaron   Yes, sir?

SS Officer   There are many officers. You will attend to their boots two—no, three times a week. You understand this.

Aaron   Yes, sir.

SS Officer   And if the job is well done, you might just find an extra piece of bread on your plate. Maybe an extra bowl of soup. You are one of the fortunate ones, Aaron. Make sure it stays that way.

VIII.

SS Officer   You are doing very well, Aaron. Very well. Starting today, however, there is one more task for you. We just got in a shipment of ladies' shoes from France. Don't ask how we got them. But they are here. They are very fashionable, but some are in disrepair. We have some women that serve the needs of our officers. It is good for morale if they are dressed smartly. It takes the men's minds off the misery that pervades this place. For a few moments, they can fantasize that they are back home—in better times— with more civilized pleasures available to them. The shoes are important. Often, that is the only things the girls will be wearing. These slippers, these heels. Very fashionable. In Paris before the war, they would have cost a small fortune. You do this well, and from time to time, we might give you a bit of ersatz jam for your bread and maybe once a week, an egg. You are one of the lucky ones, Aaron. Your services are useful. And as long as you remain useful, we might keep you around a bit longer. We just might do that. You and the seamstress and the wig maker. One of the lucky ones, eh, Aaron.

IX.

SS Officer

We have another job for you, Aaron. That pile of shoes there. Children's shoes. They won't be needed by their original owners anymore. But there are children back home for whom these shoes would be very useful. We will ship them back home. In times of war, things like shoes can be in very scarce supply. Things are hard back home these days. Our children are suffering enough. The winter will be long and cold. There is no reason for our children to be without adequate shoes, Aaron. You will check these shoes, make whatever repairs are necessary. Shine them up well and put them in these boxes for shipping. We will let you train a few helpers to speed up the process. We'll let you pick five—maybe, ten helpers. Train them well. I think we'll have enough shoes to keep you busy through the winter. Your helpers will get extra bread rations. Maybe some tea. I don't want them to get sick on us. Then the time you spent training them would be lost. You'll submit the list of names tomorrow morning. Ten names. People with nimble fingers who can learn quickly. Our children are in great need, Aaron. There is no time to be lost.

X.

[The Voice of God. Heavenly setting. Angels. Aaron is seated in front of the same pile of shoes as in IX.]

Voice

Look at him there. He is repairing shoes, as he did in life.

Angel 1

He is very skilled at what he does.

Voice

His is a rare skill—a rare talent, refined by many years of experience.

Angel 2

Why do you have him repairing shoes? This is supposed to be a place of eternal rest.

Voice	There is work to be done even here. Watch him. Look at what he is doing. Look carefully.
Angel 1	He is repairing shoes. He is banging new soles on the shoes.
Voice	You still don't understand, do you?
Angel 1	What is there to understand? He is repairing shoes.
Voice	Any job that people do, if they do it in fear and reverence and love, can become a sacred act, an act of healing. Any act. Watch him as he bangs the nails, as the soles become securely fastened to the shoes. He is repairing the split between the heavens and the earth. Watch him as he goes from one pair to another and slowly the pile is diminished. Do you see?
Angel 2	We see that. But we do not understand what that means.
Voice	You do not understand. But people can come to understand. Slowly, slowly the pile is diminished. And when Aaron has finally finished, the rift between the heavens and the earth will be completely mended. It will be time then for the coming of the Anointed One.
Angel	Is this truly so?
Voice	I have said it. It is so. This will be the moment which the prophets foretold. The ushering in of an age of peace. Each of these pairs of shoes is like a witness to an evil whose time has come and gone.
Angel 2	The pile of shoes is like a mountain. Is there no one else to help him? Must he do all this alone?
Voice	He is the one who has been chosen to do this task. There is none other.
Angel 1	But it will take centuries for him to complete the task.
Voice	Then it will take centuries. He is the one chosen. He is eminently qualified. And when all of the shoes are mended, they will be placed on the feet of those who

wore them, so they can walk on the golden streets like menschim,[1] not like animals.

Angel 2   We don't have shoes.

Voice   You don't need them. But people do. And at least every one of them will have his shoes back. The children. And their parents. Everyone. And everyone shall walk the golden streets like the menschim they were created to be.

FINIS
2002

---

[1]   Human beings.

And Then There Were Two

Scene is a dilapidated room that takes up the whole stage, part of a building that has seen better days. The cast is as large as it needs to be. In the play, singers have to double up, since they are singing/acting in various performances under different directors and it is obvious that personnel are in short supply. Similarly, actors double up on roles and mirror the need for fast shifts by sometimes not finishing costume changes in time. This pressure to find people for secondary roles can also be reflected in apparently inappropriate choices, the use of older people for younger characters, and even for gender differences. Some of the awkwardness and inappropriateness should be made manifest in the studied effort to adjust to these casting difficulties and in some frustration when the demands of the inappropriate role assignments prove to be too great. The director has a great deal of latitude in making this process obvious without letting this device overpower the play itself. The play opens with snatches of music from Smetana's *The Bartered Bride*, from the overture. On stage are two directors (any age, sex) plus a chorus of three to five singers (any age, sex). [The dress should suggest dire poverty.]

Chorus:	[speaking] Why should we not be rejoicing When we have the best of health? Only he is truly happy Who possesses this great wealth
Director:	I think you have that one down. Let's go on. Get the words first. We'll get the music afterward.
Chorus	Come, my darling Start the pounding

Still is sounding
Hands entwining
Eyes in trances
Let the whole world
Join the dances
Set in motion
All the band
In great commotion
All the earth
Is moving fast
Let us dance
While life does last.

Director 2: I like that last line.

D1 The whole thing would work really well if—

D2 If what?

D1 If I had enough of a cast to do it right.

D2 I can appreciate that.

D1 I have my main players set. I'm a little short on props. Where in the world am I supposed to come up with a bear costume? And people keep getting sick. Or get shipped out. And there's no heat in this place for rehearsals. But aside from all of that, things are going pretty well. We should be finished by our deadline.

D2 Good. Because I have to take most of your chorus now.

D1 Now?

D2 You had them for an hour. They have another production to rehearse.

D1 I haven't finished with them yet.

D2 An hour. You get them for an hour. I have a deadline too, you know.

D1 What can I do in an hour? We barely get warmed up, in a manner of speaking. [Indicates he's still cold.]

D2 Rehearse your principals. I've got dibs on the chorus, at least on those three. [Enter Director 3.]

D3   And I have dibs on the other two. Good basses are hard to come by these days.

D2   Another thing.

D1   Yes.

D2   This space.

D1   What about this space?

D2   Since you're just going to work with the principals.

Dl   What are you trying to say?

D2   Could you do it somewhere else? We need to start blocking the chorus and our dance numbers.

D1   I need this space.

D2   Do the solos and the duets somewhere else. We've got the stage for this hour.

D3   About those principals.

D1   Yes?

D3   Your Marie turns out to be my Giulietta, and your Wenzel turns out to be my Spalanzani. I am going to need them now.

D2   Now that you mention it, your Hans is my Escamillio and your Ketsel is my Zuniga.

D1   This is ridiculous. How am I supposed to get a production off the ground without principals or a chorus?

D2   You'll get them again, tomorrow, for their scheduled time. Meanwhile, I can't waste time with you. [A few more people enter, haphazardly, dressed pitifully.] OK. Take it from the top. Words first. [A few snatches of the overture from Carmen.]

Chorus   In the square
What a clamor
Some are coming, some are going
Strange indeed they are to see
At the gate
Each one stops to kill time
Talking, smoking, looking out
To watch the passing crowd.

D2	Good. Good. You need to be a bit livelier. Mill about as if you were in the town square. You're supposed to be happy, carefree.
Chorus Member 1	How are we supposed to be happy? The soup was like water today.
Chorus Member 2	The soup is always like water.
CM1	And the bread was moldy.
CM2, 3, 4	The bread is always moldy.
D2	You don't have to *be* happy. Just *act* like you're happy. The audience won't be any happier than you. They're going to have to act like they're enjoying your production. Make it easy on them. Pretend that your soup had meat in it.
CM3	How good an actor do you think I am?
D2	Pretend that your belly is full and that you have a warm apartment to go home to.
CM1	He doesn't want actors. He wants geniuses.
CM2	Or madmen.
D2	Get the girls on. We need the factory scene. Where are the girls?
Girls 1 and 2	Enter We're here.
D2	That's it? Where are the others?
G1	One is out sick.
G2	One is burying her mother.
D2	OK, two is better than nothing. Say your lines.
G1, 2	Raise your eyes to the skies
	Smoke
	Upward it rises in perfumed clouds
	Smoke
	Smoke
	Smoke
	Rising gently
	Soothing the weary soul
	To bliss from pain
	The soft talk of lovers
	Their rapture, their words.

	All is smoke.
G2	Moments fly and ne'er return
	Our joys, alas, are fleeting
	Only memory's torch will burn
	For hours that ne'er return.
D2	That last part is not from our opera.
G2	Whoops. I forgot. That's from the other one.
D2	Well, don't forget. Keep your lines straight. This is no amateur production we're putting on. We're professionals. The audience is not made of country bumpkins who don't know anything. They know this piece backward and forward.
G2	So what will you do if we get something wrong? Fire us? Lower our wages?
D2	No. I am not going to fire you. It's a question of pride. For a few hours, you have a chance to transform this place—to take us to another world. OK, so it's a fantasy world. But two or three hours of fantasy sometimes is worth a whole loaf of bread, especially if you can't get your hands on the bread anyway.
D3	Time!
D2	What do you mean "Time"?
D3	What I mean is that your hour is up.
D2	I barely got started.
D3	Check your watch. Time passes quickly when you're having fun. There's a room offstage. Work with your principals. You'll get the chorus back tomorrow at the scheduled time. [D2 leaves. From time to time, snatches of a *Carmen* aria come from offstage—use an English recording.]
Carmen	If thou didst love me a little
	Together up yonder we would go
	Officer no more commanding thee
	No captain then forced to obey
	No more the trumpet wouldst thou hear
	Forcing lovers fond to part

	For roof, the sky—a wandering life
	For country, the whole world
	And above all—most prized of all
	Liberty! Freedom—the most exhilarating thing
	Freedom—Liberty—
	Free I was born! Free will I die!
D3	OK, now. We don't have much time. Who is here? Stella?
Stella	I'm here.
D3	Giulietta?
G	I'm here.
D3	Antonia?
A	I'm here.
D3	The Muse?
M	I'm here.
D3	And the men are all here?
Voices from offstage	We are all here.
D3	Amazing. First time in days. What happened?
S	They want this ready for the Red Cross visit, really ready. We're supposed to impress them.
G	We did it before. Why is this so special?
A	There are going to be VIPs here. They want it to be really special.
G	What kind of VIPs?
A	The big boys. We're supposed to convince them that we're living in an artists' colony.
D3	Well, in a manner of speaking, we are.
A	Not just a collection of artists holed up together trying to survive, a pleasant little village. An idyllic, Edenic place maintained for us by our benevolent hosts.
S	Who carry their machine guns just for the exercise.
G	On the other side of the barbed wire fence.
A	To make sure no nasty folk from the outside would try to invade our sanctuary.

S   Disturb our concentration, as it were.

G   Our creative inspiration.

A   Our ability to perform on par with companies in Berlin or Paris.

S   Better even.

G   After all, don't they get complacent? They overeat, smoke too much, drink too much, gallivant around too much, burn out too fast. No danger of that for us. We can't overeat or drink too much. So we can preserve our voices for years and years.

A   Or until we get shipped to the East.

G   Or contract TB or typhus or pneumonia. We can stay at our peak.

S   And perform for them as if nothing were wrong.

A   The best acting job of all.

G   Farce.

A   Tragedy.

S   Same thing.

D3   If you're trying to get out of rehearsals, it won't work. The consequences of not being ready for this visit are a bit too disastrous for me to think about. Much easier to think of your arias. Let's focus on Act III today. [Snatches of arias from Act III of *The Tales of Hoffmann* punctuate the spoken words.]

Various People on Stage   Like a ray of flame
                     Flashes your beauty
                     Will thou see the summer
                     O flower of my soul
                     It would be a pity truly
                     To leave death so lovely a prey
                     From the death that awaits thee
                     I shall know, poor child,
                     How to tear thee away, I hope
                     You will sing no more?
                     Do you know what you sacrifice—
                     Grace, beauty, talent, sacred gift

All these blessings that heaven has bestowed on
you—
Have you not heard, in a proud dream,
Like unto a forest moved by the breeze
The soft murmur of the besieging throng
Which speaks your name and follows you with its
eyes?
That is the ardent joy and the eternal fete
Which is the flower of your years you are about to
abandon
I give way to a transport that maddens
What flame is it dazzles my eyes?
But a single moment to live,
And my soul flies to Heaven.
I am mad—
For us the crazy joy
Which dwells in alcohol, in beer and wine,
For us intoxication and frenzy
And oblivion that drowns all
[Of all the musical snatches, the most prominent
should be that of the Muse which comes at the finale.
This can be repeated several times to make the point,
particularly during the speaking of the last lines.]
The man is no more. The poet revives . . . .
Let the ashes of thy heart kindle thy genius,
In serenity smiling on thy sorrows . . . .
Love makes thee great, but tears make thee greater
still

Enter Director 4	Can I bother you for a moment?
D3	I'm in rehearsal. It can't wait?
D4	Not really. No. It can't wait. I need to talk with someone.
D3	So . . . I'm a someone. Speak. [Arias go on in the background. There can be repeats of the last speech as needed.]

D4	The subject has come up for us to do a religious work.
D3	So? There is nothing special about that. We do religious works all the time. There are composers here that set sacred texts—art songs, choral pieces.
D4	I know that. This is different. It is . . . a Christian work.
D3	Interesting.
D4	A Requiem. A Requiem Mass.
D3	A Requiem Mass. How—
D4	Ironic?
D3	OK. How ironic.
D4	The Verdi Requiem.
D3	Ah, yes. Well, we've done Oratorios before.
D4	Yes. Haydn. Mendelssohn. This is . . . somehow . . . different.
D3	How . . . different?
D4	The Haydn celebrates creation. The Mendelssohn expresses yearning for the Messiah. A Requiem—
D3	You underestimate the power of the words as well as the music.
D4	I don't understand.
D3	The struggle to remain loyal to our tradition in the face of the tyranny of Ahab and his idolatrous practices.
D4	Well, yes.
D3	So. The prophets of Baal are all overthrown. How clear can you say it without getting into serious difficulties? This is militant stuff.
D4	A call to arms, as it were.
D3	Not precisely. We are not quite in a position to advocate what would turn out to be mass suicide.
D4	So instead we calmly wait for starvation and disease to take their toll.
D3	We do what we can. We encourage resolve.

Though thousands languish and fall beside thee and tens of thousands around thee perish, yet it shall not come nigh thee. Be not afraid. Thy help is near.

D4 What help, divine intervention?

D3 At this point, what else is there to hope for, or to tell them to hope for? I don't see any human help on the horizon.

D4 So they should just be patient?

D3 What other chance do we have at this point?

D4 I'm sure our honored hosts don't mind hearing these words. I don't see them quivering in their boots at the prospect of divine retribution. They don't mind sly allusions to Ahab and the priests of Baal as long as we tell everybody to be patient and long suffering.

D3 Different forms of resistance are appropriate for different circumstances.

D4 This form of resistance can't be terribly effective if the Germans are encouraging us to take it.

D3 I'm not sure they know the impact of the words on our resolve.

D4 Without food, medicine, or weapons, our resolve won't get us very far. Besides, the theology—

D3 What about the theology?

D4 Pain and suffering are due to sin. Are you really trying to tell the people here that we're here because of divine retribution for our sins, that the Germans are agents of the Lord to do his bidding?

D3 I'd have problems with that interpretation.

D4 Not to mention all that Christian stuff at the end.

D3 That goes with the territory. If you want to perform an oratorio, there are a limited number of Jewish themes. You get to those sections, you can concentrate on the music.

D4 Which brings us to the Verdi. It's a church work.

D3 The message isn't bad, divine retribution for evildoers. Mercy for the faithful. Salvation. Peace.

D4   Why would the Germans want us to sing these words?
      And they do, for the foreign dignitaries. The word is
      that Eichmann himself will be at the premiere.

D3   I'm not sure that I can figure out the German mind.

D4   I'm not sure that I want to, but then again, a Requiem
      Mass—

D3   So?

D4   It's like we'd be singing for our own funeral before
      we're dead. It's almost as if we're acknowledging that
      the struggle is over and the final killing is only a
      formality.

D3   Singing a work this beautiful is not an act of futility,
      whatever happens. The only act of futility is in not
      singing.

D4   So you would go ahead with it?

D3   Under these circumstances.

D4   Namely.

D3   We have no real choice.

D4   These is always a choice.

D3   Sure, we could choose not to sing, and the German
      would then have no use for us anymore.

D4   True. Either way, we wind up in the transports. We
      don't sing, and they get us sooner. We sing, they
      convince the visiting dignitaries we're OK, and we
      get to go a bit somewhere down the line.

D3   Unless—

D4   What?

D3   Unless somewhere down the line, the Germans lose
      the war and we get liberated.

D4   What do you think the odds are of us getting
      liberated?

D3   I don't know.

D4   *So* we're stalling for time?

D3   Yes.

D4   Being useful.

D3   Yes.

D4	Hoping beyond hope.
D3	Yes.
D4	For God or man.
D3	Yes.
D4	Well then, I suppose we should proceed. In Latin?
D3	Yes, Latin.
D4	Why?
D3	It's stronger in Latin. And we can get by with more. We can say almost anything as long as they think no one will understand. As long as most of them don't understand.
D4	So. I'll drill them in the Latin.
D3	Yes.
D4	Starting now.
D3	Hey, we haven't finished our practice yet.
D4	What can I tell you? Your hour is up.
D3	Most of it was spent talking to you.
D4	Tomorrow is another day.
D3	I better get more done tomorrow than today. Time tends to disappear quickly around here.
D4	Faster than you think. Where's the choir?
D3	You mean my chorus?
D4	The last hour, your chorus, this hour, my choir. [They congregate.] We need to go over the pronunciation. Repeat after me. Dies irae.
Choir	Dies irae
D4	Dies illa
C	Dies illa
D4	Solvet saeculum in favilla
C	Solvet saeculum in favilla
D4	Quantus tremor in futurus
C	Quantus tremor in futurus
D4	Quando Judex est venturus
C	Quando Judex est venturus
D4	Cuncta stricte discussurus
C	Cuncta stricte discussurus

D4	Tuba mirum sporgens sonum
C	Tuba mirum sporgens sonum
D4	Per sepulchra regionum
C	Per sepulchra regionum
D4	Coget omnes ante thromnes
C	Coget omnes ante thromnes
D4	Mors stupebit et natura
C	Mors stupebit et natura
D4	Cum resurget et creatura
C	Cum resurget et creatura
D4	Judicante responsura
C	Judicante responsura
D4	Liber scriptus profertur
C	Liber scriptus profertur
D4	In quo totum continetur
C	In quo totum continetur
D4	Un demundus judicetur
C	Un demundus judicetur

D4   Good. Your pronunciation is improving. I've written out a translation so you know what you are singing. We're going to start with the first part. Try to get into the mood. You are petitioning God Almighty for eternal rest and light. Requiem aeternum. Dona eis, Domini, Et lux perpetua luceat eis. Te decet hymnus, Deus, in Sion. Exaudit orationen meum. Ad te omnis caro veniet.

Chorus member It would be easier petitioning for food. How are we supposed to go through three straight hours of rehearsal on a bowl of water someone calls soup, and a bit of moldy bread? For what? To satisfy some foreign dignitaries that we are happy people, singing and dancing while the world around us lets us burn.

D4   What would you have us do? Go out on strike? Singing and performing is what keeps us from dying.

C2   And what we do convinces our visitors that our brothers and sisters, our parents and our children are not dying. We perform. They die. I don't think I can perform at that price.

D4   I can't force any of you to sing. All I can tell you is that those who can't sing anymore and those who won't sing anymore don't seem to stay around for very long.

C3   Is that a threat?

D4   It is not a threat. It is our reality. I don't make the rules. I don't enforce them either. I am as trapped as any one of you. As long as I can get you to sing well, I have some hope in keeping you alive for a few days. Maybe until the next performance. Who knows, maybe the Russians or the Americans will get here by then and you won't have to sing anymore. Libera me, Domine, de morte aeterna in die, illa tremenda, quando coeli movendi sunt et terra. Dum veneris judicare saeculum per ignem. Tremens factus ego et timeo, calamitatis et miseriae, Dies magna et amar valdi.

Cl   What are you saying?

D4   I'll translate for you tomorrow. [All exit.]

II

[Woman 4, the main character, a pianist. In this first scene, Women 1-3 come on as wispy figures, to suggest that they are part of the waking dreams of Woman 4. Their monologues can overlap, using a Sprechstimme mode of delivery (halfway between talking and chanting, eerie). Their speeches can be cut up, can overlap, be treated chorally. They can add dance movements, modern dance movements, to complement the words or separate women/men can be used as dancers while the women intone their words.]

W1   How it . . . was. Like yesterday. Parts so vivid. And yet. We awoke. And they were already upon us. No mercy. The men first. Every one of them. Women

93

too. After many of them were . . . well, you know. They were soldiers. What can you expect? Mothers in front of children. Children in front of mothers. Boys as well as girls. I awaited my turn. Like a starving prisoner yearns for a piece of moldy bread. And finds it sweet to the taste, like a piece of holiday cake remembered from childhood. My turn never came. I just stood there. We just stood there. There was one other like myself. We begged them for death. And they laughed. They tossed babies out on the rocks below. And they laughed at us as they led us away. We did not die. They watched us closely. You cannot stop the eye from seeing or the ear from hearing, the echoes reverberating in the brain. Sounding. Resounding. The heart from pounding. Day after day. I prayed. To God. To men. To no avail. They treated me kindly, in their way. And I lived. And yet do I live. Year after year. To no purpose. Blood pumps through my veins that should have drenched the arid soil of Gamla. My heart still beats that should have fed the vultures that still circle this place waiting for me to die.

Woman 2   You want to know how it was. You can never know how it was. Even if I told you every minute detail, you would not know even the smallest fraction of what occurred. When they came with their banners, proclaiming the reign of the Prince of Peace. And in his name, they cut us down. Town after town. They set fire to our houses. Watched us burn alive. Those that escaped the flames did not escape for long. Women full with child. Old men. Children. For the sanctification of the Name. All. Except for me and one other. They rode around us as if we were not there. I begged them to finish their work, to no avail. I wandered off, alone, to eat the bread of the slaughtered ones, to eat the meat of dead men. To wait. To die.

Woman 3   We thought. If we tell them what they want, they will leave us alone. If we profess to be what we are not. And we did. But they did not. They peeked in at our windows to catch us being what we were. They swooped down upon us like wolves and devoured our flesh. We disappeared, one by one, family by family. Some left in the dark of night. Others were snatched up, never to be seen again. They burned some in the public square. They savored our screams as if they were some great delicacy. The fragrance of our burnt flesh somehow sated their appetites and sharpened them anew. In the end, there were just two of us. I wandered off, alone. Hidden. Almost invisible. And then I hung the star about my neck. To no avail. I sewed it on my clothes, front and back. To no avail. I spat upon their churches in full view of the multitudes. It did no good. I tell the tale now, to the birds of the field, to trees and rocks. To the night wind. I. Alone. [The three women dancers wander off.]

Woman 4   It is not so hard these days to find time to play the piano. Many of the others are gone now. I too before long. Perhaps. Once there was nothing to play on, until they discovered a piano just outside the camp. Not much of a piano really. A box with keys and strings. You would have thought at first that it was made of solid gold. They brought it in, propped it up on old crates. It would not hold a tuning for very long. Some notes stuck. The tone was . . . terrible. But we fought among ourselves to play on it—an hour every other day. We gave concerts on it. Everyone was ecstatic. We played Haydn. Mozart. Beethoven. Solos. With strings. We used it for operas. And then, another piano came. A real one. This time with legs.

A concert grand. A Bechstein. We fought for that one too. And then another piano came, and then another. We didn't need to fight among ourselves anymore. I spent two hours every day—to prepare, to play for them, for us. I practiced. Hard. The études. I prepared myself to play them all. Time after time, until all who wished to would hear them played at least once. I can choose which piano I want now. I play from memory. For those who are not here, I fill the air of empty halls, waiting to be applauded by hands that instead wave farewell. I hear the voices of children singing in the darkness. There is time to play now. Endless time. To play. Anything at all. Perfectly. Or not at all. In empty halls, halls emptied, of all but memory. [Her area of the stage darkens. Enter two children. They can be eight plus. If older, they should affect an air of innocence and naivete. They are dressed in peasant garb.

Pepicek and Aninka   [They seem hesitant at first to enter the woman's reveries. Another child enters with a tin drum, and the children urge him/her to initiate the processes of recall. It should be clear that over the passage of time, the specific words of the opera *Brundibar* have been lost except for fleeting passages. Even parts of the plot are jumbled somewhat. But the initial memory of the first songs start the process of recall.]

Child 1   Beating the drum, singing. [Check CD of *Brundibar*, the melodies oft times are closer than the words.]
Come and get your ice cream
It's so cold, it pleases all
Everyone loves ice cram
Young and old, big and small
Vanilla, strawberry,
Chocolate, raspberry
Boys and girls everywhere

Hurry here, get your share.

[Child bangs for a while, waits—no clear response. Child begins again with a new instrument, a new voice. Check CD for melody.]

Rolls, buns, bread, cakes, donuts, pastry
All delicious, full of flavor
Strictly fresh, straight from the oven
Taste it! Do yourself a favor!
Satisfy your appetite
With my goodies. Try a bite.

[Child plays for a while, waits—still no clear response. Child begins a third time, new instrument, new voice. Check CD for melody.]

Milk, milk, fresh milk, butter, cheese
Come and buy some, if you please
For the children and their mothers,
For the pets and all the others
Milk, milk, fresh milk, butter, cheese
Come and buy some, if you please.

[Woman looks up, stares into space. Child nods, turns to the other two children, waves them to occupy center stage in front of the woman, and then exits triumphantly, occasionally banging on the drum.]

Pepicek (M)   Do you have the money?
Aninka (F)   Yes. It's all here, wrapped up in my handkerchief.
P   Mama will be so pleased.
A   Now we can buy her milk, like the doctor said, and she will get better.
P   We have enough to buy her milk for a whole month.
A   I am so happy. [They sing. Refer to CD.]
    Milk and cream the jolly milkman

Gladly pours into your milk can
But if you don't have a quarter
Your kitten must lap water.

P We'll take just enough to buy her milk today, and we'll hide the rest.

A Where?

P Let me think.

A I know. You remember the loose stone near the well?

P That is a wonderful idea. No one will think of looking there.

A Let's go now.

P Yes. We wouldn't want some wicked man to find us with all that money and take it from us.

A Like that old meanie, Brundibar.

P Yes. We have to hurry. [They exit. A moment later, Brundibar enters. He is crotchety, surly old organ grinder with huge clown shoes. As much as is possible, given his huge shoes, he goosesteps as he walks.]

Brundibar Ah, you scalawags. You thought you could get the best of me. Dancing and singing next to me so you could wind up getting all the coins that were meant for me. That was a nasty thing to do, wasn't it? But I will pay you back for that. I heard where you hid the money. And I will go to that stone and take it all for myself. I will. Or my name isn't Brundibar. [He exits.]

[Reenter P and B]

A Mama was so happy.

P She is going to get better now. I just know she will.

A Let's go back to the well.

P Why?

A Just to make sure the money is still there.

P Why wouldn't it be there?

A I don't know. But I just want to check.

P OK. You go check. [She exists and returns a moment later.]

A   Oh, Pepicek!

P   What is the matter, Aninka?

A   The money is gone!

P   How could that have happened?

A   The stone was pulled out. And the money was nowhere to be seen.

P   Why did I listen to you?

A   You thought it was a good idea to hide the money.

P   But it was your idea to hide it there.

A   You thought it was a good idea too.

P   Who do you suppose might have taken it?

A   I don't know. But there were footprints in the mud next to the stones.

P   Footprints?

A   Big, big footprints. The biggest footprints I have ever seen.

P   There is only one person I know with feet that big.

A   It couldn't be.

P   It must be Brundibar!

A   What are we going to do? Without the money, we can't buy milk for Mama, and she will get sick again and maybe die.

[Singing. Check CD for tune.]

Dear Mommy, you should see how
We grew strong and fair
To think about the past
Maybe you do not care.

Mom rocks a cradle
Which time left empty, cold
And wonders what will be
When she is frail and old.

P   We will have to follow his trail.

A   But even if we follow him, even if we find him, what can two children do with such a person? He is so big and strong. He is like a mountain.

[Together]
No matter how loud we try
Nobody can hear our cry
There are only two of us.

P   Well, we do have our friends.

A   That's right.

P   The cat.

A   The dog.

P   And the sparrow.

A   They will help us.

P   With all of us working together, we can do almost everything.

A   Call the dog. [P barks.]
I'll call the cat. [She meows.]

P   And now the sparrow. [They both whistle. The three animals enter. Costumes stylized. Size of actors not critical.]

A   Friends. We must go off together and find Brundibar. For he has stolen the money we needed to buy milk for our mother.

P   And the doctor said, without milk she will not get better.

A   She might get worse and worse.

P   And even die.
[They all sing. Check CD for melody.]
Voice to voice, and we'll be strong
Become members of our band
Right and justice we'll defend
The dictator will be defeated
United we'll win our stand
We shall give a good example
To all people in this land.

Sparrow   I will fly up high and see where he is.

Cat   I will sneak up on him and scratch his eyes while he sleeps.

Dog   And I will bite his ankles until they bleed.

P   We will find him.
A   We will get our money back.
P   So we can buy milk for our mama.
A   And she can be well again.
Sparrow   We are all friends.
Cat   And we will stay friends.
Dog   To the end of time.
P   To the end of time. [They all exit and return a moment later.]

[Singing. Check CD for melody.]

We won a victory
Over the tyrant mean
Sound the trumpets, beat the drums
Show us your esteem
We won a victory
Since we were not fearful
Since we were not tearful
Because we marched along
Singing our happy song
Bright, joyful and cheerful.

P   We are a team.
A   We can do anything.
Sparrow   You can buy milk for your mother.
Cat   She will be well again.
Dog   And we will be happy and gay.
P   Till the end of time.
A   All who love justice.
Sparrow   All who will abide by it.
Cat   All those who are not afraid.
Dog   They can be our friend.
P   They can play with us.
A   Forever and ever. [They bow to the woman and exit skipping and dancing.]

Call from a Voice Offstage   Are you finished? We need you for a rehearsal—*The Bartered Bride*. Hurry. They are waiting for you.

Woman	Memory. Getting a little fuzzy. You don't eat well, the memory goes. The concentration. You get to a passage you've played nearly all your life, and you draw a blank and sit staring out into space. And then two hours later, it comes to you when you're peeling potatoes. Nothing is ever lost. It just has to be retrieved—from the darkness. [Enter the Kaiser, dressed regally, and Death, a tall, angular man—strong, but almost apologetic for his power.]
Death	You have done very well of late, my Kaiser.
Kaiser	And you as well, my friend. You have been kept busy on the field of battle.
D	War is a busy time for Death.
K	Corpses blanket the fields.
D	That is true.
K	Only—
D	Only what, my lord?
K	The corpses seem to be evenly divided on the opposing sides of the field.
D	That is true.
K	That is a sore point with me, my friend. At the rate the conflict is going, I will barely have enough soldiers left by next week for the next invasion.
D	Your men have always been courageous. They charge into the very center of conflict. I must admit, however, they have not always been careful in following a strategy once it has been laid down.
K	We can change that.
D	A little training can go a long way.
K	That is not quite what I had in mind.
D	What did you have in mind?
K	Well, you know we have been friends for a long time.
D	Yes. You have certainly supplied me with my share of young men.

K	Well, turnabout is fair play. I do for you, and you do for me.
D	What did you have in mind?
K	That we become allies. Partners.
D	You don't realize what you are asking?
K	I do indeed. Spare my men, and I will wage war after war. I will provide countless people for your pleasure—soldiers, civilians, women and children, the aged, the defective, the crippled, thousands, nay, millions. Whole nations and races will fall victim to your swinging scythe.
D	Death works for no one man, Kaiser, not even such a man as you. You overstep yourself. From this day forth, I shall absent myself from the world. You will have to do without me.
K	You can't do this.
D	What can you do to stop me? You can't kill Death.
K	Leave then. I am not such a man as can be intimidated even by Death itself. [Death exits, the Kaiser stands for a moment, then a messenger enters.]
Messenger	Kaiser.
K	Yes.
M	I came from the battlefield.
K	Give me a report. How are our troops faring?
M	As usual, sire. They charge to the very center of the conflict into the maelstrom of blood and gore. They would march to the very gates of hell to defend the honor of Atlantis and its benevolent ruler.
K	Of course. Of course.
M	But something very strange is happening, sire.
K	Tell me, quickly.
M	Never have I seen such happenings in all my born days, and I am far from being a young man.
K	I await your message.
M	In fact, these grey hairs have adorned my head for more years than I would care to tell.

K	You will not have a head to adorn if you do not deliver your message this very instant!
M	Yes, sire. One must keep one's head about him at all times. The message is that, soldiers are being hacked to bits by sabers.
K	That is to be expected.
M	Chopped by hatchets.
K	Of course.
M	Shot by rifles, pistols, and machine guns.
K	So?
M	Shredded by shrapnel and blasted to smithereens by cannon, howitzers, and mortars.
K	Yes, yes—
M	But no one is dying.
K	That is . . . impossible.
M	Impossible or not, it is true. I saw one man with a hole in his chest as big as a melon. Another had his whole face blown away. I saw two soldiers burnt to a crisp—unrecognizable. Others with limbs missing. One without a head. They were all walking around as if nothing had happened to them. No one is dying anymore. The shooting has stopped now. The soldiers are gathering together—thousands of them that should be dead. They are marching—here.
K	Here?
M	It seems so.
K	What do they want with me?
M	I do not know.
K	What is to be done?
M	I do not know. I am only a messenger. But I would not wish to be around when they got here, sire.
K	They cannot . . . kill . . . me.
M	They are rather pungent, sire.
K	They rot, but they don't die
M	It would seems so, sire.
K	And they are coming here—you are sure of that?

M	It is not a pretty sight, sire.
K	How long could they last like that?
M	If Death does not take them anymore—forever.
K	That was man's most fervent dream, once—to achieve eternal life.
M	But if no one dies, the earth will soon be filled with disease-ridden, decrepit people and animals and plants.
K	The situation is intolerable. I must rouse Death from his lassitude.
D	[Enters, M leaves hastily] You called?
K	You have got to resume your old function.
D	My old—impartial function?
K	Your old—impartial function.
D	I could do that.
K	I knew that you would listen to reason.
D	Under one condition.
K	Name it.
D	You're sure you want to hear this?
K	Of course.
D	Fine. I will resume my normal duties—if I can choose my first victim.
K	Is that all? It is a small request.
D	Are you sure of what you say?
K	Of course.
D	Then, I choose you as my first victim.
K	Oh.
D	There is no other way.
K	And if I don't agree?
D	You will have a few companions at your table for dinner, at your bath, in your bed.
K	You drive a hard bargain.
D	Compliments will get you nowhere. Is it agreed?
K	It is agreed.
D	Then I agree to resume my normal functions in this world. [He puts his hand on K, who collapses in

agony and writhes on the floor.] I did not promise you that your death would be quick or painless. Yours will take a while. When the time comes, you will consider it a blessing. [Death acknowledges the woman's presence, takes a step toward her, and bows. She almost welcomes him, but he laughs, steps back, and bows again. He snaps his fingers. The messenger comes back and, at Death's bidding, drags the Kaiser offstage, feet first.]

Voice from Offstage   Hurry. The rehearsal for the Requiem begins in ten minutes. Ten minutes.

Woman   All this is terribly disheartening—depressing, in fact, hardly the kind of entertainment one would want to see on a night out on the town. You will have to forgive me. Memory is a selective affair. And my mind tends to dwell on the morbid these days. Forgive me. Not all of my memories are quite so grim. I could tell you the story of the glass mountain. It's one of my favorites. It was a favorite of the children who lived here until they are gone now. The story remains. Stories tend to live longer than people here. There is no end to the stories to tell. So few people remain.

Once upon a time, there was a peaceful little kingdom tucked away in a little corner of the world. It was not a very rich kingdom or a very powerful kingdom or even a very beautiful kingdom. But it was a very pleasant place in which to live. People worked hard every day to provide for their families, and they loved their king, who worked very hard for the common good.

The king had a daughter—a beautiful woman who was very wise and learned and had a very kind heart. The time came when the king wanted to find someone very special for his daughter to marry. He dreamed of the grandchildren that he could dandle on his knee. The word spread far and wide that the princess was searching for a worthy partner, and soon princes came from many miles away to win her heart. Among the many men who came to see the princess was an arrogant wizard from the neighboring kingdom. He thought himself to be rather good-looking, intelligent, and charming. He thought that if he married the princess, he could gain control over the peaceful kingdom, and so he set out to sweep the princess off her feet, into his arms, and into his power. The first day he spoke with her. The princess listened politely, bowed to him, and went off to tend her garden. The second day she listened to him politely, bowed, and went off to read some ancient books and parchments. The third day she listened to him, bowed, and went off to visit the children's hospital. The wizard grew impatient. He asked for the king's help. The king said that he had raised his daughter to think for herself and he would not ask her to do anything she didn't want to do. The wizard began to get angry. Who were these people who would stand in the way of something he wanted? They were obviously not of a quality worthy of his attention—except that he did want to marry the princess so he could control her kingdom. Being a wizard with an evil nature, he soon found a way to further his plans. He began to spread rumors among the people that the king and the royal family were actually foreigners who had seized power many years ago. They stole money from the people and lived in a palace with rich food and elegant clothes and jewels while the people had to slave away to earn enough to feed their families. They had even changed the customs and beliefs of the people, and now the ancient gods were angry and ready to show their displeasure. The wizard said the earth would begin to shake and wondrous things would happen. Being a powerful wizard, he was, in fact, able to make the earth tremble. The people were afraid. The trembling got stronger. The people's fear soon turned to anger toward the king and his family. The wizard announced that a great sign would appear the very next day. And the very next day, he created a huge mountain of glass that enclosed the entire palace—with the king, the princess, and the whole royal family inside.

The people could see inside the glass mountain. They could see as the days passed by that the people inside were starving to death. But they were afraid, and they were angry. They pretended not to see, as one by one all the people in the royal family died—except for the princess. They pretended not to see her sitting in the garden every day and pretended not to hear the mournful song she sang. The wizard watched the people not seeing and not hearing, and he laughed in his heart. He told the people that there was a hole in the top of the mountain that led to a stairway that led down to the royal treasury. Anyone who could climb to the top of the mountain could become rich forever and ever. He watched people trying to climb up the mountain. They would climb up the stairs right in front of the princess singing in the garden. But the stair ended one-quarter of the way up the mountain. And no one could figure out how to climb the hard, smooth walls beyond that point.

One day an ordinary-looking young man, dressed in ordinary-looking clothes, rode into the kingdom on an ordinary-looking brown horse. He rode straight to the glass mountain. The evil wizard was there at the moment, talking to the princess through a tiny crack in the mountain. [Enter a wizard-like character with clothing hinting at a cross between Merlin and an SS officer. A screen can block the princess from

	the general population, represented by two or three people. The woman can play the princess.]
Wizard	Who are you?
Man	That's not terribly important.
W	What are you doing here?
M	I am here to set the princess free.
W	That's a rather-difficult task for a nobody like you to accomplish.
M	Perhaps. I have my ways.
W	I'm not sure you know who you're dealing with.
M	I know who you are.
W	Then you must know of my powers?
M	Your reputation is known to me.
W	And yet you still dare to challenge me?
M	Yes, I do.
W	You realize, of course, that someone who can make the earth tremble and cause a mountain of glass to rise up from the ground in an instant can also destroy you in an instant.
M	I am not devoid of special powers myself.
W	We shall see what we shall see.
M	Could you please assemble the population to witness our confrontation.
W	With great pleasure. It would serve my purposes for them to see another example of my powers in action. [He claps, two to three people enter as representative of the population.]
Person 1	The people are assembled, my lord.
W	Excellent. This gentleman here thinks he can destroy the glass mountain and set the princess free.
Person 2	The princess—ah, yes. The princess.
W	He thinks he can take the royal treasures that rightfully belong to you.
P1	That would not be just. The people would not stand for that.
M	I will not take a single coin from the royal treasury.

W Ah, he promises this and that. But can you trust such a man? A stranger, who appears suddenly out of no place.

M Not very long ago, you appeared suddenly out of no place. Why should the people trust you?

W Enough of this chatter. The people will watch you fail. Then they can give you a thrashing for bothering them, any maybe then a tarring and a feathering, and then maybe a little burning at the stake or a drawing and quartering [He pounds his staff on the ground, and the earth trembles. The people show their fear.]

M That is a nice trick. [He pounds his staff on the ground. It trembles even more.]

W Impressive, but inconsequential [He pounds the ground harder. It trembles more. Sound of ooh's and aah's from unseen population.]

M Not bad. [He pounds harder. More ooh's and aah's.]

W I may have underestimated you. See what you think of this. [He throws his staff on the ground. It turns into a snake. P1 and P2 visibly frightened.]

M Not bad. [He tosses his staff to the ground. It becomes a snake and swallows W's snake. He picks up the snake and turns it back to a staff.] I can see you are getting a bit worried, so worried, in fact, that you are beginning to sweat blood. [He does]. And considering what a louse you have been to the royal family, it is only fair that you be joined by a few of your kind. [W start scratching vigorously]. And considering the boiling rage you must have by now, a few boils might be in order. [Add pain to scratching.] And considering how you have kept the people in the dark for so long, maybe a little darkness would be appropriate. [W is struck blind.] I think that will be enough—for the moment. You may leave now. Here is your staff. You can use it to find your way back to your own kingdom. If you ever return, I have

<table>
<tr><td></td><td>some more surprises I can give you that will be a lot less pleasant [W wanders off, tapping his cane before him.]</td></tr>
<tr><td>Voic from Offstage</td><td>Rehearsal beginning for The Tales of Hoffmann.</td></tr>
<tr><td>W</td><td>So what happened, you ask? The young man stood before the tiny crack in the mountain, and he listened to the princess as she sang. Then he began to sing with her. The crack in the mountain began to grow and grow until finally there were cracks all over the mountain, and suddenly it just fell apart and came crashing to the ground. The princess was unhurt. The palace was undamaged. But, of course, everyone but the princess had died.

The young man married the princess. They ruled the kingdom wisely for many years. They had children that were attractive, intelligent, and compassionate; and they were loved by everyone in the kingdom. The princess would still go into the garden to sing. There was a sad quality to her singing the people pretended not to hear. She told stories about her life in the glass mountain that no one listened to, and no one seemed to notice one day that she stopped singing and telling stories ever again.

Did you like that story? It doesn't have such a happy ending. I'm not sure if the story really ended that way or if it got changed in my mind over the years. Lots of things have changed in my mind in the past few years. Sometimes I don't even know if it is me telling you this story. [Man enters—one of the "citizens" of Theresienstadt.]</td></tr>
<tr><td>Man</td><td>Do you sing?</td></tr>
<tr><td>Woman</td><td>A little. That is not what I do best. Do you play the violin or the viola or the cello or the flute?</td></tr>
<tr><td>M</td><td>No. I am the choral conductor. I am looking for voices.</td></tr>
</table>

W	I am a pianist. I am looking for instrumentalists.
M	Pity.
W	Yes.
M	We were rehearsing for the Verdi Requiem. Gave one performance for some international visitors who kept calling this place Theresienbad. Can you imagine?
W	That's what they call this place when they want to impress people. The only exotic waters here are laced with typhoid and dysentery.
M	The name worked with some of our German coreligionists. They came here actually expecting to find a spa here. Got some awfully good musicians that way. Should have seen the look on their faces when they had 80 percent of their possessions taken from them when they got off the trains, when they were assigned to the excrement wagons or the garbage detail or the carting away of the dead.
W	Many good musicians did come here somewhat less than voluntarily.
M	Some magnificent soloists. But after our first performance of the Verdi, almost all of our choir members were shipped out. I gathered together a second choir, gave a few more performances, and they did it to me again. I'm a good conductor, but I can't get boards and stones to sing. They want more performances. Where am I supposed to find the singers?
W	I wish I could help you, but I need to practice my own pieces to find others to play quartets, to replace—
M	I understand.
	[Enter demented old woman.]
O.W.	Lo! The book is exactly worded
	Wherein all hath been recorded
	There shall judgment be awarded
	When the judge his seat attaineth
	And each hidden deed arraineth

	Nothing unavenged remaineth.
W	Hey, that's pretty good. She's got the words already. Is she a soprano or an alto? You better get her before she wanders off.
M	Miss, over here.
W	She looks a little frazzled. [O.W. wandering aimlessly.]
M	We need you for the next performance of the Verdi Requiem.
O.W.	Hey, Tomorrow, life starts over

And with it the time is approaching

When we'll fold our knapsacks

And return home again

Everything goes, if one wants

And on the ruins of the ghetto we shall laugh.

M	That's not Verdi.
W	It's from the other Requiem.
M	Yes. I remember now.
W	Maybe you could do that one as well.
M	First things first. We'll be lucky to get the Verdi off the ground.
W	How much time do you have?
M	Thirteen days.
W	Not much.
M	The capos are not really musicians. They think that putting a performance together is like building a latrine.
W	And if you don't get it together in thirteen days?
M	There is no if. One way or another, the performance will go on. They'll find people. Give them work exemptions and special food allocations, and trust we will put on the performance of our lives. And they're right. We will. We won't let anyone think we are second-rate as musicians. The Germans will acknowledge that, at least. The Red Cross folks will go off satisfied that the Germans are treating us well, and within a week, they will ship us off to Auschwitz.

We are singing our own Requiem. The Germans know it. We know it. They know we know it. But the show must go on.

O.W.   But once the day will arrive
When we'll walk out of the ghetto
And life will smile at us
In defiance of the Hamans
We will break the bars
Forward our hope leads us.

M   Where is that from?

W   Last Purim.

M   Ah, yes. You have a head for all of this. Quite a memory. Nothing escapes you.

W   There are times I wish my memory were less competent. It seems to have a life and will of its own.

O.W.   Do not lament
When things are bad
Do not lose hope
But work, work. [She is joined by an old man who begins to harmonize with her.]

M   Not bad.

W   A tenor.

M   Second tenor. Maybe a baritone. First tenors are hard to find these days. Do you recognize the piece?

W   Al S'fod. It's a song based on the poetry of a writer from Palestine.

M   She seems to be a compendium of all that was ever sung here.

W   She and her friend here. Maybe if we just stand around long enough, they will attract a crowd. You might get your whole choir here.

M   Am I doing them any favors?

W   Getting them to sing the Verdi?

M   It's like the kiss of death.

W   You think they might escape otherwise?

M   Maybe.

W	Look at their faces. They're already half-dead as it is.
M	The mind has a large recuperative ability.
W	There are some things even the mind can't do. You might be showing them the ultimate act of mercy.
M	Put them out of their misery?
W	End on a high note, as it were.
M	In hope for divine justice and retribution?
W	I was thinking more of music than of the theology.
M	Oh.
O.W.	Theresienstadt, Theresienstadt When will the suffering end and when Will we be free again?
M	Soon enough, my dear woman. The Russians are advancing. The Americans as well.
W	Not soon enough.
O.W.	Let us not perish, us and our descendants, St. Wenceslaus.
M	St. Wenceslaus?
W	It's an old Czech song.
M	Oh. She's got quite a repertoire.
W	Too bad she won't get a chance to use it.
M	Except for the Verdi.
W	If you can get her to focus on any one thing.
M	Trust me, I've been a choral conductor for over thirty years.
W	She's yours. Now if you could find me a violinist.
M	If I find any of them, I'll send them your way. Where exactly?
W	By the bandstand or at the Bechstein.
M	Ah, yes. An excellent instrument. Surely beats the one we started with, doesn't it?
W	Funny. Then we had pianists with nothing to play on. Soon we'll have all the instruments and no one to play on them.
M	Except the guards. I caught one of them at the Beckstein the other day. They are not devoid of

	musical talent. He was playing one of the themes from the Göttedämmerung.
W	Maybe you can get some of them to sing for you.
M	They wouldn't sing Verdi. Besides, they have more important things to do. And I'm not so sure I want them singing the Requiem.
W	And then they could join you for the next leg of the journey. A small price to pay for singing such heavenly music.
M	A small price to pay.
W	If they would let me, I would do it in a minute. [She begins to move off.]
M	Where are you going?
W	To practice Chopin. The Etudes. For a concert.
M	When?
W	I'm not sure. Maybe January or February.
M	I hope that I'm still around to hear it. [He exits with O.W. and O.M.]
Film Director Enter B2	Excuse me. You are . . . the pianist?
W	Yes. I am a pianist.
F.D.	The one working on Chopin?
W	Yes.
F.D.	Well, I am the director—from Prague.
W	The director?
F.D.	Yes. For the film.
W	The film?
F.D.	About life here in Theresienstadt.
W	I heard something about that.
F.D.	We still have some footage to shoot for the film—not to mention the soundtrack.
W	Life here in Theresienstadt, the food lines?
F.D.	No, not that.
W	The disposal of human waste?
F.D.	No, not that either.
W	The removal of the dead?
F.D.	No.

W	The cattle cars en route to Auschwitz?
F.D.	You are making things more difficult than they have to be. We want to focus on the arts. That is what this place is known for.
W	The arts, of course. And you are making this film for whom?
F.D.	That is not terribly important at this time—just people.
W	The ones not shipped to Auschwitz?
F.D.	People.
W	And you want—
F.D.	To film you playing Chopin, the Etudes on that wonderful piano you have at your disposal.
W	The Bechstein.
F.D.	Yes.
W	To show the world how wonderful it was to live here?
F.D.	To share your music with the world.
W	There are other ways.
F.D.	What ways?
W	Let me go on concert tours.
F.D.	That is not politically feasible at this time.
W	Possibly never.
F.D.	I am a film director, not a prophet.
W	So I should be a good little girl and just play?
F.D.	Yes.
W	And you will want to record the conversation we just had?
F.D.	With some careful editing, yes.
W	And—
F.D.	Enough music to use a background for the film in general.
W	And why me?
F.D.	You are an excellent pianist.
W	One of the few pianists who are still around.
F.D.	Well, yes.
W	You know, of course, where the others went?

F.D.	Yes.
W	And what became of them?
F.D.	Yes.
W	And still you ask me to help with the film?
F.D.	Well, yes.
W	You know what will become of me after I help you?
F.D.	In all probability, yes.
W	And still you expect me—
F.D.	It didn't hurt to ask if you wanted to be remembered.
W	Oh.
F.D.	You would want that?
W	*Hmm.*
F.D.	In the name of the others who won't be in the film.
W	In the name of the others.
F.D.	Yes.
W	You are a persuasive man.
F.D.	I try to be, yes.
W	In the name of the dead, a Kaddish.
F.D.	A what?
W	A memorial.
F.D.	Oh.
W	Whatever else happens, I will play for them.
F.D.	Good.
W	A lone voice crying in the wilderness.
F.D.	What?
W	Nothing. [Sound of a Chopin Etude in the background.]
F.D.	I have been authorized to offer you something—in appreciation for your cooperation.
W	What?
F.D.	This.
W	How wonderful. A can . . . of . . . liver pâté.
F.D.	You don't see much of this around these days.
W	No, you don't. Much better than thirty pieces of silver.
F.D.	A joke?

W	Yes. A joke.
F.D.	Come. Let's finish this segment. I have three more to shoot today.
W	To shoot.
F.D.	To get on film.
W	Oh.
F.D.	You thought I meant—
W	Hardly.
F.D.	Another joke?
W	Of course.
F.D.	Too bad we can't get that on film.
W	I have a favor, maybe . . .
F.D.	A favor?
W	There is some other music I would like to play.
F.D.	Besides the Chopin?
W	Yes.
F.D.	I'll get it on film. I don't know about the final editing. I'll do what I can.
W	I'd appreciate that.
F.D.	What exactly did you have in mind?
W	Some pieces, they were composed here.
F.D.	Nothing too modernistic. Might not go over too well.
W	Nothing too modernistic. Some children's pieces.
F.D.	That sounds good.
W	For the children.
F.D.	Yes.
W	Who are no longer here.
F.D.	That's too bad.
W	Yes.
F.D.	It would have been nice to get some footage of them playing the pieces composed for them.
W	Yes. Very nice.
F.D.	We might be able to sneak one or two of them in.
W	One or two.
F.D.	A snatch, a melody.

W   A fragment.

F.D.   Yes.

W   For the children.

F.D.   Yes.

W   Who are no longer here.

F.D.   And then—

W   Yes.

F.D.   Some scenic shots.

W   Oh.

F.D.   Since the beautification project got under way.

W   That too.

F.D.   A backdrop for the music. Beautiful music deserves no less.

W   To achieve the effect.

F.D.   A very nice effect. In the middle of a war, flower gardens and open space.

W   Achieved—

F.D.   By conscious, conscientious efforts.

W   Leveling dwelling places.

F.D.   Eliminating eyesores.

W   Shipping thousands out of sight.

F.D.   Preserving the healthiest, the most creative.

W   Out of mind.

F.D.   The fires of imagination.

W   The ashes of memory.

F.D.   I have a group in mind for the segment. It is a bit daring, I know. A new beat—dynamic, forceful, reflective of the new political reality for the modern world. A balance to the classic mode, the culture of the past—delicate, ornate. The new regime— masculine, confident, brash at times—making room for itself midst the ruins of the old order.

W   You wax eloquent.

F.D.   I am most impressed by the new. Not the precious, decadent, esoteric, sterile cacophonies of modernism, but the earthy tone of the common man, triumphantly

	guided by the Führer's hand. Jazz—there is a group here.
W	I know.
F.D.	The ghetto swingers.
W	Yes.
F.D.	The music is catchy, positive—even though—
W	Yes.
F.D.	Well, you know.
W	What?
F.D.	The musicians themselves.
W	Ah.
F.D.	One is short, bespectacled, with red hair.
W	So?
F.D.	We don't have to actually put him on film.
W	Hardly.
F.D.	Just the music.
W	Without the musicians.
F.D.	Distill the essence.
W	Discard the husk.
F.D.	Thank you for your time, the day is short.
W	Yes.
F.D.	Time is of essence.
W	Yes.
F.D.	My work must be complete in the next few days.
W	Before the husks—
F.D.	The husks?
W	The chaff.
F.D.	Ah.
W	Are scattered to the winds.
F.D.	I suppose.
W	Please remember, my playing their improvisation.
F.D.	Yes?
W	Das Recht der Auffuhrung bleibt dem Komposisten bei Lebzeiten vorbehalten.
F.D.	To be sure.

W   The rights remain with the players and composers for the duration of their lives.

F.D.   I can attest to that.

W   For the duration.

F.D.   To the very end. Of course.

W   One more thing.

F.D.   Yes?

W   The movie?

F.D.   Yes?

W   What do you call it?

F.D.   Der Führer Schenkt den Juden eine Stadt.

W   Oh.

F.D.   The Führer grants the Jews a city.

W   Yes. Yes. I understand. [He exits.] [She calls out after him.] Will you include the children in the movie?

F.D.   [From offstage.] Of course, children. What would the movie be without children playing in the newly landscaped park?

W   The theater.

F.D.'s VOICE Of course, the theater. [Enter children—a boy and a girl pantomiming idealized bucolic love. He leaves. She is brokenhearted. Director should utilize sections from Mozart's *Bastien und Bastienne* as background for this section.]

Bastienne I am forsaken, and with him gone both sleep and rest
Naught can I do, by big sorrow shaken
Vision and mind are so depressed
Deep agitation stirs my soul
This dire need takes death as toll.
[Enter Colas, a Wizard, dressed accordingly.]

Colas Diggi, daggi, schurry murry
Hurum, harum
Lirum, Larum
Raudi, maudi
Giri, gari

               Posito besti, basti

	Posito besti, basti
	Saron Froh
	Fatto, motto
	Quid pro quo.
	He makes appropriately grandiose gestures. Bastien reappears and tries to make up with Bastienne. She repulses him at first; then there is a reconciliation.]
B and B	We're reunited, love's crown thus sighted, and saved from hopelessness, by loyal tenderness.
	[Enter chorus of children (2).]
Chorus	See how after showers dawns a fairer day.
Colas	Now your happy future flowers, thanks to my great magic might.
B and B	Souls a-turning, full of gladness
	Hand in hand press
	Naught of sadness you e'er confess
	All our heart wounds he hath healed
	Truly, wonders he has done.
	[At this point, officials in quasi-Nazi uniforms come in and lead one of the two children in the chorus off. The opera ceases, music stops, children in turn read poetry addressed directly at the audience.]
Remaining The Chorus Member	last, the very last
	So richly, brightly, dazzlingly yellow
	Perhaps if the sun's tears would sing
	Against a white stone
	Such, such a yellow
	Is carried lightly way up high
	It went away I'm sure because it wished to kiss the world goodbye.

For seven weeks I've lived in here
Pinned up inside this ghetto
But I found my people here.
The dandelions call to me.
And the white chestnut candles in the court.

Only I never saw another butterfly
The butterfly was the last one
Butterflies don't live here
         In the ghetto.

[Bows seriously to the audience. Prompter comes
in with a cue card, shows it to the audience: CLAP.
At this point, the officials return and lead that child
offstage.]
Bastienne   I'd like to go away alone
Where there are other, nicer people
Somewhere into the far unknown
There, where no one kills another
Maybe more of us
A thousand strong
Will reach the goal
Before too long.

[Prompter returns, holds up cue card for applause,
Bastienne bows, officials come and lead her off.]
Bastien   [Puts on glasses to read. During the reading, Prompter
in the background is heard to say repeatedly,
pleadingly, despairingly, "Will someone please tell
him to take off his glasses before it's too late?"]
A little garden
Fragrant and full of roses
The path is narrow
And a little boy walks along it.

A little boy, a sweet boy
Like that growing blossom.
When the blossom comes to bloom,
The little boy will be no more.

[Prompter holds up card, boy bows, is led off by
officials.]

Colas   The heaviest wheel rolls across our foreheads
To bury itself somewhere deep inside our memories . . .
[Officers interrupt his reading and lead him off. Prompter drops cue card.]

Prompter   I have to go now and deliver the mail. There is usually not much. We are a bit cut off, you know. The Danes get packages from home. Little else gets through—except once in a while—from Birkenau, a whole package of post cards assuring everyone that all is well. Better even than here. Well—
You'll have to excuse me. I have to finish delivering them before . . . Well, there are all kinds of spectacles in this place. The dramatic is everywhere. Even in the public square. Would you believe, today, a public hanging for assorted crimes, smuggling in a letter, trying to talk to a wife when she was being sequestered. Other things like that. No tickets needed for this performance. Admission is free. Required actually. The families get the front row seats. Front row, center. No coming late for the performance. The management sets the rules. No room for ad-libbing either. If you'll excuse me, I'll be back before long. These impromptu performances keep you on your toes. You rehearse what you think is the script, and then suddenly you get a new author preempting your rehearsal schedule. We scrape for casts, never manage to get enough people to cover the parts. But they somehow managed to get everyone they need with no difficulty.
Like a few months back. The census. They had all of us out in a muddy field for hours. Very dramatic. Planes flying overhead. Sound of machine guns in the hills off to one side. No food. No water. No toilets. Now that's real drama. A cast of thousands. Forty thousand or so at last count, though to tell you

the truth, we lose about 150 a day to malnutrition, disease, exhaustion, beatings, and what have you. And people are shipped out to the East. New people are shipped in. Hard to tell about the exact numbers. The cast for that drama was diminished a bit at the end. By a couple hundred, give or take a few. The price you pay for art.

I have to go now. Running late. The mail, such as it is, must be delivered on time. Oops. I almost forgot. Cardinal principle of the theater. Can't leave the stage empty. So I present to you one of the singers from the ghetto swingers and his rendition of "Ol' Man River." [Singer enters, having only partially completed applying shoe polish so as to appear in blackface. Adapts weird Southern pronunciation. Starts softly.]

You and me, we sweat and strain
Body all achin' and wracked with pain
Tote dat barge, lift dat bale
Get a little drunk
And you're thrown in jail
I gets weary and sick o'tryin'
I'm tired o' livin' and scared o' dyin'
But ol' Man River, he jes' keeps rollin'—along
[Bows. Lights.]

III

Prompter   Glad to have you back. Things are rather hectic at this point. The International Red Cross is coming for an inspection. There is a beautification project going full tilt. Streets are being cleaned. Houses are being painted, pastel shades, nice. Well, not all of them. Just the ones in the central area of town. Gardens are being planted by the children. Yes, there are still children here. In new clothes. Well, not quite new. Close enough. With new tools—rakes, hoes, shovels, and the like. The children are learning new songs for the occasion. No. You don't want to know the words. Kitsch. Pure kitsch. I won't tell you who wrote the words or the music. It would be an embarrassment. There are new flowers on the lawns. Everything is being mowed, hand trimmed. A couple of cafes have been opened. A few jazz groups are lined up to perform. The audiences are being lined up to attend. Vouchers are being issued for food and drinks and cigarettes. Some empty stores have been converted into bakeries. Bakers have been called into service, white gloves and all. There are going to be produce stores as well, with real vegetables in them. The orchestra is set to play an all-Mozart concert. A soccer game has been scheduled. And a swim meet. And a high dive contest, with a film crew to capture the thrill of victory and the agony of defeat, with soldiers in boats downstream to make sure the contestants don't get carried away with enthusiasm or disoriented and swim the wrong way after they make their dives. There will be a clothing store—where people can buy back at discount prices objects confiscated from them when they got here. And general stores, where people can buy things that look a lot like things that belonged to people who are no longer here. An opera is scheduled for the gym—by a Jewish composer, no less. There is a garden party set up with local dignitaries. The leader of the community will arrive in a limo driven by an SS officer who will open the door for him when he gets in and out and will bow appropriately—the same one who beat him mercilessly only yesterday. That's poetic justice for you. There will be new linens for the hospital and new uniforms for the nurses. Of course there will be fewer patients for them to attend to. Wouldn't want to give the impression of overcrowding. And the orphans will be gone. Wouldn't want to suggest that families had been dislocated. There will be a carousel for select children in freshly laundered clothes to ride on. Oh, and a bank. I forgot to mention the bank, with its freshly minted bills of 1, 2, 5, 10, 50, and 100 koruna. With a picture of Moses carrying the Ten Commandments on the front of each bill, a nice touch. There will be a fresh load of children from Holland arriving, with the camp director himself there to greet them and lift them off the train—to set them down on the soil of their new home.

This is high drama, wouldn't you think? Extremely well orchestrated down to the slightest detail. Not exactly strict realism, but it doesn't seem that realism is required for this performance. Not even a semblance. A suspension of disbelief is all that is required from the audience, which is nothing new for the audience in question. They are conditioned for such exercises and will play their roles admirably.

Now I should mention that even the best-laid plans of mice and men sometimes go awry. It rained here heavily last week. The river eroded the banks down by the cemetery. Some coffins were seen floating down the river and some bodies in various states of decay. Hardly a sight to show visitors not accustomed to that kind of thing. But that occurrence was a fluke. The director assures us that nothing like that will occur during the visit. He must feel confident that he can predict the weather or control it. Nothing would surprise me anymore. [The woman enters.]

Woman	The Etudes. They will be ready.
Prompter	No Etudes. The director has been explicit. They are too melancholic. Too tempestuous. Too unsettling. Your time will come—later.
W	My time will come later. [She wonders off, some indication of the passage of time.]

Prompter   As I told you, the production was well staged, and as I expected, it was well received. The international committee was supposed to go on over to Birkenau as well, where they had a drama of similar character and caliber to show them. But our production was sufficiently impressive that they didn't feel the second stop was necessary. Too bad. That would have been a challenge for any director. To convince a person of any intelligence at all that Birkenau was a pleasant haven, built as it is only a few hundred yards from the crematorium. Now that would have been a tour de force. Speaking of which, I need to inform you that the head director is here. Eichmann himself. Now that doesn't happen every day. I'll bow out at this point and let the principals take over. [Eichmann enters with a man of scholarly appearance in peasant garb and with an assistant in Nazi uniform.]

Eichmann   I am gathering together a group of Jewish scholars for a major project. I would like you to help me with it.

Scholar   I am a laborer, Herr Eichmann, a simple worker in the fields.

E   I know who you are. I have a project I wish to complete as quickly as possible. I have always been interested in your books of learning. You might say that I am a student of your traditions. It would please me greatly to be able to offer the public an edition of your Talmud in German translation. Your books are a mystery to those who don't read the arcane languages they are written in. I already have a committee working on this project. You would be welcome to join them.

S   A worker, Herr Eichmann. I am just a simple worker.

E   Think about it. I'll give you a few days. You would be freed for the duration of the project from all manual labor. from the sun beating down on your head in summer, from the freezing winds and rain of winter. Think it over carefully. There are times when unskilled workers are judged to be expendable. You understand me. Yes. I knew you would. You are an intelligent man, a highly intelligent man. I'm sure you will come up with an appropriate decision. You may go now. [He exits.]

Bring in the artists. [The assistant leads in three men dressed in rough clothes.] So you are the three. Let me look at you. I am an excellent judge of character. I can tell by a man's face, by how he carries himself. You three look honest enough, intelligent enough to know what is good for you. You were brought to Theresienstadt because your artistic talent was recognized. You are among the privileged few. I'm sure you realize that. Others have it much worse. Times are very difficult during a war. Many of our own German citizens are finding it more difficult to make ends meet than you are here. Here, the meals are predictable, the workloads are light. I have provided you with paper, pens, ink, charcoal, paints. Do you realize what luxury items these are? Many a German artist would do almost anything for free access to such materials, to draw, to paint. To what end? What I ask you is the true purpose of art. I am waiting for an answer.

Artist 1	Art is an effort to portray a reflection of the artist's vision of the world he lives in.
E	Ah yes, of the world he lives in.
1	Yes, Herr Ecihmann.
E	You would agree?
Artists 2, 3	Yes, Herr Eichmann.
E	And if the artist chooses to turn his back on the real world, to substitute for the world a myopic, distorted view, a self-indulgent caricature of the world. What then?
Al	The artist creates for an audience.

E   Exactly. And if the audience is not there?

Al   He does not get to sell many of his works.

E   He goes hungry, you might say. You don't answer. And who, might I ask, is the audience for these works of yours that we have found—look at them! "Quarters for the Aged." That is . . . grotesque. "Waiting for the Worst"—what is that supposed to mean? "Going to work"—look at the grotesque distortions in their faces. Real people don't look like that. "Mass Burial"—you are leading your people to despair, not hope. And your picture, "Hunger"—people scratching at heaps of garbage for potato peels—that is propaganda of the worst kind.

I know you artists. You are elitists, all of you— wounded by the smallest disappointments, like little children throwing tantrums because your lollipop was the wrong flavor. I even know who your audience was supposed to be. You thought you could outwit us, didn't you? That you could smuggle the pictures out, get them to the other side. Convince the people out there that things are far worse here than they really are so they could think us monsters. It won't work, of course. The International Red Cross has come and gone. They have written up a glowing report of their visit here. They won't be back for quite a while. If and when they return, they won't miss the people we have found it useful to relocate. And they won't miss you either after you are moved to your new quarters in the Kleine Festung prison. I think you'll have adequate time there to muse on the errors of your ways—you and your families. Take them out of here. [They are led off.]

These Jews. People of a certain degree of talent, that is true. But what can you expect from a degenerate race? A twisted view of the world—poisoning the imagination of the people. We will finally cleanse the world of their pernicious influence. After all these centuries. It is a matter of months, not years. Of weeks, perhaps. [He leaves and returns with two to four people in formal attire. He himself is dressed more formally—perhaps suggested by a simple change of jacket.]

E   So happy to have you visit us again—so soon.

Man   It is good to be back. We are under some pressure to make sure things are OK. We are getting reports that are frankly quite disturbing.

E   Feel free to look around. The town is very much the way it was the last time you were here.

Woman   Somehow it seems there are fewer people in the streets than last time.

E   It was a difficult winter. There were shortages of rations and medicines. In wartime, everyone suffers. And then, we had to deploy many of the people here—for work details. And the front approaches. Some were moved for their own safety. But don't worry. We still have enough on hand for the performances.

W   Ah yes, the performances.

E   The Tales of Hoffmann—by a Jewish composer, you should know.

W   Yes, Offenbach.

E   And a repeat performance of the Verdi *Requiem*.

M   That's impressive. Such a powerful work. It takes a good choir and a good orchestra—and an excellent conductor to make it sound like anything at all.

E   We are very fortunate in that regard. We have excellent musicians here. You will be pleased once again. And this evening, after dinner, a piano recital, Chopin.

M   My favorite.

E   So while the Germans prepare for the Allied assault, the people here lead a life most ordinary people would envy.

W   Even the barbed wire?

E	For protection. Many among the local population are not too friendly to the Jews. We keep them out. We can walk around the center of town to the performance hall and see how the rehearsals are going. [They walk]. Listen. The Verdi. It is quite . . . superb. [They stop to listen.]

Voices	[Recorded music] Quid sum miser
	      Tunc dicturus
	      Quem patronum rogatorus
	      Cum vix justus si securus.

M	Their pronunciation and elocution are excellent.
Voices	Lacrymosa dies mosa Huic ergo parce Deso.
E	Yes, they do a remarkable job in everything they undertake. I am very proud of what we have accomplished here.
Voices	Libera animas de poenis inferni et de profundo lacu Ne absorbat eas tartarus ne cadant in obsurum— De morte transire ad vitam.
E	I think you will be pleased with the final production—this evening. It should be quite memorable.
Voices	Benedictus qui venit in nomine Domini.
E	We've had our problems, you should know. The choral director is no longer with us.
W	I'm sorry to hear that. I remember the last performance. It was quite moving.
E	We have had to be rather resourceful with our personnel of late.
Voices	Dies irae Dies illa Solvet saeclum in favilla Quantus tremor est in futuru Quando Judex est venturas.
E	But the results, I can assure you, will be most satisfying.
Voices	Dona eis requiem

Lux aeterna perpetua luceit eis.

E Most satisfying.

W And the Offenbach?

E Also doing quite well, under rather trying circumstances.

W It is one of my favorite works. I remember when I first saw it in Paris. Those were happier times.

E This performance should then bring back happy recollections. [They walk. Verdi's music disappears and is replaced by Offenbach.]

Voices The sky its radiance lends to beauty
But hidden in iron hearts is hell.

M I remember the last performance. Stella was superb.

E Her replacement does very well.

M And Antonia.

E Her replacement is also quite an accomplished singer.

Voices Like a ray of flame
Flashes your beauty.
Wilt thou see the summer,
O flower of my soul?

W I remember Spalanzoni.

E We had some difficulty finding someone to take that role.

W And Dr. Miracle. A very demanding part. Not only the singing, but the acting as well.

Voices From the death that awaits thee
I shall know, poor child
How to tear thee away, I hope.

W And Hoffmann. What a dimension of pathos he gave to that role.

E Ach. Hoffmann. We have made a real discovery there. A talent hidden from view.

Voices 'Tis her voice, do you hear
A talent that the world has lost.

E One never knows what is possible until one has been pushed to the very edge.

Voices	But a single moment yet to live, and my soul flies to Heaven.
M	And the Muse. The last aria. The dazzling conclusion to it all.
	The man is no more, the poet revives
	Let the ashes of thy heart kindle thy genius.
E	Yes, a pretty work, when all is said and done. We had the score shipped here, especially to please the . . . inhabitants. A Jewish composer and a Jewish cast. Most appropriate.
W	The ending, the tone, the irony reminded me flittingly of the tone at the end of the Göttedämmerung.
E	There is no basis for comparison!
Aide	[Enters] Herr Eichmann.
E	What is it? We are engaged in important matters at this time.
A	The buses have arrived.
E	What buses?
A	To evacuate the Danish Jews.
E	How dare they, at this time!
A	We tried to intervene. They said we had no right. The moment the Jews were on the buses, they were in international territory.
A	And—
A	We had to let them go.
E	You had to let them go. This is a matter not for now. I will discuss it with you later. It is time, now, for our dinner. It has been especially prepared. The table is set, with fresh fine linen. And crystal. And china. The finest silverware.
A	I should tell you, Herr Eichmann, that the servers—
E	Yes, the servers.
A	They are new, Herr Eichmann, not the most experienced. Most of the old servers left on the last transport. Some are in the opera, and some are in the chorus. We had to choose. Priorities.

E   How was I to know they would demand another visit so soon after this last favorable report? How was I to know? But we will make do. This is only a small difficulty. They will understand. How could one expect the impeccable service of a grand restaurant in a place like this?

A   How indeed?

E   Everything will be just fine. And I trust the report they make will again be quite favorable.
     [Sound of music in the background. The first music in phrases of "Deutschland, Deutschland über alles." As the music gets truncated to "Deutschland, Deutschland über" to "Deutschland, Deutschland," there are loud, discordant, cacophonous chords. The musical phrase gets shorter, more tentative, softer, more timorous, and the musical retort stronger, more strident.]

E   And another thing.

A   Yes, Herr Eichmann.

E   Silence that music, once and for all, and get that pianist.

A   Which pianist?

E   While we eat.

A   Yes, Herr Eichmann.

E   To play Chopin. Something lyrical. Nocturnes. Waltzes. My dinner guests are not to be disturbed by such degenerate modernism. They are not to be disturbed—at all.
     [The dissonant music ends abruptly. Sounds of a Nocturne. Plaintive. Halting. E and his guests exit. Lights dim to a somber level. Pace of action slows. We are in the fortress prison of Kleine Festung. A pile of dirt to one side is uncovered. The three artists enter in slow motion and begin to move the dirt from one side of the stage to the other. A guard brings in a wheelbarrow and places it center stage. He looks at

the prisoners with calm contempt. One carries the dirt from the pile to the wheelbarrow with a teaspoon. The second whose hands are crippled is forced to bite off chunks of dirt and carry them to the wheelbarrow in his mouth.

A third, whose legs are crippled, cups the dirt in one hand and crawls to the barrow. The guard watches for a while and moves off. The crawler and spoon handler continue their work. The artist with the crippled hands looks around, finds a piece of coal he has left to one side, painstakingly removes a piece of paper he has hidden on his person, and slowly begins to draw the scene. Some moments pass. The woman enters and watches the drawing in progress. At a certain point, he finishes the picture, looks around to see where he can hide it, sees the woman standing there, and gives her the picture. He then returns to his work, and the stage is slowly darkened until there is only one lit area—the spotlight on the woman herself. The impact of the slow motion should be stylized rather than melodramatic, oriental theater rather than soap opera, ritualistic.

Woman   I left Theresienstadt after it was liberated by the Russians. They came in triumph, bringing food, macaroni, and pork and bread. The inmates attacked the bread wagons like sharks in a feeding frenzy. There were some writers later. They watched and took notes about what they saw. I wanted to play for them. Chopin. But I never got the chance. I wanted to play. I have to play. Even now. The Etudes. Always, the Etudes. I could play for you now. Maybe not. You have been here for a long while. You must be tired by now. Some other time.

The critics say that I play well technically, but they fault my interpretation. Too emotional, they say. Barely controlled. At the edge. Besides, what audience would want to sit through a whole evening of just the Etudes, without other contrasting works of a less emotional bent? The audience leaves the concert hall utterly exhausted—completely spent. Such a program is self-serving, they say, and does not take the feelings of the audience into account. People wish to be entertained, not emotionally savaged. And I must admit, after an initial enthusiasm, audiences have fallen off of late. I am not invited to give concerts the way I once was. I have fallen, as it were, on hard times. And I understand. I do. Times and circumstances change. People's needs and desires change. I do not wish to impose. There are younger artists now, reflections of the current temper. They are the ones that draw acclaim. Their playing is brighter. More sparkling. Audiences come from hearing them uplifted. Excited. Entertained.

I still get my chances to perform—for people in old age homes, for refugees, for children. I still play—

I carry the picture with me wherever I go. It is getting old now. The paper is getting really brittle. It will not be long now before it falls apart, crumbles, blows away in the wind. I don't want it to end like this. You have been very patient with me. I can sense that you are tired now, that you have been subjected to more than you had bargained for. That was not very fair of me. I beg your apology. I am getting old. Sometimes I do get self-indulgent. I have to be reminded to keep things within the bounds of reason. I have to be reminded. When you get on in years, you tend to forget. A lot of things. So I will be more responsible today than I am usually. You are deserving of consideration.

I have found someone who was with me in Theresienstadt. It's true, they did ship her out to Birkenau. She was on the forced March of 1945 from

Auschwitz to Buchenwald. I caught sight of her in a supermarket last year in Detroit. I recognized her immediately. We talked about old times.

Sometimes we travel together. I brought her along for this occasion. She was always of a cheerful disposition, and I can always count on her to lift my spirits when I feel down. I don't know if you will recognize her. She was in one of the choruses in Carmen. She was one of the cigarette makers. Her voice is not what it once was. But she remembers the lines as if she had learned them yesterday. She remembers them, every word. So we will end on a cheerful note, I can promise you that. We will end on a cheerful note. [The old woman enters, takes center stage, nods for the music to begin. The appropriate music is played softly in the background, while she half-sings, half-says the words.]

Raise we our eyes to the skies
Smoke
Upward it rises in perfumed clouds
Smoke
Smoke
Smoke
Smoke
Rising gently
It soothes the weary soul

To bliss
From pain
The soft talk of lovers
Their rapture
And their words
All is
Smoke.

[The woman nods in appreciation and goes to the singer. They walk off, arm and arm, like two old ladies would. The lights are cut off suddenly as they are halfway en route to exiting.]

Finis

The Entomologists Of Lodz

[Open space in the ghetto of Lodz in 1942. There need not be much in the way of scenery. Just enough to suggest squalor. The characters are Herr Todtmacher, a Nordic-looking petty German officer in his early thirties, in uniform. Jankowicz, a Pole of about twenty-five, dressed in worker's garb, and three children, aged eleven—two boys and a girl—dressed in hand-me-downs and tatters with the yellow star on their chest. No particular effort need be made for realistic detail in the sets or realistic transition from scene to scene.]

Herr Todtmacher (T), Jankowicz = (J), Boys (Bl, B2), Girl (G)

J	I found something, Herr Todtmacher.
T	What did you find?
J	A bug, a pretty one too.
T	Are you sure it's a bug?
J	It looks like a bug.
T	Let me look.
J	Here.
T	It's not a bug.
J	It looks like . . .
T	Haven't I taught you anything at all? Look at the mouth parts. What do you see?
J	I see . . . uh . . .
T	Jaws. Correct?
J	Yes, Herr Todtmacher
T	And what do bugs have?
J	I . . . don't remember.
T	A sucking tube.
J	Yes. I remember now.
T	And the wings. Look at the wings.

J	The wings—
T	The wings are completely covered by the wing covers. In bugs, the wings are only half-covered.
J	Half-covered.
T	That's why true bugs are called hemiptera—half wings.
J	Hem-hem . . .
T	Hemiptera.
J	Hem-iptera.
T	So the wings are completely covered, and there are jaws. so we have a—
J	A beetle!
T	Right. A beetle. You are learning something after all.
J	It is a pretty beetle.
T	Yes.
J	Is it good, for your collection?
T	It is a common variety—scaribidae, a dung beetle. But it is a good specimen. Yes.
J	I am glad.
T	Where did you get it?
J	By the school.
T	Where exactly.
J	In front, on the wall.
T	Good. You must learn to be precise I matters of this kind. When did you collect it?
J	This morning
T	When? Exactly.
J	At ten o'clock, I think. Yes. When they took off the twenty-five school children. Ten, or maybe a little later.
T	You must be precise. Ten or ten fifteen?
J	Ten fifteen.
T	Good. Then record the date, time, location, and the species.
J	The species?
T	You look it up in the book.

J   There are so many pictures in the book. They all look the same.

T   The book tells you how to know which species it is.

J   Such long words, Herr Todtmacher.

T   If you want to be a real collector, Jankowicz, you have to learn those words.

J   Yes, Herr Todtmacher.

T   We will go slowly. You know the difference between bugs and beetles now?

J   Yes, Herr Todtmacher. You look at the wings and the mouth.

T   Good.

J   Is it a good specimen?

T   Yes, Jankowicz. You have done well.

J   I did exactly what you told me. I put the jar under him and just flicked him. I put the lid on before he could fly away. And then I watched him till he stopped moving. It took a long time, Herr Todtmacher.

T   With beetles, it takes a long time. Flies, butterflies, moths—they go quickly. You learn these things with experience. Which insects die in moments. Which linger. Some beetles are really stubborn. They close off their spiracles—breathing tubes. They can last for an hour or two. That's amazing when you think about it, an hour or two in a cyanide jar. A person wouldn't last for more than a minute or two at most.

J   Can . . . I watch you?

T   Watch me?

J   Put it in the collection.

T   I wasn't planning to do that until tomorrow evening.

J   I'd like to see you put it with the others—stick the pin through the belly and attach it to the board and label it.

T   Not tonight, Jankowicz. It is my wife's birthday.

J   Oh.

T   We are planning a special dinner—not that you can find much that is special in this godforsaken place. But . . . there are ways . . .

J   Yes, Herr Todtmacher.

T   Dinner. Candlelight. Some music, Wagner perhaps. *Tristan und Isolde.* Her favorite. And then—

J   And then?

T   Well, you understand, Jankowicz. Her birthday. Poor dear. There isn't much for her to do in this town.

J   No, I suppose not.

T   Not for a city girl who is used to the night life. Cafes. Dancing halls. Well. Once the war is over, we will return to her home. She'll be happier there. She wanted to be with me. I told her how it would be, but she insisted. It is not exactly a beautiful town, is it?

J   No, Herr Todtmacher, may I come to see you pin the specimens tomorrow?

T   We shall see, Jankowicz. Meanwhile, be on the lookout. Insects are everywhere. Sometimes you find the most beautiful specimens in the most unlikely places. Have you seen any butterflies, Jankowicz?

J   No, I can't say that I have, Herr Todtmacher.

T   Be on the lookout, Jankowicz. There are some rare specimens that have been reported in this area. I would love to have them in my collection.

J   Yes, Herr Todtmacher.

T   Check with me tomorrow and show me what you have captured. [He exits. A boy of eleven enters, dressed poorly.]

J   You. Over there.

B   Me?

J   Yes. You.

B   Me?

J   There is no one else around, is there?

B   I supposed not.

J Then it must be you.

B I suppose so.

J What are you doing by the fence?

B The fence.

J Of course. The fence. This fence.

B I was . . . just walking . . . on my way home from work.

J From work?

B In the leather factory.

J Yes. I can smell. And where do you live?

B On *Zbozowa* Street.

J That is not by the fence.

B I . . . like to look out . . . sometimes.

J Don't fool with me, boy. I know why you're here. Smuggling.

B Me? No. Not me. I wasn't smuggling.

J I know everything that happens around here. You know. I could have you shot.

B For walking by the fence?

J For smuggling. Even for walking by the fence.

B I . . . did not know.

J Of course you knew. Don't try to fool me.

B Why would I try to fool you?

J Because you think I am stupid. But I am not stupid. I know all kinds of things. All kinds of things. You can't fool with me.

B No . . . I . . .

J What?

B You . . . are going to let me go?

J To let you go. Well, now. That depends.

B Depends on what?

J Depends on whether you can be of service to me.

B How?

J I . . . am a collector.

B A collector?

J Of bugs, insects.

B   Oh.

J   You did not think it possible of me, eh? But I am a collector of insects. All kinds of insects: of beetles and bugs. You know the difference?

B   Beetles, bugs.

J   You look at the wings and the mouth.

B   The wings and the mouth.

J   I will show you later.

B   Later.

J   But more than beetles and bugs.

B   Yes.

J   I am a collector of moths and butterflies.

B   Moths and butterflies.

J   Yes. And I could overlook your smuggling, if you could find me some beetles and bugs and some butterflies.

B   Butterflies—here in Lodz?

J   There are some rare types around. If you find me some good specimens, I could overlook your . . . walking by the fence. I could even overlook anything you might do by the fence, if you get my drift.

B   I get your drift. But I have not seen any butterflies.

J   I can be patient—for a while. Meanwhile, I could be satisfied with beetles and bugs.

B   How about flies! They are everywhere. Flies. All kinds.

J   Flies. I'm not sure.

B   I'll catch you some. You'll tell me after if they're what you're looking for!

J   Flies.

B   Sure, flies. They're insects.

J   I suppose.

B   Sure they are. And some of them are pretty. Almost like butterflies.

J   Butterflies.

B   I mean, I'll try. But in the meantime, beetles and bugs and flies.

J   OK. But they had better be in good shape, or your little walk by the fence just might get you a bullet in the head. Then, I suppose, I can let you lie there and I'll get all the flies I want, hey. [Boy exits, running.] They should all be shot. But maybe he can find me a butterfly. Wouldn't Herr Todtmacher be surprised? Then he'll teach me all kinds of thing from his book. But those words. Those long words. I don't think I'll ever learn those words. Not in a thousand years. Meanwhile, I'll have to find something to show Herr Todtmacher by tomorrow, or he will lose faith in me. This is a good place. By the light. Insects are attracted to light. They fly around until they bang into the light and their wings get singed and they fall to the ground. They never learn. I can get a lot of insects without having to look very hard at all. But Herr Todtmacher won't like it if their wings are singed. And if they're already dead, I don't get to put them in the jar. Now, if I had some sugar water. But sugar is harder to come by in this place than gold. Herr Todtmacher might give me some sugar—even a little bit. What could I tell him? Meanwhile, let me pick up the bugs by this light. This one is no good. It's singed. This one too, and this one. Singed. Stupid insets. [He stomps on them.] No use collecting them. No need to put them in the killing jar. Useless. Useless. Not even worth the energy to crush them underfoot. The boy better find me something, or he'll find himself in big trouble. I'll watch him as the guns are raised and tell him that he brought it on himself. They don't bother with a firing squad these days. Like the crazy woman at the fence yesterday. The guard made her dance for fifteen minutes and then shot her in the face. He had better find me something to show Herr Todtmacher—or else. [He exits.] [Boy returns with another boy and girl of the same age.]

B1	I'm telling you.
B2	It's crazy.
G	Are you sure?
B1	I'm telling you. That's what he said. Bugs.
B2	Bugs.
B1	That's what he said.
B2	Bugs.
G	You've got to be kidding.
B1	I'm not kidding. He wants bugs.
B2	I've got a few here he can have. [Picks a few lice from his head] Where does he want me to put them?
B1	He gave me a jar.
G	He can have some of mine too. [Picks at her head.]
B1	I think he wants all different kinds.
B2	Oh.
B1	Especially butterflies.
G	Where are we supposed to find butterflies? There are no butterflies around here.
B2	Are butterflies bugs?
B1	Insects, not just bugs.
B2	I can find him some roaches. Do you think he'd want some of them?
B1	I don't know. The man definitely has some screws loose somewhere. Get him a few roaches. I don't supposed that would hurt.
G	But what good will it do, getting him bugs?
B1	He said that if we get him his bugs, he would overlook our trips to the fence.
G	Oh.
B1	And he might manage to get us some extra bread. Maybe even some potatoes.
B2	And if we got him a lot of bugs . . .
B1	I don't know. Maybe a lot of bread.
G	So I guess we have to get him a lot of bugs.

B2   That shouldn't be hard. Bugs are just about the only things that are doing well around here. They are everywhere.

G   Do flies count?

B1   I suppose.

G   There are flies everywhere.

B1   Remember. Not all the same kind. We need all different ones.

B2   Who looks at flies? Flies are flies.

B1   If you want bread, you'll look at the flies.

B2   I suppose.

B1   There are a lot worse things to do in this world than to look at flies.

B2   I suppose.

G   We have only one jar.

B1   You'll have to find a way of killing the bugs so they don't get damaged. Get a rag or something to wrap them in till we get together again. Then we'll put them all in the jar. Meet here tomorrow after work.

B2   My mother is going to worry if I'm not home in time. I can't tell her I'm out looking for bugs. She'll think I'm crazy.

B1   Make up something. Anything. Till tomorrow.

B2   Till tomorrow. [They exit and return—stylized motion to indicate the passage of time.]

B1   What do you have?

B2   I got ants—three different kinds. Do ants count?

B1   I suppose. How am I supposed to know what Jankowicz wants. It's worth a try.

B2   And I got some flies. Never noticed how many different kinds of flies there are—blue, green. Hard buggers to catch. Took me a long time. This had better be worth it.

B1   How about you?

G   I got some flies too. I've been thinking. We could make a fly trap. Then we wouldn't have to work so hard.

B1   A fly trap?

G   Yeah. There was a dead rat in the street covered with flies, and there was a piece of metal over it. The flies would land on the rat. Then when they got disturbed, they would fly up into the metal. They never seemed to learn how to escape, even though there was a way out. I got gobs of them.

B1   Hey. That's a good idea. A fly trap. Let me see what you got here. Hey, that's good, but there are a lot that are the same.

B2   Make up a story. Tell Jankowicz that they're all different. He won't know.

G   Talk about little spots, hairs, different colors on the wings.

B1   I suppose.

B2   Look. Try it out. See what happens. What do we have to lose?

B1   We have a lot to lose. If he gets angry, he can do almost anything.

G   He won't get angry if you keep a straight face. Make the story sound good. I don't think he has too much upstairs to work with.

B1   That's true enough.

B2   So what did you get?

B1   Some roaches, different sizes, some with wings and some without. A big water bug. Some moths I got by the light. It's nice they turned the lights back on. You can get a lot of bugs under the light.

B2   That one is all broken up and torn.

B1   Look, he'll take what he wants. The rest he can throw away. Here he comes now, [B2 and G exit.]

J   So how is my little bug collector.

B   I have a lot for you.

J	Good. Good. Let me see.
B	Here are some ants.
J	Ants?
B	Sure. Ants are insects.
J	Ants?
B	And some roaches.
J	Roaches. I didn't need you to find me some roaches.
B	And a big water bug.
J	[Looks closely.] Yes. That is a bug.
B	How can you tell?
J	[Proudly.] Look at the mouth and the wings.
B	What about the mouth and the wings?
H	See, a tube. No jaws. And the wings are only half-covered.
B	Oh.
J	That's why they're called . . . um . . . I forget. But that's a true bug.
B	I'm glad.
J	What else?
B	We got flies. Gobs of flies. All different kinds.
J	They don't look like all different kinds.
B	You have to look closely. They are all different. When . . . do we get or bread?
J	I have to make sure these are OK. Only . . .
B	Only what?
J	You didn't write down where you found them . . . and when.
B	You didn't tell me to do that.
J	I . . . forgot.
B	Well, I do remember where they all came from. And when I got them. I can write that down for you. Do you have a pencil and paper?
J	I can get it. I'll be right back. You wait here. [He exits, B2 and G enter.]
B1	He needs to know where and when we got them.
B2	That's easy.

G	I got all of mine in the same place.
B2	I got mine down near the school. What we don't remember—
G	You can make up. He'll never know the difference.
B1	That's true enough. You go now. I'll tell you how I make out. [They exit.]
J	[Enter.] I got the pencil and paper.
B1	I'll need something to lean on.
J	That rock.
B1	Something smooth—like a book.
J	A book?
B1	Or a flat piece of wood.
J	A flat piece of wood. OK. I'll be right back. [He exits and returns with a plank of wood.]
B1	OK. I'll start with the flies. [Begins to write.]
J	Hey. That's no good. I can't understand that.
B1	Well, I can't write in Polish.
J	What are we going to do now? If it's not written out, Herr Todtmacher won't take any of the specimens. Then I'll have to throw them all away, and you won't get anything at all.
B1	I can tell you, and you can write it down.
J	That's a good idea.
B1	So. The flies. They all came from a dead rat on *Dworska* Street at seven this morning.
J	You're talking too fast. Give me time. Dead rat on Dworska Street at—seven this morning.
B1	And the ants—all came from that collapsed building on Franciskanka Street.
J	The ants on the building on Franciskanka Street. When?
B1	At noon.
J	At noon. This is going to be so good. Herr Todtmacher will be so surprised.
B1	And the bread?
J	After I see Herr Todtmacher.

B1	OK. But if I don't get the bread, I won't go on any more hunts.
J	You'll get the bread if Herr Todtmacher is pleased. If not, you get nothing. You didn't happen to see any butterflies, did you?
B1	No. No butterflies.
J	That's too bad. There would be a special reward for a butterfly.
B1	I did not see any butterflies.
J	Keep looking. I'll talk to you later. [B1 leaves, T enters.]
T	So, Jankowicz. What's new?
J	I have some specimens for you.
T	Specimens. Very good. You have specimens. A lot of specimens. I see. You must have spent a lot of time collecting, Jankowicz.
J	Not *so* much time, Herr Todtmacher. If you know . . . how . . .
T	Ach—a real collector. Already with collecting protocols. Very good, Jankowicz. I have underestimated you. Let's see now. Roaches, not so rare, ants, and flies. A lot of flies—some interesting ones here. Let me see—off a dead rat on *Dworska* Street at seven this morning. Very good, Jankowicz. Maybe later I will show you how I pin them to the board. You'd like that, eh, and how I identify them and put the names on the labels. You show promise, Jankowicz. There might be something in this Drecknest after all. The vermin of Lodz. The six-legged vermin of Lodz. No butterflies, Jankowicz?
J	No, Herr Todtmacher. Not yet.
T	Keep looking, Jankowicz. I could be made very happy with some butterflies. I reward people handsomely who can make me happy.
J	Yes, Herr Todtmacher.
T	I will talk to you later. [T exits, B1 enters.]

B1	Well?
J	He was . . . surprised
B1	Pleasantly surprised?
J	Very pleasantly surprised.
B1	And the bread?
J	Here.
B1	Just one loaf.
J	One loaf.
B1	For all those bugs?
J	Be happy with what you got. I don't have to give you anything.
B1	No. But I don't have to find you the bugs.
J	I could have you shot.
B1	But you won't. If I die, you have no one to get the bugs for you.
J	There are other children.
B1	But they won't be as good as I am. I can promise you that.
J	One loaf today. We'll see about tomorrow.
B1	I have a large family. One loaf doesn't go very far.
J	Tomorrow. If you find me some . . . specimens. [Exits.] [Enters B2, G.]
B2	Well?
B1	He was pleased.
G	And.
B1	One loaf of bread.
B2	That's all?
B1	He said he'd see about tomorrow . . . if . . .
G	If?
B1	If we got some more specimens.
B2	A loaf of bread isn't much for three families.
B1	It's more than what we normally have. It's a beginning. Something is more than nothing. Miracles begin slowly. Think of it. Some people try to turn lead into gold. We have learned to turn flies into bread.
G	I have an idea.

B1	Nu?
G	If we had more workers—
B1	That is an idea.
G	But we can't get more workers if we have nothing to give them.
B2	I don't think it is wise to tell Jankowicz that you are not working alone.
B1	No. Not yet.
G	So you have to get more bread if we are to get more workers.
B1	Yes.
B2	Meanwhile we'll keep hunting for more specimens. You work on Jankowicz.
G	Or we'll have to spend time on the other side of the fence.
B2	And that is dangerous.
G	Masha was shot yesterday trying to get back in.
B1	Masha?
G	Yes.
B2	It would be easier to get bread from Jankowicz.
G	Safer.
B1	Nothing is safe these days.
G	Safer.
B1	Even Jankowicz. He could turn in a second.
B2	Bread is bread. Even for a few days, it's worth it.
B1	Like getting water from a rock.
G	Talk to him.
B1	You collect. I'll talk. [B2, G exit and then return.] Well?
B2	Well what?
B1	Don't play coy. What do you have?
B2	I don't know exactly. I was over by the woodpile by my house. I was climbing. I knocked down one of the timbers. Amazing what you can find in rotting wood.
B1	Would you look at that!

B2	Three different kinds of beetles, and this squiggly thing with horns on its end. I don't know what to call it. A few more ants.
B1	That's really good. Put them in the jar.
B2	What did you get?
B1	More flies. Different kinds. Never realized there were so many different kinds of flies in the world. And a cricket.
B2	Let me see. Yep. That's a cricket all right.
B1	I know a cricket when I see it.
G	Look what I got.
B1	What?
G	Crawling on my father's books.
B1	That is strange. Never seen one like that before.
G	There were a lot on the books. I got two of them, and these tiny beetles. They were on the books too.
B1	Don't give me too much at once. I'm not sure what Jankowicz will give us. He may not give us any more if we give him twenty insects than if we gave him ten. This way we can stretch things out for days when we don't find anything.
B2	I don't think there's any danger of that happening. There are bugs everywhere.
B1	I suppose.
G	You don't think, maybe, we should get a few more helpers.
B1	I don't know. If we get more helpers, we have to split the bread more ways—unless I can get more bread from Jankowicz.
B2	Do you think he will go for that?
B1	One way of really impressing his Herr Todtmacher.
G	It's worth a try.
B1	I'll feel him out. See any butterflies?
B2	No. No butterflies.
G	None for me either.

B1	Too bad. I could probably get us a real bonus for a butterfly. [B2, G exit, J enters.]
J	Well, my little collector. Do you have anything for me today?
B1	Yes. Do you have anything for me today?
J	You show me first. Then we'll talk about rewards.
B1	Just remember. If I don't get food, I just might not feel strong enough tomorrow to add to your collection.
J	Watch it. Just remember, I could still have you shot.
B1	Who would get you your specimens?
J	You've got a lot of cheek, you know. It will wind up getting you in a lot of trouble.
B1	Look here.
J	Specks of dirt.
B1	Look more closely. They're beetles.
J	Beetles?
B1	Yes. The kind that eat paper.
J	Are you sure?
B1	Got them off some old books.
J	OK. What else?
B1	Look at these.
J	OK. Anything special?
B1	Look at this one with the horns on his back.
J	What do you call that?
B1	I don't know. Never saw one like that before.
J	What else?
B	This.
J	Hey, that's pretty.
B1	It's only a beginning. What do you have for me?
J	Two loaves of bread.
B1	Not bad for starters.
J	For starters.
B1	I was thinking. I could get you some really nice specimens if I had a few more workers with me.
J	More workers?
B1	You know, more kids.

J	I don't know about that.
B1	Sure. We could have a whole troop of them going through the ghetto street by street. No insect would escape us. But I'd have to be able to give them something.
J	Like what?
B1	Like bread and potatoes.
J	I'll have to think about that. As it is, I have to sneak the bread out. We can't have dozens of you little tramps running around getting extra rations. It would be noticed.
B1	How about just ten?
J	How about just five. I think I could handle that. A loaf per worker, but only if the catch is good. Let me have these specimens. I'll bring them to Herr Todtmacher. I'll talk to you tomorrow. [Exit Bl, enter T.]
J	Herr Todtmacher?
T	Yes, Jankowicz.
J	I have something for you.
T	Just leave them on my desk.
J	That's all?
T	I'll look at them later, Jankowicz. I'm rather busy now.
J	I understand, Herr Todtmacher.
T	I'm not sure that you do, Jankowicz. All these regulations, this paperwork. These changing directives. These timetables. Having to get this much food and this much material for the factories. What a mess. All to keep a bunch of vermin alive for a few extra months until . . .
J	Until what? Herr Todtmacher.
T	Nothing, Jankowicz. Forget I said anything.
J	You are still interested in adding to your collection?
T	Yes, Jankowicz. I will look at your specimens. I will talk to you about them in the morning. I should have

	time then to show you the boards and have you pin a few.
J	And show me the pictures in the big book?
T	I'll show you the pictures in the big book.
J	And teach me the names.
T	I suppose so. Leave me now. I'll talk to you later. [J exits]. The man is a genuine pest. [Looks into the jar.] But he is beginning to find some interesting specimens—an earwig, by Jove. And a silver fish. Not bad at all. I'll have to encourage him a bit. It's just all this paperwork. And my wife. Why did I have to bring her to this Drecknest in the first place. [Exits, B1, B2, G enter.]
B1	How did you do?
B2	Not bad. The lights attract a lot of bugs—all different kinds. These evening performances are helpful.
G	Yes. I even managed to get a few moths, but their wings are torn or singed. I don't think Jankowicz will be happy with them.
B2	Pull the wings off. He won't know the difference.
B1	But Todtmacher.
B2	Yes. Todtmacher.
B1	What else did you get?
B2	Some beetles.
B1	Good, and you?
G	Something with wings. They don't look like flies.
B1	No, they don't, do they?
G	What are they?
B1	I don't know. It doesn't really matter. As long as they're different.
G	I got two more kids to help us.
B1	Good.
B2	Not so good. You didn't hear?
B1	Hear what?
B2	About the shooting.

B1	I don't listen to such news. It happens almost every day. Someone gets shot. Just careless. Or stupid.
G	Or unlucky.
B1	Or unlucky. Who was it got shot this time?
B2	Jakov.
B1	Which Jakov?
B2	The one with the big ears.
B1	I know him.
B2	You knew him. I got him to join us. I told him where it was safe to go and what places to avoid. I told him not to go near the fence.
B1	So.
B2	He was near the fence. Stupid. Just plain stupid. Just for a few bugs.
B1	It was not for a few bugs. It was for bread. Besides, he might have been down there for other reasons.
B2	Like what?
B1	He sometime gets stuff by the fence. Sometime he would sneak through and get stuff from the other side.
B2	Well, he won't be doing that anymore.
B1	Is he dead?
B2	Dead.
B1	That's too bad. He was a nice kid.
G	I got someone too.
B1	Who?
G	Leah.
B1	The one with the pushed-in nose?
G	Yes.
B1	I don't know. That one is always sick.
G	I feel sorry for her.
B1	It's not good enough to feel sorry. If someone is on our team, they have to be able to help us. Otherwise, they'll cost us bread instead of helping us to get more bread. We have to be practical. Where is she?

G	She is sick. Maybe with typhus. Her mother was crying. I don't know whether she will make it through this time.
B1	So we have to get some new workers.
B2	Yes.
B1	Reliable workers.
G	Yes.
B1	Meanwhile, let's put our insects together.
B2	What did you get?
B1	The best one is the beetle with a curved thing for a mouth.
B	That's weird.
B1	Don't knock it. This may get us something special. The weirder they are, the better Todtmacher will like it.
G	Any butterflies?
B1	No butterflies.
B2	No moths.
B1	So we'll make do with what we have. Leave it to me. I'll deal with Jankowicz. [Exit B2, G, enter J.]
J	Well?
B1	Well, I have a few things.
J	They had better be good.
B1	They're good.
J	These are no good. Their wings are singed and torn.
B1	How about these?
J	These look interesting. Flies?
B1	I don't think so.
J	They have wings.
B1	But they seem different.
J	We'll see. What else?
B1	How about this?
J	That is strange.
B1	I thought so too.
J	Herr Todtmacher should be pleased.
B1	That should be worth a bit extra.

J   Like what?

B1   Like maybe . . . some potatoes.

J   How many potatoes.

B1   Maybe three or four, for each of us.

J   For just one beetle?

B1   And the thing with wings.

J   Let Herr Todtmacher see them first. If he's really pleased, maybe. But not three or four potatoes each. Where do you think I would get them from? Two maybe. No more. [B1 exits.]

These Jews. Always trying to get the best of you. A dozen or so potatoes for one beetle and a few flies. They must think I'm really stupid. Even if Herr Todtmacher is pleased. I wouldn't give them that many potatoes. It would spoil them. I have to be careful. Next thing you know, they'll be asking for butter or meat. Wouldn't want to get into trouble over one beetle. [Enter T.]

J   Herr Todtmacher.

T   Jankowicz.

J   I have some interesting specimens for you to look at.

T   I hope so, Jankowicz. It has been a very trying day. All these reports, whenever there is an incident by the fence. I have to write it up. I am tired of writing all these reports, Jankowicz. Tired. Why do they need them? What do they do with them anyway? One kid more or less. What is that compared to the numbers we ship out every week for labor in Germany. Show me the specimens, Jankowicz.

J   Here they area, Herr Todtmacher.

T   Very interesting, Jankowicz. A lacewing, a mayfly, and a weevil and a very interesting weevil at that. I'll have to check the species. I'm not familiar with this one. Where did you get it, Jankowicz?

J   I'm . . . not sure, Herr Todtmacher.

T	What do you mean, Jankowicz? After all I told you about labeling.
J	That's it, Herr Todtmacher. The labels. I left the labels at home.
T	At home, Jankowicz. That's not very careful of you. You sure you have the labels?
J	Very sure, Herr Todtmacher.
T	Good. Have them for me tomorrow. Meanwhile, I'll look up this specimen in my book and tell you about it when I see you. You are finding some very interesting specimens, Jankowicz. But you still don't think like a scientist. [J leaves and then returns.] Jankowicz.
J	Yes, sir.
T	Any butterflies?
J	Not yet, Herr Todtmacher.
T	Make sure you treat them carefully if you find any. I would hate for you to find something and then ruin it by handling it wrong. [T exits.]
J	The labels. The kids got me in trouble. I shouldn't give them any bread today. But then they wouldn't get me any bugs for tomorrow. Herr Todtmacher expects me to come up with something new every day. I would have to look for myself, crawl in the dirt, dig in the garbage. No, it's better this way. I'll get the information from them, give them a potato or two, and let them dig in the garbage. Better them than me. It's for vermin to sniff out vermin and for me to stand by and watch them pick through the muck. Now if one of them could come up with a butterfly, that would be something, wouldn't it? [Enter Bl.]
Bl	Was he pleased with the specimens?
J	He was somewhat pleased.
Bl	Pleased enough for us to get our potatoes.
J	One potato for each of your helpers, two for you.
Bl	That's not enough.

J   You should be grateful for what you get.
B1   And you, are you grateful for what you get?
J   Look, I can get other kids to collect for me if you're not satisfied.
B1   But they won't find you beetles with curved snouts and—
J   And what?
B1   I will have some surprises for you in the next few days.
J   Like what?
B1   You'll see.
J   You bring me something special, and I'll get you something special.
B1   What?
J   You'll see.
B1   Some meat, maybe.
J   You want meat?
B1   What would I have to find to get some meat, maybe some eggs?
J   More than a weevil, I'll tell you that.
B1   OK. More than a weevil. Meanwhile, I'll just take my bread and my potatoes.
J   One each for your helpers. Two for you.
B1   Whatever. [J exits, enter B2   and G.]
B2   Well?
B1   A couple of measly potatoes.
G   That is not much.
B1   I'm doing the best that I can.
G   We're going to have to get some more spectacular specimens.
B2   How? We're doing the best that we can.
B1   I don't know. Be inventive. We've got to get more out of this effort than just a little bread and some moldy potatoes. [They exit and then return.]
B1   Well?
B2   I have something, I wrapped it up in this rag.

G	It's still alive.
B1	It's a stick.
B2	No. It just looks like a stick. See, it's moving.
B-1	Jankowicz should really like that. Should we keep it alive?
B2	Why not?
G	Here. Look what I got.
B1	God, that's huge.
G	It bites too. It nipped me when I tried to pick it up at first.
B1	Better get that one in the jar.
G	OK. How about you?
B1	I got this flying thing with a long, long tube at its end.
B2	Weird. See how much you can get for these—more than just bread and potatoes.
G	Tell Jankowicz that we have a secret way of attracting and trapping insects. He better give us some decent food, or he'll miss out.
B1	We'll see.
B2	You'll have to do better than that. My stick creature is worth more than one potato.
B1	We'll see. [He turns around to indicate a passage of time.] Bread. Potatoes. An egg apiece.
B2	An egg apiece.
G	It has been a long time since I've seen an egg.
G	But one egg for my whole family?
B1	One egg is better than no eggs.
B2	I'll bet they're all rotten.
B1	They smell OK.
G	And tomorrow?
B1	We'll see, [They all exit. Enter J and T.]
T	What now, Jankowicz?
J	More specimens, Herr Todtmacher.
T	I'm busy, Jankowicz.
J	These are special, Herr Todtmacher.

T	OK. Let me see. This . . . is . . . impossible.
J	What?
T	These beetles.
J	Yes.
T	Where did you get them, Jankowicz?
J	Let me see, on *Mickiewicz* Street. By the garbage dump.
T	That's impossible.
J	Why do you say that?
T	Get me that volume over there on the table.
J	This one?
T	Yes, that one. Bring it here. Quickly. Let me see. Yes. Here it is. Rhinoceros beetle. Goliath beetle.
J	I'm glad you found them. Do they please you?
T	These specimens are wonderful—except.
J	What? Herr Todtmacher.
T	These are tropical beetles, Jankowicz. There should be no such beetles within 8,000 kilometers of here.
J	That's very strange, sir.
T	Are you sure you're not taking them from somebody else's collection?
J	I'm sure.
T	Beetles this size don't get blown 8,000 kilometers off course, Jankowicz.
J	No, sir.
T	What else do you have?
J	That's all I have for today. Herr Todtmacher.
T	No butterflies?
J	No butterflies. Can . . . I see you pin them, Herr Todtmacher?
T	Not right now, Jankowicz. I have orders to carry out.
J	Orders.
T	We have to make this place more efficient, Jankowicz. The factories. We can't be feeding people who can't produce the goods we need, that would be wasteful. Food is hard to come by. I've been instructed to

lower the amount of food going into the ghetto by 20 percent. We will have to lower the population, ship the surplus to Germany. The children under fourteen, Jankowicz. They are to be gone by the end of the week.

J   But that is impossible, Herr Todtmacher.

T   Nothing is impossible, Jankowicz, when you have the will to carry it out.

J   But the children.

T   What?

J   It is . . . the children . . . that are finding the specimens.

T   The children, Jankowicz?

J   At least some of the children.

T   I thought as much. I didn't think you would be able to find such specimens alone. So it is the children. Which children, Jankowicz?

J   I only know of one, Herr Todtmacher. He gives me the specimens. I know there are at least a few others.

T   How many others?

J   I'm not sure. But there couldn't be too many.

T   Find out who they are. Get me their names. I might be able to make a few exceptions to the general order, for a while.

J   For a while?

T   A few weeks. A month at most.

J   That would be too bad, Herr Todtmacher. Because once the children are gone—

T   I suppose that if I am to have such specimens, I will have to preserve these children for a while. Yet who would believe that such insects were found here, in Poland? I don't even believe that myself. Get the names, Jankowicz. I must have the names. [J circles to leave and return.]

J   He won't give me the names, Herr Todtmacher.

T   What do you mean, Jankowicz?

J	I found out his name, but the others have gone into hiding. I explained the situation to him.
T	You did what!
J	I told him what you told me.
T	You idiot! No wonder they went into hiding. No matter. We'll make do with the one alone.
J	He gave me this, Herr Todtmacher.
T	That is impossible.
J	It is still alive.
T	I can see that, Jankowicz. But it can't be so large. No insect could be this large.
J	He said that one of the other kids found it. If we got rid of the others, he won't be able to get specimens like this.
T	So I am supposed to leave all of the children here just to make sure the three or four who find these insects won't be shipped out.
J	It would seem so, Herr Todtmacher.
T	And how would that look in my reports, Jankowicz? I have certain quotas to make. If the children don't go, who will take their places? The mental defects are already gone. The refugees from other towns are almost all gone. The gypsies are gone. The elderly and the very sick are gone. Who is left, Jankowicz? I can't ship out adults who are able-bodied enough to work in the factories. That would lower production. All that would be noticed.
J	Send some of the children.
T	And take the risk that the ones I want to remain won't be in the group that goes.
J	I suppose—
T	How many shall I send? Jankowicz, half?
J	Half sounds like a very good number, Herr Todtmacher.
T	I'm glad you approve, Jankowicz.
J	Sir—

T   Yes, Jankowicz.

J   The boy asked for a larger killing jar.

T   Why, Jankowicz?

J   Because one of the children asked what they should do if the specimens wouldn't fit into the jars they have now.

T   Specimens larger than the killing jar, that seems hardly likely, Jankowicz.

J   The boy didn't seem to think so.

T   That is amazing, Jankowicz. There must be something going on here that we are unaware of.

J   Like what, sir?

T   I don't know, Jankowicz. But your children are finding things that should not exist. It would be nice to find out how they are doing this before . . .

J   Before what, Herr Todtmacher?

T   Before we can't find out any more and some precious scientific discovery is lost forever. We wouldn't want that to happen, now, would we?

J   No, sir.

T   So. See what you can find out, Jankowicz. Quickly.

J   I'll do what I can do. [Exits and returns.] No dice.

T   What exactly do you mean?

J   I mean that they have covered their tracks. No one will tell me who is involved.

T   We could use certain forms of persuasion.

J   I hinted at that. He said that if anything happened to him or his helpers, the bugs would stop.

T   This is unheard of, Jankowicz. Such defiance.

J   There might be another way, sir.

T   What other way, Jankowicz?

J   A bit of extra food. My grandmother used to say, you can catch more flies with honey than with gall.

T   Your grandmother—ah, yes. Catching flies with honey. Exactly. And which flies are we to capture, Jankowicz?

J   Something like this one, Herr Todtmacher.

T   Astounding. I have never seen anything like this in my life. Where are they finding such specimens?

J   It takes a thief to catch a thief.

T   Yes.

J   It takes a bug to catch a bug.

T   Yes, very good, Jankowicz. You show some promise. So. A bit of honey.

J   Yes, sir.

T   In the form maybe of meat and potatoes.

J   Just a bit. I don't think it will take very much to achieve our purpose.

T   Your purpose. No, Jankowicz. I don't think very much is needed at all. You'll see to all of this?

J   Of course, sir?

T   Yes, Jankowicz.

J   Do you think I might be able to see you pin the specimens to the board?

T   I think you just might. And, Jankowicz.

J   Yes, sir.

T   If you find me a butterfly.

J   Yes, sir.

T   I just might let you pin it to the board.

J   That would be an honor, sir.

T   Meanwhile, leave me to my work. I still have to figure out how to make these quotas without interfering with our operations. You know, Jankowicz, when all this is over and I get the time to write about the collection . . .

J   Yes, sir.

T   I might give you a footnote to acknowledge your help in the collection.

J   I would be honored, sir.

T   It would be even better if you could figure out where they are finding these specimens.

J   I'll do my best, sir.

T   I will talk to you later, Jankowicz. You can tell me then of the success of your plans.

J   I will not disappoint you. [Exit T, enter B1.]
      I have just seen Herr Todtmacher.

B1   Did he like our specimens?

J   He was impressed.

B1   And the food?

J   Bread. Potatoes. Eggs.

B1   No meat?

J   Meat is hard to come by.

B1   Beans. Vegetables.

J   We will see.

B1   If I am to maintain the necessary energy for us to—

J   For us.

B1   For us to—

J   That is a sticking point. You still will not tell me who your helpers are.

B1   It is their choice to remain unknown.

J   You realize that this secretiveness makes thing somewhat . . . inconvenient.

B1   How so?

J   If we don't know who your helpers are, we can't exempt them from the shipment of children to Germany for the work camps.

B1   So?

J   So they may inadvertently wind up on one of the lists.

B1   I suppose then that your collection will suffer.

J   I could make it worth your while. They wouldn't have to know.

B1   Worth my while?

J   We might be able to get you some meat—to make sure that your family is protected. A small price to pay for such assurances.

B1   I'll consider it. Meanwhile, what do you think of this specimen?

J   An—

B1   Ant.

J   It is so big. I have never seen an ant so big.

B1   Probably not.

J   Where did you find such creature?

B1   The collectors have their ways.

J   That is another point, their ways.

B1   What about their ways?

J   Herr Todtmacher is very impressed with the specimens. He would like to know how and where you found them.

B1   If we told him, he wouldn't need us anymore.

J   There should be no secrets among fellow en-to-mologists.

B1   So now we are to be counted as fellows?

J   Yes. As fellows.

B1   Could we one time sit together at the same table and discuss our findings over a good meal?

J   I don't know.

B1   Isn't that what fellows do?

J   I suppose. It might be arranged. But meanwhile.

B1   Meanwhile, we are the collectors.

J   Yes.

B1   We bring in the bugs, and we receive bread, potatoes, and eggs.

J   Yes.

B1   And what do you get?

J   What do you mean?

B1   What do you get by being the go-between? I mean, you serve a useful purpose. You take what we find and

	bring them to him. That should be worth something, shouldn't it?
J	Herr Todtmacher is very appreciative of the arrangement.
B1	Of course.
J	He is teaching me the names of all of the insects from his big book. I am learning how to identify each one.
B1	That must be very exciting for you.
J	And he is teaching me how to mount the specimens on a display board.
B1	I am sure that is very gratifying for you, pinning the insects to the board. Did you bring us what I had asked for?
J	What?
B1	A new killing jar.
J	Oh yes, here.
B1	That will do for a while, but if the insects get much bigger, we're going to get into some problems.
J	Bigger than this?
B1	Much bigger. That's what my collectors tell me.
J	I suppose something could be arranged.
B1	I hope so. We can't let them just crawl around in our pockets, and if we have to stomp on them, there won't be much left to exhibit.
J	You don't suppose—
B1	What?
J	That I could watch you put them into the jar?
B1	Not really. You could get your own jar, your own specimens.
J	I suppose.
B1	We have our secret methods of finding specimens and putting them into the jar quickly so we won't get bitten or stung. Collectors get antsy when someone watches them to discover their methods
J	Well, I suppose. You haven't come across any butterflies, have you?

B1	No. No butterflies.
J	Remember, there is a special reward for a butterfly.
B1	No butterflies.
J	You'll keep trying?
B1	Yes. We'll keep trying, [J exits; B1 goes through an intricate pathway to symbolize the means taken to preserve secrecy.]
B1	You are here alone?
B2	Yes. Alone.
B1	Why alone, she—
B2	Was taken in this morning's transport.
B1	That's terrible.
B2	She told me to give you this.
B1	What is it?
B2	A bee of sorts.
B1	I would hate to have to deal with this one when it was alive.
B2	She wanted you to have it, it might be worth a few potatoes. She left with her entire family.
B1	And you?
B2	I have this.
B1	They are really pretty.
B2	Yes.
B1	It's hard to imagine something so brightly colored crawling around in the mud and garbage.
B2	Yes.
B1	Any butterflies?
B2	I haven't seen any.
B1	Pity. I could hold out for some real goodies if I had a butterfly.
B2	Not a one.
B1	I'll talk to Jankowicz. I'll see what we can get for these.
B2	I—
B1	What—

B2	I don't think our family can last much longer. My father is ill. He can't keep up with the work in the factory anymore. My mother is also ill, and my brother and sister are young. Would it be better if Jankowicz knew?
B1	Then they would take another family.
B2	I suppose.
B1	To make their quotas.
B2	Yes.
B1	If we keep him guessing.
B2	Yes.
B1	He might get scared that all of his collectors will be gone. He might leave some families with children.
B2	Yes.
B1	But if you are gone, and the other children can't find what you have found.
B2	I'll show you the places. You can teach the others.
B1	Yes.
B2	That way, maybe they will slow the process—just a bit.
B1	Maybe. Meanwhile, here is what I got from Jankowicz. I suppose now we'll only have to divide it two ways.
B2	I suppose so.
B1	It would be nice if you could find a butterfly. [B2 exits; J enters.]
J	What do you have?
B1	A bee.
J	That's all?
B1	A large bee.
J	Let me see. That is a really large bee.
B1	And these beetles. Look at the colors.
J	They are very striking.
B1	What do you have for me?
J	The usual. There is a promise of more if you cooperate.

B1   Tell Todtmacher I have to have more workers. More children. I cannot keep supplying him with such specimens without workers. The children are being shipped out. How am I supposed to find more workers if all the children are disappearing?

J   Give me the names, and those children will be passed over.

B1   I cannot give you the names. If the children disappear, no more specimens will be found. Tell him that.

J   I will tell him. But there are quotas to make.

B1   No children, no insects.

J   I will tell him, but—

B1   Tell him, [B1 exits, enter T.]

T   Well?

J   Some more specimens, Herr Todtmacher.

T   Let me see. These beetles are fine, and the bee.

J   What about the bee?

T   It is of monstrous size, Jankowicz.

J   I thought it rather large myself, sir.

T   You were able to find out who.

J   No, sir.

T   Where?

J   No, sir.

T   How?

J   No, Herr Todtmacher. He refused to tell me anything. He insists that he needs his helpers. He even wants more helpers. But he won't tell me which children he needs. He seems to want all the children in place, so he can choose his helpers at his leisure.

T   That is too bad, Jankowicz. Because there is simply no more leisure for him to have. My hands are tied. The orders come from higher up. Children are, how shall I say, not terribly efficient in the factories. They are a luxury whose time has passed. We can preserve this one child for a little while—that is all.

J   But the collection, Herr Todtmacher.

T   We all have to make sacrifices, Jankowicz. I have specimens here that will hold center stage in museum exhibitions. They are valuable. But I cannot stop the work effort for the sake of a few insects, however remarkable they might be.

J   I had hoped—

T   We all had hopes, Jankowicz. Hopes sometimes must be sacrificed. That is life, man. You have to be brave. When all of this over, you will go back to your home and I to mine, and we will go on with our lives as best we can. At least we will have a few specimens on hand to remind us of what could have been.

J   It's just not fair.

T   I never wanted to be here, Jankowicz. There are other positions I thought were open to me that would have been far more exciting, more glorious, more worthy of my abilities. But they sent me here to the backwaters of the earth. I came. I had no other choice. I carried out my orders as best I could. And somewhere, in the cracks of time, I managed to get a few gems I did not expect to find. Life is like that, Jankowicz. You go along, work at whatever task is assigned to you, grin, and bear up as best you can and wait for those little cracks in time, get whatever you can, until the cracks close, and the dreams are cut short. The specimens you brought me are very special, Jankowicz. They brought me brief moments of happiness in the midst of this dreary, godforsaken place. They have taught me something—that in the midst of the mud and garbage, crawling with vermin, there can be found rare treasures. That is almost inspirational, Jankowicz. You have helped me to understand that, Jankowicz. And I am grateful to you for that.

J   I don't know what to say, Herr Todtmacher.

T   It is not necessary to say anything, Jankowicz. The crack is closing—rapidly. The children will be gone soon. Whatever treasures are still crawling through this rubble, we will get as many as we can. The world is not perfect, Jankowicz. We can't be greedy. We will get whatever is possible and then bid goodbye to the rest with our heads held high—with a cheerful heart. It is the only way to survive on this dunghill we call life.

J	I suppose so, sir.
T	Look, we can afford to be generous in these last days. Give the boy some jam to go with his bread. I know people who would pay a king's ransom for a jar of such preserves. One for you and one for the boy. Make sure he gets it—today. Encourage him in his collection. The crack is closing, Jankowicz. Animals live in the present to the very moment of their deaths. It takes a man to seize the moment, to squeeze time, to get every drop of its sweet juice and toss away the pulp and the peel. There is still room for grand gestures, Jankowicz, even in the forgotten places of the earth. [T exits; B1 enters.]
B1	Well?
J	Herr Todtmacher was very pleased with the last specimens.
B1	And—
H	He asked me to give you this. [Gives him the jar of jam.]
B1	Jam?
J	Yes.
B1	Real jam?
J	From his own private collection.
B1	Jam?
J	You can taste it, if you don't believe me.
B1	I believe you.
J	You can share it with the others.
B1	There are no longer any others.
J	Train those that are left.

B1   There is no time for that.

J   There is still time for you to find specimens for Herr Todtmacher's collection. There are other goodies in his cupboard I'm sure your family will enjoy.

B1   Yes.

J   Then you will continue your efforts.

B1   I will continue.

J   I can promise you, you will not be disappointed. [Now begins a pantomime. J and B1 exit; J and B1 return. B1 hands J some large insects; J hands B1 food items B1 exits; T enters; J hands T the insects; T hands J food items—tins of government food, boxes of candy. T exits; B1 returns with more insects— larger than before. The process is repeated three more times. J exhibits little emotion beyond being the avid courier. T exhibits increasing pleasure with the specimens, B1 increasing reluctance and hesitation in accepting the food items. After the third time, J returns, but the boy is not there. J looks around and exits. At this point, a large beetle drags itself on stage. It is OK if the costume clearly shows that the beetle is the boy who has now become an insect. The effect can be grotesque to the audience, but J and T accept the reality of the insect without question. When the beetle gets to the center of the stage, J reenters. He can hardly believe his eyes.]

J   I can't believe it. Look at that specimen. I discovered it myself. I, Jankowicz, have found it. No one else. This is the moment I've been waiting for. It is too big for the killing jar. I wonder if it bites. [He touches it tentatively. It barely responds to his taps and prods.] It seems to be near death. I will take it with me. God, it's heavy. [Pulls the back legs.] I'll have to be careful. I don't want to damage it. [He winds up lifting the beetle and carrying it in a circle and then letting it fall, belly side down. T enters.]

J	Herr Todtmacher. [Breathless.] Look. This specimen I found it. I. Alone.
T	It is truly magnificent, Jankowicz. You have done very, very well. This will be the centerpiece of my whole collection.
J	I am pleased that you are happy, Herr Todtmacher.
T	More than happy, Jankowicz. For some time, I have wanted to show you who much I appreciate your efforts.
J	Yes, sir.
T	You may help me to prepare the specimen. I will show you how it is done, soaking it in formalin, setting it upon the board. [A large board lined with velvet is on hand. T brings it to center stage. They arrange a platform of sorts on which they place the board. The beetle is then lifted onto the board, belly side up. The six legs are bent, but pointed toward the ceiling.] And now you, Jankowicz, may attach the beetle to the board. [Jankowicz is overcome with joy. He accepts a very large pin from T and seemingly puts it through the belly in the place T indicates. T carefully prepares a label to place at the foot of the specimen.]
T	This may be a new subspecies, Jankowicz. If so, the academy may acknowledge your discovery when they name it.
J	I don't know what to say, Herr Todtmacher.
T	It is a magnificent specimen, Jankowicz. Truly magnificent. In perfect condition, of all the specimens you've brought, clearly the finest. Only—
J	Only what? Herr Todtmacher
T	It would have been nice . . .
J	What? Herr Todtmacher.
T	All of these specimens, Jankowicz, all of these specimens, and not a single butterfly. [Lights dim]

Hopscotch

[Setting: a slum/barrios/shantytown or a town ravaged by war. The children's ages should be ambiguous. They have matured by necessity beyond their years, or they are arrested in their development by numerous traumas. There is the silhouette of a body drawn on the ground in yellow. The children have drawn lines in the silhouette to turn it into a hopscotch figure. They are playing hopscotch using a ball made of rags.]

I.

1	I'm on fourzies.
2	It's not your turn.
1	I come after her.
2	I didn't get to go yet. First me, then her, then you.
1	Are you sure?
2	I never forget things like that.
1	Well then, take your turn.
2	I'm on fivezies.
3	Are you sure?
2	I never forget things like that. [Throws the rag ball.]
1	It landed on the line.
2	The ball part is in the five.
1	Part of it is on the line. That's the rule.
2	That's not fair.
1	Rules are rules. You'll get another turn soon enough. It's her turn.
3	My turn.
1	What are you on?
3	I'm on threezies.

<table>
<tr><td>2</td><td>Hurry up! At this rate, we'll never get to finish the game.</td></tr>
<tr><td>3</td><td>There. I got it in the three.</td></tr>
<tr><td>2</td><td>I bet you step on the line.</td></tr>
<tr><td>3</td><td>I bet I don't.</td></tr>
<tr><td>2</td><td>You did before.</td></tr>
<tr><td>3</td><td>Watch me. [She does the three.] See. I did it. This one is easier than the one we had yesterday.</td></tr>
<tr><td>1</td><td>Yeah. That was a kid. The squares were pretty small.</td></tr>
<tr><td>2</td><td>Hurry up.</td></tr>
<tr><td>3</td><td>There. I got it in the four. I'm on a roll. [She does the four]. And now five.</td></tr>
<tr><td>2</td><td>It's on the line.</td></tr>
<tr><td>3</td><td>Are you sure? It's pretty close.</td></tr>
<tr><td>2</td><td>It's on the line.
[Enter 4]</td></tr>
<tr><td>4</td><td>Can I play?</td></tr>
<tr><td>1</td><td>We already started.</td></tr>
<tr><td>2</td><td>You'd have to start with onezies.</td></tr>
<tr><td>4</td><td>I don't mind. I'm pretty good at this. I'm sure I'll catch up with you.</td></tr>
<tr><td>3</td><td>You have to go last—after me.</td></tr>
<tr><td>4</td><td>That's OK.</td></tr>
<tr><td>1</td><td>First me, then him, then her, then you.</td></tr>
<tr><td>4</td><td>OK.</td></tr>
<tr><td>2</td><td>What are you on?</td></tr>
<tr><td>1</td><td>Fourzies.</td></tr>
<tr><td>2</td><td>Go.</td></tr>
<tr><td>1</td><td>There. I got it in. [Does the four.] Now fivezies. [Gets it in.] Watch me go. [Loses balance somewhere along the way. Steps down with both feet.]</td></tr>
<tr><td>2</td><td>You stepped. It's my turn.</td></tr>
<tr><td>1</td><td>I need to drink something. I'm so thirsty.</td></tr>
<tr><td>2</td><td>After the game is over. It's my turn to do fivezies.</td></tr>
<tr><td>1</td><td>Hah! You missed.</td></tr>
<tr><td>3</td><td>My turn. There. Right in the middle.</td></tr>
</table>

2   I'll be watching you. Better not step on the line.

3   Hah! Did it. Now six. I bet I'll be finished before you even get started. See six. [Does six]. And now seven. [Enter a big kid (BK).]

BK   Sorry. The game is over.

3   What do you mean? We're not finished yet.

BK   You are now. I'm saving this for me and my friend.

2   Where is your friend?

BK   She'll be along in a few minutes.

1   Then we can play till she gets here.

BK   You can't play unless I say you can play. And I don't want you to play. You'll smear up all the chalk lines.

2   We drew the chalk lines.

BK   That was very nice of you—to draw the chalk lines for us to use.

3   That's not fair.

BK   Fair is whatever I say is fair. If you don't like it, I got a knuckle sandwich you can eat—along with a few of your teeth.

4   There's four of us and only one of you.

BK   Just try me out.

1   Let him have the stupid game. We got other games to play.

4   I never got a chance to start.

1   Come along with us. We'll let you first in the next game.
        [They exit. BK smudges up the hopscotch figure and goes off. Fade.]

                          II.
        [Same kids. By the edge of a collapsed building, most of which is offstage.]

3   I really wanted to finish the game.

1   We'll finish it later.

4   There were four of us. We could have taken him.

1   The word is that he carries a knife and he knows how to use it. It just wasn't worth it.

4   He'll spread the word that we were chicken. Then everybody will come down on us.

1   We can prove we can fight if we have to. Even if we took him, if he carved up two of us, would that be worth it? Besides, if we did a number on him, his pals would come after us. And they wouldn't give up until we were all toast. We'll figure out a way to get back at him somewhere down the line. I know some of the places he hangs out. Let him think we're afraid of him. Then when we strike, he won't imagine it was us that did him in.

4   That's pretty clever.

1   If you're not clever around here, you're going to be dead.

2   Even if you are clever—

3   You've got to be clever and lucky.

1   Or just out and out nasty.

2   You think he's gone by now.

1   Give it some more time.

3   I wanted to finish the game. I was on a roll.

1   You've never beat me yet. I was just stringing you along.

3   You're just saying that to look good.

1   I don't have to say anything to look good. I am good. I can beat you any day of the week blindfolded with one hand tied behind my back.

3   You talk a good talk.

2   Save it for somebody else. We don't have to rag on each other.

4   What do you want to do now?

1   There's always the collapsed house.

2   It's just a pile of rocks.

1   You ever try to climb it?

2   No.

1   It's fun. If you don't watch your step, you can twist an ankle or disappear down some hole.

3   Aren't there rats around that house?

1   There are rats around every house.

2   They say that the rats feed off the people that are buried in there.

1   Rats have to feed off something. If the people in there are dead, they don't care anymore.

4   I heard that the spirits of dead people wander around until they're buried properly.

1   Dead is dead. Don't matter if you're buried under stones or dirt, whether you get chewed on by rats or worms. You going to play or not?

4   What game?

1   Climb the heap.

4   You want us to climb up this pile of stones?

1   Sure. I did it two days ago. It's no big deal. One person climbs. The others count. The one that gets up and down the fastest wins.

2   That sounds like fun.

4   I don't have shoes for climbing.

1   Neither do I. Go barefoot.

4   On the rocks?

1   Sure. Barefoot is faster on the rocks.

4   Did you do it barefoot before?

1   No.

2   We could all do it barefoot.

1   That's OK by me.

4   There's sharp things in there. You could cut your foot.

1   Breaks of the game.

4   A cut foot could get infected.

1   People get sick all the time.

2   Remember that old guy. His foot got infected. They had to cut his whole leg off. They say he screamed bloody murder for days.

1	You gonna play or not?
2	Count me in.
3	Me too. Hey, would you look at that.
1	It's just a bug.
3	A big bug. Never seen one like that before.
1	A bug is a bug.
3	This one is unusual.
1	You can look at the bug. I got a pile of rocks to climb.
3	Some people collect bugs.
2	My sister used to collect pencils. Sounds kind of crazy. She had jars full of them. Used to sort them out by color and size. A pencil is a pencil, I told her. You use it to write with. Don't matter what color it is or what size. If it has a point on it, you can write with it. That's all that matters. The point. That didn't stop her from collecting. She'd find them out on the street. They'd all go to her collection. Her damned collection.
3	Whatever happened to them after?
2	We gave everything of hers away. No use keeping what other people had a need for.
1	Hey, we going to climb this heap or not?
3	Let's do it.
2	Who goes first?
1	I'll go first.
2	OK. You go. We'll count, unless you want to keep looking at that bug.
3	I'll count.
2	Good. Then you start. Ready. Set. Go. [The climb begins on stage, and then the climber exits as he gets about head level with the other kids.]
4	He's doing real good.
2	Oops. He slipped.
3	It looks like he's in pain.
2	He's getting up.
3	Made of strong stuff.

4   His leg is bleeding.

2   It takes more than a little blood to stop someone like him.

3   Anyone like us. Any of us.

2   Yeah.

4   Oops. He fell again.

3   He's not getting up. Should we go up there and get him?

2   Wait a second. See if he can make it on his own. He's getting up.

3   Nothing going to stop him now.

4   He made it to the top.

2   Sometimes it's harder climbing down than up. You figure going up is the hard part. And you get careless coming down.

3   You got to be careful around here—every step you take, going up and coming down.

4   Hell, even walking on the ground. My cousin got a nail in his foot. It got infected. They took his leg off just below the knee.

2   No shit?

4   He was supposed to get a wooden leg—like those pirates you see in the movies.

2   Them pirates is really cool.

3   He get his leg?

4   Nope. Got some other kind of sickness. Bent him up like a pretzel. Never heard screams like that come from his mouth. I never thought anybody could scream like that. On and on. All day and all night. I guess people were happy finally when the screaming stopped.

2   Hey, you made it down.

1   Yep.

2   Didn't think you'd make it after you fell.

1   I stepped on something I thought was solid. It wasn't. I scraped my leg something awful. But I made it up

and down anyway. No cuts and bruises going to stop me now. How did I do?

2 What do you mean? You made it up and down. That was cool.

1 How fast?

2 I don't know. I stopped counting when you fell the first time.

3 I stopped when you fell the second time. I didn't know if you would make it up at all.

1 You stopped counting.

2 Yep.

4 Me too.

1 So you don't know how long I took.

2 Nope.

1 So how do you know what time you got to beat. I sure as hell am not going to climb that heap again. No way.

2 Why not? You know the way now. You'll probably make it up faster this time. You got an edge.

4 Maybe we could do a trial run too. It's only fair.

1 I'm not interested in what's fair. It's not my fault that you stopped counting.

4 We were afraid for you.

1 You worry about yourself. I can take care of me on my own.

2 You going to climb again?

1 After you guys do it. I'm feeling a bit dizzy now.

3 You must have really banged yourself up. You look like you took a real beating.

1 No big deal. I got more bruises on me than lice.

2 That's a lot of bruises.

1 You better believe it. Who's next to climb?

3 I guess I can go next.

1 Good.

3 And don't forget to count. Whatever happens.
[She starts to climb. Exits as she climbs higher.]

4   Hey, look at that girl go.
2   Faster than a rat.
1   Faster than a rat headed for breakfast.
4   She's made it to the top. Now she's coming down.
2   Oops. She slipped.
4   Where did she go?
1   Maybe she fell through.
2   That would be a bummer.
1   Ruin her time.
2   Ruin more than her time.
4   Are we going to leave her in there?
2   Couldn't do that.
4   We going in there?
1   No big deal.
4   All those rats.
1   Rats is no big deal.
2   Roaches.
1   Don't like roaches. They give me the willies.
4   How are we going to find her?
1   Just follow her screams.
2   She might be unconscious.
     [She comes out from behind them.]
3   I'm not unconscious.
2   Wow! Where did you come from?
3   From the top of the pile. I just chose another way to come down. How did I do?
4   What do you mean?
3   I mean, how much time did I take?
4   I don't know. When you disappeared, I stopped counting. We thought you had fallen through. We were talking about going in to get you.
3   So you don't know if I was faster than him. I know I was faster.
2   We stopped counting for him too.
3   This isn't going to work.
2   Let's try something else.

3   It was fun up there. I could see all around the neighborhood.

4   What could you see?

3   Nothing much. What is there to see in this neighborhood? Other houses just like this one. But it was still fun. We could play King of the Mountain.

1   You can't be king. You're a girl.

3   King. Queen. Who cares? I could stay up there longer than anyone.

1   Not if we pulled you off.

2   Three guys against one girl.

2   Isn't that the way it works? Everybody gangs up on the one who's on top.

3   I can take any of you one on one.

2   It don't work that way.

3   Three against one isn't fair.

1   It has nothing to do with fair. Nothing is fair. You see someone on top, you pull him down. Don't let anybody get over you. No way.

3   It's pretty shaky up there. I don't know if I want to be wrestling up on top.

1   You want to be on top, you got to take your chances.

2   We're a gang. Nobody has to be on top. We just got to make sure nobody else gets over on us.

3   Yep.

1   Somebody try, and we all get together and pull him down.

2   Yeah.

3   Hey, would you look at that.

4   What's that?

3   It's an eggbeater.

4   What's it for?

3   You know, when you're cooking your eggs. You got to mix them up first before you put them in the frying pan.

4   I can't remember the last time I had eggs. My mom used to mix them with a fork.

3   This is a fancier way. It kind of fluffs them up.

1   Some people like them better that way.

2   If I had some eggs, it wouldn't matter to me if they were fluffed up or not. I would eat them any which way.

4   You can say that again. What are you doing?

3   I'm taking the eggbeater.

4   Why?

3   I just like the way it looks.

2   It looks broken. I don't think you could beat any eggs with that, even if we had some eggs here to beat.

3   Probably not.

2   Then why take it? Just leave it with all the other stuff that's just lying around.

3   I told you, I like the way it looks. It's interesting, kind of pretty.

1   You're kind of weird. It's just a piece of junk.

3   Sometimes junk can be pretty.

2   What can you do with junk?

2   I like to look at things like this and try to figure out how to use it.

4   Use it for what? You can't beat eggs with it. Besides we got no eggs.

3   It kind of reminds me of a time when I did have eggs.

2   Why do that? It just reminds me of how hungry I am.

3   Sometimes, if you get into your memories, it lets you think for a while what it is like to be full.

1   And then you come back down to earth, and you feel how it's like to be empty again.

2   I'd rather not dream of being full. It makes me even hungrier.

3   Well, maybe so. But I do like the way it looks. It doesn't really matter what it's used for.

1   You want it, take it. Nobody's going to stop you. Whoever used to own it ain't here no more. And if he was, he wouldn't have any eggs to beat. And it's broke. So he couldn't use it anyway.

3   You want to see what I got. All kinds of interesting things.

2   We got nothing else better to do. We can see what you got. Then I got to get me something to eat.

3   Wait a minute. Look over there.

1   What?

3   Over there, on the ground. It's a whisk.

2   What's a whisk?

3   You use it in cooking to mix things up so there are no lumps in the mixture. To get air in the mixture. So what you are cooking is light and fluffy when you cook things like soufflés.

4   What's a soufflé?

3   It's something like a cake, only not so sweet. Maybe it has vegetables in it and eggs. Only it's not a dessert. You serve it with the meal—with lamb or beef or chicken.

2   When is the last time you ate meat?

3   I can't remember.

1   When is the last time you ate soufflé?

3   Never.

1   But you know about things like that.

3   I read about it once. Look at it. Look at the loops. At the handle. It's a beautiful thing.

4   Two of the loops are broken.

3   Yes.

4   Why would you want to keep something that's broken?

3   Two of the loops are not broken.

4   So?

3   It's amazing. After all this.

2   What would you use it for? You have no eggs, no vegetables. You can't make soufflés.

3   It's a memory. Somebody *here* used to make soufflés. Somebody here used to dine like a king.

1   Not any more.

3   No.

2   An eggbeater and a whisk.

3   Yes. And look there.

4   What is that?

3   Part of a garlic crusher.

4   What is a garlic crusher?

3   When you cook, you take a clove of garlic. And you crush it so that all of the flavor comes out—the fresh garlic juice—to flavor everything.

2   My uncle used to eat a lot of garlic. Whole pieces. Raw. On black bread smeared with rendered chicken fat. Slices of onion and pieces of garlic. He said it was healthy. That it would put hair on your chest. My aunt said it would make you smell bad, and no one would want to come near you. My uncle said it would keep peasants away. But my aunt said the peasants ate the same thing, only with lard instead of chicken fat. My uncle said blech—that would keep anybody away. Anybody but another peasant, my aunt said. Then my uncle would take a bite of the bread and fat and onions and garlic, chew it up and swallow it. And he would try to kiss my aunt and she would push him away and they would wrestle around until he got his kiss—and she would laugh and he would finish eating.

1   Black bread, rendered chicken fat, raw onions, and garlic. That sounds really good.

3   I bet your uncle never used a garlic crusher. Or your aunt either.

2   My aunt was a good cook.

1   Did she ever make soufflés?

2   No. When she used garlic, she'd cut it up really fine with a sharp knife. She tried to teach me once how to do it. But I could never get the pieces as small as hers.

3   It would have been easier using a garlic crusher.

4   This one has one of the pieces missing.

1   So it is useless. Even if we had some garlic.

2   There are some wild onions growing in the woods outside town. Wild onions and leeks.

4   What are leeks?

2   Big onions.

4   OK.

2   We could go and get some. They have a pretty sharp flavor.

1   I have a pretty strong hunger. All this talk about food.

3   Let me take the garlic crusher.

4   The broken garlic crusher.

3   Yes.

2   And the whisk and the eggbeater.

3   Yes.

4   Why?

3   I am making something.

4   What?

3   I don't know what to call it. Something like a sculpture.

4   What's a sculpture?

3   It's like a statue. Only statues are usually made to look like people—famous people like generals sitting on their horses. They're usually carved out of stone or made of metal like bronze.

4   These things are made of metal.

3   Yes.

2   You're going to make a statue out of an eggbeater, a whisk, and a garlic crusher. A general sitting on his horse?

3   No. Not a general. It won't look like a person. It won't look like anything at all.

2   Then what is it?

3   A memory—of the way things were. Of the people that were here.

2   Why would you do that?

3   Somebody here could make a soufflé. That is a nice thought.

1   It doesn't help to fill an empty stomach.

3   No.

1   We scrounge around garbage heaps looking for moldy potatoes.

3   Yes.

1   We eat them raw.

3   Yes.

1   Why remind people about soufflés when they're starving like animals locked up in a pen?

3   There may come a time when we are not starving like animals in a pen. It would be nice then to remember that we are able to make soufflés once again.

1   You are a dreamer. That is something that will never be.

3   It was once.

1   Maybe, once.

3   It happened once, it could happen again.

1   In your dreams.

3   OK. In my dreams. Sometimes it is nice to dream.

1   A dream doesn't fill the belly.

3   No.

1   I would give all the dreams in the world for something to really fill my belly.

3   We are more than animals in a pen. We need food. But sometimes we need dreams too. And when there isn't much food, sometimes dreams are all you have to make it through another day.

2   At the end of the day, I get so tired I fall asleep wherever I happen to be. I never dream.

3   You dream. You just forget.

2   Maybe it is a good thing, just to forget.
3   For you, maybe. For me it is a good thing to remember. To think about what used to be. To think about what could be once again.
2   To think about what is now.
3   Yes. That too. It is all part of what I am making.
4   Out of a broken eggbeater, half a whisk, half a garlic crusher.
3   Yes.
2   Well, we have nothing else to do. Could we see your work, this sculpture thing?
3   It's not finished yet.
2   How long will it take for you to finish it?
3   I don't know. Every day I find new things to put in it.
4   So you will never be finished.
3   I think it will be finished, next Tuesday.
2   Can we come to see it next Tuesday?
3   Yes. It should be finished by then.
       [The three boys exit. She continues looking for other things. Fade.]

III.

       [The three boys]
2   Well, it's Tuesday.
4   Yes.
2   Time to go and see that sculpture thing.
4   She said it would be finished by today.
2   I've never seen a sculpture before.
1   You saw a statue before. A general on his horse, with a drawn sword.
2   Yes.
4   She said this would be different.
2   Let's see, how different.
       [They come across the sculpture. It is an abstract piece of work made of intertwined pieces of found objects—the eggbeater, the whisk, and the garlic crusher should be clearly visible.]

196

4	Well, here it is.
2	I see the eggbeater.
4	I see the whisk.
1	I see the garlic crusher.
2	This is a strange thing.
4	Very strange.
2	If you stand close, you can see everything she put into it. But if you stand back, it looks kind of eerie. I don't know if it's supposed to be scary or sad.
4	Maybe it's scary and sad.
2	Maybe we should ask her if she meant it to be scary or sad.
1	She's not here.
2	That's strange. She told us to be here. You'd think she'd want to be here to see what we thought.
4	Maybe she's hiding somewhere just to see how we would react—in case we thought it was really bad.
2	It's not really bad. I kind of like it.
4	But I want to know what she wanted us to think.
2	Scary or sad.
4	Yes.
2	Should we wait for her to show up?
4	We could wait. She's bound to be here pretty soon. [Enter another girl. Whispers to one of the boys.]
1	Oh.
2	What?
1	She's not going to be coming.
4	Why not?
1	She's not going to be coming ever again.
2	Oh.
1	They found her out by the collapsed house. They took her away. They left a chalk picture of her on the ground. [Fade]

IV.

[They are standing by the yellow silhouette. The new girl takes out some chalk and draws lines on the silhouette for hopscotch.]

5	Want to play?
4	I don't know. The squares are awfully small.
5	That makes it more challenging. I'm really good at this. I bet I can beat all three of you, hands down.
1	I bet you can't.
5	I go first.
1	Why do you go first?
5	Ladies first, silly.
1	You ain't no lady. You're just a girl.
5	Girls go first.
1	Why?
5	That's just the way things are. I bet I get through all the numbers before any of you get past threezies.
1	Bet you don't.
	[She throws something into square one.]
5	Watch me and weep.
	[Fade]

FINIS
2006

Lamed Zayin

I

(Two soldiers, in the uniform of a foreign army, one is an officer.)

Officer How long has this been going on?

Soldier Every night.

O And you've never said anything.

S She . . . never said anything. She never did anything. So I didn't report it.

O You don't think it a bit unusual . . . worthy of reporting?

S There's a lot that's unusual that's going on around here that no one reports.

O That's true enough . . . but the woman . . . she could report what she has seen.

S Somehow that never entered my mind.

O She could be a spy . . . or a reporter.

S Spies don't just come out and stand in the open . . . dressed like that.

O Maybe that's her angle.

S Neither do reporters for that matter.

O I don't like it. There were to be no witnesses.

S There are hundreds of witnesses.

O I mean . . . besides them.

S Tell me again why we are leaving . . . these witnesses.

O Who will they tell?

S Some of them won't have to tell anyone . . . given a few months.

O   There is nothing so special here. A lot happens in war. Schoolchildren get hit by snipers. Grandmothers get blown up by land mines. Women get raped.

S   As a matter of policy?

O   This is a war of the spirit as well as of guns and bombs. We not only want territory. We want to strike at the heart of our enemies. To break their morale.

S   The sense of outrage might give our enemies greater resolve. It certainly will not win us many friends in the international arena.

O   Who gives a fig for world opinion? As long as we get our weapons. There are any number of nations in the world who are perpetrating atrocities at this very moment. Some of them are being courted for favored nation status all over the world. As long as you have natural resources and can provide markets for goods and services, it doesn't much matter what you do in your internal affairs.

S   We are not exactly a rich nation.

O   No.

S   And we don't have such a large population that we couldn't be marked as a pariah.

O   The world has a short memory. Today's pariah is tomorrow's trading partner. Meanwhile we have a policy to enforce.

S   Yes. A policy.

O   Any reservations you might have would best be kept to yourself, if you get my drift.

S   I get your drift.

O   Besides, it's not such an onerous task before you. It's not as if you were asked to kill babies.

S   No.

O   Or grandmothers.

S   No.

O   Just . . . ravish a few women here and there.

S   It is not just a few women here and there.

O   The more the merrier.

S   And with the woman watching . . .

O   I can imagine you might get unnerved. Why don't you just shoot her?

S   I thought of that. But there is something about her. The other men feel the same way.

O   You want me to show you how it's done? War is a man's business. Dirty business. It takes a real man to do what has to be done.

S   I am doing what I am told has to be done.

O   You certainly don't look like you're enjoying it. You have all the woman a man could ever hope for.

S   They're not exactly willing partners.

O   A woman's reluctance is just icing on the cake.

S   A caress or two is always nice.

O   There are different kinds of lovemaking. There is partnership . . . and there is conquest . . . sometimes a bit of both mixed together. Don't let anyone ever tell you there is no pleasure in domination and conquest.

S   There are times when it seems that all I am conquering is a slab of dead meat.

O   If that is all that is available, you can learn to find pleasure in dead meat. Use your imagination. Besides . . . think of all the sons you are engendering.

S   Sons I will never get to see. Sons that will be raised to hate even the thought of me.

O   So . . . the world isn't perfect. This is war. You manage the best you can. If we weren't screwing their women, they would be screwing ours.

S   I'm not sure of that.

O   Be sure. I know them. They have no love for us. They are certainly no respecters of our women.

S   So they are no better than we are.

O   You might put it that way.

S   And we are no better than they.

O   It's not a question of being better. It's a question of survival. Us or them. It is better that we survive than that we perish.

S   I am prepared to fight. I am prepared to defend my country. I am prepared to kill . . . prepared, if necessary, to die. I am not prepared to rape defenseless women. Night after night.

O   Then get prepared. Adjust. Those who can't adjust . . . who can't follow directives . . . don't tend to stick around for very long. Our commanding officers don't have much sympathy for people with too many scruples. They are subjected to treatment little better than the women you are called upon to service. I trust you will take what I told you to heart, I have . . . a special regard for you. I would feel bad if anything dire would happen to you.

S   I . . . appreciate your concern.

O   You are about the age my son would have been . . . had he not been killed . . . by them.

S   I understand.

O   So . . . you are to do your patriotic duty.

S   Yes.

O   And I will take care of this woman for you. You don't look very happy with my offer.

S   She hasn't done anything. She is not one of the enemies.

O   How do you know?

S   She is . . . different.

O   She is an impediment. Sometimes innocent people get in the way of something that must be done. In war, sometimes innocent people get killed when they find themselves in the wrong place and the wrong time.

S   You will . . . calmly walk up to her and put a bullet in her brain!

O   If necessary.

S   And you will sleep well afterward?

O   No better or worse than I do every night.

S   No pangs of conscience?

O   No more or less.

S   I don't know whether to admire you or pity you.

O   You'll have time to figure that out after the war is over . . . if you don't get killed first. Meanwhile, you have a job to do. There is a fresh batch of prisoners coming in tonight. Prepare yourself for some action.

S   It's getting harder every day.

O   I don't care how you do it. Fantasize that you are with your sweetheart.

S   No one has to hold my sweetheart down for me to make love to her . . . or beat her into submission.

O   Pretend then that she is some cheap whore you've come across . . . or some adolescent fantasy.

S   My imagination is not that good.

O   Pretend that the bitch is the difference between life and death . . . that she's an enemy soldier. You have to shoot or get shot.

S   There are times the thought of death is most sweet.

O   You have someone waiting for you back home.

S   And I pay for that love by performing a mockery of love night after night.

O   Think of it as conquest . . . a knife in the heart of the enemy.

S   Yesterday the one they gave me was barely fourteen. She could have been my own daughter.

O   A hunk of meat. A knife in the heart of the enemy. Think of yourself as a hero.

S   I can no longer look at myself in the mirror.

O   A hero . . . although you won't probably be given any medals for your heroism.

S   I wash my hands at night. They are stained with blood. I scrub my skin. The odor of their fear never leaves me.

O   You do your work . . . and I will do mine. We can't let anyone interfere with our duties as patriots . . . in any way.

S   Our duties . . . as patriots.

O   We are fighting for God and country.

S   It is most strange to think that God would approve of what we do in His name.

O   You'd rather hand the country over to a bunch of heathens?

S   They are not heathens. They merely practice a different religion from ours. Some of them are Christians like ourselves.

O   Heathens. Heretics. It comes to the same thing.

S   If you say so.

O   Our leader says so. The head of our church says so.

S   I am . . . so tired.

O   The head of our church. Our justification is based on Scripture . . . on the teachings of our patriarchs.

S   So very tired.

O   We are doing holy work. You should be proud.

S   Holy . . . work . . .

O   Look beyond the moment . . . to the ultimate cause we are fighting for.

S   I cannot see so far into the future. I see only the face of one frightened girl who could be my own daughter.

O   Our noble aims. Protecting the life of your daughter from the likes of them.

S   The face . . . of that woman . . . looking at me as I follow my orders . . . looking at me with such pain.

O   I will arrange it so she will never look at you again.

S   In . . . my dreams . . . her face. Etched onto every rock. In every cloud.

O   Never, ever again.

II

(Same officer, a different soldier, slightly different uniform.)

O	You there!
S2	Yes, sir. (He comes to attention and salutes.)
O	You are on sentry duty?
S2	Yes, sir.
O	You have been on sentry duty all this week?
S2	Yes, sir.
O	Have you seen a woman moving about the camp . . . dressed somewhat strangely . . . watching . . . our operations?
S2	Yes, sir.
O	You have seen her and yet you made no report of her presence. You did not challenge her. You did not take her into custody.
S2	No, sir.
O	Can you explain your actions, Soldier?
S2	She looked a lot like . . . my sister . . . my younger sister . . . killed by a sniper's bullet . . . last year. There was a lot of sadness in her face. She wasn't doing anything, sir. Nothing at all. Just walking among our men . . . Their women. Not saying anything at all.
O	So you took it upon yourself to not follow military procedures and let a strange woman . . . a spy, perhaps . . . to wander around this camp . . . in a time of war.
S2	It was not only I who did so. The other men as well.
O	This is a strange madness . . . a disease that must be eradicated or it will destroy us at the core. I have chosen you to eradicate the disease. You can vindicate yourself, Soldier. It is either that or face court-martial for your failure to follow procedures. And you know what happens to soldiers who face court-martial. A swift trial . . . and then the firing squad. You . . . have a family, Soldier? A wife? Children?
S2	They were all killed, sir.

O   A mother?

S2   Yes, sir.

O   And how would she feel learning of your death? Learning of your death from a firing squad? Learning of the shame?

S2   I don't know, sir.

O   You don't know. Are you so stupid that you can't imagine how your own mother would feel?

S2   She would be devastated, sir.

O   So. To protect your own mother from being devastated, you will now vindicate yourself. Find that strange woman and shoot her down. And bring her body here . . . to me.

S2   I cannot do that, sir.

O   You cannot do that . . . even if it costs you your life? Even if your mother will be torn apart by the news of your death and will go weeping to her grave?

S2   I cannot do that, sir.

O   Well then, can you at least bring the bitch here to me so that I can see the strange power she seems to have over our men?

S2   I have tried to talk with her, sir. I warned her of the dangers of moving around the camp. I and the other men. She did not answer me with words. She looked at me. Her eyes seemed to speak to my very soul.

O   You are not making much sense, Soldier. What did her eyes say to your very soul?

S2   The pain. I felt her pain. I felt my own pain . . . watching what goes on in the camp . . . night after night.

O   And were you moved to stop what is going on in camp night after night?

S2   I am a soldier, sir.

O   A very strange kind of soldier, indeed . . . who picks and chooses what orders he is to follow . . . who would face his own death rather than follow military procedures.

S2   Yes, sir.

O   Well then, Soldier, at least take me to the place where this woman walks free as a bird. Let me see how she hypnotizes our men . . . turns them into lambs instead of soldiers. Let me see her with my own eyes. And then you watch me, Soldier. I will end the spell she has over you with one bullet from this gun. One bullet to the head. Take me to her, Soldier, and you will see how a real man acts in the name of his country and his God.

III

O   (Writing, alone.) It was not my custom to be in that area of the camp at that time of night. We gave the orders. Nothing is written down, of course. It would not be wise to have written records in case it should happen that our actions come under international review. The prisoners are kept in their quarters. Things happen in times of war. Soldiers are men, after all. They are away from their wives and girlfriends. They never know from one day to the next if they are to live or die. They have seen their comrades hit by enemy fire . . . wounded, maimed, or blown apart. Who would fault them for taking their frustrations out on a group of enemy women? Men have done that since the beginning of time. No one need know of our policy to have this done systematically. Knowing the enemy as we do, we realize how devastating it is for them to discover that their women are sullied . . . that they carry the children of infidels in their wombs. So the men fight during the day . . . and they occupy themselves with other activities once the sun goes down. Just another part of the war effort. As such, the presence of a strange woman watching all this was unnerving to the men and had to be stopped. It was not hard to find the woman. She moved among the soldiers and the women almost like a spirit. She made no effort to stop what she saw . . . and her presence, for the most part, did not deter the men from what they were doing. She did not seem to look directly at any one person . . . and yet she stood there as an accusing presence. I accosted her. I demanded to know who she was. I demanded that she come with me. She did not seem to understand what I was saying. I stood directly in front of her. I gestured in a way that was unmistakable. I drew my gun and pointed it directly at her. She seemed not to care. She moved past me almost as if she were floating two inches above the ground. I fired into the air. She did not respond. I got in front of her again. I pointed the pistol at her. I shot at her feet. I fired a bullet just to the side of her head. She looked at me for an instant and then moved on. I felt unable to move. It took every ounce of my strength to return to my tent. I saw visions of things that had happened to me long ago . . . things so painful I had never wanted to be reminded of them. In the end, I decided to leave things as they were. The men are doing what they have been ordered to do. If that woman wants to witness every rape that takes place in the camp, let her. She takes no notes. She records nothing. She takes no photos. Anything she might say later on, we will claim to be the ravings of a woman driven mad by the horrors of war. There is enough horror to drive more than just one woman mad. Enough horror to drive all of us mad.

I have never written to you of my childhood. The story is best left untold. I had ordinary parents . . . an uneventful childhood and adolescence. Nothing worth going into detail about. I was born. I grew up. And I am here now. I can't tell you what I am doing now . . . even the location. All that is classified information. A few months, a year or so, and this will be over. Things will return to normal. We can pick up the pieces where they lie and begin to make a life for ourselves. It will be good getting away from here. I have started having dreams of late that wake me in the middle of the night. I trust that all of that will disappear once I get home.

IV

(Two women, middle-aged. If possible they can be black, dressed in somewhat traditional garb.)

W1	What's the matter?
W2	It is not to be believed.
W1	There is an awful lot these days that is not to be believed.
W2	Eerie.
W1	The killing. Neighbor killing neighbor. People who lived next to each other for years . . . who have shared recipes . . . who have watched each other's children.
W2	What do you expect? When you consider what was done to us in the past.
W1	Anger is one thing. Hunting down a few villains. A sound beating. Some trials. Imprisonments. An execution or two.
W2	The outrage was so great. Beyond anything that could be atoned for.
W1	By babies?
W2	Babies grow up to become soldiers that can rape or maim.
W1	You could kill an innocent baby?
W2	You forget what they did to my family . . . to our people.
W1	The babies did nothing.
W2	One does not make such subtle distinctions when the time of reckoning arises.

W1	I could not act so against children . . . babies.
W2	These times require one to have a strong stomach.
W1	A strong stomach is not the same thing as a hard heart.
W2	I do not know if you are the one to talk to.
W1	We have been friends since we have been children.
W2	The time is out of whack. Lifetime friends turn on each other. Husbands and wives.
W1	We are in the same age group. We were initiated together.
W2	That is true.
W1	Such ties are stronger even than blood.
W2	You will not think evil for me for what I did?
W1	You are my age sister.
W2	I was involved . . . in the . . . retribution.
W1	Oh.
W2	They came to my house last night. It is time, they said. I took up my machete. We knew which houses to go to. Their men were away at the fighting. The women were there. The women, the old people, and the children. The babies. We showed them no mercy.
W1	My god!
W2	We went from house to house. Some of the women I had known since childhood. I attended them at their births. I dawdled their children on my lap. I showed them no mercy. Their cries did not deter me from my purpose. House to house we went. Somewhere along the way, I became aware of a presence. A woman . . . in a robe. Like . . . a shepherdess . . . from a distant land . . . pale-skinned . . . but not quite white. She was watching us as we went about our work . . . with a look that seemed to pass through us and our victims.
W1	She tried to stop you?
W2	No. She made no gesture to stop us. But as the machete fell . . . each time . . . each slash seemed to register on her face. I have never seen such a look of

pain on any woman's face . . . even those we forced to watch as their babies were cut in two. No one made a move to chase her away. No one made a move to harm her in any way.

W1   You had machetes in your hands.

W2   The pace of killing stopped for a moment. But when it became clear that she would not try to interfere with what we were doing, the killing went on . . . throughout the night. And she watched us through the night. And then in the morning as we headed for our homes, suddenly she was gone. She had vanished into the air like a spirit. I was afraid. I am afraid now.

W1   Afraid of what?

W2   That somehow I must have angered the ancestors . . . or the gods . . . and they will seek vengeance on me.

W1   She did nothing to you last night.

W2   The gods act in their own time. You are lulled into thinking they have forgotten, and then somewhere down the line something happens to tell you that the time of reckoning has finally come.

W1   What are you going to do?

W2   There is a wise man in the village who knows of such matters. I will take counsel with him. Perhaps there is yet some way to avoid catastrophe. I must know quickly, because they will come for me again tonight. There are other women in neighboring villages that are targeted. It will be hard to tell them no after what I did last night. They may think I have sympathy for our enemies. They could turn on me and my children.

W1   They could turn on me and my children. I did not go out with you last night.

W2   They knew you would not go out with them on such a mission.

W1   Am I in danger?

W2   You are a respected member of the community. You are a healer. A wise woman. You have helped to bring many children into the world. But I would advise you not to walk about for the next few nights. These are perilous times.

W1   And the lady . . .

W2   I dread seeing her again. I looked into her face for one moment, and I felt my knees failing me. I felt my arm go limp. I had to look away to regain my resolve. I did not look directly in her face again. But I knew she was looking at me. At us. At what we were doing. I fear that all will not be well with us. That some dire calamity is brewing that will come upon us like a sudden storm. I must take counsel with this sage. I must find out what I am to do when they come for me tonight.

V

(Two women, middle-aged, in concentration camp garb.)

W3   You are back.

W4   Yes.

W3   And all went well?

W4   We are back.

W3   I don't know how you manage.

W4   We manage.

W3   Under the very noses of the guards.

W4   We manage.

W3   And the women?

W4   As well as could be expected under the circumstances. If times were normal, they would have two weeks to recover . . . special food. We do what we can. The ones that recover, recover. And the other ones . . . don't. Without our "program," they would all perish. Not that it matters much. They start with the sick and the weak. In the end, we will all be sick and weak. I wonder sometimes why we continue to struggle from day to day. Sometimes I think that those that die quickly are most blessed.

W3   And yet you go on.

W4   Yes.

W3   Why?

W4   I have no answer for you. I don't know what else to do.

W3   And the babies . . .

W4   I'd rather not talk of it.

W3   I remember how it was with me. It was freezing cold. The wind blew snow in my face. It was like knives cutting into my flesh. The snow was deep. But all I could think about was the pain . . . and the fear. I was terrified that the guards would notice. You were there for me. You and the others. You stuffed rags in my mouth to stifle my cries. You took me out on a garbage cart. I felt at times that I was going to break in two.

W4   It was your first.

W3   It was my first . . . a boy.

W4   Who can remember such things?

W3   A boy. The image of his father. Of blessed memory.

W4   Why do you torture yourself with such thoughts?

W3   You bundled me up in the rags you brought . . . and wheeled me back to the barracks.

W4   Yes.

W3   And the baby?

W4   What do you want from me? We do what we have to do. Otherwise all would be lost. Mother and child.

W3   What must be done.

W4   There were two women tonight . . . within minutes of each other. I was so preoccupied I did not notice . . . until I looked up and saw her there.

W3   Who?

W4   A woman . . . dressed strangely. Not one of the inmates or the guards.

W3   Who?

W4   I don't know. But it seemed right for her to be there. I accepted her presence without question.

W3   What was she doing?

W4   Watching. Just . . . watching. Watching as we attended the women in their labor. Watching as we brought the babies out from the womb. Watching as we cut the cord and brought forth the afterbirth. Watching as we bundled the mothers up and put them back on the cart. Watching as we took the babies off to the side and smothered them with rags. Watching as we buried them in the snow. There was such a look of pain on her face. She made no gestures. She made no move to approach us. She said nothing at all, although once I thought I saw her lips moving in what might have been words from the heart. From my heart. And somehow my spirits were lifted. To know that she was there . . . that she had seen everything. That she knew what I was feeling. We began to wheel the mothers back to the camp. And she was gone. Just like that. I don't know if she will return. But I will remember the look in her eyes until the moment of my death. A warm embrace. I felt a lightness in my step. A renewed strength in my arms.

W3   The woman that you saw.

W4   Yes.

W3   I have heard others talk of her.

W4   Others?

W3   The women that clean out the shower houses . . . after the bodies are removed. One of them told me.

W4   Oh.

W3   One of the young ones too . . . fresh from the trains. She was with her mother. The guards forced them apart. She was pushed off to one side . . . taken to the quarters of one of the officers . . . to serve his needs. She looked back and saw her mother standing naked with some of the other older women. The guards looked at them and jeered. Then they were taken to the shower house. And the woman was there. The woman in the strange garb . . . as her mother was ordered to walk . . . to her death. She saw the look of pain in the woman's face. And the memory of that look of pain stayed with her that night when the officer came and used her. That night and the nights that followed.

W4 And the guards?

W3 They seemed not to notice. Her presence did not slow them down for an instant . . . if they noticed her at all.

W4 Was she . . . an apparition?

W3 I don't know. Would you say that she was an apparition?

W4 She seemed as real to me as my own mother. As real to me as God was to my father. As real to me as the blood of the mothers on my hands. As real to me as babies buried in the snow. As real to me as lice and hunger. As real to me as death.

W3 What did you make of it? Was it a sign?

W4 I make nothing of it. I felt her eyes on me, and I felt warm somehow. I felt the strength to go on for another day. You want an explanation. Explain the camps to me, and I'll explain her presence. Explain our suffering over the ages. Look up at the heavens and explain the silence. Explain how they can do this to us and then return to their quarters for a hearty meal, a glass of vintage wine, and a night of pleasure with tomorrow's corpses.

W3 I . . . don't know.

W4 Well then. Some things are better said with silence.

VI

(Two land owners, Russian, early nineteenth century.)

M1   It was the darndest thing.

M2   You look . . . puzzled.

M1   I am puzzled. This is my estate. I know everyone who lives here. Every peasant. Every man, woman, and child. Every animal. Nothing happens here without my knowledge and approval. These people live on my land at my pleasure. If I decide to take my pleasure of one woman or another, who is to tell me no. It is an honor to sleep with the lord of the manor, is it not?

M2   That is the custom.

M1   My word is law. If I do not maintain absolute control, then the whole order will collapse. At the head of the universe is God Himself. He doesn't ask His creatures whether they wish to do His bidding. His will is known. Those that disobey receive eternal punishment when they die. Is this not so?

M2   Most assuredly.

M1   And the church . . . There is a head of the church. Everybody can't just do as he pleases. You disobey the teachings, and the final penalty is excommunication. You disobey the tsar, and the penalty is death or imprisonment. Children don't dictate to their parents, do they? The result would be chaos. If a child is insolent, it is our duty to admonish him . . . to chastise him . . . and, the Bible says, if necessary, to put him to death.

M2   It is written thus.

M1   So . . . it is for the lord of the manor to give orders and for the peasants to obey. The rabbit does not dictate to the lion. I ordered the woman to prepare for my visit and she told me no. I had to show her who was the lion and who was the hare or every other peasant would think he could do as he pleased. I had to make an example of her.

M2   You did indeed. I would have done so without a moment's hesitation.

M1   I did not act impulsively. I thought the whole thing out step by step. In the end, I ordered her to meet me in the middle of one of my fields . . . at noon . . . her and her family . . . and all the other families on my land. And I took her son. I gave an object of his clothing to the hounds to smell, and I sent him out across the fields. And I set the dogs loose. They came upon the boy well within the mother's sight. They ripped him to shreds before her eyes. There was barely enough for her to bury. I let that be a lesson to her and to the others that live on my lands that I am the master here. It is my will that is to reign here and no other. Was this not a lesson that was well drawn, my friend? Could there be any mistake in the message I delivered?

M2   None at all.

M1   And then it was that I noticed a woman standing off to one side, watching the whole affair. She was not one of my peasants. She was not a member of our class. She was dressed strangely . . . in a costume better suited for wandering through the deserts than through the steppes. She stood there . . . watching. She did nothing to stop my little exercise. She made no gestures. But it was clear from her face that she was deeply affected by what she had seen. And the peasants were drawn to her. The more they looked at her, the more affected they became. The situation had the potential for becoming . . . chaotic. I was on horseback. I had a saber and a pistol. It angered me to think that this woman had taken it upon herself to trespass on my land . . . to react thus to a judgment I had every right to carry out . . . to incite and inflame the feelings of my peasants thus . . . I spurred my horse and galloped toward her. She took no notice of my approach. I felt like riding over her. In the end, I decided to strike her with my whip. As I rode up to her, she looked up at me with such eyes . . . how can I describe them? They seemed to look straight through me . . . to some distant point. There was such pain in her face. I rode past her, my whip still raised in my hand. I knew that I had to strike her now or the peasants would see me as weak. I pretended that riding past her was part of my plan of intimidation. I wheeled the horse around, more determined than ever to put her in her place. But she had vanished without a trace.

M2	What do you make of all this?
M1	I didn't make anything of it. I went home that night and ate well. I drank some fine wine. I slept well and woke up the next morning quite refreshed.
M2	And the woman.
M1	Which woman?
M2	The strange woman, of course.
M1	I haven't seen hide or hair of her since. Not me or anyone else on my estate. I have people around who are my eyes and ears in such matters. I have to know what goes on or things might get out of hand. The peasants must know that they can do nothing . . . say nothing . . . think nothing without my finding out about it and taking decisive action. If that woman ever shows herself on my land again, I will make an example of her, you can be sure of that.
M2	Well then, I guess you have the situation well in hand. Are you up for the hunt on Saturday?
M1	I wouldn't miss it for the world. What is it this time . . . boar . . . or wolf . . . or bear?
M2	Boar.
M1	Great. We haven't had a good pig roast in weeks. I'll tell my servant to ready the hounds.

VII

(Sixteenth century. A grand inquisitor and a foreign merchant.)

Merchant So . . . what do you think?

Inquisitor It's an elegant piece of equipment. It brings together what before was separate gear.

Me That's what I like about it. And it doesn't take an expert to operate it. Some of our people aren't too clever. They get caught up in the moment and overreact. The next thing you know, the subjects are gone. Before they can get a confession out of them. Of course, it is possible to announce they made the confession anyway. Who would know?

I But why bother going through the process at all? We could just garrote them and then produce a confession. It takes all the meaning out of the ritual. We want the confession. But it wouldn't be good if people thought we were executing anyone without an admission of guilt.

Me I must tell you that I admire you folks. You have gone far beyond us in getting your subjects to admit their culpability. Some of your equipment is quite ingenious. You have studied the body. Assessed the individual responses of prisoners. While we have gone beyond you somewhat in our technology, our psychology at times is rather primitive. It would be nice for us to share our expertise.

I That might present some difficulties. We are of different faiths. Technically, if any of you set foot on our soil, we would be obligated to try you for heresy, utilizing some of the very equipment you are showing me.

Me Even if I were part of an official delegation?

I It is better, I think, for us to meet like this, on neutral territory.

Me   Sometimes that proves to be rather difficult. What is neutral territory today is either in your camp or mine tomorrow.

I   It is a turbulent time that we live in.

Me   All the more reason for keeping up with current technology. We have been having a major problem with witches of late. It doesn't matter how many we catch and how many are executed. There are twice as many, it seems, to replace them. Some very respectable ladies of late have come under their sway. Only last month we had to put several of them to the test.

I   Are you still using your dunking chairs?

Me   Yes. Some traditions die hard.

I   And no one has called the logic of the process into question?

Me   Not yet. To do so would appear impious and draw suspicion that one had sympathy for the cause of the damned. Not too many people are willing to risk that.

I   That is where our methods appear to be preferable. We get confessions.

Me   But they are extracted in secret.

I   But who would doubt the veracity of our inquisitors? To do so would be to draw suspicion that one had sympathy for heretics and Satanists. So we are about in the same position.

Me   It would seem so. Except that our population seems a bit more primitive in its love of spectacles. Our peasants are impressed by the dunking chair . . . and public hangings. They come out in droves. A hanging is a cause for revelry and song-making. Balladeers show off their poetic and musical skills, traveling players put on skits . . . people eat picnic lunches on the grass. At times I wonder why we develop refinements in our techniques when the public seems

	satisfied with old-fashioned gallows, chairs . . . and chopping blocks.
I	We do pride ourselves in the intricacies of our methods. Some of our inquisitors are so skilled they can extract a confession by a look alone . . . although it does pay to keep up with modern technology in the more refractory cases. That's why the new chair is so intriguing. I will tell you that it is rather expensive.
Me	But it's specialized. Custom-made. You would expect costs to remain high for a while.
I	We can afford a few luxuries now and then. We do confiscate the property of our subjects . . . especially some of the more prosperous merchants and landholders . . . crypto—Jews and the like. Half of the confiscated assets go to the state. We get to keep the rest.
Me	It's hard keeping up with the rising tide of Satanism. Once witches operated in the dark of night in obscure corners, deep in the woods. Now they are more brazen and flaunt themselves in the light of day.
I	We must be eternally vigilant.
Me	Not a week ago, I was at a chair dunking. A widow lady, it was. Her five children were on the bank of the pond carrying on most terribly. And suddenly I looked up. There was a lady next to them on the shore. She was dressed . . . probably in the costume of one coven or another. She looked at the proceedings with such a plaintive stare. I almost lost my composure. The children stopped this shrieking for the moment, and an eerie calm fell over the assembled mass of people. It was clear to me that she was one of the devil's cohorts. Only such a person could have such an impact on the crowd.
I	What did you do?
Me	Nothing. These people have such power I myself was held in thrall. It would have been a wondrous

	opportunity to extirpate the evil from our midst. But by the time anyone could collect their wits, she had vanished into thin air.
I	Your story is all the more amazing for the fact that a similar occurrence happened at one of our autos de fé. We burned seventeen heretics at the stake that day before a large throng of people. And then a woman appeared suddenly and stood by the fires. And the shouts of the crowds were stilled . . . even the cries of the heretics as the flames consumed them. She was clearly in league with Satan . . . Who else could with the sympathy of the crowd for such profaners of the faith? I found myself carried away looking at her. I doubted my own sense of purpose. And then, suddenly, I lost sight of her. When I refocused my gaze, there were now just the heretics, all expired. The absence of their cries had placed a pall on the proceedings that could only be removed by the next such event. We pushed it forward to erase this debacle from our minds . . . to reestablish the bulwark of our faith. Let her dare to reappear on our streets and we will, I assure you, deal with her most expeditiously.
Me	With the new equipment, perhaps.
I	That would be . . . most appropriate.

VIII

(Two young Black women in tribal dress.)

1	You saw her too.
2	Yes . . . just as they held me down. The whole time they did the cutting. I looked at her face. The scream that rose in my throat never reached my lips. It froze like a leopard about to spring.
1	And they saw?
2	If they did, they took no notice of her. They cut me exactly as they did the others.
1	The way they cut me.

2   I saw her eyes before me . . . and the pain seemed to hover just outside me. I had the feeling that if I let the sight of her go, it would seize me like a great snake and strangle the life out of me.

1   I had the same feeling. Exactly the same.

2   The image of her stayed in my mind for three days. And then the pain subsided.

1   Yes. Three days.

2   Well . . . what now? We are women, my sister. They can treat us like children no more.

1   They say that the initiation is even more painful than having a child.

2   Let us hope so, sister. I could not bear going through such an ordeal again.

1   Do you think the lady will return when we have our children?

2   I don't know. No one has ever told me of such an apparition before. Perhaps the two of us have a special blessing from the gods.

1   May it ever be so, my sister. May it ever be so.

IX

(Two women, middle-aged, in Middle Eastern garb of two thousand years ago.)

1   You are not saying anything.

2   What do you want me to say? I have watched the Romans kill my sons . . . one by one . . . in front of my eyes . . . for being true to themselves and their beliefs. What is there to say?

1   I would like . . . to console you.

2   You are a dear friend. But you are not the one to console me.

1   It pains me to see you like this.

2   Then perhaps you need to distance yourself from me . . . so that you no longer have to see me like this.

1   I cannot abandon you at this time.

2   I cannot . . . respond to you . . . now. Only someone who knows such pain as I feel now . . . only someone like that . . . Your children still live. They made their choice. You can visit their homes. You can speak with them and their children. I am glad for your happiness. Take care of them. They need you. You can do nothing for me now.

1   I fear for you.

2   There was a lady at the place of execution. I saw her there. I saw how deeply she was moved . . . the way her body sagged. Her eyes. She must have seen great sorrow in her own life. As I looked at her, I knew I was not alone. I knew there were other women who had known such loss. Naomi lost her two sons. Eve lost her son. It is the way of the world. We carry our children close to our hearts. In pain, we bring them into the world. We stay up with them at night when they have fever. We bind their wounds when they fall. We watch them grow and move out into the world. And then they are taken from us. And there is an emptiness nothing can fill. An emptiness no one else can possibly know. But that woman knew. God knows what she must have lived through . . . the universe of pain and suffering in those eyes . . . the horror and the dread. I know that I am not alone in this world. That is my consolation. I wish you well. Go to your children. Dawdle your grandchildren on your knees. Taste the full measure of joy that is in the world. And those of us who know the emptiness of such loss will find each other. I have nothing else to live for. Nothing else at all.

X

(Two people—angels actually—speaking near the entrance to heaven.)

A1   Where is she now?

A2   Outside the gate.

A1	What is she doing?
A2	Just . . . sitting there.
A1	You told her she could enter?
A2	Yes.
A1	And what did she say?
A2	Nothing at all.
A1	No gesture even?
A2	Nothing. She just sits there.
A1	You're sure she heard what you said.
A2	She heard me well enough. She looked at me as I spoke. I could read in her eyes that she heard every word I said. I am rather adept at reading thoughts.
A1	You keep telling me that. What was she thinking about?
A2	Two ladies from Gamla.
A1	Which two ladies?
A2	Two old ladies who were forced to see the Romans kill all the other people in that fortress . . . nine thousand of them. The men and women were put to the sword. The babies were tossed alive on to the rocks below. And these two ladies were spared. They had to live with that vision for the rest of their lives. "I was with them. I was with them," she kept repeating to herself.
A1	That's what she was thinking about?
A2	Not that alone. There was a whole litany of such incidents. She made it her job to be at the scene of one atrocity after another.
A1	How did she come to take on such a burden?
A2	It is a long story.
A1	We have time.
A2	Not really. They are waiting for her. Everyone.
A1	Everyone?
A2	From top to bottom. That doesn't happen very often. Doesn't seem to phase her very much. We have been through this before.
A1	She has been here before?

A2	Yes.
A1	That doesn't happen very often, does it?
A2	No. There are times when people are sent back. It has never happened before that someone has refused to enter.
A1	You know why she refuses to enter?
A2	I have a good idea.
A1	So tell me already.
A2	What happens to people who enter here?
A1	Eternal bliss.
A2	What happens to their memory of pain?
A1	There is always memory . . . but not the pain itself.
A2	There is your answer.
A1	I don't understand.
A2	She does not want to be relieved of her pain.
A1	That doesn't make any sense.
A2	It does if you think about her history. What has she been doing all this time?
A1	Attending one catastrophe after another.
A2	Why?
A1	I'm not sure.
A2	To bear witness to suffering. She herself suffered greatly in her life. She is drawn to the suffering of others. It has become her very reason for being. She comes to terms with her own tragedy by acknowledging the tragedy of others.
A1	She is not the first person to do so.
A2	No. But she will not let go of her mission. As long as there is suffering in the world . . . as long as there are victims of atrocity, she will not let go.
A1	Then she will have to hold on till the very end of days.
A2	Apparently so. But her refusal is having some unforeseen consequences.
A1	Namely?

A2	She sits outside the gate. Others notice her. They wish to go out and console her. If she will not enter to feast upon the table that has been set for her, they wish to set the table for her . . . out there.
A1	That has never been done before.
A2	No.
A1	Will it be permitted?
A2	I'm not sure. There are always surprises around here. Just when you think you understand, the rules of the game are modified somewhat.
A1	People can do that?
A2	They have before . . . extraordinary people.
A1	Is she so extraordinary?
A2	How many have taken her path before her?
A1	I see your point.
A2	So. It gets interesting now . . . to see what response she will elicit . . . especially since she's not aware that she is trying to elicit any response at all.
A1	She is just doing what comes naturally to her, as it were.
A2	Exactly.
A1	Totally unaware of the impact she has on anyone?
A2	Seems so.
A1	That is extraordinary.
A2	Not so extraordinary. Great pain can produce great isolation. But somehow, even in her isolation, she has the ability to reach others, even if they can't seem to reach her.
A1	She must have an interesting life story. Who is she anyway?
A2	Her name has not come down to us. She was born in Bethlehem to someone from the house of Judah. She was the concubine of a Levite who lived in the territory of the tribe of Ephraim.
A1	A concubine?
A2	Yes.

A1   Not such a distinguished personage.

A2   No. And her behavior was not very exemplary either. She got angry and returned to her father's house. Her man wanted her back and went to the father's house. The father was delighted the man came for her and gave a feast that lasted five days.

A1   Is all of this detail important?

A2   I'm not sure. But that's all that is known about her. You asked me. I'm telling you.

A1   I thought her story might be a little more auspicious.

A2   I'll tell the story. You tell me how noteworthy it is. Can I go on?

A1   By all means.

A2   They started out for the man's house late on the fifth day. It was too late to finish the trip that day, so the man stopped at a town not far from Jerusalem . . . a town in the territory of the tribe of Benjamin. No one in the town extended any hospitality to them, and they were prepared to sleep out under the stars. But a resident of the town from the house of Ephraim found out their plight and offered them hospitality . . . the man, the concubine, the servants and the donkeys. They were about to settle down for the night when some ne'er-do-wells and rabble-rousers came to the master of the house and demanded that he turn over his guest so they might ravish him.

A1   I seem to have heard this story before.

A2   There are similar episodes recorded before.

A1   Like . . . Sodom and Gomorrah?

A2   Yes. There the entire population was involved. The guests were angels there to get Abraham's kinsman, Lot and his family, out of the city because it was about to be destroyed for its immorality.

A1   It does seem that the punishment was justified.

A2   Indeed, God rained down fire and brimstone, and the entire population was destroyed. There are other similarities.

A1   Namely?

A2   Lot refused to turn his guests over to the mob.

A1   He proved himself worthy of being saved from the general destruction.

A2   Yes. As did the host in this case.

A1   He is a man worthy of being respected.

A2   Wait till you hear the end of the story.

A1   Proceed.

A2   To placate the unruly mob, the Ephramite made the same offer Lot did in Sodom. Lot offered his virgin daughters to the mob as a substitute for the angelic guests. The mob refused.

A1   He offered up his daughters?

A2   Yes. It does seem a bit gruesome, if you will.

A1   I'll say.

A2   The text underscores the lengths a man will go to preserve the laws of hospitality . . . which go to the very heart of the ethical principles of the time.

A1   But to offer up your own daughters?

A2   The magnitude of the sacrifice was even greater than even a first reaction might suggest. If the daughters were no longer virgins, they would no longer be considered marriageable. And, therefore, Lot would be without heirs or descendants.

A1   That was Lot's sacrifice. Think of the poor girls.

A2   That's the whole point, I think. The Ephramite offered up his daughter to preserve the honor of his guest, a stranger, but he also recommended the sacrifice of the concubine. In the end, the traveler forced the concubine out of doors, and she bore the brunt of the outrage alone. They ravished her and brutalized her throughout the night. With her dying strength, she crawled to the doorstep of the house. When the morning came, the guest awoke and prepared to return to his home. He saw the concubine lying there and ordered her to prepare to leave. When he found that she was dead, he took her body home with him. Then he dismembered her, cutting her body in twelve pieces, and he sent one piece to the prince of each of the twelve tribes of Israel with a letter describing the outrage and demanding that they take action. The princes demanded that the perpetrators of the atrocity be tried so that justice could be done. But the tribe of Benjamin refused, and a war was started. After some rather bloody battles, the warriors of Benjamin were given over to the warriors of the other tribes and an oath was sworn that no daughter of any tribe would be given to a son of the tribe of Benjamin.

A1	Wait a minute. You are loading me down with historical data. I can't assimilate all of it so fast. What does all this have to do with the woman outside the gate?
A2	She was the original victim. A crime was perpetrated in a time of moral chaos. Eventually the principles of justice were reestablished, and the evil men were punished for their crime.
A1	So justice triumphed in the end.
A2	One could say that. But the soul of the concubine has not been at rest. The story is not too tidy on reflection. Why did the traveler put his concubine in harm's way to save himself?
A1	She was only . . . a concubine.
A2	She was of the house of Israel. And the host was willing to sacrifice his daughter . . . and Lot's daughters . . . not presumably his sons, if he had had any.
A1	Because they were . . . female.
A2	Exactly.
A1	So outraging a woman was less unthinkable than doing the same thing to a man.

A2   Apparently so, even though the traveler demanded that her death be avenged. Still . . .

A1   A woman's life counted for less than a man's.

A2   A woman's life. A woman's pain. A woman's humiliation. There was something about this woman . . . something about what she experienced that would not let the matter lie. She was offered rest . . . here. She was offered the reward of eternal life, and she turned it down. She had to understand . . . something. She had to resolve something on her own. She is, I must admit, not exactly an intellectual heavyweight. So she finds herself at the scene of other atrocities and tries to understand them. She makes no more sense of them than of her own demise.

A1   I must admit that when I look at the atrocities that abound in human history, I find it hard to understand . . .

A2   The purpose.

A1   Exactly.

A2   Even if the perpetrators are brought to justice.

A1   In earthly life or thereafter. Somehow the pain of one child . . .

A2   So . . . you begin to understand. She will not be assuaged. She will not be placated. She demands a reckoning.

A1   In a way, don't we all demand a reckoning?

A2   We all wish for a reckoning. We all hope it will eventually take place. We are satisfied to wait, if necessary, until the end of days until the reckoning becomes clear and all the pieces fall into place.

A1   I suppose.

A2   But this woman, it appears, is not willing to hope or to wait. In her own silent, inarticulate way, she demands an explanation. That places her on another plane, as it were.

A1   No one has ever demanded such a reckoning before? Abraham did. Moses did.

A2   There is something about the way she has gone about it that makes her unique.

A1   A nameless, illiterate concubine. A footnote in an obscure, quasi-historical record.

A2   Somehow, all of this is supposed to make sense. At some level, we all make our peace with the atrocities we encounter . . . to impose meaning an apparent chaos. Somehow she has been able to focus on outrage in its purest form. In her silence is a challenge that seemingly cannot be denied. There is talk that her presence is a destabilizing force of such magnitude that it cannot be overlooked or denied.

A1   By . . . God Himself?

A2   Indeed. According to the vision of the mystics, on Friday night, God goes through the world, searching to be reunited with His indwelling presence, the Shehinah. This union is the essence of the peace of the Sabbath, which in turn is a foretaste of the peace that will be ushered in at the end of days. When a husband and wife encounter each other at this moment, they too receive a hint of the promise of peace that is to be the portion of all Creation . . . when all will be able to lie under their own fig trees and no one will be afraid.

A1   The vision of Isaiah.

A2   Yes. The promise that everything ultimately will make sense. That no child's cry will be unaccounted for.

A1   And now?

A2   It is said that the Shehinah herself is in mourning. She is disconsolate. She has turned to face the darkness at the edge of night . . . and the union and harmony which is the very cement that holds the world together has been shaken.

A1	Because of one woman?
A2	She has somehow in her silence focused, concentrated, and borne witness to the unanswered cries of women and children . . . of innocence. She has forced a reckoning by her very presence . . . outside the gate. The seeds of pain in her own life have blossomed over the years, watered by the tears of the countless others she has seen. She can no longer be denied.
A1	And now.
A2	God only knows what will happen now.

XI

(Some time later.)

A1	Well?
A2	Well what?
A1	Well . . . what happened?
A2	With . . .
A1	The lady.
A2	Which lady?
A1	You're toying with me. The one outside the gate.
A2	Oh, that lady. She's gone now.
A1	She never entered the gate?
A2	No.
A1	Whose decision was that?
A2	A decision arrived at by mutual consent.
A1	Her and . . .
A2	The master of this place. They both agreed that she had more important things to do down there.
A1	What kind of work?
A2	The kind of work she had been doing before.
A1	She agreed to that?
A2	Yes. Does that surprise you?
A1	The look of pain she bore on her face . . . yes . . . of course. Why would anyone agree to accept even one hour of such unmitigated agony?
A2	A sense of purpose . . . of where you fit into the divine plan.

A1   The divine plan calls for her to accept a role of pain and suffering . . . to be a witness to other people's pain and suffering, and she accepted such a role?

A2   He asked it of her, and she accepted. So I suppose that is all that is important in this case.

A1   You heard?

A2   In a manner of speaking.

A1   In what manner of speaking?

A2   It was a moment almost unprecedented in the history of the world . . . or perhaps one that occurs far more often than we are aware of. One individual . . . facing the dark night of the soul, that place where ultimate chaos and ultimate meaning intersect, where one is a single step away from the abyss or the heavens. Moses was there . . . the moment he stood on the top of Mount Sinai and asked to become aware of the divine attributes . . . and was told that even he could perceive them, as it were, from behind . . . a reflection, not the thing itself.

A1   And if Moses could only see a reflection . . .

A2   The tradition says that God tried to present him with the Torah as it really was. He told Moses the truth as He understood it, and Moses was unable to grasp what he was told.

A1   What was he told?

A2   Aleph.

A1   Aleph?

A2   Yes.

A1   Silence?

A2   That silence that encompasses everything . . . that existed before Creation.

A1   And Moses?

A2   He couldn't grasp what he was told. So God gave Moses the Torah, beginning with the letter Bet, and that Moses could understand. He could hear, and what he heard, he could understand.

A1 A reflection of the essence of truth.

A2 Yes.

A1 And this woman?

A2 I saw the dark cloud envelop her. There was no thunder and lightning. Absolute silence reigned. It was not like the absence of sound. It was silence that was so complete that any sound would have felt like an intrusion . . . any sound beyond that of the beating of the human heart . . . beyond the breath of a human soul . . . beyond the ebb and flow of life itself.

A1 And for how long did the silence reign?

A2 Longer than I could have borne it, I am sure. It seemed to me like an eternity. In the end, the darkness moved away and I looked at the woman's face. The pain was still there, but there was also a sense of serenity and peace clearly marked. She arose and prepared herself for the return. She walked differently than she had before. There was a sense of resolve in her footsteps that was not there before.

A1 She received an answer.

A2 So it seemed.

A1 And that answer was . . .

A2 The answer was given to her, not to me.

A1 You have no idea?

A2 I have no idea.

A1 And that satisfies you? The drama is over, and you have no idea how it was resolved?

A2 It doesn't have to satisfy me. It had to satisfy her.

A1 God said . . . Aleph?

A2 Perhaps.

A1 To her and not to Moses?

A2 Perhaps. Each of us has to face the emptiness his or her own way.

A1 A concubine and not Moshe Rabbeinu?

A2   Who knows? I did hear a mystic talking about the matter. He seemed satisfied that order had somehow been restored to the cosmos, that the coming Sabbath would be quite special.

A1   What exactly did he say?

A2   The world is in turmoil. Evil abounds, of such magnitude, that were it not for thirty-six righteous men who bear the pain and suffering, the whole universe would collapse upon itself . . . and return to its primal state.

A1   The thirty-six righteous men. I have heard that story before.

A2   There is a commentary that God determined that the sins of parents would extend to their descendants to the third or fourth generation. That statement is in the book of Exodus. But in Deuteronomy, it is written that parents shall not pay for the sins of their children nor children for their parents . . . the commentary states that this is one of the principles that Moses taught God.

A1   That is a very bold notion . . . that God can learn from mere mortals.

A2   Very bold indeed. The implication is that people should live their lives in such a way that they too have something to say to God that matters . . . that is worth listening to, that God can learn from man.

A1   Go on.

A2   The mystic told me that when God faced the woman, He thought the universe could be preserved by the very existence of these thirty-six righteous men.

A1   Yes.

A2   But that He left with the realization that this woman was also essential to His plan.

A1   Thirty-six is twice eighteen . . . which stands for life. What is . . . thirty-seven?

A2   A prime number.

A1   So?

A2   So . . . we thought we understood thirty-six. Now we have to rethink everything . . . based on thirty-seven. Or maybe forty-one or fifty-nine. Who knows? Sometimes we think we have found meaning in numbers or things, only to discover that all we have found are partial meanings or the reflection of meanings. The universe is bigger than our understanding of it. If thirty-six righteous men can hold the key to the mystery, why not thirty-six men and a woman who understands the meaning of silence?

A1   I don't understand the meaning of silence. I don't even understand the meaning of your words.

A2   Don't we have some things we are supposed to be doing?

A1   I suppose.

A2   For the moment then, let's leave the question of understanding to someone else.

XII

(Gestapo officer and concentration camp guard.)

Guard   The girls are ready.

Officer   Showered, cleaned up, deloused?

G   Showered, cleaned up, deloused.

O   Good. Our officers are waiting. A lot is asked of them in this godforsaken place. The least we can do is offer them some creature comforts.

G   Some of the girls are not bad-looking at all. Dark hair. Gypsy eyes. Decent figures, all things considered.

O   They'll get better treatment than their compatriots . . . for as long as they are useful to us.

G   Rather nice-looking, all things considered. Not as nice, of course, as Nordic types . . . but that would be impossible here. These are the best that are available. (Enter messenger.)

M Herr Commandant, the ninety-three women are ready.

G Ninety-three? There were only ninety-two of them. I counted them out myself.

M There are ninety-three. One of them was dressed rather exotically . . . almost like a Bedouin. I thought that was part of the fantasy.

O What do you mean?

M Arab women are supposed to be sensuous and at the same time responsive to men's needs. There were women dressed as gypsies or princesses. This one, however, stood out from the others.

G An Arab woman. Intriguing. I might want to take a stab at her myself.

O I stipulated ninety-two women. Can't you men get anything right? Ninety-three is not ninety-two. We can't let extra women sneak into this special group. The next thing you know, they'll be changing places with some of the female guards. Bring me this Arab woman . . . now. (He exits and returns momentarily.)

M She was nowhere to be found. When I left her, she seemed to be consoling the others . . . more with gestures than with words. They seemed to glance at her from time to time . . . for reassurance.

O People don't just disappear. Not in this place. I want that woman found and brought here, or someone will be in big trouble. You counted them?

G Yes . . . ninety-two.

M There was no mistaking that woman. She had an air about her that was quite distinctive . . . of wisdom . . . and innocence. I can't quite explain it.

O Don't explain it. Just find her. Now. (He exits.) Nothing surprises me around here anymore. We try to run things like a camp, and they turn out to be more like a circus.

M Herr Commandant.

O   Yes.

M   The ninety-two.

O   Yes.

M   They are all dead.

O   What do you mean?

M   They are all dead. Suicide most probably. Cyanide tablets.

O   Where the hell would they get cyanide tablets?

M   There is an underground at work in the camp. It would not be impossible to sneak pills in to them.

O   Suicide?

G   These people don't take very kindly to being used for sexual purposes.

O   These people. These people will learn that they cannot play games with me. Select out ninety-two other women to take their place . . . and ninety-two others to be hanged in the public square. Our officers will get what they need one way or another.

M   Yes, Herr Commandant.

O   And put out a search for that other woman.

M   Yes, sir.

O   I will make an example of her. She will be used by all the officers in turn . . . in one night. And then we will hang her body up for the crows to eat. There are twelve sections in this camp, aren't there?

G   Yes, Herr Commandant.

O   Maybe we'll dismember her and hang one piece of her on a pole in each section of the camp. They will do our bidding here. We are the rulers here. They cannot presume to do . . . each man . . . what he pleases to do in his own sight.

Finis

1997

Lebenslieder (Songs Of Life)

[Small room, sparsely furnished. No effort is necessary to make it historically accurate. It should have a desk on which the composer, Viktor Ullmann, writes his compositions. Lamp. Some scattered books and manuscripts. The play begins in 1933. Ullmann is thirty-five. His second wife, Anna, comes in periodically with their son, Max, who is one. A calendar, on an easel or projected onto a wall, shows the years as they progress. The words of particular songs can be projected as well—possibly with their English translation. Sound of soldiers marching. Occasional brusque orders in German do not have to coordinate with words or action on stage.]

Viktor	We will be safe here in Prague.
Anna	Safe.
Viktor	For the moment. Yes.
Anna	Safe, for the moment.
Viktor	I can work here.
Anna	For the moment.
Viktor	Yes.
	[He begins to compose. The year shifts to 1935. Sound of marching and orders grows louder.]
Anna	What are you working on?
Viktor	A song.
Anna	A song, now?
Viktor	What else would you have me do?
Anna	A song—
Viktor	Schwer ists, das Schöne zu verlassen.
Anna	Oh.
Viktor	It is difficult to leave that which is beautiful behind.
Anna	Oh, Viktor.

Viktor   What can one do but write to turn pain into something beautiful. To turn the loss of beauty into something beautiful.

Anna   I am afraid.

Viktor   To turn fear itself into something beautiful.
[She leaves. 1936: She returns.]

Anna   Still working?

Viktor   Almost finished.

Anna   What is it this time?

Viktor   An opera.

Anna   Oh.

Viktor   Der Sturz des Anti-Christus.

Anna   You are not afraid that there might be trouble.

Viktor   There is trouble.

Anna   You don't have to take chances by doing such things.

Viktor   Whatever I do, if I do nothing at all, trouble will still search us out.

Anna   If there is a noose in the town square, you don't have to walk up and put your head in it.

Viktor   If there is a noose in the town square and it is meant for me, they will find a way to get me there, no matter what I do.

Anna   We could leave. We could hide.

Viktor   There is nowhere to go now. Nowhere to hide.

Anna   I am afraid. I am afraid for us. I am afraid for our son.

Viktor   I could pretend and tell you there is nothing to fear. I too am afraid. That is why I work. The fear goes into my music. The fear. The anger. There is nothing else to be done now. What will be, will be.
[She leaves. 1939: Sound of marching louder. Woman enters. Elizabeth, Viktor's third wife.]

Elizabeth   What is it this time?

Viktor   A concerto.

Elizabeth   Why do you bother? You know the new law. It will not be performed—anywhere.

Viktor	The music is in my head. I have to write it down, or it will be lost.
Elizabeth	And if you write it down and no one ever hears it. They could come here, it would still be lost.
Viktor	I do what I can do. What happens afterward, who can say? [She leaves. He puts down that manuscript, begins another. She returns.]
Elizabeth	Still working?
Viktor	A song cycle. Five poems. I am working on the third one right now.
Elizabeth	Songs . . . now?
Viktor	A lovely poem by Huch. I like his work. Sturmlied—O Brausen des Meeres und Stimme des Sturms.
Elizabeth	The sun is shining today. The weather is fine. We could go walking in the park.
Viktor	The storm is gathering around us. Our little boat is being tossed by the raging waters.
Elizabeth	The sun is shining today. The park—
Viktor	Let me finish just this one song. We will have time.
Elizabeth	Time.
Viktor	Still time. Today. For a walk in the park. [She leaves. 1940: She returns.]
Elizabeth	Working hard?
Viktor	Things are going well.
Elizabeth	With you. Here.
Viktor	Yes.
Elizabeth	Not out there.
Viktor	I can't do anything about that. It doesn't stop me from working. The Slavic rhapsody is finished. I've done as much with it as I can at this point. The piano sonata as well. I am working on another song cycle. Twelve songs of a more spiritual nature.
Elizabeth	Spiritual—
Viktor	I have my moments.
Elizabeth	You have faith that all of this will work out?

Viktor	In time.
Elizabeth	In our time?
Viktor	Perhaps.
Elizabeth	And if not?
Viktor	There's nothing I can do about that now. [She glances at the page he is working on.]
Elizabeth	Im Himmel, im Himmel sind der Freuden so viel. Do you believe that?
Viktor	Things are not so joyous down here.
Elizabeth	I know that.
Viktor	So one can fantasize. Besides, all I'm doing is setting a text that inspires my music. I don't have to actually believe the words. [She looks at another page.]
Elizabeth	Marienlied. Ich sehe dich in tausend Bildern, Maria lieblich ausgedrückt. You are thinking maybe of converting?
Viktor	Not really. It wouldn't do any good now anyway. They don't care what faith you profess. All that counts is what you were when you were born. What your parents were. Your grandparents.
Elizabeth	So why write a Marienlied?
Viktor	Part of a musical tradition.
Elizabeth	You had me worried there for a minute.
Viktor	I wouldn't do anything to worry you. [She flips a page.]
Elizabeth	Gottvater sah gemach ich gehn.
Viktor	It would be nice to ask Him perhaps what is going on right now. What He intends by all this.
Elizabeth	You think you would get an answer?
Viktor	Who knows? It doesn't hurt to ask.
Elizabeth	You are a strange man, Viktor Ullmann.
Viktor	These are strange times, Elizabeth. [She leaves. He stops composing. Picks up a book. Gets some blank pages. Begins work again. She reenters.]

Elizabeth	It is late, Viktor.
Viktor	When I feel inspired, I have to work.
Elizabeth	What is it this time?
Viktor	Poems by an English poet, Elizabeth Barrett Browning.
Elizabeth	Elizabeth——
Viktor	A nice name, isn't it? The poems are quite nice, sonnets, mostly about love.
Elizabeth	You can think of love now.
Viktor	With you by my side, yes. I can think of love.
Elizabeth	Let me read. Briefe nun mein Tod bleich und lautlos dauernd. The words are beautiful.
Viktor	Yes.
Elizabeth	A bit morbid.
Viktor	Perhaps, but beautiful nonetheless.
Elizabeth	You will come to bed?
Viktor	Just let me finish this one song, sketch it out. I can work on the rest later.
Elizabeth	I will be waiting for you. [She leaves. Time passes. She returns.]
Elizabeth	What now?
Viktor	Four songs.
Elizabeth	More songs?
Viktor	That is what seems to preoccupy me these days. Short pieces I can finish quickly.
Elizabeth	Oh.
Viktor	One has to be practical. I wouldn't want to be interrupted in the middle of a large work.
Elizabeth	Better to finish short works no one will probably get to perform than to get interrupted in the middle of a large work no one probably will ever get to perform.
Viktor	Exactly.
Elizabeth	I suppose there is some logic in that.
Viktor	Yes.
Elizabeth	Strange logic.
Viktor	Strange times require strange logic.

Elizabeth	What are these poems about?
Viktor	A bit exotic. Based on the work of a Persian poet.
Elizabeth	Why Persian? You usually use German poetry.
Viktor	Every once in a while, it pays to step outside the ordinary to get some perspective. You read work written a half a world away centuries ago, and suddenly you find a kindred soul—someone who clarifies what you were trying to express.
Elizabeth	Hafiz?
Viktor	I found a translation of his work in an old bookstore.
Elizabeth	You shouldn't be browsing around bookstores. It's getting too dangerous.
Viktor	Sitting at home can be just as dangerous. The authorities know who I am. They know where I live.
Elizabeth	There are hooligans roaming around looking for an excuse to beat someone up.
Viktor	Every once in a while, I have to get out. Walk . . . somewhere. Feel free. Read. The poems are delightful. A bit wicked, but delightful nonetheless.
Elizabeth	Vorausbestimmung—this is a bit irreverent.
Viktor	Yes.
Elizabeth	Preordained by God's goodness to drink and fornicate.
Viktor	I told you it is wicked. If you can't joke about something, maybe it isn't all that important.
Elizabeth	He doesn't take himself too seriously either. Look.
Viktor	Yes. Betrunken. That's what I feel at times. Betrunken.
Elizabeth	You don't drink that much.
Viktor	More's the pity. I would like at times to be a reeling shadow in the indiscreet moonlight. Instead, I am all too sober. And the only moonlight I get is through that window.
Elizabeth	You let yourself get drunk in your music.
Viktor	True. But sometimes there is no substitute for the real thing.
Elizabeth	Unwiderstehliche Schönheit—anyone I know?

Viktor Look in the mirror.

Elizabeth You flatter me. Hafiz is so taken by her beauty he forgets to pray.

Viktor He forgets to pray, but he doesn't forget to write.

Elizabeth Ah. And so you write.

Viktor Yes.

Elizabeth And forget to pray.

Viktor I have never been particularly devout.

Elizabeth A German Hafiz.

Viktor Not a German. Just someone who happens to write in German.

Elizabeth And reads German poetry and is inspired to write music.

Viktor That no real German will ever listen to.

Elizabeth Lob des Weins—this is strong stuff. Let this song force its way to the dancing spheres with a mighty impulse. I am the master of the world.

Viktor I feel that way sometimes when I compose.

Elizabeth And then—

Viktor Then the real world comes back to me, and I realize I am but a speck in the ocean. That anyone in a uniform can do whatever he wants with me, and I can't do a thing about it.

Elizabeth So you compose some more.

Viktor It's what I can do.

Elizabeth And feel in brief moments—

Viktor Like I am the master of my fate.

[She leaves. Then 1941.]

Elizabeth Another piano sonata?

Viktor Things come to me. I write them down.

Elizabeth No chance of getting it published.

Viktor Not now.

Elizabeth Ever?

Viktor Who knows? I've made copies, just in case.

Elizabeth Copies—where?

Viktor I sent them to a friend.

Elizabeth	They could just as easily raid his place as yours.
Viktor	He is not a member of the tribe.
Elizabeth	You trust him?
Viktor	I would trust him with my life.
Elizabeth	He could claim that the manuscript is his.
Viktor	He has his own work. A different style. Besides, if something does happen to me, the work is more important than the name that is attached to it.
Elizabeth	You wouldn't mind if it was attributed to someone else?
Viktor	It's a strange thing when I compose something. It's more like I find it or discover it than that it's mine in any sense of the word. I don't mind if it has my name on it. I work hard to get everything just so. But if it has someone else's name on it, I don't suppose I'll mind it when I'm gone.
Elizabeth	And your name is lost to posterity.
Viktor	These days that is the least of my worries. Staying alive for a bit longer, that's important. I have more work to discover, I'm working with some French sonnets now, by Louise Labé.
Elizabeth	I'm not familiar with her work.
Viktor	Read this.
Elizabeth	On voit mourir toute chose animée. That's pretty morbid.
Viktor	Sonnets tend to be somber in tone ever since Petrarch. One is always lamenting the loss of an idealized lover or the passage of time.
Elizabeth	Je vis, je meurs.
Viktor	A truism.
Elizabeth	Lut, compagnon de ma calamité. Isn't there anything more cheery to occupy your time?
Viktor	It's a challenge to make something beautiful out of such mournful sentiment. I think it helps me cope with everything out there.
Elizabeth	Just as long as it stays out there.

Viktor	To tell you the truth, I'm not counting on it.
Elizabeth	Then don't tell me the truth.
Viktor	You'd rather hear pretty little songs.
Elizabeth	Your songs are never just pretty or little.
Viktor	Still they can take your mind off what is going on out there.
Elizabeth	Yes. At least for a while.
Viktor	Good. I have two more songs to write to finish the series.
Elizabeth	I will wait to be entertained.

Elizabeth [Sound of marching gets louder. Some orders in German seem to be coming from just outside the door. 1942: There is a knocking on the door. Two soldiers and an officer enter. The soldiers carry submachine guns. The officer says, "Heraus!" Viktor and Elizabeth exit. Momentary blackout. The new scene is in a similar room, but it is smaller and more crudely furnished.]

Viktor	You know, it could be worse.
Elizabeth	Worse than this?
Viktor	This place is a showcase. Not like the other camps. They want the world to think that all the camps are like this—artists' colonies, where talented people are free to express themselves and develop their talents.
Elizabeth	So that the world can delude itself that all is fine and dandy and the Führer can put his plans into effect without interference. What's the difference if we get killed now or somewhere down the line?
Viktor	We have a chance to be ourselves. To compose. To write. To paint.
Elizabeth	And as soon as we are all gone, all the work will be destroyed.
Viktor	Maybe not. I heard talk of a museum. They did one in Germany, of what they called decadent art. The joke was on them. More people came to see the decadent art than the art sanctioned by the Reich.

	There are whispers of an exhibit of work of an extinct race.
Elizabeth	Oh good. They'll kill us and then exhibit our work.
Viktor	To demonstrate their superiority. Chances are, people will do the same thing here they did in Germany. The art the government sanctions is pretty dull stuff.
Elizabeth	So we should live with that hope.
Viktor	That's not the question for me. We are here. It's amazing how many talented people they have brought here. People I would never have had a chance to collaborate with. They have named me Director of Modern Music here. We are composers and performers. That's what we are. We will compose and we will perform.
Elizabeth	Until the day they ship you out and murder you.
Viktor	Until that very day. I'm not going to curl up and wait to die. They don't take kindly to that in any case. People who don't cooperate tend to disappear rather rapidly.
Elizabeth	So it's compose or decompose.
Viktor	Exactly. I'm working on an opera I started a while ago. Der zerbrochene Krug. If I can't get it performed outside these gates, I can get it performed here.
Elizabeth	A captive audience, as it were.
Viktor	With occasional visitors from the outside.
Elizabeth	Who want to be lulled to sleep.
Viktor	Exactly.
Elizabeth	And you can continue to do this.
Viktor	I don't see that I have any other choice.
Elizabeth	There's always another choice.
Viktor	Not one I'm likely to take.
	[She exits. He works. She returns.]
Elizabeth	I hardly get to see you anymore.
Viktor	I'm sorry. It's just that the work takes up so much time.
Elizabeth	You work harder here than you did outside.

Viktor   Outside I could fool myself into thinking I had more time. There are no such illusions here. We did a performance of the Verdi *Requiem* last month. The Germans applauded our efforts enthusiastically. They praised the soloists lavishly, and then they shipped them out. There is no understanding these people. They shed tears listening to Brahms and then condemn the very players that moved them to the gas chambers.

Elizabeth   And these are the people we are entertaining.

Viktor   We are not doing it for them. They think of us as less than human. But here at least, they have to recognize us as artists of the highest order. They are stuck on the logic of their own propaganda. If they didn't praise us for our talent and give us the opportunity to create, the international visitors might choose to visit other camps. And there is no way they could pretend these camps are artists' colonies.

Elizabeth   And if we refused to play their little game?

Viktor   There are enough talented people they could get to replace us. We are stalling for time. Germany is now fighting against the rest of the world.

Elizabeth   They have allies.

Viktor   Trust me, they cannot hold out forever. There will come a time—

Elizabeth   Will we live to see it?

Viktor   Whether we do or not is beyond our power to predict or to influence. We do what we can. As artists and composers. There is room in what we do for us to express our true feelings—in ways the Germans can't decipher.

Elizabeth   Maybe no one else will either.

Viktor   We do what we can with the people we have. I have never been so productive. I have finished a symphony, a piano sonata, a string quartet, an opera.

Elizabeth	Yes. Der Kaiser von Atlantis oder die Tod—Verwindung. It's a wonder they let you perform it.
Viktor	It is an allegory. A fairy tale. They choose not to see it as a reflection of themselves.
Elizabeth	Self-delusion.
Viktor	Not the only example I could cite. I have also been composing some songs.
Elizabeth	More songs.
Viktor	Schubert composed over six hundred songs before he died at thirty-one. I am forty-five. I have a way to go yet.
Elizabeth	Schubert died of natural causes.
Viktor	There are a lot of people here who die of natural causes—typhus, typhoid, dysentery, pneumonia, tuberculosis.
Elizabeth	Helped along by a lack of food, chilly barracks, rotten sanitary facilities.
Viktor	Some artists believe that great work can only arise from great suffering.
Elizabeth	You know, I wouldn't mind testing that idea. Let me have a happy life for a few years and see—
Viktor	Maybe in another lifetime. Look, I set these poems by Georg Trakl and Albert Steffen, and these are new—twelve Lieder based on poems by Hans Gunter Adler.
Elizabeth	Let me see. Bei dir, in Lachen und in Thränen. Hinab, hinab, die Glocke stimmt. Komm Weicher Schraf! Komm süsse Nacht. You think the end is near?
Viktor	After the next visit of the International Red Cross. There is talk.
Elizabeth	Little cakewalk. What is a cakewalk?
Viktor	Among the Negroes in the United States, it's like a strut, a competition to see who dances the best. Amazing that anyone living in such intolerable conditions could lose himself so completely in dance, could find such joy.
Elizabeth	We do that here.

Viktor   We do try, don't we?

Elizabeth   Lundi, mardi fête, mercredi peut-être. You think the end will come soon?

Viktor   All too soon. I finished this Cantata.

Elizabeth   Vor der Ewigkeit. Was sind die Dinge dieser Welt? Was sind die Sachen? You are writing religious works now?

Viktor   The singers. They ask me to write such things. It is for them.

Elizabeth   You do not believe.

Viktor   Look around you. Is it possible to believe here?

Elizabeth   They believe.

Viktor   It is good for them to believe. It helps them get through the day.

Elizabeth   And what helps you get through the day?

Viktor   Writing a cantata for them so they can continue to believe.

Elizabeth   You are an amazing man, Viktor.

Viktor   I only do what I can do under the circumstances. [She leaves. 1944: She returns.]

Elizabeth   You are working yourself into an early grave, Viktor. You don't rest. You could catch anything. It is not good, Viktor.

Viktor   I must produce what I can while there is still time. Look, an opera about Joan of Arc.

Elizabeth   Why Joan of Arc?

Viktor   She was killed for being who she was.

Elizabeth   Yes.

Viktor   And another symphony.

Elizabeth   Has the orchestra rehearsed it?

Viktor   Not yet. And another piano sonata.

Elizabeth   Will it be performed?

Viktor   The pianist who was supposed to play it was shipped out.

Elizabeth   Oh.

Viktor	And a dance fandango from another opera I am working on.
Elizabeth	Another opera.
Viktor	*Don Quixote.*
Elizabeth	Why that?
Viktor	He lived in an idealized world of his own fantasies.
Elizabeth	An idealized world.
Viktor	Untouched by sordid realities.
Elizabeth	Oh.
Viktor	And some other songs and choruses.
Elizabeth	Always songs and choruses.
Viktor	Based on Chinese poetry. Here. Read.
Elizabeth	Wanderer erwacht in der Herberge. What I wouldn't give to be able to wander through the woods.
Viktor	Yes. And twelve songs based on poems by Rilke.
Elizabeth	I don't know his work.
Viktor	I'll give you a copy. He is profound. Beautiful. He might be the greatest German poet of this century.
Elizabeth	A German.
Viktor	There are Germans, and there are Germans.
Elizabeth	I suppose.
Viktor	Besides, he died well before all this came to pass.
Elizabeth	What's this?
Viktor	Three Yiddish songs.
Elizabeth	You never liked Yiddish. You said it sounded like German spoken by ignoramuses and yokels.
Viktor	That was before here. These are my people. Sometimes they express their deepest feelings in Yiddish.
Elizabeth	And Hebrew songs. You don't know Hebrew.
Viktor	I had help with the Hebrew.
Elizabeth	What does it say?
Viktor	Am Yisrael Yivneh. The people of Israel will build. Will rebuild.
Elizabeth	Do you believe that?
Viktor	I would like to believe that. They must believe that.
Elizabeth	And this one?

Viktor	Anu Olim Artza Ba Shirah. We are immigrants moving toward our land in song.
Elizabeth	Do you believe that?
Viktor	They tell me what they have to sing to get through the next day.
Elizabeth	And this one?
Viktor	Eliahu Ha Navi. It is a religious song sung at the end of the Sabbath and on holidays. The prophet Eliahu is supposed to come to usher in the coming of the Messiah. The song says it should come soon, in our days.
Elizabeth	Do you believe that? [In the background, a solo voice sings the Ani Ma'amim—Maimonides' principle of faith. "I believe in the coming of the Messiah, and even if he may tarry, still will I believe with a perfect faith."] [Enter two Nazi guards.]
Guard 1	Viktor Ullmann!
Viktor	Yes.
Guard 2	Elizabeth Ullmann!
Elizabeth	Yes.
Guard 1	You are to get your things ready. One suitcase each. You are going to take a trip to the East.
Viktor	A trip to the East. [As the lights dim, the sound of soldiers marching. The sound does not drown out the chanting of the Ani Ma'amin which continues on in an utter darkness as they play ends. The audience lights come on gradually after about thirty seconds of darkness.]

FINIS, 2005

For Viktor Ullmann and all the others in Terezin.
For Cantor Dan Gale, whose rendition of the songs of Viktor Ullmann was the direct inspiration for this play.

Learning His Portion

[The setting is a study in the synagogue in a small town in Eastern Europe in the early 1940s. the backdrop should suggest shelves of tall slender volumes. But half of the shelves are empty. A father and son sit at a wooden table. The boy is twelve. The father in his forties, but he looks older. They are dressed in working clothes. Their heads are covered with black kippot. They both wear the fringes of the small tallises, worn by observant Jews under their shirts. The fringes should be clearly seen.]

I.

Father   It's time to begin studying your portion, my son.

Son   Yes, Father.

Father   I hoped that you would be able to study with Reb Isserlas. Such a teacher comes along only once in a hundred years. And to think that he lived in our town, our little town. Practically down the street. Who would have thought that he would accept my son as his student? What an honor. But it doesn't pay to go over what cannot be, my son. Who knows why things happen the way they do in this world? One has to make the best of what one has. And it is not such a bad thing for a father to teach his own son. So what if I am not the greatest of scholars. I am not exactly an ignoramus either. And what I don't know, there are always books. OK, not so many books now. But our father Abraham didn't have so many books, and still he managed to teach his son. So here I am, comparing myself to Father Abraham. OK. I am not Father Abraham. But I still remember something of what I was taught when I was your age. OK, my teacher was not a Reb Isserlas. And maybe I wasn't the best of students. But still I learned something. And something is better than nothing, isn't it, my son? I studied something, and you will study something. Between the two of us, we should be able to come up with enough for your speech. We will study your portion line by line, word by word. You are a bright boy, my son. You have a pleasant voice. By the time you are through, you should be able to impress even a Reb Isserlas, he should rest in peace. Your Parsha is Naso. A long Parsha. So much to talk about. How does it begin?

Son With the numbering of the descendants of the House of Levi, the Gershonites, the Merarites, and the Kohatites.

Father What do we learn from this passage?

Son The men were numbered from the age of thirty until the age of fifty. But elsewhere, it says they were numbered from the age of twenty-five. The men of the other tribes were numbered from the age of twenty. The Kohanim were numbered from the age of one month.

Father Rashi says that the Levites were numbered at twenty-five because they began their training at that point. Only those that had done well in their training were numbered again at thirty. They had five years to prove themselves. Five years should be enough time to prove yourself. I was apprenticed at the age of eight to Reb Shalom, the tanner. He was not a very patient man. If I made the slightest mistake, I would get a klop on the ear or a kick in the behind. He told me to think of everything I did as if it were going to adorn the temple in Jerusalem. I remembered that. Everything had to be as good as possible. In five years, you either learned that lesson or you were out on the street.

Son	The other tribes were numbered from the age of twenty.
Father	They were counted as soldiers. You could learn to handle a spear or a sword much more easily at an earlier age. War was not sacred work.
Son	The Kohanim could not begin their work at one month of age.
Father	That age had to do with receiving the priestly portion of the sacrifices and the tithes. The priests had no land to till. They had to rely on their portion to survive. What do we learn from the order of the families? Sometimes the order is the birth order of the sons of Jacob and sometimes the order has to do with the assigned tasks.
Son	The importance of the tasks is not dependent on birth order.
Father	Yes, my son.
Son	And each task is important. Any task that is done is important if it is done well.
Father	Yes, my son. But the temple is no more. The tasks that are listed cannot be done today. Then why do we still read about them today?
Son	Because to read them today is like doing them. Studying them fulfills the commandment.
Father	So when we study, it is as if we are doing the sacrifices and taking care of the tabernacle. We are doing sacred work. Your preparation is sacred work.
Son	I understand, Father.
Father	And sacred work sometimes can be dangerous. When the sons of Kohat were numbered initially, there were more than 8,600 of them. By the age of thirty, only a third of them were left.
Son	What happened to the others?
Father	That is not so clear. If they did not purify themselves correctly, if they touched the wrong objects, the Kohanim were supposed to wrap the sacred objects

so that the Levites could carry them. Two of Aaron's sons died when they offered strange fire before the altar. Uzzah died when he touched the ark to prevent it from falling off the cart that was bringing it to Jerusalem.

Son   I do not understand, Father. Uzzah was doing a good thing to prevent the ark from falling. Why should he had been punished for doing a good thing? Did not Abraham receive a promise from God that if even ten good people lived in Sodom and Gomorrah, the cities would be saved for their sake?

Father   Things are not always clear, my son. When Job lost his wife and children, his money, and his health, he eventually had to accept the fact that we cannot always understand the workings of the universe. He had to accept the fact that God had a plan even if he didn't understand it.

Son   Am I to accept the fact that our town is part of such a plan?

Father   I do not know, my son. What is, is. And somehow we have to make the best of it. When it is time to study, we must study. It is better to study than not to study.

Son   Even if we do not understand what we are studying, like why Uzzah had to die trying to do something right?

Father   The sagas tell us that it was wrong to put the ark on an ox cart. The ark had poles. It was supposed to be carried by the Levites, not pulled by an ox.

Son   That was not Uzzah's decision, was it?

Father   No, my son.

Son   Then why should he be punished for someone else's mistake?

Father   Sometimes that is the way things happen. Somebody builds a bridge and doesn't build it right. Someone else tries to cross the bridge and gets injured when the bridge collapses.

Son	And what happens to the person that built the bridge?
Father	We are told that all our actions are judged in this life or the next. Nothing escapes the vision of the Ultimate Judge.
Son	It was God that struck down Uzzah for trying to save the ark. How could that be, Father?
Father	Uzzah was not a Cohen. He was not supposed to touch the ark.
Son	Was he supposed to let it fall? If you were Uzzah, would you have let the ark fall?
Father	I suppose not, my son.
Son	Even if you knew you would be struck dead.
Father	Sometimes life offers us difficult choices.
Son	To let the ark fall or to save it and die.
Father	Yes, my son.
Son	And if we don't study, we know we are failing to do what is expected of us.
Father	Yes, my son.
Son	Either way, we could pay a heavy price.
Father	It is better to study than not to study. To prepare you to be a man. We cannot allow the forces of evil to silence our voices. That would be a kind of death. We must fill the silence of this place.
Son	Even if it costs us our lives?
Father	It may come to that whether we study or not, my son.
Son	So if we must die, it is better to die studying than not studying.
Father	Yes, my son.
Son	Father, what was the strange fire that Aaron's sons brought before the Lord?
Father	It is not clear, my son. Some sages suggest that they were drunk, because right after that passage, Moses is warned not to allow priests to make their offerings while they are drunk. There are numerous warnings about the drunkenness. Noah got drunk and did

shameful things in his tent. The daughters of Lot got him drunk so that he would do shameful things with them. Sages are warned not to give judgments if they have been drinking wine. Kings are warned not to drink too much, because they have power to do great harm if they give in to their urges. King Ahashverus was drunk when he ordered that Queen Vashti be killed for not dancing before his guests. He was drunk when he gave permission to Haman to kill all the Jews. One sage said that a man loses one-fourth of his wisdom for every full cup of wine he drinks.

Son Do you think the people in this town were drunk when they came upon us?

Father Some of them, most probably. Sometimes a person must drink in order to do something that ordinarily he would consider not proper to do.

Son They drink in order to get drunk so that they can do what they really wanted to do but couldn't do without drinking.

Father Yes, my son.

Son And the ones that came from far that ordered all this to be done. Were they drunk too? Did they need wine or vodka to do what ordinarily they would not have done?

Father Sometimes people get drunk with power. There are sages that say that Aaron's sons may have been drunk with devotion. They were not satisfied with the portion given to them and wanted to draw closer to the Holy of Holies than was permitted to them.

Son So the love of God can also be dangerous?

Father We are all given our place on the mountain, my son. Moses could go to the top of the mountain. Aaron, not quite. The elders could go just so far. The people stood at the foot of the mountain.

Son Or under the mountain.

Father That is one interpretation.

Son	They were given the choice of accepting the Torah, or the mountain would come crashing down on their heads.
Father	Yes.
Son	A choice of studying, obeying, or dying.
Father	Yes.
Son	Or of studying, obeying, and dying.
Father	That is also possible. To die Kiddush Ha-Shem, for the sake of God's Holy Name.
Son	It doesn't seem as if the people had much of a choice.
Father	They chose. We choose.
Son	It seems like it would be safer to go into hiding and not to study.
Father	That would be a kind of death, my son, and not one of my choosing.
Son	We are not Kohanim or Levi-im, Father.
Father	No. One must be born into this role through the father's line.
Son	They are obliged to do certain tasks, even today when there is no temple.
Father	Yes, my son. But we can choose to study. A sage can arise from any family line. In a sense, a sage can be thought of as being more important than a king or a priest. A king or a priest can be replaced if he dies. He doesn't have to be learned or wise. But a sage is a unique person. He cannot be replaced by someone who is born into a family. He must become a sage by his own efforts. We are not from a priestly line. But we can choose to become learned. We can choose to study so much and so well that we become irreplaceable.
Son	We are alone, Father. If we die, there is no one to replace us, even if we are not so learned.
Father	It is like that always, my son. If we don't choose to do something, it will not be done. Let us proceed then with the portion.

Son	The next passage talks about those that are impure.
Father	Impure in which way?
Son	Those with leprosy, with issues and those who have touched the dead.
Father	What is to happen to them?
Son	They are to be put outside the camp.
Father	Why?
Son	Because of God's presence in the camp. Their presence would defile the camp and then God might withdraw His presence from midst the people.
Father	Are all three categories the same?
Son	I'm not sure.
Father	According to the Sages, there were three camps. The area around the tabernacle, the area of the priests, and the area where everyone else pitched their tents. Those who had had contact with the dead were excluded from the sanctuary. Those with an issue were excluded from the priestly area, and those with leprosy were excluded from the entire camp. What does that teach us?
Son	God distances Himself from all that is impure.
Father	Why is the leper judged most severely?
Son	Leprosy is a disease. I read about it once. It was very common in some areas.
Father	We are not sure that the term used in the Torah refers to a disease or to something else. The sages saw leprosy as a spiritual affliction, a punishment for specific sins. Think of Miriam.
Son	She spoke against her brother Moses. She was stricken with leprosy and had to remain outside the camp for seven days.
Father	Moses himself, when he refused initially to go to the people and to Pharaoh. He put his hand in his robe, and when he took it out, it was leprous.
Son	Why?
Father	He said the people would not believe him.

Son	So he spoke against the people and Miriam spoke against him.
Father	And the staff was turned into a serpent, the one who maligned God.
Son	So leprosy was the punishment for speaking ill of someone.
Father	The sages teach us that one who talks evil of someone kills three people—himself, the person he is speaking to, and the person he is speaking about. When one is shamed publicly, the blood leaves his face and he becomes ashen, like one who has died. He has been mortified. If the act is like murder, no wonder that the person who has sinned thus becomes like one who has died.
Son	And therefore he is put outside the entire camp.
Father	Exactly. The purpose of the sacrifice is to draw near to God. One who has sinned by speaking ill of someone else has drawn away from God and is therefore marked in such a way as to cause him to be put out of the camp. The sages say that when the people gathered at Mt. Sinai, they were almost godlike creatures. All the infirmities they suffered in Egypt were gone. They all stood before the mountain. That indicates that there were no longer any cripples among them. They all saw the lightning. There were none that were blind. They all heard the thundering and the Voice. There were none that were deaf. They all answered. There were none that were mute. They all ate manna, which was assimilated into their bodies as a purely spiritual substance. They were not subject to the call of nature. But when they sinned with the golden calf, all the infirmities returned.
Son	If they all sinned, who was left who could remain in the camp?
Father	The Levites stood with Moses.
Son	But all the others?

Father	Moses understood that they were all guilty and deserving of punishment. That's why he prayed for mercy and not for justice. When he went up on the mountain the second time, he asked to know God's attributes. And God identified Himself as a God of mercy and grace. Abraham came to know God as a God of justice. Moses asked for forgiveness for the people and the people were forgiven.
Son	Is misfortune only due to sin? Is it only those who sin who suffer?
Father	The matter is not so simple, my son. Job asked that question after he was afflicted. His friends told him his suffering must be due to sin and they were afflicted for speaking thus.
Son	So what are we to make of the suffering we see in the world?
Father	Job never got a clear answer. I don't think anyone gets a clear answer.
Son	What are we to do then?
Father	The sages focus on what we can understand. They list sins that estrange us from all that is holy, cursing the Divine Name, immorality, bloodshed, false accusation, haughtiness, trespassing, lying, theft, false oaths, profanation of the name, idolatry, and ill-will.
Son	Should we be able to see the signs of leprosy in those who commit such sins?
Father	They mark themselves, my son. The sign of their evil is emblazoned on their faces no less clearly than if they were leprous.
Son	They march proudly through the world as if they themselves were gods and those they strike down were underlings.
Father	Though the wicked may spring up like grass, there will come a time when they shall be cut down.
Son	When, Father?

Father   Hopefully, speedily, in our day. There will come a time when the exiles will be gathered from the four corners of the earth. Not only us, my son, but all those who recognize the sovereignty of God. The proselyte. Those with good hearts. Look at the next passage. If a man does something evil to his fellow man, he must give a sin offering, an act of restitution—full damages, plus a fifth extra for atonement. A sin against one's fellow man is like a sin against God. If the injured person has no kinsman, with whom can restitution be made? The sages said that the person with no kinsman must be a proselyte, since every Israelite must have at least one kinsman. The proselyte has left his father's house—like Father Abraham. He is like one with no kinsman, and therefore he is called the son of Abraham.

Son   It does not say kinsman, Father. It says redeemer.

Father   The sages understood it to mean a kinsman, for it is a kinsman that is obligated to be the redeemer. This is what we learn in the book of Ruth. The closest kinsman is the first to be called on to redeem the land, and then on down the line. The same as in the case of the levirate marriage, the same as in the case of land that was used to repay a debt.

Son   Aren't we all kinsmen, Father?

Father   All Israel is one family. All Israel. All people of good heart.

Son   I search the ruins, Father.

Father   Jeremiah redeemed a portion of land just before he went into exile. He saw this as a promise of return.

Son   What do you see, Father?

Father   I see a child that has to study his portion and prepare a speech.

Son   For whom, Father?

Father   I do not know, my son. But it is not always given to us to know the impact of what we do. Just because

	we cannot complete the task, we are still obliged to begin.
Son	I am cold and I am tired, Father. I am hungry.
Father	It is a long portion, my son. We have more to do before we can rest. What is the next section?
Son	About the Sota, Father.
Father	Explain to me this passage on the Sota.
Son	If a man suspects his wife of adultery, she is subjected to the trial of the bitter waters. If she is innocent, she receives a blessing. If she is guilty, she is cursed and then executed.
Father	Let's look more closely at the passage. Why would he suspect her being unfaithful?
Son	Either because he has a jealous nature or because her behavior leads him to be suspicious.
Father	The sages were aware that some men are prone to jealousy. They wrote that only a man with a pure heart could initiate such proceedings. If such a man had cause for suspicion, he was obligated to initiate the proceedings.
Son	Why?
Father	Again, the question of purity. That is why the passage on the Sota follows the passage on the leper. An evil tongue kills three people. Adultery leads to the destruction of the nation. The relationship of God and man was seen as a marriage. Idolatry was seen as a form of adultery. Hosea understood this concept when he forgave his wife for her infidelity. He saw his act as a reflection of God's forgiveness for His people. Peace in the home was seen as so important that God could lie to preserve the harmony between Abraham and Sarah. He could allow His name to be turned to the ashes that were mixed with the water in the trial. The preservation of chastity of the Hebrew women in Egypt was seen as one reason God was willing to free the slaves from their bondage.

Son	There is a relationship here between what people do and what happens to them.
Father	Yes. The water used in the trial was taken from the lavers in the tabernacle, which were made from the bronze mirrors of the women. The sages said, let those who lived chastely in an unchaste land judge those who are charged with unchastity. The water and dust reflect the elements from which the first man was created. The priest reviews with the woman the stories of Reuven and Judah who both confessed their sins and repented—in the hope that if she is guilty, she will confess and not require that a parchment with God's name on it be destroyed. If she is guilty, the priest tells her she will experience excruciating pain in the areas of the body in which she sinned. If she is innocent, and has been infertile, she will become fertile. If she was fertile, she is assured that her future deliveries will be less painful.
Son	Was there no chance that she would pass the test if she was guilty or that the austerity of the proceedings might have an impact on her even if she were innocent?
Father	Many centuries ago, this ordeal was judged to be too one-sided. There is no evidence that the trial was used after this point—or even before.
Son	And yet we still read about it.
Father	It does emphasize the importance of purity, fidelity, and peace in the family—and a way people could demonstrate guilt or innocence.
Son	What do we have today to demonstrate guilt or innocence?
Father	What do you mean?
Son	Some way to face the world that accuses us of all kinds of crimes, of proving our innocence.
Father	They are convinced of our guilt. I don't think there is any kind of trial they would accept to prove our

innocence. There was a time they used torture to get us to confess our guilt. Under such trials, people would confess to almost anything to get the pain to stop.

Son And now even the question of guilt or innocence seems unimportant. They fault us for the very fact that we exist. It was easier in ages past when guilt or innocence meant something—when one could be assured that God Himself could bear witness.

Father We have not finished our work, my son. There is more to read and more to analyze. The next section is on the oath of the Nazarite.

Son The one who takes an oath not to eat anything made from grapes and not to cut his hair.

Father Or her hair. The oath can be taken by a woman as well.

Son And not to touch the dead, not even to bury his parents or his children.

Father The oath was taken by those who wished to reach a higher stale of purity than most people aspired to, but the sages were suspicious of such efforts. Some associated such efforts with the death of Aaron's sons. The idea that one would renounce something that was deemed permissible—like grapes and wine—was just as suspect as moving to excess in that which was permissible, like gluttony or drunkenness. Other religions could think of celibacy as a high calling. But even the Nazire was not required to be celibate.

Son There is the example of Samson. His mother was required to refrain from grapes during her pregnancy, and Samson was to be a Nazire for all of his life. But he was not celibate. He consorted with Philistine women.

Father That was the source of his downfall.

Son So the oath of the Nazire did not protect him from his own impulses. It did not save him from himself.

Father	No.
Son	Even at the end, he was more interested in exacting vengeance on his enemies than in exacting justice. And yet he was called a judge.
Father	Those were chaotic times, my son. In the period before Saul became the king, it is written that men did what was right in their own eyes.
Son	That did not mean they listened to their conscience.
Father	It meant they did whatever they felt like doing whenever they felt like doing it. There were no standards of behavior at all. There was total chaos. In the story of the concubine in that town in the territory of the Ben-jamanites, the people acted no better than the people of Sodom and Gomorrah.
Son	Like today.
Father	Very much like today.
Son	The laws of purity haven't changed much over the ages.
Father	They have kept us together as a people. They have acted as guidelines for our behavior.
Son	And what has acted as guidelines for their behavior?
Father	Things have not changed much over the years.
Son	They claim that they read the same Torah that we do.
Father	Yes, my son.
Son	Where is it written that it is good to treat people in such a manner?
Father	Some of them apply the same rules of Herem to us as our ancestors applied to the Canaanite nations and to the Amalekites. We were ordered by God to wipe them out of the Land—to kill men, women, and children. To slay the Amalekites wherever they could be found.
Son	So we are like Canaanites and Amalekites in their eyes.
Father	They say that we killed their Messiah.

Son	The one that was supposed to bring peace into the world.
Father	Yes.
Son	And so in the name of this Messiah who was to bring peace into the world, they kill us as if we were Amalekites—we who study the rules of Nazirut and strive to be pure of heart.
Father	Yes, my son.
Son	You can explain this to me, Father.
Father	No, my son. I understand it no better than you do.
Son	And still, you study. And I must study.
Father	What else would you have us do, my son?
Son	What does it mean to be holy, if they hunt us down in every corner of the earth?
Father	Would you choose to be like them—to hound others the way they hound us? Would you choose to be like a wolf searching for prey?
Son	No, Father.
Father	This portion leads to the priestly blessing. Those who conduct themselves in a pure manner are given permission to act as vessels of divine blessing. Like prophets, they can allow divine words to come through them. It is a privilege granted to humans to participate in ongoing Creation. God creates only one man and woman. They are to create the rest of the human race. God creates men unfinished. We are to remove the imperfection through the ritual act of circumcision. God sends rain, but man must still sow and raise the crops. God allows us to bless others with the words He gave us. And since there is no longer a temple to give the blessings in, each parent blesses their children with these words every Shabbat.
Son	The words are seemingly so simple.
Father	Generations of sages have tried to understand these words.
Son	May God bless you and guard you.

Father   May He bless the sons and watch over the daughters. May He guard you from the evil inclination. May He guard you from the forces of evil.

Son   Father!

Father   May He keep you in the covenant and watch over you until all your suffering comes to an end.

Son   When will our suffering end, Father?

Father   May He cause His face to shine upon you and show you grace.

Son   No man can see His face and live. Even Moses only saw God from behind.

Father   The light of His face—that is the Torah, whose light continues to shine in the darkest night. The light of His presence—that is the Shehina that we welcome every Friday evening in the prayer Le Chah Dodi. The Shabbath bride, Grace. Divine gifts offered to us even when we are undeserving.

Son   Where is that Grace today, Father?

Father   Peace. Fullness. Wholeness. Serenity. Even up to the moment of our deaths. The sense that we have done everything possible to lead a good life—to fulfill the obligations we agreed to at Sinai.

Son   And what of His obligations to us? What of His obligations to us?

Father   We have not finished discussing the portion, my son. There is the matter of the offerings of the princes of each tribe to the tabernacle.

Son   Father!

Father   The princes. According to tradition, they were the overseers appointed by the Egyptian taskmasters. They took the beatings when the Israelites could not follow the harsh edicts. The labors, they were assigned, the rigor or meaningless tasks, the switching of male and female roles, the separation of husbands and wives. They were rewarded for taking on the burden of suffering, and they became the leaders of

	the tribes. Look at the order of the princes and their tribes.
Son	Judah, Issachar, Zevulun, Reuven, Shimon, God, Ephrayim, Menasshah, Benjamin, Dan, Asher, and Naphtali.
Father	Why that order, my son?
Son	I don't know.
Father	Each time the order of the sons of Israel is presented, it is different—to show that no tribe is more important than any other. The offerings are identical. The passage describing each offering is the same. The chanting style is the same for all the tribes. No offering is more melodic than any other. And the sum of animals brought is precise. Not a single item has been left out. And when it became clear that they were, in fact, complete, only then did Moses enter the tabernacle and only then did the divine voice speak to him from the arch between the two cherubim.
Son	What do we have to offer, Father?
Father	You will chant the words, the way your fathers did before you. You are as important now as any of them were back then. Your voice is your offering. Your study, your struggle to understand.
Son	There were many of us once to give such an offering, Father. And now there is just the two of us. That cannot be. It takes at least ten men to make such an offering.
Father	What can we do, my son?
Son	Will I hear the voice coming out to me from the ark, between the cherubim?
Father	We shall see, my son. We shall see.

II.

[The boy chants from the portion, the book of Numbers 7. He reads verse 89 in Hebrew, and for the sake of clarity, it can be translated into English. He reads from a book, not a scroll, since there is no Minyan—i.e., ten men—present in the Shul.]

"And when Moses went into the Tent of Meeting, Moses heard a voice speaking to him from above the ark cover from between the two Cherubim. And God spoke to him." How are we to understand this? The princes represent each tribe. Each gives the same sacrifice down to the grains of the meal offering. Not a single grain was missing. And because the offering was complete, the Voice of God can be heard. But today there is no tabernacle. There is no more temple. What offerings then can be made?

My Father taught me that the voice of the student is the offering. We study the sacred texts. We study the commentaries. We chant the text in the traditional way. This then is deemed an acceptable sacrifice— except that the sacrifice is incomplete. The seats of the synagogue are empty. The seats in the House of Study are empty—in our town and in countless other towns like ours. There are no longer human voices to do the chanting. The voices are stilled forever. And so God is silent. And each person does what is right in his own eyes. Each person follows his own impulses, and the silence grows.

In the beginning, our sages tell us, there was silence, beyond all understanding. But the silence was filled with the seeds of Creation. This is a different silence—the silence of emptiness. How long can this silence grow before the world will collapse into Tohu Va-Vohu. Into absolute chaos. The silence of stilled voices. The silence of those who might have protested. The silence of those that never had a chance to live. The silence of God.

You do not answer me. My Father does not answer me. There is no voice to bear witness even to the memory of Sinai. There is only my voice midst the silence and the sound of the footsteps of the executioners as they approach to make the silence complete. The voice

of one child trying to become a man—without the strength to pull the place down upon the heads of those that come. And no one left when we are all gone to say the Kaddish. Ve Yitgadal Ve Yitkadash.
[Sound of approaching boots, just outside.]
Shmei Rabbah.
[Sudden blackout.]

FINIS, 2005

One Yellow Flower

[Two inmates in a concentration camp setting. They are dressed accordingly. One sad clown].

Man 1	Would you look at that?
Man 2	Strange.
Man 1	A clown—here?
Man 2	There are all kinds of weird people here.
Man 1	But a clown?
Man 2	There are doctors here and lawyers and carpenters and jewelers and water carriers. Why not clowns?
Man 1	Aren't clowns supposed to cheer people up?
Man 2	Look at him. He's sad. He's crying. How is that supposed to cheer people up?
Man 1	Some clowns are happy. Some are sad. I guess if you see someone who is sadder than you are, then you might feel happier by comparison.
Man 2	You would feel happier seeing someone cry?
Man 1	If you go to the circus. They have crying clowns.
Man 2	I can't remember the last time I went to the circus. Maybe once or twice when I was a child.
Man 1	Did the clowns make you laugh?
Man 2	I suppose. I can't remember the last time I laughed.
Man 1	Do you remember the last time you cried?
Man 2	I think my tear ducts have gone dry.
Man 1	When?
Man 2	I can't remember that far back.
Man 1	Do you remember your last steak?
Man 2	No.
Man 1	Your last *pâté* de foie gras?

Man 2	What's that?
Man 1	It's like chopped goose liver. It's supposed to be a real delicacy.
Man 2	You've never had any?
Man 1	Not really. These days, all I dream about is the taste of bread and maybe jam.
Man 2	What kind of jam?
Man 1	It doesn't matter. Just a bit of sweetness to balance out the day.
Man 2	I remember the taste of jam. It wasn't that long ago. Maybe a year or two.
Man 1	And you still remember.
Man 2	As if it were yesterday.
Man 1	If I had some jam, I would give some of it to him.
Man 2	Why?
Man 1	Maybe it would cheer him up.
Man 2	It looks like it would take more than a little jam to cheer him up.
Man 1	A steak maybe. Some pâté.
Man 2	Perhaps.
Man 1	Well, he'll have to stay miserable then. I don't have a steak to offer him, and no pâté.
Man 2	How about a gesture?
Man 1	What kind of gesture?
Man 2	Maybe a thumbs-up gesture.
Man 1	I don't think that would work.
Man 2	Maybe a hug.
Man 1	A hug.
Man 2	There are times when I think a simple hug would mean as much to me as a steak.
Man 1	Really?
Man 2	Maybe even more. I think my stomach has shrunk so much it couldn't handle a steak. I've heard about people who tried to eat too much too quickly and actually died.

Man 1   It's an interesting way to go. I've seen people starve to death. But death by steak . . .

Man 2   It's supposed to be rather painful actually.

Man 1   You've witnessed it?

Man 2   Once.

Man 1   Once is enough.

Man 2   You only get to die once.

Man 1   Once is enough.

Man 2   So maybe a hug is better than a steak. You can't die from a hug.

Man 1   It depends on who's doing the hugging.

Man 2   A bear?

Man 1   No bears around here.

Man 2   If a bear did show up around here, he would be killed for his meat.

Man 1   Bear steak.

Man 2   Possibly.

Man 1   But you could die from eating steak, so maybe a hug for him.

Man 2   From me or from you?

Man 1   I don't know. Do you suppose we should ask first? It's only polite.

Man 2   I believe in the direct approach. Hey, mister. You look pretty sad. Can I give you a hug?

Man 1   You think he'd say yes? We are perfect strangers.

Man 2   I don't think I'm perfect.

Man 1   Good enough.

Man 2   Possibly. And you?

Man 1   Possibly.

Man 2   So it's worth a try.

Man 1   What else could we give him?

Man 2   I don't have any money.

Man 1   Neither do I.

Man 2   No flowers either.

Man 1   Flowers?

Man 2   My mother always put fresh flowers on the dining room table. She said it would cheer her up.

Man 1   Your mother—

Man 2   Yes.

Man 1   Where is she now?

Man 2   Dead.

Man 1   I'm sorry.

Man 2   Out of her misery.

Man 1   That's one way to look at it.

Man 2   How would you look at it?

Man 1   I'm not sure. I know about this life. I don't know what's on the other side.

Man 2   The other side—

Man 1   You know. Some kind of afterlife.

Man 2   I don't believe in that.

Man 1   What do you believe?

Man 2   That dead is dead. Finito. Kaput.

Man 1   So this life is all we have.

Man 2   Yes.

Man 1   It isn't much.

Man 2   No.

Man 1   A miserable existence and then—

Man 2   Nothing.

Man 1   No pain.

Man 2   No joy either.

Man 1   Not much joy here.

Man 2   Every once in a while.

Man 1   Where?

Man 2   I saw a flower the other day, growing out of a dung heap.

Man 1   And that gave you joy?

Man 2   Strange, isn't it? I just stood there and looked at that flower—and for a while I forgot about all the troubles in my life.

Man 1   How long did the joy last?

Man 2   A few minutes.

Man 1	Just a few minutes? That's all?
Man 2	Look, joy is hard to find around here. A few minutes of joy is a precious thing.
Man 1	Does it balance out the hardship? The misery?
Man 2	I think about that flower from time to time. The joy returns.
Man 1	Interesting. What color was the flower?
Man 2	Yellow. Bright yellow.
Man 1	What kind of flower was it?
Man 2	I'm not sure. I never paid much attention to such things before.
Man 1	But now?
Man 2	Now is different.
Man 1	If it would happen, that we get of here in one piece.
Man 2	Dead or alive?
Man 1	Alive preferably. What would you like to do?
Man 2	I would like to buy a house somewhere.
Man 1	A house?
Man 2	Even a cottage. With a bit of ground in front and behind. I would like to plant a garden. A garden filled with flowers.
Man 1	Yellow flowers? Like the one you saw?
Man 2	Yes.
Man 1	Growing out of the dung.
Man 2	Dung is good fertilizer.
Man 1	People are also good fertilizer.
Man 2	You want I should plant my garden over the bodies of people?
Man 1	One source of protein is as good as another.
Man 2	You would like to think that your molecules would somehow become the nutrients for plants?
Man 1	Better than have them go to waste. At least flowers or a fruit tree. Any kind of tree.
Man 2	It's a pity you wouldn't be around to enjoy it.

Man 1   You don't think I would be able to look down from some place on high and somehow perceive what happened to my remains.

Man 2   No.

Man 1   So consciousness ends with death.

Man 2   Yes.

Man 1   We all sink into oblivion.

Man 2   Yes.

Man 1   And that doesn't frighten you?

Man 2   It might bring some relief.

Man 1   From all this.

Man 2   Yes.

Man 1   Are you ready to be . . . relieved?

Man 2   Not quite yet.

Man 1   You want to prolong the agony.

Man 2   I guess so.

Man 1   Why?

Man 2   It's all I know.

Man 1   You're afraid of the unknown?

Man 2   Let's just say that life is . . . a challenge.

Man 1   And you like challenges.

Man 2   I like . . . pleasure.

Man 1   And your life is so pleasurable.

Man 2   There are always surprises. Yellow flowers growing from the dung.

Man 1   And that makes up for everything else.

Man 2   I'm not sure I would put it that way. But the pleasure was there. Maybe it was all the more pleasurable by comparison.

Man 1   So we need a little misery to appreciate the joy.

Man 2   I don't think I need quite all this misery. A little misery would suffice. You don't need a lot of salt and pepper to season your food. A little pinch will do.

Man 1   Maybe he could use a little pinch.

Man 2   You think?

Man 1   To get him started. To get his blood flowing again.

Man 2	He's still alive. His blood must be flowing.
Man 1	It's a manner of speaking. An expression. An idiom.
Man 2	What does it mean?
Man 1	He needs perking up.
Man 2	And you could do that?
Man 1	And you as well. Maybe better than I.
Man 2	I could try.
Man 1	Maybe he wouldn't look so down in the dumps.
Man 2	It's hard to get someone perked up if all he has to look at is this.
Man 1	All the same.
Man 2	It's all we have. We have to make the best of it.
Man 1	We could try to change it.
Man 2	There's little likelihood of that.
Man 1	We could start a rebellion.
Man 2	With what? You need guns. Ammunition. All we have is clods of dirt. Clods of dirt don't do very well matched up against machine guns.
Man 1	I guess not.
Man 2	So at least we can change ourselves, our attitude toward things.
Man 1	You can do that?
Man 2	I do it all the time. Every minute of every day.
Man 1	Amazing. Can you teach me how to do that?
Man 2	Did you notice the yellow flower?
Man 1	To tell you the truth, I didn't.
Man 2	You could have passed it a hundred times and never noticed it.
Man 1	Probably.
Man 2	So that's the clue. You have to be open to the possibility of yellow flowers so that when you see one, you will notice it.
Man 1	As simple as that.
Man 2	Yes. As simple as that.
Man 1	And what will happen if I open myself to the possibility of yellow flowers?

Man 2	You will wake up each day with a sense of anticipation. Of hope.
Man 1	Which is most likely never to be realized.
Man 2	But there was, in fact, a yellow flower. That was real enough.
Man 1	And that is supposed to change my attitude toward being here?
Man 2	Toward being anywhere. Toward being itself.
Man 1	It's such a great thing to have being?
Man 2	It's all we have. We might as well make the best of it. That heap of dung not only gave rise to a yellow flower. If you looked at it closely, you would see there was a lot of life being generated in that dung.
Man 1	Maggots.
Man 2	Life.
Man 1	Such life feeding on shit.
Man 2	Life is life. Some things feed off nectar. Some off shit. It's our attitude that makes one lyrical and the other disgusting.
Man 1	Flies.
Man 2	Part of the web of life. They fit in. They have purpose in the whole scheme of things.
Man 1	They carry germs.
Man 2	Also a part of the scheme of things.
Man 1	Germs that cause illness and death.
Man 2	We are part of the whole scheme of things.
Man 1	This camp is part of the scheme of things?
Man 2	Maybe not. People interfere. There is no reason to think a place like this is a necessary part of the general scheme of things.
Man 1	Human nature being what it is.
Man 2	We could spend hours talking about human nature.
Man 1	I'd rather not.
Man 2	But it is part of human nature to choose. How to respond to circumstances.

Man 1   Maybe it's in the genes. Maybe you were destined to notice yellow flowers, and I was destined to see only maggots and flies. Maybe your parents raised you to notice flowers.

Man 2   You don't think you have a choice in the matter?

Man 1   Maybe my ability to choose was predestined.

Man 2   I've had this discussion before.

Man 1   As have I.

Man 2   It's impossible to come up with any definitive answers.

Man 1   True.

Man 2   But I have to believe that the ability to notice flowers is a choice that I made. It is a choice that you can make. And it makes all the difference in the world. It's like the Bible says—

Man 1   You are going to quote the Bible?

Man 2   Yes.

Man 1   You are a believer?

Man 2   There's a lot of wisdom in the Bible.

Man 1   Truth?

Man 2   I'm not sure about that. I'll settle for wisdom.

Man 1   What kind of wisdom?

Man 2   I give you this day a choice of life or death. Choose life.

Man 1   We don't get to choose in this place. They decide to select you out, and you're dead meat. You get typhus, and you are dead meat. There's not much choice in that.

Man 2   You can still choose how you react to each day. No one can take that from you.

Man 1   They barely give you enough food to get through the day. Look at us. We are wasting away. There's hardly any meat on our bones. They make you work from dawn to dusk. Our clothes are too thin to protect us from the cold. We have to stand for hours for inspection even in the driving rain or snow. We walk

around like zombies just trying to put one foot in
front of the other.

Man 2   This place is challenging.

Man 1   Daunting.

Man 2   Call it what you will. There are still yellow flowers
growing out of the dung.

Man 1   One flower.

Man 2   Even one.

Man 1   And that's enough for you.

Man 2   Under the circumstances, that's what I have.

Man 1   And that is what you will tell that clown over there.

Man 2   What else would you have me tell him?

Man 1   That we are all fated to end up as a dung heap.

Man 2   And you think that would cheer him up?

Man 1   It's the truth. Why hide the truth from him? He'd
only be disillusioned later.

Man 2   There are different kinds of truth. The yellow flower
is as true as typhus.

Man 1   Yes. Do you think he will buy into that?

Man 2   It's worth a try.

Man 1   And you will do it because—

Man 2   It's there for me to do.

Man 1   You are . . . strange.

Man 2   No stranger than anyone else.

Man 1   OK. You talk to him. It couldn't hurt. The guy looks
as sad as anyone I've ever seen in my life. If you can
take the edge off his sadness, I think that you are a
miracle worker.

Man 2   We shall see what we shall see. [He goes over to the
clown.] Good morning.

Clown   Not such a good morning.

Man 2   No worse than any other.

Clown   A good deal worse than many others.

Man 2   Here one day is pretty much like all the others.

Clown   One misery after another.

Man 2   There's not much I can do about that.

Clown	That's just the point. There's not much I can do about that either.
Man 2	So if I can't change things, at least I can change my attitude toward things.
Clown	That's easy for you to say. You're just one person.
Man 2	And you?
Clown	It's a bit more complicated than that. Let's just say I'm disappointed, again. I thought things couldn't get much worse. And then they did. Much worse.
Man 2	I can't say I'm exactly pleased to be here.
Clown	You were plucked from your home on Chobodny Ulitzi II R/A, ushered into the courtyard behind the town hall, kept there for three days with no food and little water, with no protection from the cold and no bathroom facilities, and then shoved into a cattle car with eighty-four others. It took forty-three hours and twenty-six minutes to get to this place. You had to form two lines. Those that went left got gassed and cremated. The rest of you got to work—until you would drop dead of starvation, exhaustion, or disease.
Man 2	How do you know all this?
Clown	I have my way of knowing.
Man 2	Can you guess my age?
Clown	Thirty-seven years, six months, fourteen days, three hours, and twelve minutes.
Man 2	You are good. Amazing. With that kind of insight, you could make a fortune.
Clown	Unfortunately, that kind of insight only increases the pain. I know everyone in this camp. I know all about them. I know secrets they have kept from everyone else in the world.
Man 2	How could you know this?
Clown	How do you think I could?
Man 2	Only God could know all this.
Clown	And so.

Man 2	I can't believe it.
Clown	You have struggled with belief all your life. Now you know the truth.
Man 2	If you are God, don't you belong up there?
Clown	Check your Bible. Every once in a while, I come to earth to check up on things.
Man 2	And you can't do that from up there?
Clown	It's different. There are times I need to get close.
Man 2	So now you're close.
Clown	Yes.
Man 2	You don't look very happy about it.
Clown	Why should I be happy? Let's just say that my supreme creation has been very problematic over the years.
Man 2	Your supreme creation.
Clown	Mankind.
Man 2	Oh.
Clown	Adam and Eve were understandable. I was naive to think they would want to stay childlike forever, ignorant of the difference between right and wrong, between good and evil. And Cain, he had never seen death before. But succeeding generations—war, bloodshed, carnage. I tried starting over with Noah. I made concessions. He could eat meat if he ritualized the slaughtering of animals. Things got worse and worse with Noah's descendants. People have free will. That's part of what it means to be human. They have to choose between good and evil. But they use their intellect to become more and more sophisticated in their evil. And I have to witness this all over the world age after age. And finally here in this camp, my chosen people. It's disheartening. Discouraging. I don't know if people will ever realize their moral potential.
Man 2	There are some very moral people here.

Clown	And most won't survive. Oh, eventually the people who think they are masters of the universe will be defeated.
Man 2	Really?
Clown	Yes. Really. Too late for you, I'm afraid. Most of them will slink off into some dark corner and pretend that none of this ever happened or that they certainly had no direct hand in it. And of course, somewhere down the line, it will happen again. I will have to witness it again and think that if I had arranged things a little differently, all this suffering might be prevented.
Man 2	You could do that?
Clown	I could always destroy everything and start all over again.
Man 2	Human nature doesn't change.
Clown	That is the central problem. Human nature doesn't change.
Man 2	I saw a flower last week.
Clown	A flower.
Man 2	A yellow flower growing from a dung heap.
Clown	Flowers need nitrogen. They have to get it from somewhere.
Man 2	A flower—here. I wrote a poem about it.
Clown	A poem?
Man 2	Yes. Do you want to hear?
Clown	I know about your poem. I would like to hear you read it.
Man 2	It's a simple poem. I hardly call myself a poet. But the words came to me just like that. Whenever I feel really despondent, I find myself repeating the poem. It gets me through the day.
Clown	The poem.
Man 2	Springing from a turd In a corner of the camp One yellow flower
Clown	A haiku.

Man 2	What?
Clown	It's a form of poetry that originated in Japan.
Man 2	I didn't know.
Clown	One rarely knows where inspiration arises from.
Man 2	From this place?
Clown	Yes. Even here. Your poem has given me hope.
Man 2	My poem?
Clown	Yes. If poetry can still blossom here, there is still hope.
Man 2	You still look sad.
Clown	What is happening here is not exactly a cause for celebration. A single poem does not quite balance out all the pain and suffering.
Man 2	No.
Clown	But the pain and suffering did not stop the poem from coming into being.
Man 2	No.
Clown	One must look at the positive side of everything.
Man 2	I suppose.
Clown	A yellow flower. A baby's smile.
Man 2	There are no babies here.
Clown	There will be babies . . . after.
Man 2	That is something to dream about.
Clown	And you still dream.
Man 2	Yes.
Clown	Of babies' smiles and children's laughter.
Man 2	Yes.
Clown	That has not been killed in you.
Man 2	No. Certainly not.
Clown	I will reflect on that.
Man 2	Have a good day.
Clown	Yes, a good day, [Man 2 approaches Man 1.]
Man 1	Well, did you hug him?
Man 2	No.
Man 1	He seems to have stopped crying.
Man 2	Yes.
Man 1	But he still looks sad.

Man 2   Yes.

Man 1   Not quite as sad as before.

Man 2   No.

Man 1   What did you do?

Man 2   I recited a poem for him.

Man 1   A poem.

Man 2   Something I wrote.

Man 1   You wrote a poem?

Man 2   Yes.

Man 1   I didn't know you were a poet.

Man 2   I am not quite a poet.

Man 1   But you did write a poem.

Man 2   Yes.

Man 1   About what?

Man 2   About the yellow flower.

Man 1   Could you recite the poem for me?

Man 2   OK.

           Springing from a turd
           In the corner of the camp
           One yellow flower

Man 1   That's it? It's pretty short.

Man 2   It's a haiku.

Man 1   What's that?

Man 2   A Japanese form of poetry. Three lines, seventeen syllables, no metaphors, contrasting imagery.

Man 1   You know about such things?

Man 2   He told me all that.

Man 1   You wrote the poem first and then he told you.

Man 2   Yes.

Man 1   Somehow you wrote a haiku before you even knew what you were doing.

Man 2   Yes.

Man 1   How is such a thing possible?

Man 2   If a flower can grow out of a dung heap without realizing what it is doing, why can't I write a haiku without knowing exactly what I am doing.

Man 1   You have a point there.
Man 2   So let's get back to the barracks. It's dinnertime.
Man 1   You call what we will get to eat dinner?
Man 2   It's evening. It's what we get to eat. What else would
          you call it?
Man 1   Thin cabbage soup with a moldy slab of bread.
Man 2   Out of thin cabbage soup
          And a moldy slab of bread
          One haiku
Man 1   You never cease to amaze me.
Man 2   Bon appétit! [Fade]

Finis 2011

On The Freedom Road

SCENE ONE

> Peasant's home in Germany, about 1943. A plain wooden table on a carpet. A large dresser-type cabinet against one wall. Simple furnishings. MAN and WOMAN about sixty, dressed in peasant clothes. Late evening.

MAN

A nice dinner.

WOMAN

Thank you.

MAN

It is always amazing to me how you manage to turn the simplest ingredients into delicious meals.

WOMAN

I had good practice growing up. We never had much in my family. My mother could turn scraps into a banquet.

MAN

She would have been proud of you.

WOMAN

Things are more difficult now. It is not only a question of providing for us.

MAN

I know.

WOMAN

The neighbors watch everything we do. If we get extra food, if we throw away extra trash.

MAN

We have to be careful. They give a reward to informers.

WOMAN

Our neighbors. People we have known for years.

MAN

These are hard times. People are struggling to survive.

WOMAN

But to turn us in for a sack of potatoes, for a dozen eggs. We could be killed.

MAN

Not all of our neighbors would do such a thing.

WOMAN

It only takes one. I am afraid.

MAN

I don't know what else we could have done. People come to you and ask for refuge. It is a question of life and death.

WOMAN

It could be a question of our life or our death.

MAN

We made the decision to take them in. That's water under the bridge now.

WOMAN

Are you sorry?

MAN

No. It was the right thing to do. Besides, it gives me some pleasure to know I am thwarting the government even in this small way.

WOMAN

Do we let them come to the table tonight?

MAN

I don't feel safe doing so. If someone came to the door, there wouldn't be time for them to hide.

WOMAN

It's hard asking them to spend all their time in such a small chamber.

MAN

What else can we do? If someone catches them here, it would not only mean their deaths but ours as well.

WOMAN

It is so hard to see them suffer so.

MAN

It was worse for them before. It is hard on you as well. You have to take out their pails every night. Late. Hide it in the pit behind the trees. In all kinds of weather. It is a wonder no one has seen you do it up to now.

WOMAN

We do whatever we have to. Whatever it takes. Let me get these dishes ready.

She puts some food on three plates. Puts their used plates in the sink. Suddenly there is a knock on the door. The couple looks at each other in momentary panic. The WOMAN sits down. The MAN answers the door. A Nazi OFFICER enters followed by two SOLDIERS carrying submachine guns.

OFFICER

Good evening. I hope we are not intruding.

MAN

Of course not. We were just having our evening meal.

OFFICER

Yes. Your evening meal. It is a bit late for dinner, is it not?

WOMAN

My husband works late. I wait for him to get home.

OFFICER

The way a good wife should. It is a pleasure these days to see such a happy married couple, for how many years?

MAN

For thirty-six years.

OFFICER

Thirty-six years of marital bliss. How wonderful! Do you have children?

MAN

We had two children. Our daughter died in infancy.

OFFICER

Such a pity.

MAN

And our son is fighting on the Eastern Front.

OFFICER

Ah, yes. Fulfilling his patriotic duty. It is a privilege meeting such a fine family. The fatherland is truly blessed to have such loyal citizens.
MAN

We are only doing what is required of us.
OFFICER

We could expect nothing less. Really admirable people, wouldn't you say. It is a pleasure being in your company.
MAN

We are just ordinary people leading ordinary lives.
OFFICER

Yes. Ordinary people. We talked to your neighbors about you. That's what they told us. That you were ordinary hardworking people. We like to see that. Ordinary people. Salt of the earth. Then again, sometimes even ordinary people are led to do things that are not so ordinary. You look puzzled. I will explain. Human nature is a funny thing. It is not always easy to predict what ordinary people would do. You train two men as soldiers. One charges into battle and the other one flees in terror. How are we to explain such different behavior?
MAN

I . . . don't know.
OFFICER

One comes home covered with glory with a medal on his chest. He is celebrated by his people. He becomes the stuff of legends. The other one is shamed, put before a firing squad. His parents are sorry he was ever born. How would you explain that?
MAN

I . . . really couldn't say.
OFFICER

A great mystery, human nature. Take this village, for example, an ordinary village filled with hardworking people. We are in a war. The government issues directives to its citizens. Clear directives. As is expected, most of the townspeople are loyal citizens. They follow the directives without question. This is the way it should be, is it not?
MAN

Yes.
OFFICER

And if for some reason one of the supposedly loyal citizens chooses not to follow the directives, one could expect there would be consequences following such disobedience, should there not?

MAN

I . . . would expect so.

OFFICER

So, for example, if there was an order to turn off one's light by a certain hour and someone kept his lights on in flagrant violation of these directives, that should call for some kind of penalty. The lights could attract the attention of enemy bombers who could target the village. Then many people would suffer because of the indiscretion of one person. So what looks like a minor infraction would have to be dealt with seriously, wouldn't you agree?

MAN

I can understand that.

OFFICER

You are a sensible man. Of course you understand. We are in extraordinary times. We are fighting with powerful enemies. We have to be vigilant. Extremely vigilant. It is our job as officers of the Reich to be extremely vigilant. You can understand that, can't you?

MAN

Yes. I can understand that.

OFFICER

The Reich has determined that there are internal enemies that have to be dealt with as well, enemies that for centuries have tried to sap our creative energy, that taint our blood. It is understandable that the state would want to rid itself of such parasites, is it not?

MAN

It is understandable.

OFFICER

It is like having a tumor. If you have a tumor, you go to a surgeon and you have it removed. Otherwise it could destroy the whole body. It is better to cut the tumor out then to let it grow and have the body die. Is that not the logical thing to do?

MAN

One would say so.

OFFICER

So it is with us. For centuries we have had to deal with such parasites. They have spread disease among us. They have poisoned our wells. They have kidnapped our children and used their blood in their perverse rituals. Is it not understandable that we would work to rid ourselves of such vermin? We ordered loyal citizens to help us in this endeavor. And most people have helped us. They have been rewarded for their help. But some people have not helped us. In fact, they have sheltered the members of this misbegotten race. They have gone against the clear directives of the state even in the face of dire penalties. That is quite strange, wouldn't you say? We have to search out these people and make an example of them. That is our job as officers of the Reich. And we carry out his job most thoroughly. What is it you are eating for dinner?

WOMAN

Potato stew.

OFFICER

Yes. A basic, healthy peasant meal. Solid food. Something to fill the belly and stick to the ribs. To warm a person from the inside out on a chilly evening.

MAN

Yes.

OFFICER

Now let me see. Your wife cooked the meal.

MAN

Yes.

OFFICER

She is an excellent cook, I imagine.

MAN

Yes.

OFFICER

And an excellent housekeeper.

MAN

Yes.

OFFICER

Not one to allow the house to get too messy.

MAN

No.

OFFICER

Or allow dishes to pile up in the sink.

MAN

No.

OFFICER

And there are how many people now in your family?

MAN

Three.

OFFICER

And your son is fighting for the Reich on the Eastern Front.

MAN

Yes.

OFFICER

So surely you would not expect him to make it home for dinner.

MAN

No.

OFFICER

And yet there are three plates here, and two in your sink. Two plates that have been freshly used. Interesting, is it not? You are only two people. There are two plates in the sink and three more plates on the table with more food. Perhaps you knew we were coming to your door and you prepared it for us. That is a possibility, is it not? You have nothing to say. You have nothing to say because you prepared the food for three other people, three other people you are hiding somewhere in the house. That is true, is it not? It always amazes me how you peasant folk think you can outsmart us. Do you take us for fools? We know all about your tricks, chambers hidden behind walls, under the floor. When will you learn that you cannot fool us. I can take one look at your face, at your wife's face and see what you are doing. So let's call a spade, a spade. I will tell you what we will do. You will show us where you have hidden your guests, and we will spare your lives. If not, we will rip apart your house board by board,

and we will find them anyway. Then we will take you and your beloved wife by the center of town and shoot you before the eyes of your fellow townspeople. Maybe before we shoot you, we will play a bit with your wife. She is not a bad-looking woman. Our soldiers have been deprived of female companionship for some time. She can entertain our troops for a while, and we can let you watch the fun. Then we can put you through a bit of travail and let her watch you. I think that would be entertaining, would it not? Then again, if you showed us where your guests were hiding, that wouldn't be necessary. Shall I give you, say, three minutes to make up your mind?
MAN
I will show you where they are hiding.
OFFICER
Good. You are showing some sense at last.
MAN
Behind the dresser. There is a secret compartment in the wall.
OFFICER
Good. I expected as much. Where else could they hide? In the basement. Behind a wall. There aren't many possibilities. We would have found them soon enough. OK, let's see. We move the dresser. The soldiers move the dresser.
OFFICER
Ah yes. I can see the outlines of the door most clearly. That couldn't fool anybody. OK, open the door. Tell your guests to come out, or we will shoot them through the wall.
MAN
Come out. The jig is up. There is nothing else to do.
Out a BLACK MAN, BLACK WOMAN, and BLACK CHILD dressed in the clothes of nineteenth-century American slaves.
OFFICER
What is the meaning of this? Where are the Jews you are hiding?
MAN
These are my guests.
BLACK MAN
Please, suh. Please, massah. We are tryin' to escape from our plantation. Life was real hard there. They beat us for every little thing,

so hard the blood would drip down our backside and we couldn' sit for days. The massah son use to come down on Friday and Saturday night and use our women. An' they was threatenin' to sell my wife to some other plantation. I couldn't live without my wife. No, suh. We decide to escape. Follow the North Star, they tol' us. And so we did. Through the swamp. Through the forest. But we seem to got los' somewhere along the way. These folk took us in. They hid us so the slave masters wouldn' catch up with us. They tol' us we could stay till we gets our strength back and then continue on our way.

OFFICER

Is this some kind of joke?

MAN

These are our guests. I guess you'll do with them as you please.

OFFICER

We're not interested in a bunch of niggers. We're looking for Jews.

MAN

What do you want to do with them?

OFFICER

I don't give a damn about them. You want to hide a bunch of niggers in your wall, you can do it. Of all the damn foolishness I've ever seen, this takes the cake. Come on, let's get out of here. We have a lot more houses to visit before the night is done.

The OFFICER and the SOLDIERS exit, slamming the door as they go.

BLACK MAN

Should we go back behin' the wall?

MAN

No. I think you can eat at the table tonight.

BLACK MAN

I think we be healthy 'nuf to push on tomorrow.

MAN

If that's your desire.

BLACK WOMAN

We gots to make it to Canada.

MAN

Could you help us move this table?

They do. The MAN removes the carpet, revealing a trap door that opens. They hand the three bowls down to waiting hands.

WOMAN

Yes. You can eat at the table tonight.

MAN

I have to thank you for being here. If you had not come, I don't think we would have made it through.

The WOMAN portions out three more portions which she sits on the table. The Blacks start eating. Empty bowls are handed out through the trapdoor. The carpet is put back.

WOMAN

When you're finished, could you help me move the table and chairs back?

They do. [Sound of a bloodhound].

BLACK MAN

We best be gettin' back to our hidin' place.

MAN

I guess so.

BLACK MAN

Tomorrow morning we gets an early start. And then onward to Canada.

BLACK WOMAN

(Almost singing)
On the Freedom Road.

BLACK CHILD

On the Freedom Road.

FADE TO BLACK.

The Prince Of Łodz

Stage set can be quite simple. Stage left is an office, in turn the office of a Nazi official, Herr Übermann, and of the principal figure, Mordechai Chayim Rumkowski. All that differentiates the two sets is a large wall portrait of Hitler in the former and a standing Nazi flag or a Nazi flag on the wall and some other clearly recognizable Nazi paraphernalia, both of which can be whisked away quickly and replaced by a somewhat smaller portrait of Rumkowski. In front of the portrait is a table behind which is a leather chair and in front of which is one or possibly two wooden chairs of coworkers or petitioners. There might be a map or two on the wall. Stage right is an open area. Much of the action will take place just offstage—to the right of this open area. The office and the open area are separated by a wall—with a window and a door. However the wall is set up, it needs to be quite mobile, since just before the last scene, it needs to be removed in a matter of moments.

The characters are the following:

Herr Übermann—quintessential Nordic type, tall, slim, muscular, blond, blue-eyed, precise in his bearing. Neatly dressed. More an administrator than a military person. About forty.

Mordechai Chayim Rumkowski, seventy. A stocky man with a white bushy head of hair and a full beard. These two attributes should be as realistic as possible, but removable within moments. He wears black pants and a shirt and jacket that are the worse for wear—a worker's hat. In the last costume shift, all that needs to be changed is the jacket and the hat. Rumkowski will need two capes during the course of the play—one long full-black cape and another of the same length, white, with an ornate silver collar. He has two hats of similar shape—miter-box hats with eight peaks, one black, of a type used by famous cantors of old and one blue and white. In addition, he will need an ornate cane or walking stick. These ceremonial objects need to be readily available—possibly they could be hung on a coat rack.

Hans Biebow—German industrialist, about fifty to fifty-five. Dressed for administrative office work—clothes a bit newer, better cared for. He should be less stocky than Rumkowski, but not as athletic as Übermann, tending to put on weight due to insipient dissipation.

Messenger—Young, slender, nervous, flitting between servility and contempt. It is unclear whether he is a German having to learn how to deal with Jews or a Jew learning how to cope with Germans. His identification with one side or the other is mercurial.

Two German Soldiers—dressed accordingly.

A Rabbi—about sixty-five. Dressed in traditional Chassidic garb, black suit, socks, shoes, black overcoat with a thin sash to tie it. The open coat reveals a vest, ritual prayer shawl. Rabbi is full bearded, long earlocks, broad-brimmed black hat.

Two Male Workers—in concentration camp garb.

The action of the play historically spans a period of somewhat over four years. The action and mannerisms, while realistic, have to embody change within a format of continuous action that seems to span one endless day or night. Time is telescoped. What breaks in the action are necessary for scene changes should be as brief as possible. There will be no intermission. The audience must remain as trapped in the events as the characters, particularly toward the end when the telescoping of the time is more pronounced. The locale of the play is the industrial city of Łodz, Poland, population of 750,000, of whom about 250,000 are Jews and 90,000 are Germans. The time span of the play is late 1939 to August 1944. The play opens in Übermann's office. Übermann is seated behind his table as the two German officers bring Rumkowski in—hands behind his back. It is obvious that he has been worked over by his captors, to whom, in spite of his efforts to maintain a stately bearing, he is just another Jew.

Soldier 1   [Salutes.] I have brought Rumkowski to see you, Herr Übermann.

Übermann   Ach. Yes. Mordechai Chayim Rumkowski of Łodz. Have him sit there. [The other soldier shoves

Rumkowski forward. He is a bit dazed. Übermann signals the soldiers to leave. They both salute, do the requisite heel clicks, a sharp 180-degree turn, and leave. Übermann signals for Rumkowski to be seated. He hesitatingly sits down.]

U So. You are Chayim Rumkowski?

R Yes, I am Chayim Rumkowski. Mordechai Chayim Rumkowski.

U Mordechai Chayim Rumkowski of Łodz?

R Yes. I am from Łodz.

U Mordechai Chayim Rumkowski, the insurance salesman, who made a tolerably good living, moved to Łodz in 1917, married, had no children, and is now widowed—who managed an orphan asylum, quite successfully—was a fundraiser for charitable causes. Member of the Zionist Party. They tell me that you are a great man among your people.

R I have the honor to be a leader of that community.

U *The* leader of that community.

R *The* leader of the community.

U Good. Good. Exactly as I had surmised. It could work. Yes. I believe so.

R I don't understand, Herr Obermann.

U Übermann.

R Herr Übermann.

U I will tell you what I have in mind. These are difficult times. We find it useful to have someone we can rely on to help keep things from getting out of hand. Someone with authority, acceptable to the people, who can be trusted to carry out needed directives without question. There will, of course, be certain benefits for the man who fills this position.

R Certain benefits?

U You will have unquestioned authority in the ghetto. Your word will be law. You will be in charge of supply, health, welfare, education, culture, the press, labor, housing, finance, taxes, purchasing, communications, mail, the courts, transport, the relocation of people as it becomes necessary. You will work with our agent, Hans Biebow, to provide us with needed textiles for our troops. Certain considerations will be given to you . . . and to your family. We will keep you posted as to what is expected of you. You alone of all of the Jews of Łodz will have access to this office. Is that clear?

R   Herr Übermann, how is it possible to maintain control without police to enforce your directives?

U   You may have your police.

R   With uniforms?

U   With uniforms.

R   Special forces for gathering information for protecting my person?

U   Special forces for gathering information and for protecting your person.

R   And how will they be armed?

U   Armed?

R   To maintain control.

U   With clubs.

R   Clubs?

U   Clubs should do very nicely.

R   And how will they be paid?

U   Paid?

R   They will have to be paid.

U   So pay them.

R   Pay them?

U   You will have the power to tax the residents of Łodz, and if necessary, to confiscate money and goods. You will be able to print money and declare it the only legal tender in Łodz. People will exchange their other moneys at any rate that you determine. They will have to . . . to buy food. You can pay the police with the money you print. That should keep them loyal.

R   Paper money only or . . .

U   Paper money, coins—whatever. We can work out details in due time. If you are agreed. You are, after all, the most obvious person to be in charge of the Łodz ghetto. Der Älteste. Der Leiter.

R   Yes, that is true.

U   So. It is agreed then.

R   It is agreed.

U   You will be hearing from me. You have two weeks to set up your administration, your counsel of advisors. You will let us know what you need. We will let you know what is possible.

R   I understand, Herr Übermann.

U   Our people will escort you back in a style more in keeping with someone of your station. A car perhaps, maybe a horse-drawn carriage with a police contingent.

R   That would be most gratifying.

U   Then we understand each other.

R   I believe so.

        [One of the soldiers returns. Übermann whispers instructions to him. The soldier shows signs of disbelief, followed by a subtle smile. He nods to Rumkowski who exits with a show of great dignity and self-importance.]

U   [Shrugs his shoulders.] What do you expect from a Jew!

        [Blackout, quick change of scene to Rumkowski's office. Rumkowski is talking to Hans Biebow, who sits in the chair in front of table at which Rumkowski now presides. Rumkowski thinks of Biebow as an ally or confederate. Biebow knows that as a German and a Nazi loyalist, he is in a far more secure position than Rumkowski. Rumkowski is dressed in a weirdly ornate uniform with fancy buttons on it and ribbons in his black cape and black miter hat. Whenever he can, he gives his commands imperiously. The tone may not always be appropriate to the circumstances or to the person he is addressing. The ornateness of Rumkowski's costume is clearly in contrast to that of Biebow, which is businesslike and conventional.]

Biebow	I have come to talk to you of production figures.
R	Is there a problem?
B	The army wishes to get stipulated production from each factory. We are falling short.
R	If the army wants to have its production quotas met, it will have to ensure that our workers are fed adequately.
B	That is your responsibility. You know that food is scarce.
R	Polish workers get twice the food allowance that we do. We produce half again as much as they do. I am sure that the soldiers get enough to eat.
B	Probably.
R	The people here are on a starvation diet. How can you expect full production quotas from a starving workforce?
B	Certain conditions cannot be changed.
R	Perhaps.
B	They pressure me. All the time. The ghetto must prove its usefulness to the Reich or it will be resettled, as it were.
R	I will see what I can do. You are looking at the portrait?
B	Yes.
R	A very nice likeness, isn't it?
B	You have very talented people here in Łodz.
R	You have no idea—artists, musicians, poets, playwrights.
B	Amazing.
R	Why should that be so amazing? Because we are Jews?

B	No, not that. You would not think to see the squalor, the hunger, the disease that people would have the energy, the desire.
R	You do not understand human nature, my friend. If the inducements are right, creativity will flow—like a mighty stream.
B	Inducements?
R	Surely. The artist who painted this portrait was hungry. He did this for me for bread rations. One extra half loaf of bread for a whole month. An extra flour ration or two. And every time he came into my office, he got to see his masterpiece hanging boldly on the wall. Every time he saw someone else come in, he knew that they too would see his work.
B	That is, I suppose, inducement enough.
R	It was.
B	What other projects do you have him working on now?
R	The artist is, unfortunately, no longer here in Łodz.
B	Really?
R	It seems that he could not confine his energies to appropriate channels. He was caught handing out leaflets that were creating agitation that was potentially detrimental to our regime.
B	And—
R	At first, I had my men bring him here and I spoke to him, softly but firmly. That did no good. Then I had my men accost him on the street, to indicate our displeasure somewhat more forcefully. That did not work either. Artists are a temperamental lot—unpredictable, as it were. Not amenable to reason.
B	And so?
R	What would you have me do? If there is an insurrection in the ghetto, the Germans would have an excuse to come in and suppress it—their way. There have already been demonstrations against our handling

of ghetto affairs. The Bundists and Zionists can't stand each other, but they agree on their hatred of us. Tailors have demonstrated. Carpenters, nurses, even gravediggers, fishermen, butchers, coachmen, youth groups, even Chassidim—they want more food. They want fewer hours. More say in how the ghetto is managed. Such rabble rousers must be put in their place—if necessary, by extraordinary means—for the good of my people, my workers, my children. It was for the good of the people that he be relocated. Along with his family. He is no longer among us. In matters like this, one must act courageously, decisively. Hesitation would be interpreted as weakness. Fortunately—

B   Yes.

R   There are others here who are equally talented. Have you seen the new coinage?

B   I have some of the coins here. They are admirable.

R   All our work. From the design to the actual minting.

B   Your likeness on the coins is excellent. On the bills as well.

R   With the Star of David in the background, the menorah, my signature to ensure that this is the only legal tender in the Łodz ghetto. Did you check the paper on the bills? Real watermarked paper from Berlin. The exact same paper they use for deutsch marks.

B   German watermarked paper. Amazing.

R   Of course, I might have chosen a different watermark to put in the paper.

B   I can see that. [Holding the bill up to the light.]

R   But this is wartime. One could hardly suppose that they would take the time to make paper especially for the Jews of Łodz.

B   Hardly.

R   But it is somehow gratifying to know that the currency of this small corner of Poland is as fine as any printed in the entire Reich.

B   Indeed. Your artists must be very proud.

R   More than proud. Each day they get a chance to hold the product of their creativity. They can run their fingers over it, smell it, and of course, to spend it for extra bread rations for their families. I hear no grumbles from them.

B   I would not suppose so.

R   I have a whole army of creative minds working for the glory of Łodz. Look at these stamps.

B   Stamps too.

R   We are our own little world here. People need to communicate with loved ones outside these walls. We have our own post office. We have our own stamps. Look.

B   Nice touch, the light coming from behind your head. The star. The symbols of industry, the smoking chimneys of our factories, the compass, the carpenter's knife, the bobbin. Who could forget the bobbin? They allow you to mail letters to the outside?

R   The mail is picked up by a German postal worker. Who knows what happens to it afterward? The people get mail from outside, letters, some of them opened. Packages. Money. We check for money and valuables, record them, for future use. These are hard times. The people know that they have their own stamps to put on letters which they send out through their own post office.

B   I really like the stamps. Especially the light from behind your head. That is a nice touch.

R   The light of hope and faith.

B   Hope and faith?

R   What else?

B   You are doing very well.

R   Under the circumstances, pretty well. What I could show you—

B   I am afraid I have little enough time today for such enumerations. I must arrange for the shipment of the fabric and the other finished goods. We have fallen short of our quota again. Herr Übermann will not be pleased.

R   We are getting closer to the quota every day.

B   Close is not good enough. You know how these people are. They want no excuses.

R   We are only human.

B   Sometimes being human is not enough.

R   They ask for the impossible.

B   Then you must do the impossible. [Messenger enters.]

M   It is time, Herr Rumkowski.

R   Have I not taught you how to address me?

M   I am sorry. I was rushing. It slipped my mind.

R   Try again. You will learn that I am not to be trifled with.

M   It is time, Herrliche Rumkowski-Prezes Rumkowski, Jüdenälteste of Łodz.

R   That is better. Time for what?

M   Time for the transport.

R   Again? So soon?

M   It is the same time every day, mein Furst.

B   Mein Furst, that is a nice touch. You have trained him very well.

R   I train him. And the Germans train us. How many do they want today?

M   The same as always, allmächtige, three hundred.

R   That is not the same as always, you worm. Last week it was only two hundred a day.

M   Two hundred, three hundred. Close enough. What are your instructions?

R   The same as usual. The very old. The very sick. Defectives, smugglers, speculators, antisocial elements. Those convicted of misdemeanors and their families. And the newcomers. The ones they keep moving into Łodz from all those godforsaken places that clog our streets and make demands for housing and schooling and food and—

M   Are they ready for transport, prächtige Prinz?

R   Talk to the captain of the Überfallkommandos. He will have them ready for you in thirty minutes. He has the list of who are eligible for relocation. Go. Go already. You know the routine.

M   We cannot keep the trains waiting. You know that Herr Übermann likes to have everything—down to the minute.

R   Talk to the captain. Don't just stand there. Move. Time is wasting. Don't you see I have an important conference going on here?

M   As you wish. Only make sure the numbers are correct today. Last Tuesday, you were short two in one shipment, and we had to take the first two people who happened by.

R   Leave me. You know what to do. Out!
     [Messenger clicks heels, begins a Nazi salute. Checks himself. Does a 180-degree military turn and leaves.]

B   Heavy weighs the crown.

R   You have no idea. Every day, now three hundred. Where do they expect me to find three hundred every day? The foreigners will run out soon. The gypsies. The undesirables. The dying and the dead. I will soon be forced to go to the orphanages—and then to the schools.

B   You do what has to be done.

R   You do not understand. The schools. We have special programs set up. New curriculums: Hebrew, Yiddish, Bible, Jewish history. We have established a gymnasium, with science programs. Technical training for the factories. Special programs for the deaf and mute. For cripples. And art. And drama. And poetry. In the midst of all this suffering. To go into a school and hear the children's voices raised in song. Adonenu Ha-nasai, they sing to me. Atah, nasi, de-ag lanu—provide for us, o prince, o dove, who brings order and praise through his strong arm. Purim. It was my birthday. They sent me a book wishing me well—signed by over fourteen thousand pupils, over seven hundred teachers. It moves me to tears even to think of it now. They draw posters. They put on plays. Original productions.

B In which you, no doubt, play a prominent role.

R You don't understand. These are difficult times. We must use extraordinary means to keep their spirits up. I get messages from the teachers when the plays are ready. I come to the schools in my carriage, drawn by my grey spotted horse. The children have bands. They play special music for the occasion. They march around waving banners. They put on these plays for their leader—their prince, the president of Łodz. I give them special certificates with my signature on them to bring home and show to their parents. The day of the performance they get special sweets, special ration cards for their families—for flour and sugar. For an extra half loaf of bread. Their creativity never ceases to amaze me.

B We may need to lower the age of the workers to increase the workforce, to raise production.

R Lower the age? By how much?

B By one or two years—maybe three.

R That is not so bad. For maybe four hours a day?

B Maybe six.

R Okay, six then. But that's the upper limit, do you hear me? That means they can still go to school in the morning.

B As you wish.

R I will send out an edict tomorrow. All able-bodied children thirteen years or older will report to the factories at one to receive their work assignments. One o'clock. Promptly.

B Better make it twelve thirty to be sure.

R OK, twelve thirty. Just to be sure.

B I must make the established quotas that are given to me.

R I understand. [B gets up and exits.]

All able-bodied children [he begins to write out the edict] who are not involved in religious studies are to report to one of the following factories tomorrow for work assignments: textiles, leather, furniture, plumbing, fur. Failure to show up for work assignments can lead to curtailment of food rations for the entire family. That should do it, nicely. There is nothing like writing an edict on really good paper, having the printers put on an appropriate design, affixing an appropriate signature. They couldn't do better in Berlin. They think of us as inferior human beings. But even in such adversity, we can do things with style, panache. First-class ink. First-class paper. First-class printing. And my signature—the Honorable President of the Lodz ghetto, Der Älteste, Mordechai Chayim Rumkowski. The president must have a distinguished signature. I have been practicing to get it to look really fine. My name must command respect. I will have my ink and my paper. My printing presses. My talented, loyal workers. And the people must listen intently to my words and follow them exactly. The children had better be at the factories on time, or food rations will be cut as promised. I know how to act with authority. My special forces are in place to see who complies and who does not. They all depend on me no less than the people of Egypt depended on Joseph during the seven years of famine. That is me, the Joseph of Łodz—second only to Pharaoh himself. Every document sealed with a royal seal. Sealed. Yes. I must have an official seal for myself. I will have my artists begin working on it today, this very afternoon. Who can I get? The one who designed the stamp is gone now—typhoid or dysentery. Who knows these days? The designer of the coin also got ill and could no longer work. He was put on the trains last week. What could I do? It's hard to make the daily quotas. The incurables are selected out by my special forces. We can't continue giving food to those who will die soon. One of the special forces got a little overzealous and selected him. I myself would not have done so. But I cannot watch over each and every selection. I was upset after I found out what had been done—in my name. I found out who was responsible and docked him on his food rations for five days—no flour, no sugar. I admonished him to be more careful in the future. But he is a valuable member of the forces—usually very reliable. No need to go overboard and disaffect the rest of the group—create dissention. Besides, what's done is done. Once someone is relocated, he can't be returned. The trains leave full. They return empty. The rules are not mine to make or alter. What's done is done. There are others who can make the design. I will set up a competition with the usual incentives. The winner will be honored with a ceremony, with music played by my official brass band. He will get extra bread—for a time—for his family, even if one of them happens to be a little sick, just a little. If they are very sick, that is another matter. I have my quota to fill. If there is no hope for someone, he goes. No room for sentiment here. Three hundred a day. The order is clear. The population of the ghetto must not increase. The seriously ill must go first. Those that eat and cannot work. The crown rests heavy on my head. But this is my calling. I will do what is required of me. Like Joseph. And his brothers bowed down to him. Yes. And the people. Yes. Second only to Pharaoh. In Łodz. Second only to Pharaoh himself. [Messenger enters.]

M	The soldiers are here. And the trains.
R	Of course. Is it that time already? They are never late—the trains. Is the quota met?
M	The quota is met. I think that you should know—
R	What?
M	That sixteen of the nineteen members of your council have been selected for relocation, by orders from high up.
R	They would not dare!
M	The orders have been given. The men are at the trains with the others—them and their families. The trains are due to depart in exactly thirty-one minutes.
R	They cannot do this to me. They will not get away with it. I have a mandate from Herr Übermann himself—an absolute assurance the council would not be touched. This is my purview. I will brook no interference whatsoever. Where is my cape, my cane? This is something I cannot, I will not abide. [He exits into the open area. Marches to the far end of the stage (near the trains), where two Nazi soldiers bar his path.] I must have those men removed from the selection—them and their families. There has been a serious mistake made, Herr Übermann himself told me.

Soldier 1   There is no mistake, Your Lordship. No mistake, Jewish pig. We are under direct orders from Herr Übermann.

R   There must be a mistake. These men must not be put on the train.

[The two soldiers begin to rough him up, to punch him in the stomach, in the face. He falls to the ground and just lies there as they kick him and butt him with their rifles. They spit at his prone figure and then contemptuously exit. Some moments pass. Slowly Rumkowski comes to himself, struggles to his feet, and dusts himself off—first his pants. shirt, and then the cape. He reshapes his cap, which has been stepped on or rolled over, dusts it, replaces it on his head, readjusts his clothing, looks around to see if anyone else is watching, and in a dignified manner, limps back to his office. He sits down at his table and begins to read a document that he finds has been placed there for his perusal.]

"It has come to our attention that your council was not acting in the best interest of the ghetto of Łodz to produce peace and harmony. They were unilaterally countermanding your orders. Fomenting strife among workers. Our agents became aware that they were hoarding food, valuables, money. We deemed it advisable, therefore, to disband this council. You will appoint a new council. Make sure that these new appointees are more willing to carry out your orders promptly and completely. Submit their names and profiles to us as soon as your selection has been completed. Hold the first meeting of the new council immediately thereafter and inform the members of their duties and responsibilities. Inform them of the consequences of noncompliance. We trust that you will do a better job in the selection of this council than you did with the first."

                                    Herr Übermann

[The table is noticeably more cluttered with papers than before. B enters and adopts a matter-of-fact business-like tone that would be appropriate for a normal business conference—as if nothing has happened.]

R	There is no end to these reports. Herr Übermann wants to know everything.
B	He has a reputation for being thorough.
R	How much food we are receiving. how much surplus is left over.
B	That should be easy enough to calculate. There is never anything left over.
R	What is our industrial capacity. how many enterprises, how many spindles?
B	Food allocation is down 33 percent in six months. Production up, 130 percent. It's amazing.
R	Do you have an itemized report of all the machines that were confiscated and shipped to Aryan firms?
B	I have the report here.
R	Let's see. Confiscation of foreign currency, jewels, and other valuables. How are we supposed to use the revenues when Übermann confiscates 80 percent of what we confiscate? Or more.
B	There is still a steady stream of people from other ghettos. Even 20 percent of what you confiscate lets us meet expenses.
R	Utilization of raw materials. Bought on credit. Paid for by other confiscations.
B	At the moment, we have enough raw materials to operate at near capacity of the workforce.
R	We need to increase the size of the workforce. Let's see, number of workers, age of workers, ghetto conditions, lost hours due to sickness, lost hours due to strikes and labor agitation, current wage levels, number of people sick, births, deaths, causes of death. That's easy. Causes of death.

B   Be careful.

R   Why? Everybody knows why people die in the ghetto of Łodz. They die of hunger.

B   You can't write that in your report.

R   Why not?

B   Trust me, it would not be well received.

R   I can't say everyone died from epidemics. That wouldn't look good either.

B   Come up with something that doesn't seem to blame Übermann's policies. He would not be pleased.

R   I'll think of something. I suppose I can't say overwork either.

B   You know that would be disastrous.

R   So I have to figure out some clever way of explaining why people are falling off their work benches and are not able to get up again.

B   Yes.

R   How to not blame the number of deaths on the lack of medicine.

B   Yes.

R   Or the lack of doctors and nurses.

B   Yes.

R   Any luck in attracting doctors from any other communities?

B   In six months of trying, we got a total of five doctors and two nurses.

R   That is something.

B   But, of course, some of ours have died in the meanwhile.

R   I don't know how much longer we can continue this way,

B   What is the problem?

R   Labor disputes are continuing. Growing every day. I go to the factories. I plead with the workers. We are the model for all the other ghettos in Poland. They are being shut down. We are at the same level of population as we were when the walls went up and they stopped us from working in the non-Jewish areas of the city. Work is our salvation. As long as our labor is useful to the Reich, they will preserve us. I give the artists and intellectuals trades so they will appear to be useful in German eyes. I offer to teach practical skills to religious students, so they will not be relocated. Think of the heritage you will be leaving to future generations. I tell them the pride that we alone were able to steer our course away from the rocks. I make the workers' resorts as pleasant as I can under the circumstances, but what do they do in return? They accuse me of treason. They rail at me for the extra hours they must work and the low pay they receive. They shout insults at me. They march, chanting slogans against me. I open hospitals for them—three hospitals, two clinics, an emergency aid station. I open a soup kitchen, five orphanages, an infants' home, a home for the aged, three shelters for the homeless, and still they condemn me. I encourage the musicians to give concerts—three of them last week alone. I give special rations to painters, printmakers, sculptors, playwrights. Last week, there were two new revues that played to full houses. And still they attack me. The journalists have a paper to write in, and they object if I change a word or two so as not to anger the wrong people. Look at this paper. In the middle of a war, we have not missed a single issue—with poetry even. And still they rail against me.

B   [Picks up the paper and begins to read some of the poetry]
"You lay down your life for us
The end of your striving
You are stern of visage, but mild of heart
Your blood is shed for every child

From purest well, the hearts of children,
Flow a thousand blessings upon your handsome head
[R shifts into a state of reverie. B looks at him,
intrigued, and reads on.]
And now his fine, grey spotted horse
Suddenly comes to a halt
And the masses are lighted up
By his head of silver hair.
All eyes and all hearts
Turn to him
And the people strain and stretch
With petitions in their hands
But the President is busy
And he sees no one now.
He has spied and stopped to chat
With a tiny child of seven."

B   Not exactly Heine, not exactly Goethe or Höldelin,
        is it?
R   [Coming to himself.] They never had to write under
        such conditions. But the sentiment is sincere.
B   As long as the bread keeps coming.
R   What is that supposed to mean?
B   You yourself talked about the appropriate
        inducements.
R   The inducements are somehow not enough. The
        protests are growing stronger every day. My special
        forces have gathered information I need about scores
        of subversive elements in the ghetto. It is time to
        crack down. The tribunals are in place. We shall have
        speedier trials. No need for fancy procedures. A simple
        presentation of evidence. Those judged guilty of
        rebelliousness will be shut out from work, cut off from
        food rations. They and their families will be open for
        selection in the next relocation. Independent culture
        clubs will be abolished. The Bundist and Zionist

groups will be abolished. Youth groups—abolished. Religious groups that cause problems—disbanded. Independent soup kitchens—closed. I will brook no opposition. I have appealed to the tribunal for the power to jail—to issue death warrants.

B What did they say?

R Jail is possible—though only as a last resort. No capital punishment.

B They told you this?

R They said they would resign if I pushed the matter.

B So let them resign.

R I think that they are about as cooperative as I could expect any group to be. A wise leader knows when not to push too hard.

B I suppose.

R So forced labor with no pay will have to suffice. These days it all comes to the same thing one way or another.

B I suppose.

M [Enters out of breath.] Herrliche Rumkowski.

R Speak.

M Herr Übermann here informs you that twenty-five thousand are to be selected for a mass relocation on Friday. You are to get up the lists of those who are to go.

R No. This is not possible. He promised.

M This is the message.

R Bring back this message: I cannot release such a number for relocation. It would cripple our industrial capacity. I cannot abide by such a figure. Maybe, maybe with the new arrivals, maybe with the old and the very ill, the gypsies—maybe five thousand. Maybe six thousand at the most. I shall write him this memo. Take it to him with the greatest speed possible. I must have an answer by tomorrow. By today, if possible, early. I have a wedding to attend tonight. I have to give the bride away, her parents are no longer here. I have to get my special cape ready, with the silver collar, my special hat and my special cane. I have to arrange for the food. [Messenger has slipped out during the harangue and returns with an official document he hands to R.]

B   What does it say?

R   [Glosses the text.] Six thousand will suffice for this Friday. Six thousand will do.

B   And the wedding?

R   I will go tonight, only not in my carriage. No more. I no longer feel quite safe anymore. The demonstrators are everywhere, shouting, shaking their fists at me. They write graffiti on all the walls.

B   I have seen examples of it.
"King Chayim"
"Emperor Mordechai Chayim"
"You will be Emperor, Mr. Chayim"
"The German has a little Jewboy
And the Jews a little Caesar"

R   King Chayim, you know, there is a bit of the royalist in me. Royalist. Fascist. Communist—all rolled into one. I don't believe in private property. Then again, I would never give power to the masses, the rabble. By the time they finish squabbling, we would all be dead. No work, no survival. Mark my words. Within two years, we will be the only ghetto left in all of Poland. In all of Poland [He muses, takes out a notebook in which he is writing his ideas for posterity. He begins to write and narrates aloud as he writes.]:
A few years ago, I wrote a book that resembles Hitler's *Mein Kampf.* Hitler will win this war, and then we will be faced with the problem of solving the Jewish question. Hitler will set aside for us some stretch of land where the Jews of Europe will be able to settle. I have taken care to establish good relations

with certain influential people, and they even know my name in Berlin. They will give us authority over the Jews. I will create there a model state. We will be well represented there. We people of Łodz. In two years maybe the only ones left.

[He breaks out of his reverie.] We must have more funds to keep ourselves going. There is a letter here from one of the Jewish agencies abroad. The Jews from outside Europe must know of our plight. They must help us with funds. They must. They . . . [Scans the letter.]

B   You look upset?

R   They will give us funds.

B   That is good.

R   But only if they maintain control over how the funds are utilized. How dare they! How dare they presume to dictate to me how the funds are to be used. How can they know, they sit safe and comfortable in their boardrooms, with their posh leather seats. How dare they!

M   [Enters with another document.] A letter from Herr Übermann for the relocation of twenty-thousand more people by next Tuesday.

R   No. Not this. Bring him this letter.

M   [Just before he leaves.] And the Chassidim are protesting.

R   About what? I saved their precious Torah scrolls from the fire.

M   And here is a copy of some of the songs they are singing about you.

R   I don't need to read them. Give them to my special forces to track down the authors.

M   And the children of the gymnasium that was closed—

R   To accommodate the old people, they sent us from three ghettos they razed to the ground.

M   One of your special forces told me to relay to you a song he heard them sing as they left the school.

R   I don't think I . . .

M   Rumkowski, you are our misfortune. You are our tragedy.

[Messenger leaves hurriedly with the letter. R looks to B for an answer. B shrugs his shoulders and looks back at a pile of figures he is working on. Messenger returns.]

M   Herr Übermann says that ten thousand will suffice this time, but you personally must make the selection.

R   The ones from outside Łodz are almost all gone. That leaves the very old and the very young. I must see the Rebbe. Bring him to me. I must see him now.

[B picks up his figures, nods to R casually, as if all were going well routinely. He exits. The Rebbe enters.]

R   Rebbe, I have a problem. I am not a very learned man. What do our sages say about times of great danger, times of persecution and famine and suffering? Is it permissible to sacrifice the weak, the very old, the very young so that a remnant might survive. Is that permissible?

Rebbe   Maimonides writes that it is not permissible. Every living person should have an equal chance at life. You cannot value one life against another. That is in God's hands.

R   Rebbe, help me. Take counsel with other learned men. Believe me now. Matters are no longer in God's hands. The matter cannot wait. I must know.

Rebbe   Who are we to contradict someone of the stature of a Maimonides?

R   Help me, Rebbe. Maimonides did not have to make the decisions I must make.

Rebbe   Things were hard for the Jews in his day as well. He wrote his Responsa to people who were in great travail and anguish.

R   These are not usual times, Rebbe. Even Maimonides did not know of such times. Talk to the greatest of your teachers. Write to them. Think. Pray. I must know, Rebbe. I must know. [The Rebbe leaves, R pores over stacks of papers.]
I have only five thousand. I must find five thousand more to be ready for next Tuesday. [He begins to write a new message to the people of Łodz.]
People of Łodz. I know what I ask of you. Give me your children. Let them go to the trains. The older children may stay, the ones who can work. Let the infants go so that some of us may survive. A remnant. I beg you.
[The Rebbe returns.]

R   Tell me.

Rebbe   These are extraordinary times. To save a remnant, it is permissible to sacrifice. Those who are weak, the very old, the very young. [He leaves.]
[Rumkowski dresses up in his white cape with the silver collar—the blue and white hat. He picks up his cane deliberately and moves to the door.]

R   It is for me alone to do this thing. [He leaves his office, goes to the far side of the stage—the area just before the train station. Sounds of children's voices, a cacophony of sounds: laughter, crying, screaming that increases in volume. R stands there, alone as (offstage) the soldiers bark orders, some in Yiddish, some in German. Sound of the cattle car doors closing. Slamming. Of the train beginning to move and then to move off. Fading into the distance. R stands there alone, trying to control the weeping that struggles to come out. He finally turns and makes his way back to his table. He begins to pore over his papers again. [Messenger enters with a list of matters to be discussed.]

M   Herrliche Rumkowski, a group of Christian refugees has been moved into the ghetto.

R   Yes.

M   They demand separate religious education.

R   Request denied. We have had to stop religious education in our schools. We teach only industrial skills now. There are too many of these Christians. They will be gone soon.

M   Herr Übermann informs you that you must now pay for all forced labor.

R   Where am I to get the funds?

M   That is your problem. He informs you, furthermore, that your request for flour for baking matzos for Passover is denied. Flour is now scarce and will not be used for such purposes.

R   Well, that is a small matter.

M   He further informs you that you will no longer be able to buy food and raw materials on credit. You will have to pay in cash and valuables in advance.

R   How can I pay when he takes most of what we confiscate? Besides, there are few enough refugees being relocated here anymore. My sources tell me what is happening to the Jews of Poland. They are being machine-gunned. Buried in mass graves. Shipped to death camps, gassed. How are we to maintain production quotas if we cannot get raw materials or food? Give this letter to the head of my special forces. There are still sources of money and valuables I can get a hold of when the time comes for final resettlement. Only those most qualified will escape death. Have you brought the gifts I gave you to the German informants?

M   I brought them what you gave me.

R   All of it?

M   All of it.

R   Good. There is a special consideration here for your
       good work. Without information about what is going
       on, we would be lost. What else do you have?

M   Some of the religious groups are complaining again.
       They wish to continue studying and do not want to
       send their students to the factories. They do not like
       the idea of having to petition you for the right to
       hold services.

R   They do not like!

M   That is the word I get from the head of your
       intelligence corps.

R   Take this message to the heads of these religious
       groups. From now on, all able-bodied men are to
       report to the factories for work assignments. They
       are to shave their beards, to cut off their ear locks,
       to dress like other workers, or they will get no food
       rations. Any rabbi acting to countermand these orders
       will be liable for relocation. Rabbis may maintain a
       traditional appearance and garb. All others—no. Do
       you have all that?

M   Yes.

R   Take it to my chief of police to deliver. They will be
       at work tomorrow in appropriate dress or they will be
       gone. Anything else?

M   One thing more.

R   Yes?

M   Herr Biebow has countermanded your orders to keep
       your clerks off labor details.

R   He has countermanded my orders?

M   Yes, allmächtige. He has done so. They are to report
       to labor details at 8:00 a.m. tomorrow.

R   He dares?

M   And—

R   What else?

M   Herr Übermann will see you immediately.

R   Immediately?

M   You are to go at once. There is a car waiting for you.

R   A car?

M   A car.

R   If I must, then I suppose, I must.
      [He leaves the office with the messenger. The messenger goes off one way, he exits another. The office is blacked out. Moments later he reenters the now-lit office of Herr Übermann—Nazi banner, et al., in place.]

R   You asked to see me? Herr Übermann.

U   You must understand, Rumkowski. Order and adherence to regulations, however minute, are of utmost importance. Any failure to follow directives undermines discipline and respect for authority and cannot be tolerated.

R   I cannot imagine, Herr Übermann, what . . .

U   To begin. You are aware of the directives relating to publications. All publications relating to governmental procedures are to be published in German.

R   Yes, Herr Übermann.

U   Here is one of your leaflets, Rumkowski. You recognize it?

R   Yes, Herr Übermann.

U   Does this look like German, Rumkowski?

R   It is Yiddish, Herr Übermann.

U   Yiddish is not German, is it, Rumkowski?

R   Very few of the people understand German, Herr Übermann. If the pronouncements are to be understood by the people, they must be in language the people can understand.

U   I don't seem to be getting through to you, Rumkowski. You publish your pronouncements in German and Yiddish. That takes paper. Paper is scarce. Do you know what it takes to supply you with paper for your announcements? The directive is clear enough. All governmental papers are to be published in German. Only in German. Is that clear?

R   But the people?

U   How you get the people to understand your pronouncements is of no concern to me. Am I making myself clear to you, Rumkowski, or do I have to explain it again to get it through your thick Jewish skull?

R   It is clear, Herr Übermann.

U   It is obvious that a person who can't follow simple directives may have difficulty following, more difficult matters.

R   I don't know what you might be referring to, Herr Übermann.

U   A man who might be hiding secret messages to his people, hoping that we would not know what he is talking about. Eh, Rumkowski? You might be capable of that.

R   I have not done so, Herr Übermann.

U   We have ways of finding out, Rumkowski. Such acts would be foolhardy, would they not would lead to most dire consequences? Do you understand, Rumkowski?

R   Yes, Herr Übermann. Is that all?

U   Not quite. It has come to our attention that your council members and some of your special forces are—how shall I say—skimming off the top.

R   I don't understand, Herr Übermann.

U   You don't understand. How could I expect you to understand, you innocent babe of the woods, skimming, putting moneys and valuables into their own pockets. Falsifying documents to cover up their misdeeds. This money should be going into the running of the Łodz ghetto and, more importantly, to help finance this office.

R   I didn't know, Herr Übermann.

U You are supposed to know, Rumkowski. You are also supposed to know about the discrepancies between raw materials received and finished goods. Someone is diverting raw materials or finished goods from their intended destination.

R How can that be possible, Herr Übermann? There is only one person that regulates raw materials and tabulates final production levels—only one person responsible for comparing production with the quotas we receive.

U One person, Rumkowski?

R Hans Biebow. But he—

U Biebow. I should have known that he would try to get over on someone like you.

R I don't know what to say, Herr Übermann.

U Rumkowski, either you get your government into shape and follow the directives given to you to the letter, or we shall find someone who can do it right. Do you understand me?

R I understand you, Herr Übermann.

U You may go now, Rumkowski. We will let you know our decision in due time.

R Herr Übermann—

U You may go now, Rumkowski!

[He leaves. Exits right stage. Office is blacked out, and the portraits are exchanged. Rumkowski returns to his office to a pile of papers that has grown considerably. Biebow appears in the open area outside the office. He is obviously drunk and furious.]

B Rumkowski! Rumkowski! Get out here. Der Leiter of the ghetto of *Łodz, Hans Biebow* is calling you, ordering you to get your ass out here.

R [At the window.] What is wrong, Hans?

B Hans. Hans, you call me. You kike. You worm. You Zhid. You dare call me Hans? You backstabber. You traitor.

R	[Going outside.] What is wrong, Herr Biebow?
B	Herr Biebow, is it now. You call me Herr?
R	What is wrong, Herr Leiter?
B	What is wrong? You toad, you pond, scum. Is that you told Übermann about my little skimming operation, that's all. Übermann called me in. He threatened me. Me, Hans Biebow, a loyal member of the Nazi Party. He threatened me. Do you know what he could do, you cretin? I could lose this comfortable little post here in Łodz and be put off in some dark corner of the Reich to push a pen over meaningless documents. He could even move me to the front lines, where I could be captured by the Russians. Do you hear that, you moronic pickle brain? All that nice stash I have been saving these many months would be gone in a second. All this time for naught. Do you know what the Reich pays me, you pea brain? I volunteered for this job, for the glory of the Reich. I volunteered. Doing my patriotic duty to get Jewish skeletons to turn out their quota of finished goods for the Armed Forces of the Vaterland. And what thanks do I get? This nincompoop, this son of a nincompoop that would not have been fit to polish my father's shoes, shouts at me as if I were some naughty child caught with my fingers in the cookie jar. He shouted at me. He threatened to send me up to bed without any dinner, all because you had to go and snitch on me, turd that you are. You snitched on me, after all I did for you and the other lice of Łodz. I helped to prolong your miserable lives. How long do you think you would have survived if I hadn't convinced Übermann and his kind that you were useful to the Reich, you ungrateful hyena. It is I that make you look indispensable, I, Hans Biebow. [He becomes maudlin and is close to tears.] I have done this for you and what is my thanks, you lecherous monkey,

you baboon's ass? Do you think that I could not have told Übermann about how you run things, about all those young women you gather about you from the schools, the teachers, the nurses, the personnel who run your orphanages. I have stories too, you viper's piss. I have worked too hard to make this job pay off. I will not have it ruined by the likes of you. [He begins to hit Rumkowski, and it is no small beating he gives him. He uses his fists about the head and face. Rumkowski falls; he kicks his prone figure numerous times and then storms off, stage right. Rumkowski is slow to get up. He stumbles toward the door of his office. He falls again. The messenger happens by and helps him offstage (right). Moments later, he returns. He is bandaged in some significant way. He goes back to his office. The papers are piled significantly higher. He begins work. Biebow returns and takes his usual seat. He is quite sober now.]

B You are back, Rumkowski.

R I am back, Herr Biebow.

B You were—

R In the hospital.

B Yes. I see. I see. You are—

R Better. Yes, Herr Biebow.

B There is nothing serious as a result?

R Nothing serious. Some bruises. Nothing more.

B I am happy for that, you know. We can then get back to the work like before.

R We can do that.

B There are, after all, important things to accomplish that will benefit us all.

R Indeed.

B You, me, your people.

R Yes. That is true.

B I was drunk, Rumkowski.

R I know, Herr Biebow.

B	I am not in the habit of getting drunk.
R	I know, Herr Biebow.
B	It was the shock, the possibility of losing it all. You understand, don't you?
R	I understand.
B	I mean, a man can take just so much before he cracks.
R	That is true, Herr Biebow.
B	I drank a bit too much. A lot too much. It was not like me. Trust me. You know what I am saying.
R	I know what you are saying.
B	I have work in one of the factories that has to be attended to. I am glad that you were not seriously hurt.
R	I can see that.
B	I will be back as soon as this work is completed. [He exits. The messenger arrives with a pile of directives to deliver to Rumkowski.]
M	The shop classes are closed as you ordered. All students will henceforth be working fulltime.
R	Good.
M	From now on, by directive of Herr Übermann, the ordering and distribution of food, the purchasing of raw materials, and the management of the police will be under the leadership of David Gertles and Aaron Jacobowicz.
R	He told me I would get another chance. He promised.
M	And next Thursday, there will be a relocation of three to four thousand people—to be selected by Herr Übermann himself. The relocation will include all of the remaining gypsies and—
R	And . . .
M	All remaining children under ten.
R	No. I will be down at the trains. I will be there to save at least a few. You will see. At least a few. [He moves toward the doors. Sound of a train whistle. He goes

out and stands in front of the door, addressing the empty space before him.]
People of Łodz. This is your president speaking, the älteste of Łodz. I have told you in the past to trust me in these difficult times. If my manner has seemed harsh, it has always been a question of necessity. If I do not carry out the directives that are given to me, the Germans will step in. They will be harsher, more ruthless. [He moves forward to the right edge of the state.] No, not that one, he is protected. Not that one or that. Quickly children. Get over to that side over there. Quickly I tell you. Listen to me when I talk to you and listen to the German soldiers when they talk to you. Stand up in their presence. I want only the best for all of you. [He turns from the train and walks slowly back to his office. Sounds of angry voices as he walks, like blows hammering at his head. He saves none of the children of the Bundists. None of the children of the Zionists. He sends rabbis off for relocation. He would be king. He would be emperor!]
The German has his little Jewboy and the Jews a little Caesar.

R   [Seated at his table.] Three thousand more children gone, three thousand innocents, three thousand angels. I have their food rations here to use for the others, three thousand angels flown away—three thousand more.

M   [The pile of papers on Rumkowski's desk is suddenly, noticeably smaller.] Hans Biebow has changed the day of rest for the factories.

R   I do not understand.

M   The Germans and the Poles who come to get the finished goods are Christians.

R   I see.

M   From now on, everyone is to work on Saturday.

R	Oh!
M	Herr Biebow said that we are beginning to fall short once again in our production quotas.
R	How is that possible? We have more workers. When we started, only 15 percent of the residents worked in the factories. Now nearly 90 percent of the residents are working.
M	There are fewer residents.
R	Oh.
M	The amount of raw materials has fallen off since you can no longer buy them on credit.
R	Oh.
M	There is less money and fewer valuables to confiscate.
R	Oh. What does Herr Biebow recommend that we do?
M	There are all these holidays on which the workers are idle and produce nothing at all.
R	I will order the workers to come to the factories on holidays.
M	Herr Biebow has already done so.
R	Oh. All the holidays?
M	All the holidays. You are to post the notice in the usual places.
R	Oh.
M	The special forces must be informed so they can explain the new regulations to the people.
R	Yes.
M	They will not like the new regulations.
R	That is of little importance. I have ordered it. They will do it. It is a matter of life and death. There is a role for us in history. Some huge drama is being played out, and we have been given our part to play. Providence has handed me my role to play as well, to save a remnant of our people. And I will play that role. It matters little whether the people approve or disapprove of what I do. The ones who are selected

for relocation will not complain for long. The ones who survive may or may not come to appreciate what I have done. The Rebbe told me that it is permissible to sacrifice the old and the young to save the few who are still capable of work. I have walked with the children to the trains. I have helped them to get into the cars. If I tell them to, the people will work on Shabbas. They will work on Rosh Hashanah and Yom Kippur. The ones who refuse can join the others in the trains. Do you hear what I have said?

M   Yes, mein Furst.

R   Do not miss a word. Tell the council.

M   They have already been informed. They are not too pleased with your actions of late, mein Prinz. They wish you to appear before them to answer for certain actions that you have taken.

R   I do not wish to appear before them. I will not appear before them to answer any charges. [He begins to write.]

Members of the council, you charge me with issuing pronouncements which you feel are too burdensome to the people of Łodz, too burdensome on them. My burden has become too great for me. In normal times, I would come to you because what I have done, what I have had to do horrifies me beyond all reckoning. Were I not ashamed to do so, I would come before you and cry like a baby. I would beg for your help, your support in bearing the burden of this impending disaster, a disaster much greater even than you can possibly imagine. But it is my burden as your president to bear this burden alone. I will not weep before you. I will not beat my breast. I will not bow down to the ground and ask for pardon or compassion or understanding. I will do whatever is necessary, and you will carry out my bidding until the final scene is played out. Signed, Präses Mordechai

	Chayim Rumkowski, De Älteste of the ghetto of Łodz. Take this letter to the Council. I have spoken.
M	Herr President?
R	Yes?
M	Herr Biebow has taken control of the economic matters of Łodz—food procurement and distribution, the confiscation of money and property. He has called in a contingent of German troops to help enforce his edicts.
R	Oh.
M	He has taken charge of the selection process for relocations.
R	Oh.
M	The speech that you gave to the people.
R	Yes, the speech.
M	Where you told the people to give you their children.
R	Yes.
M	They did not comply willingly to your words.
R	No.
M	The Jewish police tried to enforce your directives. They were taunted and jeered. Stoned. They retreated. The Germans were called in to help meet the quotas.
R	Yes. The Germans. It had to come to this.
M	The schools are now officially closed.
R	Yes.
M	There are reports that some schools are meeting clandestinely.
R	I know.
M	You will do something about this?
R	I will take it under advisement.
M	Your forces are under instructions to permit no demonstrations or resistance.
R	Good.
M	Is there anything else you would like me to do now?
R	No. You may go now. You have your orders.

M   Yes, Herr President. [He leaves. Rumkowski sits at the table, immobile. The messenger returns shortly with a new set of matters to be discussed.]

M   The German police have come to confiscate all the musical instruments that remain in Łodz. All concerts, plays, and public gathering are now forbidden.

R   Yes.

M   Herr Biebow has declared himself Ghettoleiter. He has reduced your staff. All those who have been relieved of their duties have been reprimanded for idleness and have been assigned to forced labor camps.

R   Yes.

M   Herr Übermann has decreed that relocation will now be set at two thousand per week.

R   Yes.

M   The roundup of those deemed incapable of work will utilize all available vehicles left in Łodz: trucks, wagons—

R   Yes.

M   Herr Übermann has set the relocation for five hundred per day.

R   Yes.

M   Herr Biebow has stated that of those remaining in Łodz, *95 percent* are fully capable of working a full day in the factories.

R   Yes.

M   Herr Übermann has decreed that relocation will be set at three thousand per day. The German police are taking whomever they find—workers and nonworkers alike.

R   Yes.

M   Herr Übermann has declared that the ghetto is to be totally evacuated. The Russians are advancing along the Eastern Front. It is only a matter of time before they overrun this area. They are to find nothing here when they arrive. Nothing at all. Herr Biebow will address the populace about what to expect. [Spotlight shifts to the opening area, where a platform has been erected by two German soldiers. Biebow hurries over and gets up onto the platform and begins to speak.] People of Łodz. The Russians are advancing on the Eastern Front. There is no telling how quickly they will arrive. There is no telling what atrocities they will perpetrate once they get here. Herr Übermann has instructed me to help facilitate the relocation of all of the remaining workers of the ghetto of Łodz. They will be sent to Germany—far away from the front lines—in an effort to save lives. Turn in all of your money to the central office. It will be converted to deutsch marks. I promise you on my honor as a German officer that all that I have said is true. I have worked with you for over four years now in the most difficult of circumstances. You know that you can trust me. Your cooperation is requested in effecting these orders. You will gather up only those belongings stipulated in the posted directives. Due to the current emergency, all those not complying will be liable for summary execution. Your Jewish police will be aided in the relocation process by German forces. Those of you who volunteer for the German work detail brigade will be given special consideration. You may sign up on these lists. You may sign up, but whether you sign up or not, the ghetto of Łodz will be totally evacuated. A workforce of eight hundred will remain behind temporarily to confiscate remaining valuables—to keep them out of Russian hands. They will tear down houses and factories so that there will be nothing left to aid the invading Russian hordes when they arrive. I will need a special work crew to dig trenches, pits. to bury what cannot *be* burned. In addition to these men, there will be a small cadre of women who will be given special assignments that will be stipulated in due time. The list of those who are to remain to finish the work in Łodz will be posted. All others are to report to the trains. Those who do not report to the trains willingly will have to answer for their own actions.

M   This is a list of those who are to remain in Łodz.

R   My brother is not on this list. My brother and his family are to be relocated. This cannot be. I must see Herr Übermann at once.

M   He is not available.

R   Take this message to him at once. My brother and his family must remain to help in the cleanup of the ghetto of Łodz. They must—

M   Herr Übermann states that there can be no exceptions made at this time. The list stands as printed. You, however, may remain in Łodz.

R   I cannot see my brother go on the trains.

M   You may join him in the final relocation to Germany where it is safe.

R   Are they to put him in the cattle cars? With all of the others? Is the brother of the president of the ghetto of Łodz to be crammed into the cattle cars, he and his family—like a bunch of animals?

M   In consideration of the station and the social position of the Älteste and his service to the Reich during these extraordinary times, a special car will be provided. A limousine. It will be placed on a flat car behind the rest of the train. The president of the ghetto of Łodz and his family will be given all of the honor which is appropriate. He will be given sealed letters and documents relating to special treatment he is to receive once he arrives at the final destination.

R   I must make final preparations. My young wife, my brother, his family, my cape (the white one with the silver collar), my hat (the blue and white one with the

eight peaks), my cane with the brass handle—I must prepare myself for the final selection. I must prepare myself. [He gathers his regal paraphernalia and stands there for a moment with a dignified air about him. He marches slowly from his office to the open court and exits right to the train. There are three train whistle blasts, which echo the sound of the shofar [ram's horn]. Tekiyah. Tekiyah. Tekiyah gedolah—a long whistle blast of two notes. The second higher note is held longer; the third time it lasts for thirty full seconds—after which time there is a total blackout and the set is cleared of all props. Rumkowski is to appear at that point on the empty stage, in the spotlight. There should be enough light to indicate that the rest of the stage is bare. Rumkowski is wrapped in his white cape, like a prayer shawl. As will become evident in the last scene, he wears nothing under the cape. He is barefoot. The long cape covers his naked legs. He has been clean shaven. The beard is gone. The hair is gone from his head. As will later become evident even the hair under his arms and in the upper pubic area has been shaved. He faces the audience—still with a regal air about him.]
Seventy-four years old. It is not for nothing that the Bible sets the span of a man's years at seventy. I will tell you quite honestly that I could have done without the last four years. When all is said and done, I could have done without them quite easily. But we must play out our roles to the end. They tell me to prepare for a shower, for delousing. I know what is to come. They know that I know. Still they maintain their pretense—with a straight face. They let me maintain my pretense as well. I will wear my cape and crown to the very shower house door. Then they will relieve me of my last burden, and the democracy of death will reign. There will be no marker on my grave.

There will be little enough left to mark—nothing to distinguish the place where my ashes lie from among all of the others who are gassed and burned. Nothing to distinguish the odor of my burning flesh from all the others they process in this place. We are not supposed to know about all of that ahead of time. So we know. They know that we know. But they carry their pretense to the very end. As do we. They know that the Russians and the Americans are advancing at this very moment and will take over these camps. They pretend not to know this either. They pretend that they can burn us to ashes and that no one will ever find out what has happened here. The truth is that they have already discovered what is happening here, and the Germans know that they know. But the Germans must carry their pretense to its final, logical conclusion, and we must pay the price for their maintaining their pretence to its final, logical conclusion.

This makes for wonderful theater, really. They hand you a role. Call it what you will—prince of the ghetto, the Älteste of the ghetto of Łodz, president. They hand you your lines to learn—work for the Reich and you will be free, free from the selection. You may hop about like a flea, crawl about like a louse for a brief season or two until it is time for the final disinfecting. Work. Prove your usefulness to the Reich, and you will be free for a brief time from the shower houses and the ovens and the mass graves. You know they are lying. They know that you know they are lying. You read your lines. Sometimes you even convince yourself that they might be true. Then they change the script. You read new lines. They change the script again. It becomes more and more bizarre. You know that. They know that you know. Until the end. Until the trains carry you here. You bow and they nod. They shout and you jump through hoops of fire—forward, backward, upside down. You jump, and the hoops keep getting smaller and smaller and the fire hotter and hotter until finally there is no way to get through one of the hoops and they look at you and shake their heads. It is a pity they say, but you have failed to leap through this last hoop. And the penalty for failure is always the same.

Two hundred and fifty thousand we were in Łodz. More if you count the others that were sent to us from the other ghettos in Poland. And now we are a mere eight hundred—pretending to raze the ghetto to the ground so that when the Russians come finally, they will supposedly get no inkling that we ever existed at all. If the workers are deliberate enough, if the Russians are fast enough, perhaps a few will still be around to be liberated. To survive. That's what it comes to after all this long drama, one large holding action to slow the process down so that perchance there might be a handful left—a remnant. All of that posturing, that pleading, that groveling. All the subterfuge, and I will never know if it came to anything at all. I will never know if even one survived. And if only one or two, can I say that the whole show was worth it? I put children on the trains myself. I patted them on their heads to quiet them, to assure them that everything would be all right. I led them to their deaths, day after day, and they knew. And I knew that they knew. King Mordechai. The Emperor Chayim is our tragedy. They knew all along. The Zionists I crushed, the Bundists. They knew. And the rabbis that finally were packed into the trains like animals. They knew. And they reviled me. The Germans pretended to show me deference. To mark me apart. They pulled my strings, and I danced like a fool. And as soon as I left their presence, they laughed briefly at my performance and went back to more serious matters of preparing for the end, and I would do it all over again. If only I knew that some would survive. Even a few.

In the end, it is all a chess game. And death is the great chess master. I saw the look in Hans Biebow's eyes as I walked toward the train for the last time—as I got in my limousine. He played his role rather well. All that business about partnership and common purpose. And I am here. And he is there. And both he and I knew all along that it would come to this. And both of us know that the other one knew, and we both pretended that we knew nothing. He got as much out of his role as he could get, as did I. And he now waits for a new role to play. A decent chap, Biebow, until the end. He really started to believe all that claptrap about the dignity of our labor—turning rags to new fabric—for the Reich. Arbeit macht frei. At the end, the power got to him—the frenzy of power and death. The pits he ordered to be dug by the very men he knew would fill them after a time. There was a gleam in his eye. The harem he collected at the end. I saw. He would not look at me finally. He knew that I had seen him. That I knew. It will not end for him the way he expected. He is out of his depth. Some way or other, he will drown in the tidal wave that is coming, and he will protest that he was, after all, a rather decent fellow. He should not have to die like this. [He drops his cape and stands naked before the audience.]

There will come a time when you stand before the door of your shower house. And all of your posturing will be of no avail. The naked truth will hit you finally. The rules of the game are set. And you learn them and play by them. And then the rules are reset and replayed and reset and replayed, and suddenly, the door is before you and you wonder—as you betray one principle after another, as you send one beauty after another, as you send one angel after another to the cattle cars—whether anything is left to be rescued after you are taken and if there is anything rescued by chance, whether what is left will stand as a testament to your posturing to your chicanery, to shout "Infamy!" over your grave. If anything is left. By chance. Anything at all.

It is too much to think of anymore. I am tired of playing my part. Death holds no terror for me that has not been played out already thousands of times. If I am called to account in some divine tribunal, I will have nothing to say in my own defense. I understand less today than I did the day that I was born. Why should it be so hard for a Jew to lead a normal life, to be a child, to jump with joy to see the sun rise up at dawn over the houses of his town. I no longer wish to understand anything at all. I should write to Herr Übermann to thank him for his final gift. One final scene before the curtain falls. One brief moment to end it all.

To stand before the door of your designated shower house, stripped finally of your cape, your special hat (he takes the hat off and drops it unceremoniously onto the ground). But the children. They had no lines to parrot, no posturing. The children brought there before they learned how to posture and betray. All so that one small remnant might survive. And I shall never know. [He turns from the audience and raises his arms over his head. There is a hissing sound that grows in intensity until it is unbearably shrill. Rumkowski sinks to the ground slowly, ending up in a heap that is not particularly dignified in its final position. The hissing ends abruptly, and there is silence. Two workers in concentration camp garb enter with a wheelbarrow or flatbed cart and hoist his body onto it like a piece of meat. They are not used to dealing with such heavy carcasses, and in their emaciated state, they struggle to lift him and get him positioned securely on the cart.]

1   I say, that was a meaty one.

2   Don't find too many like this these days.

1   You're right. Good thing too. Almost put my back out lifting him, old turd that he was.

2   Any bigger and they'd need to build a special oven for him.

1   You'd think he was some kind of prince or other, living off the *fat* of the land.

2   Yeah. A regular prince of the ghetto, with his own special oven.

1   Maybe they'll separate out his ashes, give him a special urn.

2   Ship them to Berlin.

1   To fertilize Hitler's rose garden.

[They cart the corpse off with some difficulty, stopping periodically to rest.]

2   Hitler's rose garden.

[They exit. The stage remains empty. There is no blackout. No drawn curtain to indicate the end of the play. Silence. The actors begin to file in for the curtain call. Herr Übermann first, then the messenger, then Hans Biebow, then the soldiers and other minor characters. Then the two camp inmates. In character, they indicate their displeasure at having to do one extra task. They wheel in Rumkowski's inert form and present him to the audience. The others file out, and they are left once again, reluctantly, to wheel him out for his final exit.]

Finis

1992

This Side Of Kansas

[The setting is a typical small town, U.S. home—the living room/ dining room area. The residents are a man and his wife and their teenage son and daughter, and their guests, a man and wife and their son and daughter. The dress of the latter four should be a touch old-world, a bit the worse for wear.]

I.

Martha   The shades. You forgot to pull down the shades.

Matthew   Aw, Mom.

Martha   Don't you "Aw, Mom" me. I don't ask you to do that much that you can't remember to pull down the shades. You wouldn't like it if I forgot to prepare dinner, would you?

Matthew   No, Mom.

Martha   Everybody has to do his share in this house. It's not asking too much of you. You pull the shades down. Your sister draws the curtains. Then we can set the table for dinner.

Matthew   Yes, Mom.

John   You shouldn't shout at the kids that way. You're too hard on them.

Martha   That's easy for you to say. You're at work all day. You don't have to deal with them.

John   Work isn't such a pleasant place to be these days. The supervisor is on you for every little thing. He's already let a few of the men go. If I lost this job, I don't know what we'd do.

Martha   You won't lose the job. You've been there for over twenty years.

John
: The ones they let go were also there for over twenty years. I think he's just waiting for an excuse to let the old-timers go. The young ones will work for less. Much less.

Martha
: They need experienced workers like you to keep production going smoothly.

John
: You tell them that. I don't think they care one way or another.

Martha
: If they produce shoddy goods, they might lose some contracts.

John
: There is no oversight these days. People cut corners. They get away with murder, and no one says anything about it. Last month they cut our pay five dollars a week. It wasn't much, but prices keep going up.

Martha
: Tell me about it. I'm the one that goes shopping. It gets harder and harder to put food on the table. I have to make three trips to three different stores so no one will notice.

John
: You are a clever woman, Martha.

Martha
: It's like a game, figuring everything out. But in this game, if you make one mistake, it's all over. All the time, I imagine that people are studying my every move. People do that these days. This is a small town. People notice things. They know your habits. They notice changes.

John
: I know. It must be awfully hard for you.

Martha
: By the time I come home, I am a tangle of nerves. Even the smallest things can set me off. The kids don't seem to care. You ask them to do something small, like pulling down the shades. It's the least they can do. I can't take care of everything myself.

John
: I'll talk to Jimmy about it.

Martha
: You do that. He always listens to you.

John
: After dinner. I'm famished. It gets dark late these days. By the time dinner is on the table, I feel like I could eat a horse.

Martha   We're not serving horse tonight.

John   What are we serving?

Martha   Meatloaf.

Matthew   Aw, Mom. Meatloaf again?

John   You watch your tongue, boy. Your mother just happens to make the best meatloaf this side of Kansas.

Matthew   Maybe she used to. But now it doesn't taste like there is any meat in it.

Martha   Meat is expensive these days. And we have a few more mouths to feed. I have to stretch things out a bit more.

John   That's what meatloaf is all about. When I was a child, we were pretty poor. The meatloaf was more like bread crumbs and mashed potatoes with a hint of meat. But it was spiced so well with onions and garlic that we thought it was the best eating ever. The fish patties as well.

Matthew   We haven't had fish for ages.

John   Fish is hard to come by now. It has to be trucked in from the Coast. They've got other things to do with trucks these days.

Martha   I wish you wouldn't talk of such things.

John   Why? The children are old enough to know. We're not just playing games here.

Matthew   I've got a game on Saturday, Dad.

John   I'm sorry. I'm going to be at work.

Matthew   You used to come to all my games.

John   I'd give anything to be able to see you play.

Matthew   I got two hits last week—a single and a triple. Knocked in three runs. I'm batting over four hundred. And I made a catch running out into center field. They had two on and one out. I caught the ball over my shoulder, rolled over, got up, and doubled one of the runners at second base to end the game. The coach said it was the best play he's seen all year. The guys carried me off the field on their shoulders.

John	I wish I could have seen that, son. I really do.
Matthew	You work all the time. Even on Sundays. You never even go to church any more.
John	I miss that too. I really do miss being with you all.
Matthew	You work seven days a week.
John	I have to, son. It's the only way we can make it.
Matthew	You never had to before.
John	Things happen. Times change. We can't always do what we want to.
Martha	Your father is holding down two jobs now. And he's one of the lucky ones. Mr. Jenkins down the street has been out of work for weeks now. I don't know how they're managing. The Thompsons a block over, the same thing. These are hard times. You do what you have to survive.
Matthew	We don't go anywhere any more. We used to go to the mountains for a week.
John	There won't be any trips this year. We can't afford gas money with prices being what they are.
Matthew	We could go by plane. We did that once. I remember.
John	Well, you keep on remembering. It will be a long time before we can do that again.
Matthew	It's not fair.
Martha	A lot of things aren't fair. Sometimes I think all life is unfair.
John	Just get over it, boy. As long as you think things are supposed to be fair, you're going to spend all your time being sad or angry. You're going to wind up spinning your wheels and getting nowhere fast. Life isn't fair. That's just the way it is. You cope or you don't cope. If you want to grab a few moments of happiness here and there, you first have to cope with what life brings you. You were happy when you caught the ball and doubled up the runner at second base. Not everyone gets to enjoy moments like that,

	especially these days. Just enjoy those moments and don't go moping around for what you don't have.
Matthew	I would have been even happier if you and Mom had been there.
John	And don't you think I would have been happy to have been there? If I let that get to me, I'd start feeling so sorry for myself, I couldn't get out of bed in the morning. And then where would we all be?
Martha	The minister said you have to have faith that all of this is for the best.
John	He said that?
Martha	Last Sunday.
John	Well, maybe he said that to make everyone feel better, to give people hope. It's hard to think that all of this is for the best.
Martha	He said that the harder it is to believe, the stronger your faith has to be. He said faith wasn't easy. That's what separates believers from nonbelievers. The nonbelievers lose their faith the first time something bad happens to them.
John	Well, the nonbelievers surely do have a lot to work with these days.
Martha	He said that too.
John	Maybe I should have become a minister. At least the work is steady.
Martha	It doesn't pay so well. I saw the minister looking at the collection plate. There wasn't much in it.
John	Hard times hit everybody. If you're worrying about where the next dollar is coming from, you can't be putting all your loose change in the collection plate.
Martha	We always put something in. There are people worse off than we are.
John	A lot worse. We do what we can.
Martha	And we'll pull through this—if we all work together. And that means doing chores. Pulling down the shade when you're supposed to.

John   And not sassing your mother. We have to keep cheerful in here. We have to keep our spirits up. That's the only way we're going to make it.

Matthew   For how long?

John   For as long as it takes.

Mary   Mom, Jaime asked me if I could come over to her house for dinner tomorrow night.

Martha   I thought we discussed that.

Mary   I always used to go over to her house before.

Martha   You'd go over to her house, and then it would be her turn to come over here.

Mary   So?

Martha   You know that's impossible now.

Mary   She's going to think I don't like her anymore. And she's my best friend.

Martha   She can still be your best friend. Although I'll tell you, her mother pushes her nose into other people's business. And her father's politics. People say he was responsible for what happened over at the Smiths' place.

Mary   Jo Anne stopped coming to school. I liked her a lot. There wasn't anything about bugs she didn't know.

Martha   The Smiths moved after their garage burned down. The police said it was an accident. But that's not what people are saying. They had the garage all fixed up. Mrs. Smith's mom lived there until she died about three years back. There was talk that other people were living there.

Mary   Other people?

Martha   That's what I heard tell. Whoever was in the garage surely isn't there anymore.

Mary   Neither are the Smiths.

Martha   It was just by chance that they managed to get out before the house caught. One of the kids had a fever, and Mrs. Smith was up with him all night. She smelled smoke. Mr. Smith managed to keep the fire from spreading to the house. They called the Fire Department. For some reason, they were very slow about getting there. If Mr. Smith didn't have fire extinguishers and a hose handy and if Mrs. Smith hadn't been up, the whole family might have died.

John	What happened to the people in the garage?
Martha	I don't know. I just don't know. I don't know much of anything anymore. People don't really talk to each other anymore. They go into their houses and lock the doors and hope no one will come knocking. It's really getting to me. Yesterday, the mailman rang the bell. He had a package for me. It took every ounce of courage I had to look through the peephole and then open up the door.
John	We're OK. You shouldn't be so fearful.
Martha	You don't read the papers anymore or listen to TV. There are new rules and regulations we're supposed to follow—or else.
John	What is that supposed to mean?
Martha	They talk of stiff fines, even jail sentences. John, I am afraid. Every minute of every day.
John	After dinner, I'll massage your back.
Martha	It will take more than a massage to get me unwound.
John	I'm ready if you are.
Martha	John! Not in front of the kids.
John	I have no I intention of doing anything in front of the kids.
Martha	Come. Let's get the table set. I don't want the food to dry out or burn. Now, Mary, you set the table.
Mary	With the paper dishes?
Martha	We can't do that anymore. People start noticing if you have more trash than usual. Don't look at me like that. It's true. They check all kinds of things. How much electricity you're using, how much water. You have to be careful about everything. I soak the dishes, and then I rinse them. I don't use the dishwasher

anymore. We shower every other day. And I told you about flushing the toilet.

Mary	You told us all kinds of things.
Martha	And I'll be telling you a lot of other things before this is over. It's not a game that we're playing. Bad things are happening to people. Horrible things. I hear people whispering about it in the supermarket. And they stop whispering if they think you're listening. They think you might be a police informant or something.
John	I don't want to think about that now. It's dinnertime. I'm hungry. All I want to think about is meatloaf, mashed potatoes, and greens.
Martha	No greens tonight. Two of the stores I went to had run out. In the other one, the greens looked like they should be thrown out and the price they wanted for them was unreal. We're having carrots instead.
Matthew	Carrots again. I hate carrots.
Martha	You'll eat what we have, or you can march yourself straight to bed. Be thankful for what you've got. Besides, you can do all kinds of things with carrots. Maybe tomorrow, I'll make a carrot casserole. I haven't done that for a while. When I was growing up, my family was really poor. We never realized it because your grandmother could take food no one else wanted and turn it into dishes fit for a king. She did the same thing with scraps of material. She made all our clothes. We were the envy of the neighborhood. And my father could take scraps of metal and wood and make toys for us. I wish I had some of them to show you. They were real works of art.
John	You remember that trip we took to the Smokies? We stopped at that general store. Remember the toy duck I showed you made out of sticks and baling wire. And the tops carved out of wood. We can get

by with a little patience and cleverness. Be thankful that your mother is such a good cook.

Matthew   I am thankful. But it would be really nice every once in a while to have steak or pork chops.

John   We won't be having steak or pork chops for a while.

Martha   Maybe I'll get some stew meat for Sunday dinner.

Matthew   Stew meat is not steak.

John   When things get better, I'll buy us all some steaks to celebrate. But the way things are, that's just not going to happen any time soon. Meanwhile, I want you to show your appreciation to your mom for what she does. Now you set the table, girl.

Mary   For eight?

Martha   Yes. For eight. Just like last night and the night before. Maybe next week, I'll make carrot soup with onions in a chicken stock. I haven't done that in quite some time.

[The table is set. The family sits down. The guests come in and sit down. Martha comes in with a platter of meatloaf—a large bowl of carrots, another bowl of mashed potatoes, and some white bread. She sits down.]

John   Now let us bow our heads. We thank you, Lord, for the food we are about to eat, for our family, and for our guests.

[Matthew begins to reach for the meatloaf.]

John   Now, son. Remember your manners. Guests get served first.

[The food is portioned out.]

Martha   Oh, dear me. How could I have forgotten. I made fresh lemonade to go with dinner. Lemonade and fresh iced tea.

[She gets up, returns with two pitchers, and sets them on the table. Everyone eats silently. At the end of the meal, the doorbell rings. The guest family rises without a word and leaves the room quickly.]

Martha	Quick. Take their dishes, glasses, silverware. Put it all in the box in the kitchen the way I told you. Throw the napkins in the trash quickly. And move the chairs back. I'll get the door. We've rehearsed this any number of times. Make sure everything that should be is out of sight. I don't want to keep them waiting too long. I'm coming! I'm coming! [Martha goes and returns with a neighbor from down the street.]
Neighbor	Hi, John, Mary, Matthew. I'm sorry. I'm interrupting your dinner. Kind of late for dinner, isn't it? I thought you ate early.
John	You know how it is. Sometimes I have to work late.
Neighbor	And you like to eat as a family. That's good. Families these days don't do anything together. Then they wonder why they're not there for each other in times of crisis. And these certainly are times of crisis, aren't they? Times that try men's souls.
John	You could say that.
Neighbor	I must say that you're doing better than most. Still able to put meat on the table.
Martha	Meatloaf.
Neighbor	Good old meatloaf. Been eating a lot of that myself lately. Maybe you and my wife could exchange recipes some time. You used to do that a while back. She told me about that. My wife makes good, wholesome food, but she's not adventurous. Especially with spices. Her mom didn't use spices. It was a religious thing. She thought spices were a temptation of the devil. You start spicing up your food, and the next thing you know, you'd be trying to spice up your life. Doing sinful things. She was pretty straight-laced. She wore plain clothes. No bright colors. But she raised kids that knew right from wrong. More than you can say about a lot of families these days. They don't teach kids morals. They don't discipline their

	kids when they do wrong. Next thing you know, the kids have no respect for their parents and no respect for authority figures. No respect for the law. You wouldn't expect that in a neighborhood like ours. But you never know. People you think of as being on the up and up do all kinds of things behind closed doors.
John	People do what people do. I don't suppose that has changed much over the years. People talk about the good old days. But the way my grandma told it, times were just as hard back then. People stretched the limits back then just the way they do now.
Neighbor	I don't know about that. Seems like things are going down. Morals. People don't go to church anymore.
John	I'd love to go to church on a regular basis. I'm working seven days a week and barely getting by.
Neighbor	Sometimes you have to make sacrifices. Keep things in perspective. But there I go, getting preachy again. And your food is getting cold. That's a pretty hefty bowl of carrots you have there. Your family must really go for carrots in a big way.
Martha	Carrots are healthy. They're still pretty cheap. Whatever we don't finish will get used in a carrot casserole tomorrow.
Neighbor	Boy, I'd give anything to have my wife cook me a casserole. You might give her the recipe sometime. You know, we don't get to see you that much anymore. It's like you all have drawn back into a shell or something.
Martha	We've been trying to keep together as a family. You know, with John working such long hours. The kids have activities and homework. And if you don't watch the kids doing their homework, their grades tend to slip.
Neighbor	All work and no play, you've got to let up sometimes. Next thing you know, life has just slipped on by and you feel kind of empty.

John	We are hanging in there. Doing the best we can.
Neighbor	I'm sure you are. Expecting someone for dinner?
Martha	No. Why?
Neighbor	An extra fork.
Martha	Must have fallen out of the meatloaf or something.
Neighbor	Salad fork.
Martha	We don't get to each much salad these days.
Neighbor	My family was never big on salad. I'm a meat and potatoes man myself.
Martha	Around here we're a meat, potatoes, and carrot family.
Neighbor	I can see that. Well, I won't bother you anymore. I know you all must be hungry. Good seeing you. My wife asked after you, and I just wanted to know you were OK.
Martha	You can tell her that we're fine. Just getting by.
Neighbor	I'll convey the message. You know, you're welcome to stop by any time. We're homebodies. I spend most of my free time in the garden or fixing things up. I also make model boats. Big ones. Your son might be interested in seeing my collection. I'm working on an aircraft carrier now. Accurate to scale.
John	Thanks for the invitation.
Neighbor	Well, I'll be seeing you. [They show him to the door. He exits.]
John	Well, that was interesting.
Martha	He was snooping. I can tell. That business about the carrots and the extra fork.
John	That was really sloppy of you kids leaving that fork on the table.
Matthew	You were rushing us. I didn't see it.
John	You have to understand. There are people who check up on things like that. Anything that looks unusual. The next thing you know, there's a policeman at your door. A whole gang of policemen checking everywhere.

Martha	John, I'm scared. Maybe we shouldn't be taking such risks. There's talk about people they catch. You know, it's not really fair to the children.
John	Sometimes you have to take certain risks. There is no other choice.
Martha	Other people make other choices.
John	I'm not other people, and neither are you.
Martha	But the children didn't make that choice. It affects them too.
John	Children don't make certain decisions. Their parents do. That's what parents are supposed to do. Children have to learn the way things are. It's our job to teach them.
Martha	They can't go over to their friends' houses. They can't invite other kids in.
John	Matthew gets to play ball with other kids. He sees them in the schoolyard. Mary has her Brownie troop. It could be worse.
Martha	And they have to watch everything they say. You know, they had someone speak at the school last Friday. About keeping your eyes and ears open for unusual things. About talking to the appropriate authorities if they see anything. They are turning our kids into spies.
John	You don't think our kids . . .
Martha	I don't think so. But kids don't like to keep secrets from everybody. It wouldn't take much for them to blurt something out to one of their friends and then ask them to keep the secret.
John	Children, come here now. You've heard your mother just now. I've told you that there are family secrets that you can't share with anybody else.
Mary	Yes, Father.
John	You understand what I said.
Matthew	We understand.

John   Not a word. Not a single word to anyone. You have to promise.

Matthew   We promise.

John   Cross your heart and hope to die.

Mary   Cross our hearts and hope to die.

John   Good. Let's finish dinner then.

[The other family reenters. The table settings are redone. The guests sit down and finish eating without a word.]

John   Have you finished your homework yet?

Matthew   I did everything but math.

John   You always save math till the end. Half the time you're too tired to finish. No wonder your math grades are so poor.

Matthew   I don't like math.

John   You don't like it, or you don't understand it?

Matthew   I can't figure it out.

John   Maybe we should get you a tutor.

Martha   We can't afford it, not now.

Guest-Father   I could help, maybe. I used to teach math once.

John   That's an idea. You see, I told you it would be a good thing. After dinner. After you help with the dishes. Your own private tutor.

Matthew   I don't like math.

John   Once you understand what you're doing. You'll see.

Matthew   I don't know why I have to do that stuff.

John   To sharpen your brain. These days, if you're not sharp, you don't make it.

Matthew   I'm sharp at all kinds of things. Just not math.

John   Well, when you're through with being tutored, you'll be sharp in math too.

Mary   I finished everything but reading.

Martha   You always save that for last.

Mary   I like to save the best for last. I got an A in reading last quarter.

Martha	Well, you finish up. You have to take your bath before it gets too late.
John	I think it's their night to take a bath.
Martha	That's right. I forgot. Every third day.
Mary	You used to make us bathe every night.
Martha	We can't be using too much water. Remember?
Mary	Yeah. I remember. How could I forget. By the third day, I feel like my skin is crawling. And my hair!
John	We still have water. Be thankful for what we have, not for what is lacking.
Mary	I'll try to remember that when people back off from me because I smell.
John	Watch it, girl. You don't have it so bad.
Mary	But before—
John	Before is before, and now is now. You'll adjust. It would be nice if you did it cheerfully.
Guest-Mother	Maybe, we should leave. It would make it easier for you and the children.
John	You are our guests.
Guest-Mother	It has already been so long.
John	You are our guests for as long as it takes.
Guest-Mother	It has already been—
John	For as long as it takes. Now you kids finish up and clear the table.
Matthew	Are we having dessert tonight?
Martha	I baked some cookies. I thought cookies would be nice. Nothing fancy.
John	Sugar, flour.
Martha	I save a little each day. It's nothing much. Enough for two cookies each. Every once in a while, it's nice to end a meal with something sweet.
Matthew	You used to make chocolate chip cookies.
Martha	I didn't have any chocolate chips. I'm sorry.
John	There's nothing to be sorry about. This is a nice surprise. Cookies. It's almost like the way it was before.

Guest-Mother These are very good cookies.
Martha I'm glad you like them.
Guest-Mother I used to make cookies. Fancy cookies.
Martha These aren't very fancy. I used to make some with colored sugar sprinkles on top for the holidays. Red and green sugar. This year, I don't know.
John We'll do the best we can to celebrate.
Matthew To celebrate what?
John We are still together as a family.
Mary Jodie's father is in the army. He was sent off somewhere to fight.
John Fortunately for us, the army doesn't want me.
Matthew Bart's father too. He's in the national guard. He comes home every weekend.
Martha They're lucky.
Matthew William's father was killed in the war.
Martha Yes.
Matthew Jack's father is missing in action.
John There, you see—
Matthew Robert's father—
John I'd rather not talk about that.
Matthew Robert was one of my best friends.
John When things like that happen, it does no good to keep talking about it. These are hard times. All of us are affected one way or another.
Matthew You never want to talk about things that happen.
John It's hard enough to get through the week without being dragged down by dwelling on things we can't do anything about.
Matthew I can't talk about things to anyone.
John Sometimes you just have to be strong. These days, that's the only way to survive.
Martha That's enough now. You have your homework to complete. Your math. I want to see your completed assignment by eight o'clock.
Matthew I'll never finish it by then.

Guest-Father   Don't worry. You'll finish by then. It gets easier once you understand.

Matthew   I will never understand.

Guest-Father   Give yourself a chance. You will understand. I promise you.

Matthew   Life sucks!

Martha   Don't you go saying things like that! You see what's happening all around us. There are people who would give anything to be in your shoes. Your father still has work. We still have a roof over our heads. We eat a good meal every evening.

Matthew   We're stuck in the house all the time.

John   No more or less than everybody else. There are restrictions on travel. The curfew. It's the same for everybody.

Mary   It's not the same for us. We don't have any privacy anymore.

John   It's a small adjustment to make—everything considered.

Mary   I don't want to have to make adjustments like that.

John   What would you have us do? Make them leave? You know what would happen then.

Mary   It's not fair. None of my friends have to go through this.

John   You don't know that to be true. There are other families who are doing exactly what we are doing. They just can't talk about it. You never know. You think someone is your best friend. Someone you could trust with your life. And the next thing you know, there's a knock at the door.

[There is a knock at the door.]

Mary   Whoops!

Martha   Who could that be at this hour.

[The guest family disappears without a word.]

John   Check. Make sure everything is right.

Martha	The dishes! Take the dishes! The glasses! The silverware! The napkins! Put them in the sink.
John	In the dishwasher.
Mary	We don't use the dishwasher anymore.
Martha	Nobody else has to know that. Now answer the door. We can't keep whoever it is waiting. They might think something strange is going on. [John answers the door.]
John	Well, look who it is! Mrs. Cranshaw from down the block. Welcome. Come in. Make yourself at home. Sit down. Relax.
Martha	Let me get you something. Coffee? Tea?
Mrs. Cranshaw	You still have coffee?
Martha	A little bit. I save it for when guests drop in.
Mrs. Cranshaw	I couldn't.
Martha	Please. I insist. You like your coffee black as I recall. With two sugars.
Mrs. Cranshaw	I've cut down on my sugar these days.
Martha	You're on a diet? You look so slender.
Mrs. Cranshaw	We're saving sugar. In case things get much worse.
Martha	Never enjoy today what you can enjoy tomorrow.
Mrs. Cranshaw	It's not a question of enjoyment. It's a question of survival.
Martha	Everybody is feeling the pinch. I have to go to three markets just to get basic food items. Three markets. Three long lines.
Mrs. Cranshaw	I haven't found the shortages that bad yet. The prices are getting pretty steep, and the lines are long. But I can get everything I need at the Supersol. I get a little extra. You never know when the supply will dwindle.
Martha	No.
Mrs. Cranshaw	And some people are getting more than their share. They're hoarding.
Martha	You can't blame them entirely. If you have to feed your family. It's hard to think of others' needs when

<table>
<tr><td></td><td>you don't know when your family's well-being is at stake.</td></tr>
<tr><td>Mrs. Cranshaw</td><td>Some people are feeding more than their own families.</td></tr>
<tr><td>Martha</td><td>What do you mean?</td></tr>
<tr><td>Mrs. Cranshaw</td><td>Strangers. Taking strangers into the house.</td></tr>
<tr><td>Martha</td><td>Why?</td></tr>
<tr><td>Mrs. Cranshaw</td><td>People who would get detained by the police. Certain people have been targeted. I feel sorry for them. I really do. But there's not much to be done about that, is there? We're just little people. You break the law and you take your life into your hands. You know what happened to the Naismiths?</td></tr>
<tr><td>Martha</td><td>No, I hadn't heard.</td></tr>
<tr><td>Mrs. Cranshaw</td><td>They were sheltering two children. There was a police raid. They took away the children. The next day, the Naismiths were gone. Just like that. No one has heard anything about them.</td></tr>
<tr><td>Martha</td><td>The Naismiths are good people.</td></tr>
<tr><td>Mrs. Cranshaw</td><td>It's not a question of being good anymore. It's a question of being safe. Have you read the new ordinances?</td></tr>
<tr><td>Martha</td><td>I'm always as busy. What with my husband working two jobs. There's so much I have to do these days. With the kids and their activities.</td></tr>
<tr><td>Mrs. Cranshaw</td><td>You can get penalized not only for doing something you shouldn't, but if you know someone else is doing something and you don't report it.</td></tr>
<tr><td>Martha</td><td>They're going to turn everyone into spies.</td></tr>
<tr><td>Mrs. Cranshaw</td><td>And in school, they're telling children to report anything suspicious in their own homes. That it's the patriotic thing to do in a time of crisis.</td></tr>
<tr><td>Martha</td><td>They'll have kids turning against their own parents.</td></tr>
<tr><td>John</td><td>It's happened before.</td></tr>
<tr><td>Mrs. Cranshaw</td><td>Are you afraid for your own children?</td></tr>
</table>

Martha   I don't know what to be afraid of anymore. They're giving rewards for people to do their civic duty. Not much. But these days, you don't have too much to turn supposed friends against each other. Even the suggestion that you might get more lenient treatment somewhere down the line.

Mrs. Cranshaw   We are living in troublesome times.

Martha   More coffee?

Mrs. Cranshaw   No. I couldn't.

Martha   I'm sorry I can't serve you something with the coffee. What kind of host am I?

Mrs. Cranshaw   It's understandable these days.

Martha   You are managing pretty well, all things considered?

Mrs. Cranshaw   Yes.

Martha   Your kids?

Mrs. Cranshaw   A bit shaky at school. It's like that with kids these days. They can't concentrate on English or math, what with all that's going on. My son is talking about dropping out of school and joining the army.

Martha   That would be a shame. He's in his senior year, isn't he?

Mrs. Cranshaw   Yes. I want him to finish. But he says it won't make a difference one way or another. We can't afford college tuition. He says the army will take care of his education. But you hear stories about the army these days—going into towns like ours and taking over. Can you imagine your own son being asked to do things to people in his own neighborhood. It's not to be believed.

Martha   Is he eighteen already?

Mrs. Cranshaw   Next month. That means he can do whatever he wants and we can't stop him. He'll be considered an adult.

Martha   I remember when he was just a little boy. It seems like only a few years ago.

Mrs. Cranshaw   Sometimes it seems that time passes quickly. Sometimes it seems like time is standing still. By the time you figure out one set of rules, they're no longer in effect. You wait for the nightmare to be over. And it goes on and on. It gets worse and worse. And there's no one you can talk to about anything. It used to be that you could talk to neighbors and friends. Now everybody is afraid their best friend will turn against them.

Martha   I don't know what to tell you. We're all in the same boat.

Mrs. Cranshaw   But it doesn't feel like it's the same boat anymore. It feels like everybody is in his own little boat. We should be pulling together, not pulling apart. I'm afraid sometimes even to confide in a priest.

Martha   Aren't they supposed to keep everything in strictest confidence?

Mrs. Cranshaw   They're supposed to. But I heard tell that the government was putting pressure on the church. That some churches have made accommodations. There was talk of someone who made confession one Sunday, and the next week got arrested for some illegal activities.

Martha   Like what?

Mrs. Cranshaw   Harboring someone. Rules on that are getting very strict.

Martha   I know.

Mrs. Cranshaw   The priest gives a sermon one week about helping one's fellow man and the next week talks about obedience to civil authorities. I asked him what to do when one's conscience goes against the rules of the government and he looked at me very strangely and just shrugged his shoulders. I didn't feel like I could tell him anything.

Martha   Sometimes it's best to remain cautious.

Mrs. Cranshaw   But if you can't talk to a priest. You know, when you were growing up and you had some secret sin to confess, you could always go to the priest. He'd tell you to do penance, to try not to sin again. Then he'd tell you that you were absolved, that everything now was OK. I'd always leave the church feeling relieved. I can't do that anymore. I just can't.

Martha   There's more than one priest.

Mrs. Cranshaw   But if I can't trust the priest I've known since I was a child, I certainly couldn't trust a stranger.

Martha   A member of your family?

Mrs. Cranshaw   And if they were interrogated somewhere down the line. I wouldn't want to put them in that position.

Martha   It's hard to trust anyone these days.

Mrs. Cranshaw   Yes. Very hard.
[Silence.]

Mrs. Cranshaw   Well, I know that you are probably very busy—all that shopping for your family and all.

Martha   Yes.

Mrs. Cranshaw   All that cooking and cleaning.

Martha   It was good of you to drop in. We don't get many visitors these days. Drop in any time.

Mrs. Cranshaw   Do you mean that?

Martha   Yes. Of course.

Mrs. Cranshaw   Any time?

Martha   Well, maybe not after ten thirty. My husband needs his sleep.

Mrs. Cranshaw   We could talk together, sometime, just the two of us together.

Martha   We could do that.

Mrs. Cranshaw   It used to be I'd just pick up the phone and call someone. I don't do that anymore. You never know. You hear strange sounds. Someone might be listening in.

Martha   It has been good talking to you.

Mrs. Cranshaw   I'll visit again. Soon. If that's OK.

Martha   Surely.

Mrs. Cranshaw   Well. OK. Goodbye.

Martha   [Leading her to the door.] Goodbye.
                [She exits.]

John   I'm not sure I trust that woman.

Martha   Why not?

John   You saw how nervous she was?

Martha   Everybody is nervous these days.

John   It was like she was doing something she was being
                forced to do.

Martha   Like what?

John   Like trying to win your confidence so you would
                tell her things and then she would spill the beans to
                someone and our goose would be cooked.

Martha   You really think so? I thought she was trying to find
                out if we could be trusted. She might be doing the
                same thing we're doing.

John   Or she might be pretending to find out what we're
                doing. You shouldn't have encouraged her to come
                back.

Martha   I was afraid if I didn't she might think we had
                something to hide. It's so hard to figure things out.
                I used to be able to trust my own instincts on things
                like this. There were people I trusted and people I
                didn't. And now, even with my friends.

John   You still have me.

Martha   Yes. I still have you.

John   And I wouldn't turn you in for all the money in the
                world. We're in this together. All the way. For better
                or for worse. That's what we promised each other
                when we got married.

Martha   People promise each other all kinds of things. They
                say till death do us part, and then they get divorced
                over petty little things. It's like promises were like a
                shirt you bought because you thought it looked nice.
                And then it got a small stain on it or a tear or the

style changed, and you toss away the shirt without a
second thought.

John   You're not going to get rid of me that easily. I'm here
             for the long haul.

Martha   Till death do us part.

John   Yes.

Martha   Come hell or high water.

John   I think we're in for a little of both.

[Reenter Matthew and Mary.]

Matthew   Who was that?

Martha   Mrs. Cranshaw from down the block.

Matthew   That's Joey's mom.

Martha   Yes.

Matthew   Joey's on the baseball team. He's not very good. They
             always put him out in right field when they can't get
             anyone else to play. His father rides him pretty hard.

Martha   Why?

Matthew   I guess he wants him to play better. He says some
             pretty nasty things when Joey strikes out. Joey does a
             lot better when his father is not around.

Martha   That happens sometimes. The pressure—

Mary   He's not too nice to Marsha either. She's in my class.
             She's kind of skinny. He calls her all kinds of names
             in front of other people. He does the same thing with
             her mom.

Martha   I never liked him too well. I've wanted to get to know
             Mrs. Cranshaw better, but I don't know how to invite
             her over without asking him. And he doesn't like it
             when she goes out by herself.

John   Some men are possessive that way.

Martha   A bit violent too, I've heard tell.

Mary   Marsha says she never knows when she's going to get
             hit or why. He gets real upset sometimes at dinner
             if something isn't cooked just right. He shouts and
             rants and raves. Sometimes he throws things.

Martha	When you think you have it bad, sometimes you find out other people have it much worse. Did you finish your homework?
Matthew	Yes. I think I'm understanding it better now.
Martha	See, I told you. A little tutoring and things would come easier for you.
Matthew	He has a way of explaining things that makes it easier to understand.
John	It's not such a bad thing to have your own private tutor in the house.
Matthew	He showed me some tricks I could use. They never teach you that stuff in school. We cut through the problems in no time at all. He gave me some other problems to solve. I did them too. No sweat.
Martha	You did extra work?
Matthew	I wanted to make sure I really understood.
Martha	So you might come to enjoy math after all.
Matthew	It's like walking through a fog. Suddenly the fog lifts and you can see things clearly again.
John	You thanked him for his help.
Matthew	Yes.
John	Good. Now it's time to get to bed. You have to get up early in the morning.
Matthew	Boy, will the teacher be surprised when I start doing well in class.
Martha	A pleasant surprise. It's always nice when a student catches on to what you're trying to teach.
Matthew	He'll probably ask me how I managed to figure things out. What am I supposed to tell him?
Martha	You could tell him we sent you to a tutor.
Matthew	And if he asks which tutor, what do I say? He might want to send one of the other students to the same tutor.
Martha	Oh.

Matthew	I could always fake it. Get a few problems wrong for a while and then gradually get better. That way he could think I figured all this out on my own.
Martha	You could say you worked with your dad.
Matthew	Dad's not very good in math.
Martha	Your teacher doesn't have to know that. And there's no chance your dad could tutor anyone else, not with his work schedule.
Matthew	You want me to lie to my teacher?
Martha	Just stretch the truth a bit. You did work a little with your dad.
Matthew	It didn't help much.
Martha	You don't have to say that. Sometimes you have to stretch the truth to avoid problems. These are difficult times. It's not like you would be lying about losing your homework to get out of a difficult situation. If someone was angry with your sister and wanted to do her harm, would you tell them where she was or would you lie and go for help?
Matthew	I'd lie to save her neck.
Martha	So—
Matthew	She is my sister.
John	We are all in this together. Call this a kind of math problem we all have to solve—together. In this case, we all have to come up with the right answers each and every time. Failure is more than getting a bad grade. It would be a total disaster.
Matthew	It's hard enough trying to get the right answers in school.
John	Think of it this way. You go to school to learn how to think. The information isn't so important, because by the time you graduate, most of the information will be outdated. But if you can think straight, analyze, you can solve new problems when they arise. That's what you learned tonight. You solved the problems in your homework and then you solved some new

problems. And you felt good being able to do that. Consider facing your teacher a new problem that you have to solve. You have to demonstrate that you can do the work now without revealing how you made the breakthrough. That shouldn't be so difficult a problem to solve.

Matthew   I could do that.

John   Good. Get some dessert and get to bed.

Matthew   Dessert. Wow!

John   A small reward for what you've learned tonight.

Matthew   Ice cream?

Martha   There's a little left in the freezer. Make sure you wash your dish.

Matthew   Ice cream. Wow.

Martha   Enjoy it now. I'm not sure when we'll be able to get some more.

Mary   Is there any for me?

Martha   Share it with your sister.

Matthew   I knew there was a catch to it.

Martha   Savor it. Put a little on your tongue and get the flavor of it. You don't need to stuff yourself to enjoy something.

Matthew   Shall I leave some for you and dad?

Martha   No. That's OK. The two of you can finish it off.

Matthew   Are you sure?

Martha   Yes, I'm sure. Enjoy.

Matthew   What flavor?

Martha   Chocolate.

Matthew   That's good. Chocolate.
             [Matthew and Mary leave.]

Martha   You handled that well.

John   I'm doing the best I can.

Martha   I think he understood. He connected what you said about solving problems and stretching the truth in a crisis situation.

John	It is so hard to do the right thing. I don't want him to think it's OK to lie for something small.
Martha	I think he understood. He'll be all right.
John	I didn't want to scare him or anything. But he has to know the seriousness of all this.
Martha	He has an immediate payoff. His own private tutor. He was really happy knowing he could do his math now.
John	We'll have to find ways to make the inconvenience of having guests look like an opportunity, not a burden.
Martha	Can you think of it that way?
John	I have to. If you see someone drowning and you are the only person close enough to save him, wouldn't you see that as a kind of opportunity?
Martha	I suppose so.
John	Well, we have that opportunity every day. Besides, the way things are going, I get a kind of pleasure knowing I'm doing something to get around the new ordinances.
Martha	Like doing something your parents didn't approve of.
John	I had good parents. When I did something they didn't approve of, I would always feel guilty. I don't feel guilty doing what we're doing. It feels like the right thing to do. The only thing to do.
Martha	And if we get caught?
John	We'll cross that bridge when we come to it. Hopefully it won't come to it.
Martha	But if it does.
John	We've faced problems before.
Martha	Nothing like this.
John	A new problem, a new challenge. That's what we just told our son.
Martha	We're not talking about a grade in math.
John	We'll face whatever we have to face.
Mary	Mom?
Martha	I thought I told you to go to bed.

Mary	I was going to bed. I had brushed my teeth. I was going to the bathroom. I guess I forgot to lock the door.
Martha	How could you forget something like that?
Mary	I never used to lock the door before they came.
Martha	Things are different now.
Mary	Sometimes I forget.
Martha	What happened?
Mary	He came in while I was wiping myself.
Martha	What happened?
Mary	Nothing. He came in. He saw me. He mumbled something, and then he left.
Martha	I told you about the door.
Mary	He wasn't supposed to come downstairs yet.
Martha	You were going to be a little later than usual. How was he supposed to know?
Mary	How am I supposed to remember things like that? Sometimes I forget that they are here. I think that things are the way they used to be.
Martha	Nothing is the way it used to be. Nothing.
Mary	He saw me naked. He saw me.
Martha	You'll survive. Accidents happen. I'm sure he didn't do it on purpose.
Mary	Why can't things be the way they were before?
Martha	You'll just have to be more careful in the future about locking doors.
Mary	I don't want to have to be more careful. I want to be the way I was.
Martha	Maybe, one day.
Mary	I want it to be normal. Today.
Martha	Between your lips and God's ears.
Mary	What?
Martha	It's just an expression. I want the same thing you do. We all want the same thing. This can't last forever.
Mary	It feels like forever.

Martha   I know it's hard for all of us. Now get to bed. You'll feel better in the morning.

Mary   I won't feel better in the morning. I won't.

Martha   Let me tuck you in.

Mary   You'll tuck me in?

Martha   Yes. I could do that.

Mary   You used to do that every night.

Martha   That was when you were a little girl. You're getting more grown-up now.

Mary   Sometimes I feel like a little girl.

Martha   You're afraid of what might happen.

Mary   Yes.

Martha   It's funny. Sometimes I feel like a little girl too. I remember what it was like when my mother used to tuck me in. She'd read a story and sing songs to me. I felt safe. I could go to sleep, and the monsters I thought lived in my closet couldn't get to me anymore.

Mary   I feel safe when you tuck me in.

Martha   Good.

Mary   Could you sing to me?

Martha   I can sing to you.

Mary   Who will sing to you when you go to bed?

Martha   Maybe your father will sing to me.

Mary   Then you won't be afraid of the monsters in the closet?

Martha   Then I won't be afraid of anything anymore.
      [Fade]

II.

[A stark cell. Middle-aged officer is grilling Martha, who looks the worse for wear.]

Officer   Now let's go over this again. The people you had in your house, they're not family. They're not related to you in any way?

Martha   No.

Officer   Then why did you have them in your house?

Martha	They came to us. They pleaded with us. They said they had nowhere else to stay.
Officer	And you knew who they were?
Martha	I had met the parents before at the school at PTA meetings.
Officer	You weren't friends?
Martha	Not really.
Officer	More like strangers?
Martha	Yes.
Officer	You took strangers into your house?
Martha	They said they had nowhere else to go.
Officer	You knew the rules?
Martha	There were all kinds of rules. They change every day.
Officer	They were made quite clear. Every day. On TV. In the newspapers. You can't claim to be ignorant.
Martha	I read the rules.
Officer	So you knew that what you did was illegal?
Martha	I guess so.
Officer	You broke the law. Willingly. Knowing the consequences. To you and all of your family?
Martha	I guess so.
Officer	You endangered your family for a bunch of strangers.
Martha	At church. The minister said that we are to be concerned with the welfare of our fellow men.
Officer	The minister also said you were to follow the law.
Martha	You know this?
Officer	We know what we have to know.
Martha	Yes. He did say that.
Officer	So you went against the teaching of your minister.
Martha	I asked him what to do if caring for the welfare of our fellow man went against the laws of the land.
Officer	And what did he tell you?
Martha	He didn't say anything. I took that to mean that I would have to decide for myself.
Officer	And you decided to break the law?
Martha	Yes.

Officer	You and your husband?
Martha	Yes.
Officer	And the children as well. You taught them it was OK to break the law?
Martha	Under certain circumstances.
Officer	So they could pick and choose which laws they wanted to break?
Martha	This was different. This was a question of saving lives.
Officer	The lives of people the government has decided are dangerous to the well-being of our society. Whose very presence is like an epidemic—a cancer.
Martha	They were good people. Ordinary people. Just like us.
Officer	There's no way that they could ever be just like you. Unless you are hiding something from us.
Martha	There is nothing to hide from you. You know everything now.
Officer	Something perhaps about your parents or grandparents—
Martha	What about my parents and grandparents?
Officer	Maybe they were not all you made them out to be. Maybe one of them was one of them.
Martha	No. That's not true.
Officer	We'll find out, of course. We have access to records. It would go easier if you would tell us now.
Martha	There's nothing to tell.
Officer	We'll let you know about that soon enough. In any case, you were harboring fugitives. Knowingly harboring fugitives. There is a penalty for that. A severe penalty.
Martha	What happened to them?
Officer	They'll be taken care of appropriately.
Martha	Where is my husband?
Officer	He is being interrogated—to make sure that what you are saying is accurate.

Martha	When will I be able to see him?
Officer	When we think the time is right.
Martha	And my children?
Officer	That is a serious question. You taught them to break the law. Children are our future. We can't have them be taught how to undermine the society they live in. If everybody did that, there would be total chaos in the land. People would start breaking all kinds of laws. Stealing from each other. Killing each other. We can't trust you anymore to take care of these children. They will be put in a special class and be reeducated. They will be raised by people who will teach them right from wrong.
Martha	We taught them the difference between right and wrong.
Officer	You don't get the picture, do you? You taught them how to be subversive. You taught them how to lie. How to lie to their friends, their teachers, the authorities. That's not very good parenting, is it? We will have to see how pervasive your pernicious teaching was. If they can be reeducated, all well and good. They can be watched carefully. If everything works out, they can become useful members of the state. If not, well, you will bear the consequences of what you have done to your children.
Martha	They are good children.
Officer	Good children who lie. Good children who help their parents break the law. That doesn't sound very good, does it? The matter, in any case, is out of your hands now.
Martha	I want to see my children.
Officer	You may—somewhere down the line. After they have been reeducated. It will be a test for them to see how well they have learned to be useful members of society. If they have learned how to put the well-

being of society above the whims of individuals. The love of country above accidents of birth.

Martha   Accidents of birth?

Officer   One doesn't choose one's parents.

Martha   I don't understand.

Officer   You will, soon enough. Meanwhile, we have to get to the business at hand. For any society to function, people have to know that those who follow the law will be rewarded and those who break the law will be punished. What you did is now common knowledge. People must understand the consequences of what they do. You will help us to reinforce that principle. In that way, you can atone for the sins you have committed.

Martha   We committed no sin. We did what we thought was right.

Officer   Not everyone has a good idea of what is right. You broke the law. Obviously the decisions you made were illegal. They were wrong.

Martha   They may have been illegal. They were not wrong.

Officer   I can see that you are going to be difficult. We will have to take that into account.

Martha   What do you mean?

Officer   You will see soon enough.

Martha   When will I get to be with my husband?

Officer   When we are finished interrogating him. Someone who has taught his children to lie cannot be trusted to tell the whole truth unless he is persuaded to do so.

Martha   Persuaded—how?

Officer   We have our ways.

Martha   Where is my husband? I want to see him. Now.

Officer   Maybe. If you cooperate. If he cooperates.

Martha   Cooperates, in what way?

Officer   You were not the only people in town that were hiding fugitives. We have tracked down many of them. We know there must be others.

Martha	If you say so.
Officer	This is not the kind of thing people decide on their own. They usually talk to each other. Encourage each other. Share ideas.
Martha	We did this on our own. We didn't speak with anyone else. We were afraid.
Officer	That is what I expected you to say, to protect the others in the network.
Martha	We never discussed this with anyone, even members of our family. We didn't want them to be exposed to any risk.
Officer	But it was OK to expose your children to such a risk.
Martha	It was a question of life and death.
Officer	For strangers. You chose strangers over your own children.
Martha	We didn't see it that way.
Officer	You thought you could get away with it.
Martha	Actually, yes. We thought we could.
Officer	For how long?
Martha	For as long as it took. If there was an opportunity down the line, maybe they could leave—later.
Officer	An opportunity. What do you mean by that?
Martha	Somewhere else they could go.
Officer	Like where? A place with someone from your network?
Martha	There was no network. That's why they were still with us.
Officer	You expected to find a place from thin air—just like that?
Martha	I was hoping we would hear about something.
Officer	From whom?
Martha	I didn't know.
Officer	This is getting us nowhere. We will have to use some more persuasive tactics.
Martha	What do you mean?
Officer	We have specialists in interrogative techniques.

Martha	I don't understand.
Officer	You will, soon enough.
Martha	You took us from our home before we had a chance to pack. I don't have any clothes with me.
Officer	That's too bad.
Martha	Personal items.
Officer	You'll learn to do without.
Martha	Medications.
Officer	There is a price to be paid for everything in this world.
Martha	What do you want from me?
Officer	A few names, for starters. Even one would be nice.
Martha	What kind of names?
Officer	Of others like yourself.
Martha	I don't know of any others.
Officer	Well then, I guess you'll have to tough it out.
Martha	Thyroid medication.
Officer	That's too bad, isn't it?
Martha	What kind of people are you anyway?
Officer	People who protect the nation from subversives like you.
Martha	By depriving them of clothing, medicines?
Officer	You can have your medicines. Give us one name.
Martha	I don't know of anybody else.
Officer	We'll see if you feel the same way after a week or so.
Martha	I don't think it's legal to deprive someone of their medications.
Officer	We'll let our legal experts look into that. In times of emergency, extraordinary methods are permissible to protect the general welfare.
Martha	How does depriving me of my medicines preserve the general welfare?
Officer	We will get the names of the other subversives one way or other. It's up to you how far we have to go to get what we need.
	[Fade]

III.

[Similar cell—can be the same set. Another officer. John, looking very much the worse for wear.]

Officer 2   Well, I have to admire your fortitude. You've gone through a lot of interrogation without giving us a single name of your co-conspirators.

John   I have no names to give you.

Officer 2   That's what you've said up to now.

John   It's the truth.

Officer 2   We'll see about that. We've only begun our investigation. You'll save yourself a lot of pain and trouble by giving us the information we need. We might find the information by other means, and all your heroics will be for naught.

John   I have nothing to tell you.

Officer 2   You might have something to say to your wife.

John   Where is she?

Officer 2   We have taken good care of her. She is as stubborn as you are.

John   What have you done with her?

Officer 2   We have questioned her.

John   You tortured her.

Officer 2   Nothing quite that dramatic. We have questioned her.

John   And she gave you no name. Because there are no names to give.

Officer 2   We know there are others.

John   None that we know of.

Officer 2   We'll see about that.

John   When will I get to see her?

Officer 2   Rather soon. Today, in fact.

John   You will let me see her today?

Officer 2   Oh, you will see her all right. You will see a lot of her.

John   I don't understand.

Officer 2   You will. We will be bringing her into this very soon. You'll be chained to this post—just to make sure you don't do anything rash.

John   I'm locked in a cell. What could I possibly do?

Officer 2   Something rash. Secure him.

[Two big jailers come in and chain him with a very short tether to the post.]

Officer 2   OK, now bring the bitch in.

[The jailers go out and bring Martha in.]

Officer 2   Good. You see that she is perfectly fine.

[Her movements are a bit sluggish and erratic.]

John   Her medications. She can't go without her medications.

Officer 2   She's done just fine without them to this point. Just look at her.

John   She is not well.

Officer 2   Look at her closely. Strip her so that he can look at her more closely. Do whatever you want with her. I'll be back in forty-five minutes. I told you we would get the information we wanted one way or another. You resisted our efforts before. Now let's see how well you handle this.

[They begin to strip her. Sudden blackout. Screams. Then silence. When the lights go on, the two of them are resting in the middle of the floor. John is holding Martha. Rocking her like a baby in his arms.]

John   Oh, baby. What have they done to you? I'm so sorry. You were right. We shouldn't have taken such a risk. I never thought anything like this could ever happen—here.

[Fade]

IV.

[The two officials. In a stark bureaucratic office.]

Officer 1   Miserable weather we're having.

Officer 2   It's beastly hot.

Officer 1   Bad news for farmers. It hasn't rained for weeks.

Officer 2	The corn crop will be hit hard.
Officer 1	Third year in a row.
Officer 2	Hard on chickens as well. Greg Brown told me that more than half his chickens died from the heat last week. They're doing everything to try to cool the coops down. They brought in big fans. The cost of electricity is staggering.
Officer 1	It's a major problem for us at the bank. Most of the farmers are up to their ears in debt. They can't even pay the interest on their loans. We don't want to foreclose on the farms. These are our neighbors.
Officer 2	We had to shut the public library last week. Couldn't keep the A/C going. We were way over budget for electricity. It forced all the workers to go on vacation without pay.
Officer 1	Things are bad down at the firehouse. The fields are dry. Anything could set them off. We had some lightning strikes last week. We had the clouds, the lightning, the thunder. Everything but the rain.
Officer 2	We all share the good times. We all share the bad.
Officer 1	We do what we have to do to get by.
Officer 2	Well, we're here to take care of the problem that has arisen among us.
Officer 1	Let's go down to the business at hand. Our prisons are filled to capacity.
Officer 2	Mostly with subversives.
Officer 1	Bob Raines is in for drunken driving, again. We really ought to think about suspending his license. He almost hit two kids Saturday night. Fortunately, a telephone pole managed to get in his way.
Officer 2	George Flanders is in again for hitting his wife.
Officer 1	She's a bit of a shrew. She would try the patience of any man.
Officer 2	No excuse for what he did to her. Broke her cheekbone in two places.
Officer 1	She keeps coming back for more.

Officer 2	I don't know what gets into some people. They should never have gotten hitched in the first place.
Officer 1	Till death do us part. I don't know which of them is going to do the other one in.
Officer 2	He has all those guns hanging around.
Officer 1	She's no slouch on the firing range either.
Officer 2	OK. We have a few regulars. But we've got all the others. We have to do something about that.
Officer 1	They all flaunted the new ordinances. They knew what they were doing. The penalties were crystal clear.
Officer 2	I thought if the penalties were stiff enough, people would back off from breaking the law.
Officer 1	There's no accounting for why people do what they do. I think sometimes that if you put in an ordinance against chewing gum in church, the number of gum chewers would triple.
Officer 2	Some people would rebel as individuals, and some would act together as conspirators.
Officer 1	That's what we have here. People who acted alone and people who conspired together.
Officer 2	The law doesn't make any distinction between the two. We had a problem we had to address. To get rid of the vermin in our midst.
Officer 1	The cancer.
Officer 2	If you have a cancer, you have to cut it out. It's as simple as that.
Officer 1	I don't know why some people can't see things that clearly.
Officer 2	Denial. Pure denial. If you don't look at the problem squarely, you can pretend it doesn't exist. Remember Daisy Melhouse? She had a lump in her breast. By the time she finally went to the doctor's, it was too late.
Officer 1	We're not going to let that happen to us. You discover a problem, you take care of it expeditiously.

Officer 2	We accepted the responsibility of handling the problem. The people trusted us. We will do the job we promised to accomplish.
Officer 1	The only question is how to do it.
Officer 2	They committed capital offenses. Our obligation is clear.
Officer 1	What we have to do, not how we have to do it. We haven't had an execution in this country for longer than I can remember.
Officer 2	I've read the town history. Back in the 1880s, they hanged a couple of sheep rustlers.
Officer 1	We don't have an electric chair.
Officer 2	I've been reading upon what it takes to do lethal injections.
Officer 1	It takes a doctor and a chemist or a pharmacist.
Officer 2	I don't think we have any doctors or pharmacists on the central committee.
Officer 1	You don't need a doctor or a pharmacist to do a hanging.
Officer 2	You do need a carpenter.
Officer 1	Back in the 1880s, they just used a horse, a noose, and a tree.
Officer 2	I've been reading this book on Italy during the war. At one point, they executed about 335 people in a cave outside Rome in a few hours. You get the right angle, and all it takes is one shot to the head.
Officer 1	How many people do we have?
Officer 2	At my last count—87.
Officer 1	That's a lot of people in a community this size. Do we have to do them all in? Some of them weren't so flagrant. The Jones family just let one couple stay over for one night. I don't think they knew the couple was on our list. They got some kind of cock and bull story about the couple's house being under repair.

Officer 2   But they were interrogated. I'm not sure we want anybody to know the methods we used to get at the truth.

Officer 1   You have a point there. If we let them go and they talk, things could get sticky.

Officer 2   You've got to cut out a few good cells to get at a tumor. That's just the way things are.

Officer 1   So it's agreed then. They all have to go.

Officer 2   Yes.

Officer 1   Who gets to do the job?

Officer 2   We took on the responsibility. It's up to us to take care of the problem.

Officer 1   I've never done anything like this before.

Officer 2   What would you have us do—hire some people? If we only had one or two, we could get the sheriff and his deputies to do the job. If the crime was flagrant enough, the people would be with us.

Officer 1   In a firing squad, they used to give live ammunition to only one person. That way nobody knew who fired the fatal shot. They did that for hangings too. Three levers and only one actually released the floor under the prisoner. Or two switches to set the juice going into the electric chair.

Officer 2   I think it's harder if you don't know.

Officer 1   We can't ask others to do the job for us. They might break down under the pressure.

Officer 2   That's what happened in Italy. Even with soldiers. They got so jittery, their aim was thrown off. Sometimes they lost their cool completely and started firing any which way. And some of the soldiers got their kicks doing it. We don't want to get anyone started on that track. The next thing you know, we'd have some psychopathic killers on the loose.

Officer 1   There are only the two of us. We can probably get George and Bryan to help us. They're on the committee. That makes four of us and 87 of them.

Officer 2	We could take them in small groups.
Officer 1	Groups of, say, four or five.
Officer 2	How do we make it seem like all this is ordinary so they don't get suspicious?
Officer 1	They'll have to be shackled. That won't seem extraordinary after what they've been through. We can tell them that the facility is overcrowded. That should be obvious. That they're being transferred to another facility.
Officer 2	Where would we take them? We have to have a site for our operation.
Officer 1	There's a fair-sized cave south of town.
Officer 2	They won't believe that a cave is the new facility. They'll figure things out if we start marching them toward a cave.
Officer 1	We inject 10 mg of Valium before we move them. They won't care what is happening. When I had my kidney stone, the pain was excruciating. They couldn't cut the pain, but with Valium on board, I didn't care. They could have told me they were going to cut off my leg, and all I would have asked them is which one.
Officer 2	It shouldn't be hard to get Valium.
Officer 1	The pharmacist should be cooperative. After all, it's not such a bad thing to calm some prisoners down— to keep things under control.
Officer 2	A hundred Valium shouldn't cause any suspicions.
Officer 1	Do we get a clergyman involved in this?
Officer 2	That is a problem. A lot of these people are pretty religious. They would want to make their final peace beforehand. We've got some Catholics here. They would want to make a final confession, get absolution—all the things they do before they die.
Officer 1	I don't know any clergymen we can trust on this. They've been pretty ambivalent about our program. I've listened to a lot of their sermons.

Officer 2	So have I. I can't tell you how many churches I've been to. People have started to think that I've become a religious fanatic.
Officer 1	Bugging the churches was a good idea. Once a week to go to church is enough for me.
Officer 2	So we don't get any clergymen involved in this.
Officer 1	I don't think it would be wise. Not with the numbers we're dealing with.
Officer 2	We might be criticized down the line. People come to expect certain things, giving people last rites and all.
Officer 1	We'll figure out something to tell them.
Officer 2	Maybe that we got clergymen from another town— that might work.
Officer 1	Do you think we can keep the site a secret?
Officer 2	There's a lot of rocks above the entrance. It wouldn't take much to dislodge them and seal the entrance.
Officer 1	But the smell.
Officer 2	You use lime on the bodies. I have access to lime. That's what they did in Europe.
Officer 1	OK. So we get the supplies ready. Bring them to the site. And the guns?
Officer 2	I have a luger my father got after the war. I've kept it in good working condition.
Officer 1	One gun won't be enough. If it fails for any reason, we'd be stuck.
Officer 2	It's not hard to get guns in this town.
Officer 1	It might be better to get the guns in another area. Not to raise suspicions.
Officer 2	Maybe, not all the guns in the same town.
Officer 1	So each of us gets one or two guns in a different area.
Officer 2	Luckily the three-day waiting period isn't required anymore.
Officer 1	And we do have credentials. It's pretty logical for public officials to have at least one weapon in their possession.
Officer 2	One weapon and at least one or two boxes of shells.

Officer 1   Have you ever fired a pistol before?

Officer 2   I used to go hunting with my father.

Officer 1   So did I. With shotguns. We hunted for quail. Sometimes for ducks.

Officer 2   This isn't exacting using a shotgun and aiming at birds.

Officer 1   We took on a job. We have to carry it through. Better us than someone we didn't trust.

Officer 2   We have to work out the logistics. Moving all those people.

Officer 1   We could do maybe ten a day.

Officer 2   That sounds good.

Officer 1   Morning and evening.

Officer 2   OK.

Officer 1   There's still the problem of the bodies. It's not that big a cave. Even with the lime, by the last day—

Officer 2   Five per trip. That comes to—

Officer 1   Eighteen trips.

Officer 2   If we did six trips a day, we could finish in three days.

Officer 1   That's a bit of a push.

Officer 2   Three days of push, and then we can relax. One trip every two or three hours. We could do that.

Officer 1   My wife doesn't like it when I come home late. I'm usually the one that puts the kids to bed.

Officer 2   Three days and then it's over. You can keep banker's hours after that. We can give ourselves leave afterward for maybe three days.

Officer 1   You contact George and Bryan. We'll get together tomorrow and set everything up.

Officer 2   Until tomorrow.

Officer 1   Right.
              [Fade]

V.

[Same scene as IV.]

Officer 1   How many left?

Officer 2   Two.

391

Officer 1   Shouldn't there be three?

Officer 2   One of them had a heart attack. He went pretty quickly.

Officer 1   Saved us the time and effort.

Officer 2   Yes.

Officer 1   So. Just two left.

Officer 2   Yes. A couple. They harbored a family of four. They claimed they acted alone. Couldn't get them to implicate anybody else no matter how hard we tried.

Officer 1   Some people can be very stubborn.

Officer 2   You have to admire their fortitude.

Officer 1   It's a real pity. Such fortitude in the service of the community would be welcome.

Officer 2   Well. They made their bed. They'll have to lie on it.

Officer 1   We bring them to the cave?

Officer 2   Maybe not. It's getting a bit funky there. The smell is almost overpowering. We had to use some extraordinary means to get the last group to cooperate.

Officer 1   The cave might not have been such a good idea after all. In Europe, they got prisoners to dig deep ditches.

Officer 2   They also had a lot of soldiers with machine guns. We are only four people with pistols. I don't think we could have handled it if a whole group resisted us. In any case, it's too late to resort to anything else. The job is almost finished.

Officer 1   We could finish the job here.

Officer 2   We don't want the regular prisoners to know what's going on.

Officer 1   Maybe in the wagon. There are only two of them. And they'll be shackled.

Officer 2   What do you suggest?

Officer 1   We do the man first. The woman is in no shape to put up a struggle.

Officer 2   We can surprise the man. The woman isn't likely to turn her head at that point and let us finish the job.

Officer 1	It won't matter much by then. Maybe two shots. One to take her down. The other to finish her off.
Officer 2	A sordid business, this.
Officer 1	We do what we have to do. We took care of the others. Two more won't kill us.
Officer 2	I'll be glad when this is over. I'm going home. I'm going to take a hot shower. And then I'm going straight to bed. The way I feel now, I could sleep for a week.
Officer 1	I'd like to do the same. Can't. It's my son's birthday party tomorrow.
Officer 2	How old is he now?
Officer 1	Seven.
Officer 2	Wow. Time really flies. I remember when he was born. It doesn't seem that long ago.
Officer 1	Other people's kids grow quickly. Yours seem to just inch along.
Officer 2	Yeah. It always feels that way. What are you going for the party?
Officer 1	The skating rink. Cake. Ice cream.
Officer 2	You're getting away easy. These days, people compete with each other. Things get fancier and fancier. My neighbors hired a magician.
Officer 1	My neighbor took all the kids to an amusement park. By the time he paid for the admissions and the food, they almost had to take out a bank loan.
Officer 2	And the price of gifts these days. Minimum twenty dollars. What did you get for favors?
Officer 1	No favors. Skating, cake, ice cream. That's enough.
Officer 2	There are going to be some complaints from the kids and their parents.
Officer 1	Let the chips fall where they may. There's a limit to what one can do. Somebody has to take a stand, have the courage of their convictions.
Officer 2	Better you than me. If I suggested something like that to my wife, I'd never hear the end of it.

Officer 1	You let your wife wear the pants in your family?
Officer 2	In small matters. In big things, I have the final say.
Officer 1	Love, honor, and obey.
Officer 2	I'm pretty traditional when it comes to family matters. People I know let their kids run wild. Then they wonder what happens when their kids get to be teenagers and start experimenting with drugs and sex.
Officer 1	Well, let's get this show on the road. Maybe we'll stop for something to eat on the way back. I'm really famished.
Officer 2	I could eat a horse.
Officer 1	A whole horse?
Officer 2	With mashed potatoes on the side.
Officer 1	Who serves horse around here?
Officer 2	The diner across town. As long as it gets hit by a car, they'll serve anything—possum, coon, skunk.
Officer 1	I'm not sure I'm up for skunk or raccoon. My grandma used to have a great recipe for possum though. Haven't eaten any since she got sick and died.
Officer 2	Memories of childhood. Whatever you had as a child, nothing can match it.
Officer 1	My mother was a terrible cook. Nothing she ever made was worth remembering.
Officer 2	I guess you don't choose your parents.
Officer 1	You have to take whatever you get. [Slow fade.]

FINIS
2006

Two Thousand Five Hundred and One

[A young woman and old woman in a small village in Poland.]

Paula   Irena Sendler?

Irena   Yes.

P   My name is Paula Misciewicz. I've come a long way to see you.

I   To see me?

P   Yes.

I   I'm honored of course to welcome you to my house. I'm sorry that things are not prepared. If I had known.

P   I'm sorry that I have dropped by so suddenly. I didn't really know how to contact you, until I got to town. You don't have a telephone.

I   I live very simply. I try to keep my expenditures at a minimum.

P   I should explain to you why I am here.

I   That isn't necessary. You are a guest. That's enough for me. Paula, isn't it?

P   Yes.

I   Misciewicz.

P   Yes.

I   A Polish name.

P   Yes.

I   Jewish?

P   No.

I   I have had a few visitors over the years. Almost all of them have been Jewish.

P	I was raised Catholic. My great-grandparents came to the States from Poland in 1910. As far as I know, they were Catholic.
I	I too am Catholic.
P	I know that.
I	You know of me?
P	Yes.
I	How?
P	I have read accounts of your history.
I	I am just one poor soul, an unlikely person to find herself in any history book.
P	There was one history book about the war. It was written by a Jewish author. There was a chapter called "The Righteous among the Nations." I saw your name. I wanted to read more about you. I did a search on the Web. It had your story.
I	It is not much of a story.
P	You and your friends risked your lives to save Jewish children—2,500 children.
I	I told myself that we had to do what we could. But afterward I realized that we could have done more. Much more.
P	You were able to go into the ghetto. You smuggled the children out, 2,500 of them.
I	The real heroes were the parents and the children. They had to cope with the separation—knowing that they would probably never see each other again. The children had to accept new names. They had to pretend to be other than who they were—to renounce their names, their parents, their families. I tried to make sure that I was not only saving their lives, but retaining their identities as well so that once the war was over, they could take back their names, so they could remain Jews.
P	I read about the war. I became obsessed with it. By what happened to the Jews of Poland. I read about

how my people collaborated with the Nazis in their genocide. I was ashamed. The shame grew in me year after year. If someone asked me about my name and the country of origin of my ancestors, I wanted to lie about it. But I couldn't lie. My name is so obviously Polish. I thought if I could change my name, people wouldn't know my origins. I wanted to flee from my religion. I wanted to be someone other than who I was.

I   There are others like me in Poland. The man who would become Pope John Paul II saved Jews.

P   I knew that. But somehow that was not enough for me. One man among so many others who collaborated, who actively pursued Jews, who participated in pogroms even after the war was over and a few survivors came back to reclaim their homes. The church was not free from guilt. I thought maybe if I became a Jew, I could somehow atone for what was done.

I   You did nothing wrong. There was nothing for you to atone for. You were born after the war was over.

P   I wanted to atone for my people. I started visiting synagogues. I wanted to be among Jews, among survivors. I decided to go to Israel, to see the state that was born from the ashes. I found myself in Jerusalem. I went to the Yad Ve-Shem the museum that commemorates those that died in the Holocaust. I couldn't tear myself from the exhibits. I was overwhelmed by the images of those that died in Poland. I felt that I was drowning in the blood of the innocents. And I wanted to drown. I felt guilty for being alive. I couldn't take it anymore. I fled from the museum and found myself walking on a path dedicated to the Righteous among the Nations. There were trees planted to honor them, plaques with names. I looked for names I knew to be Polish.

I sat down under one of the trees. And I caught my breath. I thought that if these people could be decent at the risk of their lives, maybe there was hope for me too. Maybe it was OK to be who I was. I read the names on the plaque of the tree I sat under. I read your name. I decided to find out more about you—every detail about your life and the work that you did, about the dog you got to bark and snarl so the Nazis would not search your car. I decided that it was not enough to sit under your tree. It was not enough to read about what you had done. I had to meet you. I had to see your face.

I   You are suffering, my child, for crimes that you did not commit.

P   I had to hear your voice. I had to feel your embrace. I had to hear the language of my ancestors from your lips. I had to hear you tell me that it is all right for me to be who I am. You told the children it was important for them to retain their names. You told them it was important to remain Jews. Tell me it is important for me to retain my name. Tell me that it is all right for me to pray as a Catholic. I need to hear it from your lips. You saved Jewish children from death. Save me too.

I   It is all right, my child.

P   Can we pray together?

I   We can pray together.

P   Teach me how to pray in my native tongue. [She utters each word of the Our Father, and Paula repeats each word after her.]

Ojcze nasz, któryś est w niebie
święć się imię Twoje;
przyjdź królestwo Twoje;
bądź wolaTwoja jako w niebie tak I na ziemi;
chleba naszego powszedniego daj nam dzisiaj;

i odpuść nam nasze winy, jako I my odpuszczamy
naszym winowajcom;
i nie wódź nas na pokuszenie;
ale nas zbaw od zlego. Amen.

P   The words are hard for me. I could understand what my grandparents said to me. But I could never answer them. Somehow the words would not come easily. Teach me. So that the words can flow from my lips like a mountain stream.

I   Zdrowaś Maryjo, łaski pełna
Święta Maryjo, łasko
Zdrowaś Maryjo, Matko Boża
Maryjo, módl się za nami
Maryjo, módl się za nami
Zdrowaś Maryjo, Matko Boża
Maryjo, módl się za nami
Maryjo, módl się za nami
Módl się
Módl się
Módl się za nami
Módl się
Zdrowaś Maryjo, łaski pełna
Świę.

[Irena cradles Paula in her arms and rocks her as one might rock a young child. Slow fade.]

Finis
2013